MIAMI BURN

JOHN D PATTEN

MIAMI BURN

Cover design: www.noveldesignstudio.com

Editing: Gabrielle Drake

This is Book 1 of the Titus Florida Crime Thriller Series.

Books in this series include:
Miami Burn (Book 1)
Miami Chill (Book 2)
Miami Storm (Book 3)

www.johndpatten.com

SPECIAL THANKS

To Mom, as always, for all your love and support in everything.

To Andrew Goffman, for always encouraging me to do what I do best and kicking me when I get sidetracked into idiot things.

To William Miller (www.literaryrebel.com), author of the Jake Noble books *Noble Man* and *Noble Vengeance,* for your expert advice.

To Derek Murphy (www.creativindie.com), author of *Guerrilla Publishing,* for sharing your vast knowledge about this industry and your infectious enthusiasm for helping authors to make a living selling books.

To David "Woody" Woodworth for publishing my first detective story "The Lonely Hunter Part 1" in our high school newspaper thirty-one years ago. Oddly—but not oddly, come to think of it—Titus is a very similar character.

To Robert B. Parker, Raymond Chandler, and John D. MacDonald for lighting the path.

MIAMI
BURN

PROLOGUE

I WALKED DOWN the three steps to the tiny dumpster area on the side of the bar and opened the gate. I flipped up the big plastic lid and tossed in the trash bag. A bundle of nerves fluttered in my neck. Sometimes it's a twitch in my toes. Sometimes it's a tightening in my shoulders. Tonight it was nerves in my neck.

They say there's no such thing as extra-sensory perception, but any experienced cop or criminal knows we develop a sixth sense that warns us of danger. It can grow stale. Mine failed me the other day with Tommy Nero's boys, but it was on tonight. Still sluggish, but on.

I dove to my left as a crowbar slammed into the metal rim of the dumpster with a loud clang. The lid crashed down onto it as I aimed my left elbow at the spot where my instinct told me a head would be and threw all my weight backward into it.

I heard the sickly cracking noise of bone against bone. I spun, my hand reaching for my gun.

My sixth sense didn't help me with the next one. Before I could get my gun, a fist fell from the sky and smashed into the right side of my face, knocking my left shoulder hard into the dumpster. Another fist pounded my kidney from the side and then something struck the back of my neck and I was on the ground. The blows came from multiple sources.

My head on the wet pavement, I saw three sets of boot silhouettes in the dim streetlights walking toward me. One grew big and slammed into my nose. I heard the bone crack and felt a stream of hot wetness trickling down my face. Everything went dark.

As I lay there wheezing, head spinning, stars popping, it occurred to me this is *not* what I came to Miami for.

I came to this steaming hellhole full of vengeance to kill a blond man who wears five-thousand dollar suits and lives in a big bayfront house on West Lido Drive. One goal, one objective. Point, shoot, done.

How the hell did I get side-tracked into *this* mess?

It was my damned curiosity that got me into this trouble, that's what it was.

In fact, it all started right here on this very spot. Right in front of this dumpster. This was exactly where I stood three days ago, smoking a cigarette when I first saw Pam Hayes standing outside the bar as she pondered walking in . . .

1

I'D HAVE BET good money that the middle-aged woman in the coral dress would have walked right on past Cap'n Jack's Seafood & Bar, but she paused at the entrance. I watched her as I smoked a cigarette in the fenced-off dumpster area where I had just unloaded the trash from the lunch shift. She took a tentative step toward the old oak door, and then another one back.

She stood in the hot South Florida sun for a solid minute—not an easy feat in July—contemplating the ancient wood carving of a sea captain with a bushy white moustache smoking a pipe, like he might give her some advice. She was in her mid-fifties with a not un-pleasant face under stately reddish-brown hair with flecks of gray. Some makeup, not too much. Pearl necklace and earrings with a wedding ring. Elegant purse and shoes that perfectly matched the dress. I could almost smell the money.

Three construction workers barreled out of the bar into the afternoon heat and crossed to the site across the street where yet another condo complex was going up. There wasn't much space for high-rises left in "SoFi"—the trendy area of South Beach between 5th Street and South Pointe—but the developers won't be happy until the sun is blotted out completely. The woman observed the dusty hard-hatted men as if they were exhibits in a museum. She frowned, turned to leave, stopped, turned back again, and placed her hand on the door handle. She lifted her shoulders, opened the door, and went inside.

I inhaled some cancer and wondered why a middle-aged woman, who looked like she should be nibbling on lobster quiche at a fancy restaurant with a dainty little fork, would visit a haven of foul language and deep-fried immaturity such as Cap'n Jack's Seafood & Bar in the middle of a Thursday afternoon. Our clientele skewed toward sailor-wannabes, bloated tourists in over-size shirts covered with little palm trees, desperate mid-lifers looking to score with other desperate mid-lifers, and a handful of beer-guzzling sports fans.

I told myself to forget the woman in the coral dress. Curiosity only brings me trouble, and Lord knows I've had enough trouble the past couple of years.

A volley of sweat trickled down my back, encouraging me to hurry up and finish my cigarette. This place is unfit for humans. Can't figure out how people live in Miami year-round, seriously.

I'm out of this outdoor sauna soon, I swear. I'm punching my own ticket once I complete the one task for which I came: to kill the blond man in the thousand-dollar suits who lives in a bayfront house on West Lido Drive—the man responsible for Ariel's death. She was all I ever truly loved in this vile world. Now, she and our unborn child are gone because of him.

The bar job is only to cover the rent for my one-room studio—more closet than apartment—in a grimy old lime-green building on Meridian Ave. Paulie, the owner of Cap'n Jack's, needed a bartender who knows how to handle his more troublesome patrons, a task at which I suppose I excel. Plus, my longish hair, goatee, and muscular stature tend to make me 'unemployable' in most trendy SoBe boutiques. Cap'n Jack's Seafood & Bar's days are numbered, though. My bet was that Paulie would sell in a year or two when the next towering monstrosity needs to be built. I hadn't known him long, but my gut said he'll take the money. Hell, I'd take the money. Not to mention the old-school bar's rugged nautical theme doesn't quite fit in with SoFi's organic juice bars, art galleries, and yoga studios.

A bright orange 1976 Olds Cutlass with a white vinyl roof and gold rims on ridiculously oversized wheels stopped at the light. It rocked up and down on hydraulic extensions to a heavy bass beat. I half-expected it to tip over. The vibration was nerve-rattling, loud enough to make the wooden gate jump on its hinge and jiggle what's left of my brain.

I swear, one task and I'm gone. Point, shoot, done.

So why haven't I done it yet?

As I pondered that question, the light changed, the Cutlass bopped away, and I finished my cigarette. I tossed it in the bin, opened the gate, went through, and closed it behind me. I shot a finger gun at the wood carving of Cap'n Jack. He didn't shoot one back.

I stepped inside and paused for a moment, allowing my eyes to readjust to the cool dimness. Three booths lined the left-hand wall opposite six stools along the bar on the right. One lone round table with two chairs sat by the window in front.

The woman in the coral dress had sat at the table, as far as possible from the three afternoon regulars gathered around the Marlins game on the flat-screen TV.

Jenny, the day bartender I was replacing for the nightshift, was taking the woman's order. Jenny was substantial in all the right ways, her Daisy Duke outfit highlighting perky attributes: red plaid shirt tied in front under large breasts to expose her perfectly tanned midriff, a sparkly belly-button ring over jean cutoffs that housed a delightful roundness over bronze girl thighs and calves all the way down to white cross-trainers that nobody noticed. Oh, and did I mention a red biker bandanna on top of her tied-back blonde hair? Yeah, she was difficult not to stare at.

I reminded myself that she's too young for me. Although, it's hard not to wonder what it would be like to remove those jean cutoffs with my teeth.

I walked behind the bar, grabbed some lemons and limes from the low refrigerator, and began to slice. Jenny slid over and pressed her round right buttock to my left leg as she filled an ice glass with soda water. I tried not to lop off a finger as my eyes drifted down to the thin pink line of thong right above where the low-cut shorts sat on her hips, the alluring top of her crack just visible under a line of blue denim. Lucky denim. Then, she flicked her long blonde ponytail in my face with a big smile as she pranced away with the drink on a tray. I caught a hint of lavender—or was it vanilla?

I tried not to look, but it was impossible. I glanced over at Jenny's arched rear over the fringe of the cutoffs as she placed the soda water in front of the woman, who asked Jenny something. Jenny leaned down, the woman said something, and then they both glanced over at me, catching me looking. I focused my gaze on the fruit I was slicing.

The small crowd erupted in a cheer as the Marlins snapped a tie with two runs against Pittsburgh. Bottom of the fifth and the score was now 6-4.

Marty from Jersey nodded at me from his perch at the end of the bar. I poured a tall Bud Lite and placed it in front of him on a napkin.

"Did you see that play?" he said. "Fucking amazing."

"Yeah," I lied as Jenny sidled up next to me.

"Somebody wants to talk to you," she said, linking the front of her right foot with my left ankle, drawing it up the back of my calf. I cleared my throat and glanced over at the woman, who hadn't even touched her soda water.

"Not interested," I said, finishing the lemons and moving on to the limes. "Too old for me."

Jenny leaned in, chin down, eyes up, and licked her lower lip. "You're always saying I'm too *young* for you. Maybe granny over there is more your speed."

"I'm thirty-six, not sixty. As for you, I'm not even sure you're legal, darlin'."

"I'm twenty-one."

I threw her a dubious squint with my eyebrows raised.

"Fine," she said with a pout. "I'll be twenty-one in December. God, you're such a dork. But one of these days, you're going to give in to me." She moved her mouth to my ear to whisper, her hot breath on my face as heady whiffs of young girl drifted up my nostrils. "And I do mean *into* me."

I cleared my throat again, fighting off primal urges.

"Not going to happen," I said. "So what's with Jackie Onassis over there?"

"She was asking about you," Jenny said. "She wants to 'talk' to you." Jenny put air quotes around *talk*.

"About what?"

"Didn't say. Just asked your name and if you were trustworthy."

"What did you tell her?"

"I said you're the biggest lying scumbag around. Oh, and a serial killer in your spare time."

"Oh, good. Thanks."

Jenny undid her apron and headed to the kitchen. "Okay, I'm punching out. It's all yours. Try not to miss me."

"I'll do my best," I said with a wink.

I looked over at the woman, catching her looking at me. She visibly jumped, put her hand to her mouth, and turned her head to look out the window.

I glanced around at my three customers. They all had beers and were fully ensconced in the game, so I walked over to the table, noticing she tensed up as I approached.

"Hello," I said. "Can I help you? Jenny said you wanted to talk to me."

"You are Titus?" she said in a shaky voice.

"Last time I checked, yes."

She flushed and took a sip of her drink, her hand shaking.

"I'm sorry," she said. "I'm a little nervous. My name is Pam Hayes. I was told you might be able to, uh, help me with a matter."

"Told? Who told you?"

She hesitated, then looked me straight in the eyes for a good long beat before she said, "Clark Erwin."

My muscles tensed and my heart skipped a beat. I got a flash of Clark Erwin's eyes under the harsh interrogation lights in a cold damp room in a place far away and now long ago. I could still feel the burst of joy when my fist smashed into his pudgy face. It cost me, but it was worth it.

"Clark Erwin?" I said.

"Yes," she said.

"How do you know Clark Erwin?"

"The FBI helped my husband and I with a matter and Agent Erwin was in charge. He said you were from Boston, but you don't have the accent."

"Spent the first twelve years of my life in Georgia."

"Oh."

She trembled. Tears welled up in her eyes. I handed her a napkin. She took it and wiped them.

"Please forgive me," she said, "I'm just not used to coming into places like these, nor talking to people like—I'm sorry, this is coming out wrong."

"People like me," I said. "It's okay. Not being used to talking to people like me is a worthy ambition in most circles."

She didn't laugh. She was about to speak again, but jumped up, almost knocking over the chair.

"I'm sorry," she said as she removed a twenty-dollar bill

from her purse and placed it on the table. She tucked the purse under her arm and darted to the door. "I just can't do this. I'm sorry. I shouldn't be here."

"Wait!" I said, but too late. She was outside.

Jenny had emerged from the kitchen, her bag slung over her shoulder. She was halfway across the room, headed to the door.

"Bye, guys," she said with a general wave to the room.

"Bye, Jenny," said the guys nearly in unison as they all turned away from the game to stare at her backside.

"Hey," I said, standing in front of her. "Cover for two minutes? I've got to catch that woman."

"Why?" Jenny said. "What happened?"

"I don't know. I just know I have to catch her before she drives off."

"I'm supposed to meet Matt in five minutes."

"I'll be back in two."

Jenny narrowed her eyes and gritted her teeth, attempting to look mean.

"Okay," she said with a sly smile, "but it'll cost you."

"Fine," I said, tossed her my apron, and ran out.

2

PAM HAYES WAS a block up, about to get into the back of a tan Mercedes. The door was held open by a tall man with gray hair in a tan suit and cap.

"Wait," I said as I approached. "Mrs. Hayes, please."

She went pale, one foot in the car. The driver sneered at me.

I raised my hands, smiled, and did my best to project warmth and trustworthiness. Mr. Harmless, at your service.

"Mrs. Hayes," I said, "I need to ask—why did Clark Erwin send you to me? Is it something to do with Ariel?"

Her eyes narrowed.

"Ariel?" she said. "No. I don't know anything about any Ariel. It's nothing to do with that. I'm sorry, I must go."

I debated with myself how to play this. What was Clark Erwin up to?

"You're in some kind of trouble," I said. "You could use a little help." She started to speak, but no words came out. "How about we just sit over there?" I motioned to the flimsy outdoor tables outside a convenience store. "Out in the open. Your driver can keep an eye on you."

She glanced over at the tables and bit her lip.

"You need to talk to someone," I said. "I can see it in your eyes."

The driver sneered at me again.

A tear ran down her cheek and she wiped it. She nodded, closed the car door and turned to the driver.

"I'll be right over there, Chester," she said. "I won't be long."

Like Chester had big plans. He nodded and got in the car.

Pam Hayes and I walked across the street and sat at one of the five little empty tables. We were the only ones there besides an old man with white hair in a green polo shirt smoking a cigar. He rubbed a quarter on a scratch ticket. A small stack of them sat on the table in front of him.

Pam Hayes removed a handful of tissues from her purse and dabbed her eyes.

"Agent Erwin said you'd be like this," she said.

"Like what?" I said.

"Like a pit bull. Once you decide something, you grab hold and don't let go."

"Character flaw."

I scratched the back of my neck and caught the eye of the old man in the polo shirt. He quickly looked away and resumed rubbing.

"What did Clark Erwin tell you I could help with?" I said.

"He said you used to be a police detective," she said.

I looked down at the seagull droppings on the pink sidewalk, and then up to the slightly darkening sky.

"Yeah," I said. "Once."

"You don't look like a police detective," she said.

"Part of why I'm not a police detective anymore."

"Agent Erwin said you were—how did he phrase it? 'One

of the good ones.'"

I laughed, unable to imagine those words coming from his mouth. "Clark Erwin said that?"

"Yes."

I shook my head, folded my arms, and laughed again. "What else did he say?" I said.

"Well, you see, Mr.—" she said. "I'm sorry, I didn't catch your last name?"

"Just call me Titus. I'm very informal, as I'm sure you've noticed."

"Well—Titus—I need some help finding my daughter Allie. The thing is—the reason I came to *you* is—nobody can know about it, especially my husband. Also, I need someone who can look in places in which an average person might feel somewhat, uh, threatened."

Her words flowed with an educated lilt.

"And I look like I wouldn't feel threatened?" I said.

She blushed.

"You look like you can handle yourself," she said. "The last time I needed a private investigator, he appeared brilliant on paper but lacked certain—ah—skills of resiliency. Agent Erwin assured me you possess these skills in abundance. You just proved it to me by following me to my car. You are indeed a pit-bull."

A gentle hot wind kicked up. Far away in the sky, thunderheads gathered. The daily deluge that hits Miami at approximately 3:17 every summer afternoon would soon be upon us.

"I'm not a cop anymore," I said. "I'm not even a licensed investigator. I sling drinks at a dive bar."

"I can make it worth your time," she said. "My husband and I are—please don't take this as bragging—we are quite well off. I can offer you a retainer today. Just tell me your price."

I glanced over at the old man. His arms were folded. His lifeless tickets lay in a little forlorn pile on the table next to him.

The blank look on his face was a million miles away. I decided to play along with Pam Hayes, out of curiosity.

"Tell me about your daughter," I said.

She nodded and removed her phone from her purse. She scrolled and turned it toward me. A montage of a very attractive young woman appeared on the screen.

"That's Allie," she said.

Allie likes skin-tight dresses, that's for sure. There were pictures of her in a yellow one, a green one, a red one, and a blue one. All appeared to be taken in bars or clubs.

"When did Allie go missing?" I said.

"Two months ago," she said. "Right when the spring semester ended. Allie is a freshman at the University of Miami. Or was, anyway. She stopped attending classes three months ago and didn't come home when the semester ended. God, I hate that school. Rex and I wanted her to go to his alma mater Yale, but, ah, that wasn't in the cards. It was all we could do to get her to sign up for classes at 'the U', as they call it."

"What does your husband do?"

"Oh, you must have seen him on television. He's a real-estate developer, very well-known. He's running for the Senate."

"I don't watch TV and I don't follow politics. Your husband sounds like he's in a position where he likely knows people who could find Allie. Has he hired anyone to look for her?"

She pursed her lips and glanced away.

"Well," she said, "you see, that's another reason I wanted to hire you discreetly. Rex thinks Allie is with friends. That's what I've told him, anyway."

Alarm bells went off in my head.

"I'm confused," I said. "Why wouldn't you want your husband to know his own daughter is missing?"

"My husband has important work to do and I don't want this to get in the way. Plus, I think I know who Allie is with, and it might cause Rex to become very angry. I wouldn't want him to hurt anybody."

"Your husband has a temper?" I said.

Her fist clenched.

"Sometimes," she said.

"Who do you think Allie is with?" I said.

Her fist unclenched and she hid it under the table. "His name is Jake Preston. He's from a troubled family. He and Allie met a couple of years ago. They dated for a while, and then broke it off. I was so excited when Allie met another boy at an event I sponsored at the Leucadendra Country Club—a sweet decent boy from a very good family, just graduated from Yale. I was certain she was falling for him but then she broke that off too and vanished. I believe now she's back with that awful Jake Preston. In fact, I just *know* she is."

"What makes you so sure?"

"Mother's instinct." I saw a flash of something nasty behind her eye, then it vanished.

A hot breeze grabbed hold of the palm tree across the street and shook loose a dead brown frond. It fell in the middle of the street.

I leaned back and folded my arms.

"I don't know what to say," I said. "I'm not in the business of finding missing college girls."

"I know," she said. "That was part of the appeal of hiring you. I just want to know where she is, that's all."

"If I find her and she's safe and she doesn't want to come home, I won't be able to make her. She's over eighteen."

"I understand. I just want to know where she is."

"She may not even want to talk to you. I can't make her do that, either."

"I understand."

I looked over at the sky, now nearly black in spots. There was a distant flash of lightning. Before my eyes returned to Pam Hayes, I noticed a black SUV parked with its engine running a block up at the corner.

"Won't your husband realize Allie is missing when school resumes in the fall and there's no college bill to pay?" I said.

Pam Hayes frowned.

"Yes," she said, "which is why I'd like to get this handled now, before the fall. Rex is very focused on his election campaign. Busy all day long—morning, noon, and night—planning committees, fundraising luncheons, thousand-dollar-a-plate dinners. There's one tonight over in Coconut Grove."

"Sounds like he doesn't spend much time with his daughter."

She nodded. "Yes, unfortunately that is true. Allie is closer with me. Rex is a very busy man. Don't get me wrong. He's a wonderful man. He's just not—oh, how do I say this without sounding cruel?—he's not your average American dad. He doesn't spend much time at home."

"Strikes me as kind of odd you want to keep this from your husband."

Her nostrils flared. "He needs to focus on his campaign. He lost last time because he wasn't focused enough. In politics, you need to be focused twenty-four hours a day. This time, he *will* win. No distractions like six years ago."

"But it's your daughter."

"I know, but it's important to the country that Rex be elected to the Senate. We must save South Florida from what's going on in Washington, D.C."

"Have you called the police?" I said.

"The police must stay out of this," she said. "It will leak to the press, and the press are vile. Titus, let me be blunt with you. I know Allie is with this Jake Preston. Right here in South Beach. I just want to know *where*."

I noticed her hands were clenched again. She noticed I noticed and unclenched them. She put them underneath the table on her thighs, and a soft lovely smile reappeared on her face.

"Tell me more about this Jake Preston," I said.

"He's from a wealthy family," she said, "but they lost everything. His father is in prison for securities fraud and his mother is in some kind of mental institution. Jake is a piece of work. He's slick."

"Slick?"

"Slick as a whistle. A fast-talker. He could sell hamburgers to McDonald's and they'd be thanking him for the opportunity. He also likes to 'party' as the kids say."

"Drugs?"

"I presume so. He spends a lot of time in those awful dance clubs."

"How do you know this?"

"Back when Allie started dating him a couple of years ago, I hired a private investigator to check up on him."

"The not-so-capable one?" I said.

"Yes," she said.

"What was his name?"

"Tom Langston."

"Here in South Beach?"

"Yes, but he's, uh, no longer with us."

"Dead?"

"I'm afraid so. I saw it in the papers about a year after I last spoke with him."

"Huh. What did this Tom Langston find out?"

She gritted her teeth.

"That Allie likes those awful places, too," she said. "She likes them a lot, as I'm sure you can deduce from those dreadful pictures."

The old man stood up with difficulty, picked up his pile of scratch tickets, dropped them in the trash, and slowly walked away.

"So you think Jake Preston has corrupted Allie?" I said.

"Yes," she said.

"Does Allie have brothers or sisters?"

"No, she's an only child. I wanted another, but I—decided

16

it would be best not to."

"Where did Allie go to high school?"

"She started off at a preparatory school, but her grades were somewhat, ah, lacking, so despite our protests she graduated from—oh, God—Coral Gables High School." She nearly spat the words out.

"Tell me about Allie's friends," I said.

"She had a couple of close ones in high school," she said, "but they went off to big colleges up north. I don't even know if she had any at the University of Miami. Allie was never good at keeping friends. She'd get one or two close ones, but then they'd drift away. Allie always liked hanging around with older kids, especially boys. Especially club boys."

"She do drugs?"

"Never. Well, I shouldn't say that. All parents say that, but who knows? You see so many parents on the news these days saying, 'My sweet girl would never do drugs.' Yet, there they are in the morgue after an overdose."

I glanced over at the threatening sky. Pam Hayes was lying to me. I wasn't sure what the lie was or if she was just leaving something out, but my experience as a cop told me so. The pieces didn't fit.

I should walk away. That would be the smart thing to do, right?

The girl was probably fine, probably happier away from her prissy mother and politician father. Maybe even better off.

My guess was dear daughter Allie just couldn't take it anymore, sick to death of haughty parties with tiny plates of lobster under tents posing for pictures with Mr. Future Senator Daddy. Hell, I'd run away from that too.

But sitting there at that outdoor table with the storm closing in, I felt something. Something I hadn't felt in a while.

This is how it always starts. A puzzle that needs to be solved, challenging me. I start lining up the pieces and then just can't let go. Like a pit bull, according to Clark Erwin, apparently.

Then, I usually end up knee-deep in shit with guns pointed at me.

Don't get involved, Titus. Go back to Cap'n Jack's Seafood & Bar, throw out a few drunks, collect your tips, and finish your task.

I moved to get up and leave, but I saw a picture of a picture in my mind—the ugliest one I ever saw—Ariel's lifeless body on the medical examiner's table, her beautiful eyes open, looking at nothing. If only I had followed the lie back then, maybe my angel would still be alive. I couldn't save her, but maybe I could save someone else.

No, Titus. Stop the heroics. You fucked it up before, you'll fuck it up again. You've proven you can't save people. Stop trying. Let it go, finish your task, and get out.

"I'm sorry, Mrs. Hayes," I said. "I can't take this offer. You'll have to find someone else. Tell Clark Erwin I said to go—uh—well, just tell him I said he was wrong."

Her face dropped. I felt a pang of remorse. I had to leave before changing my mind. I stood up, the first raindrops hitting the ground.

"Name your price," Pam Hayes said, standing up now. There was the steely determination of a politician's wife in her voice. "Whatever it is, I'll double it. I'm very very wealthy, Titus."

I paused at that for a moment. Chester, ever vigilant, was out of the car with an umbrella walking across the street toward her.

"I'm sorry," I said. "I have no price. I don't do this anymore. I'm not that person anymore. I wish you the best."

I turned and walked back to the bar. Halfway there, the storm kicked up and I sprinted. By the time I reached the door and stepped into the cold air conditioning, I was soaked.

Great way to start a shift, huh?

18

3

I DRIPPED WATER everywhere. Jenny pretended to be mad at me for causing her to miss time with her on-again off-again boyfriend Matt, who was apparently on-again this week. But that didn't stop her from drying me off with bar towels while feeling my muscles and suggesting naughty ways I could make it up to her.

Tempting, but I'm a grand champion master of discipline and self-control. Or so I keep telling myself.

After she left, it was the usual slow build, picking up between five and eight. Pablo, who works all by himself fourteen hours a day, seven days a week in the hot little kitchen out back, did his usual amazing performance art of creating several plates simultaneously while screaming at himself in Dominican-accented Spanish.

Paulie once told him to stop because it was scaring customers, but Pablo kept it up so Paulie installed a thicker door between the bar and the kitchen. It didn't help. Everyone could still hear Pablo. Now, it's just part of the accepted ambience of Cap'n Jack's. Even a review on *Yelp!* mentioned it as a positive.

I served beer-battered fish n' chips, shrimp scampi, fried catfish, French fries, burgers, crab soup, conch chowder, and seared grouper. A couple of martinis, a handful of scotch-and-sodas, and a metric ton of beer.

Only one loud drunk, but I didn't need to throw him out. One hard stare with a sharp "Hey!" stopped the argument between him and another patron before fists went flying.

The owner Paulie strolled in at midnight with his girlfriend Trina. He was about sixty, pale, mostly bald with clipped hair of an indeterminate color on the sides. He was in his typical white polo shirt, black slacks, black socks, and black shoes. I had never seen him without a fat lit cigar stuck to his lip.

Trina was Jenny after thirty years of daily South Florida sun exposure. She was in her usual jean cutoffs and a yellow halter top that was having a hard time propping up her large round breasts. Her leathery brown shoulders were covered in freckles and sunspots and deep wrinkles formed canyons around her eyes and everywhere else. She carried a huge orange knit bag.

Paulie nodded at me as they passed, heading for the tiny office in back behind the kitchen. I nodded back.

"Hi, Titus," said Trina, stretching the phrase into three sing-songy notes with a girly wave and a glossy pink lipstick smile.

"Hi, Trina," I said, repeating the rhythm.

A guy in a five-dollar captain's hat watched her rear as it, she and Paulie vanished through the kitchen door. He chuckled and said, "She shouldn't wear those at her age. Nobody wants to see that."

I lowered my voice and said "Hey" with a hand motion like I wanted him to move closer to me. He did and I leaned down with my forearms on the bar. Bro talk, on the downlow.

"Yeah?" he said with an eager smile and wide eyes, expecting a joke.

"Shut the fuck up," I said coolly and evenly with my hard stare, then went back to putting glasses away. His mouth hung open and he trembled. He downed his gin-and-tonic in one gulp and made a beeline for the door.

By one-thirty, there were only two customers left.

"Last call," I said.

Marty from Jersey had his final Bud Lite draft of the night, although I always suspected he moved up to The Abbey after here. They're open until five a.m.

When the place was empty, I added my receipts. Then. I turned off the TV and cleaned the tables. I emptied the trash, locked the front door, and went out back.

Paulie sat at his ancient metal desk, smoking and adding numbers on a noisy yellow adding machine that may have once been white. Trina was on the small couch to the side chewing gum and sipping a Diet Coke while watching the TV that sat atop a green metal filing cabinet. She mindlessly twirled her stringy blonde curls.

I put the evening's take on the desk. The ancient office chair on the other side of the desk creaked and squealed when I sat down on it.

Paulie hadn't been in for three nights so papers were everywhere. He could use a secretary or a computer, but he refused to get either. He even used those old thick ledger books with a No. 2 pencil and square erasers.

Paulie stared at me over his bifocals, puffed the cigar, and said, "You look different tonight."

"Good different or bad different?" I said.

"Can't tell. Like you got something on your mind. What do you think, Trina?"

"Huh?" she said, fully absorbed by the TV.

"Never mind."

"This documentary is shocking," said Trina. "It's all about human trafficking and how these rich guys in Eastern Europe breed girls to be personal slave whores and then ship them all over the world."

"Hm," I said, an image of Allie Hayes in multi-colored tight dresses flashing in my head. I had been so busy I hadn't thought about Pam Hayes at that outdoor table since I ran in from the rain. Paulie pressed the total button and the machine coughed and spat some paper. He glanced at the figure and then up at me.

"Not a bad three nights," he said. "You made a few, huh?"

"Did okay," I said.

"This is for you." He counted out my regular pay. I stuffed it in my right front pocket with my tips. "I guess that's it. Good week. Go home."

"Thanks," I said and stood up. The chair made a loud cracking noise.

"You're off the next two nights, right?"

"Yeah."

I walked to the door, turning to catch the face of a crying girl on the TV. In a thick Slavic accent, she explained the things rich men forced her to do when she was a prisoner in their lavish homes.

"This is your first night off in weeks," Paulie said, "since you started here."

"Huh?" I said. "Oh, right, yeah. But I think Bruno will do fine on his own."

Paulie had just hired a new guy who looked like a minotaur just up from the labyrinth, covered in tattoos. I spent a couple of nights training him.

The girl on the TV walked the journalist hosting the documentary through the "dungeon" of a jailed billionaire's mansion with her therapist. Strange objects covered the walls. The girl burst into tears and hugged the therapist when nearing something. The camera panned down to show what looked like an elaborate sexual torture table with heavy chains and spikes.

"What you got going on for your two big days off?" Paulie

said, oblivious to the TV. "Any plans?"

"Huh?" I said. "Oh, hadn't thought about it."

He stared at me again and took another puff. "Any closer to completing your task? The one you came all the way down here from up north for?"

I flashed back to the night I arrived in Miami, laser-focused on the coral-colored door in the coral-colored fence of the house on West Lido Drive—the house of the man I came here to kill. I heard the police officer's voice talking me out of it.

I forced myself back to the present by focusing on a fake knot in the imitation wood paneling that lined the office.

"Working on it," I said.

"Wish you'd tell me what it was," said Paulie. "I know a lot of people. I could help."

"Appreciate that, Paulie. Appreciate the job, too."

"Just remember, time waits for no man."

"Chaucer."

"Huh?"

"Nothing. I'll see you."

I opened the door.

"Bye, Titus," said Trina sing-songily.

"Bye, Trina," I said.

I was halfway out the door when I turned back, the girl on the TV describing more horrors. She talked about some girls she knew who had vanished, only later to find out they had ended up in snuff films.

"Come to think of it, Paulie," I said, "maybe you *can* help me. You got any contacts in the club scene?"

Paulie removed the cigar from his lip and let out a plume of smoke.

"Club scene?" he said.

"The kids," I said. "You know, loud music, dancing."

He shrugged. "I know Tony V. Not very well, but I know him. He actually owes me a favor, come to think of it."

"Who's Tony V?"

23

"Owns that place over on Ocean. You know, the hot spot. They shot that movie there a few years back, the one with Colin what's-his-face. I forget what it's called. Trina, what's that club called over on Ocean Drive with the line out and around the block?"

"Which one?" said Trina. "There's like ten."

"Tony V's place."

"Sinz," said Trina, not taking her eyes off the TV. Still fondling her curls.

"Yeah," said Paulie, "that's it. Sinz. Sinz with a z at the end." He laughed. "Why? You want to go dancing, Titus? Shake a leg? Bust a move?"

Trina giggled, snapping her fingers over her head and swaying side-to-side. "Get-down—boogie-oogie-oogie."

"Yeah, sure," I said, " 'cause look at me. I'm all about the rhythm."

Both of them laughed hysterically. I forced myself to chuckle along.

"Seriously, what's the score?" said Paulie.

"No score," I said. "Just thought maybe I'd check out the nightlife in town, seeing as I'm here anyway."

Paulie squinted and puffed. He knew I was lying, but he also knew when was a good time to press and when wasn't.

"You want me to call Tony V?" he said. "He can get you in, set you up with one of those VIP tables. But I got to warn you, you're going to be a senior citizen in there. I wouldn't go anywhere near. Trina and I would feel dead and buried."

"Speak for yourself, old man!" said Trina. "I could still make a young horny brute stand up at attention."

"You can't make lasagna stand up at attention. Falling all over the plate like the other night."

Trina looked at me and rolled her eyes. "I followed the recipe, asshole."

"You couldn't follow a recipe if it was going five miles an hour."

24

"Titus," Trina said, "why do I stay with this bald freaky loser?"

"You two should get married," I said.

"Naw," said Paulie, "takes the fun out of it."

"Oh."

"So you want me to talk to Tony V about getting you into Club Sinz with a *z*?" said Paulie.

"Yeah," I said.

"When?" said Paulie.

"Tomorrow night?"

"I'll talk to him and get back to you tomorrow."

"Thanks."

"Good luck."

I went out the security door in the back and cut into the night air, silently cursing myself.

4

MIAMI IN THE summer is a pungent brew of steamy haze simmered in sweat with a dash of hot sauce, all masquerading as air. At night, it becomes a noxious and yet aromatic medley of midnight jasmine, blooming gardenias, and toxic mildew—like getting smacked in the face by a wet punch of flowery gasoline, even at two in the morning.

I paused at Jefferson Ave and decided to take the long way home, turning left. I enjoy my middle-of-the-night walks home. It's the only time South Beach seems real to me.

Rows of square sliding doors and balconies lit by track lighting from within. Meaty leaves on big plants swaying to-and-fro in the sultry breeze, occasionally blocking the view of late-night merrymakers on balconies. Hints of laughter and tinkles of glass. Neat little dark courtyards lit from below by nebulous lights that change colors, surrounded by meticulously trimmed hedgerows.

I fired up a cigarette, adding my own toxic contribution to

the acrid murk, and inhaled a small taste of death.

Something bothered me tonight. Maybe it was that TV show Trina had been watching. Allie Hayes is definitely hot enough to fall into the world of sex for money—prostitution, porn, or worse. The only problem with that theory was that Allie Hayes didn't need money—unless there were other reasons. Or hell, it could be as simple as she was just living with a boyfriend she loves and her parents hate.

Three college-age boys in brightly colored polo shirts, plaid shorts, and Top-Siders headed toward me. They took one look at me and crossed the street. I'm used to it. I wouldn't want to see me heading toward me at two a.m. either.

So why does Pam Hayes want to find Allie so secretly? Why does she want to keep it from her husband? What is she afraid he'll do? Hurt Allie? Hurt Jake Preston? Kill Jake Preston?

It's probably not a good image for voters to have a daughter with a boyfriend who hangs with celebrities and gangstas at SoBe nightspots. Although it's a worse image to be the deranged dad who kills that boyfriend, so why would he do that?

What if there's an abusive father-daughter relationship there? I saw enough of those as a cop. Is Allie running away to escape her dad?

I need to stop. I'm speculating now. I have no evidence. I'm only going by my gut. Although, my gut is right every once in a while.

No, Titus. Stay out of this. Remember why you're here. Point, shoot, done.

I stubbed out my cigarette and dropped it in a trash can. Then, I heard a noise from behind a thick bush to my left. I stopped and listened. It was a jingle-jangle sound.

I peered into the bush. A skinny black kid struggled with a bicycle next to several others on a bike rack in front of a house. He was maybe fifteen, red t-shirt, baggy shorts, Nikes, big Afro with red highlights.

I went on past and ducked behind a banyan tree. The jingling continued and metal twisted until it snapped, finishing with a hard clang on the pavement. In a flash, the kid had the bike out and was on it, rolling into the street.

I casually stepped from behind the banyan tree and raised my left arm straight out. The kid's chest collided with my forearm and he went backward onto the pavement. I grabbed the handlebars, preventing the bike from rolling further.

The kid lay on the ground, dazed, wondering what happened. There was a cut on his temple where his head had grazed the pavement. He put his hand up and felt the blood trickling down.

He looked up at me.

"Shit, man!" he said. "I'm bleeding! What the fuck?"

"Shouldn't steal bikes," I said.

The lights came on in the house.

"Get out of here," I said.

"You made me bleed, man."

I let the bike fall, reached down, grabbed his t-shirt, and yanked him up onto his feet. The front door of the house opened.

"Genius," I said, "the people in that house probably just called the cops. Get the fuck out of here, go home, and don't even think about stealing another bike. If I catch you again, you'll have more than a cut on your forehead, understand?"

The kid's eyes went wide and he nodded. I pushed him away. He ran off around the corner and was gone.

Three college-age girls came out into the street. One was talking on her iPhone.

I picked up the bike and walked it to them.

"Kid tried stealing your bike," I said. "I was walking by and stopped him. Here you go." I placed it in front of the first one and she steadied it with the handlebars.

"Did you get a look at him?" she said.

"No."

"Where did he go?" said the second girl, backing up at the sight of me.

"That way," I said and pointed in the opposite direction of where the kid ran.

"How did you *not* get a look at him?" said the first girl, crossing her arms with narrowed eyes. "Didn't you say you stopped him?"

"Hey sunshine, just get a better bike lock. One that garden shears won't cut."

The third girl held up her iPhone and tried to take my picture, but I ducked behind the banyan tree, turned while walking away.

"Hey!" she said. "Wait! I'm calling the police."

I cut behind a row of bushes, crossed the street at the corner, and doubled back over to Washington Ave, where I went north for a couple blocks and then back over to Meridian. A minute later, I was inside my apartment.

I just can't help it. I know I shouldn't get involved, but something inside me takes over and I start messing around in other people's business, barreling into trouble.

5

I HOVERED ABOVE the outdoor pool of a house facing the Miami skyline, lights from skyscrapers distant over moonlit water, red taillights passing on the Venetian, gun in my hand pointed at the man who lives on West Lido Drive. His blond hair glowed above his usual thousand-dollar suit. He laughed a heady stream of laughter that echoed across Biscayne Bay.

The dream vanished, my eyes shot open, and I was back on the airbed on the cracked linoleum floor of my studio apartment. A tiny lizard stared at me eye-to-eye for a long moment and scampered away.

Breathing hard and covered in sweat, I sat up. The couple that had recently moved in upstairs were at it again. They followed a consistent pattern—Act One: yell at each other for an hour, finishing with a door slam. Act Two: get very quiet for ten minutes. Act Three: have very loud sex with lots of screaming and moaning for another hour. Right now, they were about halfway through Act One.

Wait, why am I covered in sweat? I looked over at the ancient air conditioner. It made no sound. Shit, not again.

I reached over and looked at the time on my phone. 3:06. I've been home less than an hour. Looks like no sleep for Titus tonight.

I got up and walked over to the air conditioner, the back-and-forth yelling from upstairs reaching a crescendo that ended with a door slam. Cue Act Two. I inspected the unit. A vein of liquid streamed out under where it was built into the stucco wall, flowing past several brown stains in parallel lines where it had obviously done so many times before.

I turned it off, waited, and turned it on again. It hummed for a few seconds, rallied back to life for a brief moment of promise, and wheezed back into a coma with a final fizzle. Welcome to my world.

I moved to the slat windows in the corner, pried a couple of them open, and waited for even a hint of a breeze. All I got was a thick whiff of cat urine.

Then, the upstairs couple entered Act Three. Sounded like a wild boar attacking a rabid hyena. For a moment, I considered walking to the park bench on which I slept my first night here. Either that or maybe find a new place. But no—I'm only here to complete one task. I should just go do it right now, get it over with. I tell myself that every night, and yet I never do it.

Why? Why don't I just do it?

Do it, Titus. Point, shoot, done. One shot and it's all over.

I ran my hands through my hair and looked out the window at the silhouettes of palm fronds dancing in the glow from the Meridian Ave streetlights. I pictured the blond man in his bayfront mansion on West Lido Drive. My pulse raced. My breathing intensified.

I pulled on my jeans, threw on a camouflage head wrap, and went to the makeshift stash spot hidden in the left-hand wall of the closet. First thing after moving in, I had installed a tiny shelf onto the wall and covered it with a piece of plywood cut to fit the measurements of the closet. Next, I had cut a hole in the plywood for a small flip-open door on a spring hinge. It opens almost exactly onto the shelf, but I screwed up my measurements so there's a gap underneath the shelf. Okay, so I'm not the most handy guy ever. Whatever. It works. I can put things on the shelf and hide them from the world. Then, I finished it with some paint so you can't even tell it's there in the back of the tiny closet. Looks like just a plain wall. Always good to have a stash spot.

I pressed on the spring hinge and it popped open. I placed my "day gun"—the Smith & Wesson 9mm M&P Shield I normally carry around—onto the shelf with its holster and removed my Sig Sauer P229.

I did a press check, inserted a magazine, jacked a round into the chamber, and tucked the Sig and its holster onto my gun belt. I flipped the door up, the spring hinge clicked back into place, and I went outside, heading up Meridian Ave toward my final destination.

Do it, Titus. Get it done. Point, shoot, done.

I walked with a mad furious determination. No more wasting time. No more waiting.

I pictured the surprise on the blond man's face as he looks up at me, sipping a martini by his pool overlooking Biscayne Bay. I felt the joy of pulling the trigger and watching his blood splatter all over his suit.

At the 5th Street intersection, a large Latina woman stood on the divider in the middle of the street. She held a sign that read in large block letters:

HAVE YOU SEEN
MY DAUGHTER?

Taped underneath was a picture of a teenage girl in pigtails.

I had seen the woman before, yesterday up on Washington Ave at 13th Street in the hot sun in the middle of the afternoon, wearing the same clothes and holding the same sign in the divider over there.

As cars stopped at the light, she walked past their windows with so people could get a good look at the picture. Some kid in a Ford Mustang shouted, "No, I haven't seen your daughter but if I do, I'll ask her to suck my dick!" The light turned green and the car sped off as the woman shouted profanities in Spanish at him.

Now there's a mother who cares about finding her missing daughter, standing at three a.m. in the middle of an intersection holding up a sign and suffering assholes. She can't afford to hire people to run around looking for her daughter like Pam Hayes. So unfair.

I pictured Allie Hayes' eyes looking at me from that montage, one in particular where her eyes glowed. The image morphed into the girl on the TV Trina had been watching. By the time I reached 6th Street, I was again deep into the puzzle of what happened to Allie and lost my motivation to continue on to West Lido Drive.

Fuck.

I turned right and headed over to the 24-hour Walgreens on Collins Ave. I bought a 750ml bottle of Rebel Yell, a spring water, and a plastic-wrapped roast beef sandwich from the big oval bin by the cash registers.

I tried not to look at the woman holding the sign as I passed her again on the way back. I wanted to go tell her I'd find her daughter but I don't have the time nor the money.

I rammed my apartment door open, not even bothering to close it behind me before I poured a thick finger of bourbon into a red plastic cup, downed it, and then poured another.

I closed and locked the door. Then, I returned the Sig to its perch in the stash spot and switched back to the smaller Smith & Wesson again. I sat in one of the plastic chairs at the plastic table and sipped my drink.

My head began to clear a little.

Upstairs was silent. I must have missed Act Three, thank God.

I fired up the "refurbished" Chromebook laptop I bought for twenty bucks from a Cuban electronics mart and unfurled the plastic wrap from my sandwich. I took a bite and looked up Jake Preston online via somebody's unsecured WiFi while nearly retching at the taste. Whatever the meat is, it's *not* roast beef. I sipped some bourbon to help it go down.

According to online search engines, there are a million Jake Prestons in the world, a few hundred in Miami. I narrowed it down until I found some articles referencing his parents.

Nothing I didn't already know. Sanford Preston in prison for securities fraud. Lorena Preston in a structured program at West Palm Behavioral Research Institute. Jake is only briefly mentioned.

I ran a search for Allie Hayes and found her Facebook page. Her picture was the same one that had stuck in my mind, the one with the glowing eyes. I right-clicked and downloaded it. Last post on both Facebook and Instagram was three months ago. I was in a cell at the time, counting the hours until my release. Allie had been in the habit of posting the usual Facebook inanity, nothing to indicate what had happened to her or where she was now.

I found Allie on Snapchat, but have no idea how to use Snapchat. I'm not up on the newer social media platforms, nor do I want to be.

I ran a search for Rexford J. Hayes. Typical politician. Silver hair, big gut, dishonest smile. Links to FoxNews and CNN interviews full of the usual empty promises and blather. Ran for Senate six years ago and lost. Up and running anew, attacking the woman who beat him last time with a variety of accusations.

He reminded me of a guy I once arrested when I was a cop in a ripped green tank top with a hairy belly who had been raping his own ten-year old daughter for six months. When I rescued her, she was tied up in the attic. He begged me to shoot him instead of bringing him in. I declined, knowing what happens to guys like him in prison. Somebody later told me he died there—badly.

Take away the tank top and put that guy in a suit and he would look somewhat like Rexford J. Hayes.

I slammed the laptop shut, tossed the remaining half of stale whatever-it-is sandwich into the garbage can, and finished my bourbon. I poured another and sipped it.

The world took on a nice glow. The old dripping air conditioner became an artsy photograph. The dancing palm frond silhouettes became the backdrop to an old noir movie.

That reminded me of something. I booted up the Chromebook again and did a search for Tom Langston, the failed private investigator Pam Hayes had hired before. I found a death notice from two years ago. I dug deeper and discovered a news article. Found dead in his car in the parking lot of a Coral Gables strip mall. One bullet to the head. Clean and neat.

Hm.

What did you uncover, Tom? Was it related to Allie Hayes or was it a completely different case you were working on?

I set Allie's picture as my home screen. I stared into her glowing eyes for a good long minute.

I shut down the computer again and sipped some more bourbon.

If Paulie could get me into Sinz, I could look around for Allie. Sure, at thirty-six I'm way too old for those places, but I'm off for a couple of days so why not, right?

Shit, wait. I have no nightclub clothes. Just a handful of Army-Navy store basics. I didn't pack before driving here and I didn't plan on staying.

Hm, I could call Pam Hayes and tell her I'll take the job, ask for a retainer, and buy some high-end nightclub clothes so I can search for Allie.

Then what? Show Allie's picture around and ask? I can't really think of much else to do. Just watch and look and hope I'll run into Allie or Jake, talk to them, and that's that.

The bourbon hit me full force. I finished it, dove onto the airbed, and closed my eyes.

I was half-asleep when I heard a voice.

"You're wrong this time," said Ariel.

I jumped up, my eyes open. Nothing in the room but me and the steamy air.

I could have sworn I heard her voice. But it must be the booze. Or my imagination.

"Wrong about what, Ariel?" I said out loud, but there was no reply.

I closed my eyes and went to sleep.

6

AT PRECISELY 11:00 A.M, a black Mercedes pulled over to the entrance to Lincoln Road Mall on Alton Road. Several horns blared.

Out stepped Chester, today in a matching black suit and cap. As he marched toward me, his arrogant sneer was again turned up to high.

"You might want to go somewhere private before you open that," he said and handed me a thick manila envelope. He turned to the car in a snit and was back in Alton Road traffic without another word.

Chester really likes me, huh? I wondered if he had a pink suit and cap to go with Pam Hayes' pink Mercedes.

Earlier that morning, I had looked up Pam Hayes' cell phone number on an information site, called her, and accepted the job. She was effusive in her thankfulness and said she had to attend a charity golf tournament and wouldn't be able to meet me, but she'd send Chester with my retainer.

Seeing as I'm not a licensed private investigator, I had no idea how much to ask for. So I factored in the Mercedes, the chauffeur, the Gables Estates address in Coral Gables, and the rich politician husband. I said an amount I thought was high. She agreed without flinching. I probably should have aimed higher. Story of my life.

My second phone call was to someone I've been reluctant to talk to since our last encounter, but I figured she might be able to help me. She agreed to meet me at Starbucks at the Lincoln Road Mall, which is why I was here. And to buy a suit.

At Starbucks, I bought a large coffee and sat outside at a table under a green umbrella. I opened the manila envelope and looked inside. My heart skipped a beat. The last time I saw that much cash in one place was on a drug bust in a low-rise tenement when I was a cop.

Damn, Pam Hayes kept her word. There was double the amount I asked for inside.

Holy shit.

I closed the envelope gingerly and looked around. Nobody seemed to notice my sudden fortune. I stuck it in my back pocket, then reconsidered and stuck it in my belt next to my gun. Cash like that is trouble.

While I waited, I tried to forget about the cash and will my hangover away by watching the swarthy outdoor sales guy with thick black hair in a loose white linen shirt from the overpriced beauty boutique across the way as he preyed on passers-by. He had great instincts. He could pick a wealthy tourist out of the crowd with ease.

"Where are you from?" would begin his pitch to the unsuspecting sap who would take the bait by answering. Then, he would say, "Oh, I have something for you!" and disappear into the shop for some sort of expensive-looking sample. If the tourist was still there when he came out with the dinky "free gift", he was halfway to a sale.

And then I saw her.

There are beautiful women everywhere in South Beach. Probably more than in the rest of the world combined.

But Detective Sergeant Sofia De Jesus-Montero of the Miami-Dade Police Department has the unique ability to make the universe dissolve around her. I felt a click in my solar plexus as she neared me. Same click I felt my first night in Miami when she pulled me over for a broken taillight—and then talked me out of murdering a blond man.

Sofia was in her usual black polyester pantsuit. I bet she has a closet full of them. Her thick black hair was piled up on top her head. Dark sunglasses. Zero makeup, not that she would ever need any. Thick lips, skin the color of burnt amber. I could just make out the bulge of the gun on her well-rounded hip.

"You know your black polyester pantsuit screams cop, don't you?" I said as she sat down. My voice echoed in my head, stinging my hangover. I sipped some more coffee. It tasted like jet fuel, only stronger.

"What do you want, Titus?" she said.

"I mean, why not just wear a uniform? It'd be more subtle."

"You look like shit."

"Ouch. Nice to see you too, Detective Sergeant."

She stood up. "Well, if that's all—"

This wasn't going at all like the movie I had played in my mind.

"Sit," I said. "Please. Coffee?" She shook her head and sat again.

"I was in the area when you called," she said. "I have to get back. Make it quick."

"All right," I said, trying not to admire the way the fabric of her pants bunched above her thighs. "I have a favor to ask."

"You owe me, not the other way around."

"I'll let that slide because I did identify that Antoine Diego guy for you at The Betsy Hotel, remember?" I flipped my phone around to a picture of Jake Preston. "Your turn. Know him?"

She removed her sunglasses. I fell into the sea of her big

brown eyes for a few heartbeats and then swam back out. She studied the photo of the good-looking blond twenty-two year old. No expression.

"No," she said. "Are we done?"

"Name's Jake Preston," I said. "From a wealthy family, but he's hit hard times. Dad's in the clink for securities fraud, mom's at the funny farm. Only child."

"Sanford Preston. It was all over the news a couple years ago. Ponzi scheme similar to Bernie Madoff. Mother chose fruit loop city rather than get a job."

"Bitch to go from billionaire to homeless."

"What's Jake Preston to you?"

I glanced over at the sales guy. He was pitching a woman in a large yellow hat carrying a Zara bag.

"I'm, uh, helping a woman find her missing daughter," I said. "She seems to believe the girl is with this Jake kid."

Sofia's eyes narrowed and her jaw tightened.

"You'd better not be doing any kind of amateur detective work," she said. "Leave that to us."

"Because Miami-Dade has the time and the budget to find every missing kid?" I said.

"Because that is *our* job, not yours. You're not licensed."

"Nor approved. Nor stamped. I have no certifications, no authorization. But as I recall, you found me to be quite efficient not too long ago when I helped you get back to plainclothes. By the way, what were you on uniform probation for anyway?"

Her stare veered somewhere between Cruella deVille and Satan. Most men probably piss their pants when she does that, but I held my own.

She studied the picture of Jake Preston again.

"Got one of the girl?" she said.

I turned the phone back and showed her the montage of blonde hair, big eyes, and colorful tight dresses.

"Seen her?" I said.

"Nope," she said. "Big city. What's she into?"

"SoBe club scene, apparently."

"Looks about right. Bet she's popular."

"Safe assumption."

"How about a private investigator named Tom Langston?" I said. "Ring a bell?"

"No," she said.

"Pam Hayes hired him to find Allie the last time she ran away when she was in high school."

"So?"

"Tom Langston turned up dead two years ago. Smells like a pro job. One bullet to the head in a Coral Gables parking lot."

"Private investigators turn up dead sometimes."

"I seem to recall reading that in *The Total Idiot's Guide to Becoming a Private Investigator for Fun and Profit*, Chapter Ten."

I caught a whiff of Sofia's perfume and momentarily got lost in a thread of black hair that tumbled around away from her head.

"Titus," she said, "I don't know what to tell you. I'm OCS, not missing rich girls unit."

"OCS?" I said.

"Organized Crime Section."

I laughed. "Do you ever bust through a door and shout 'Freeze, Miami Vice!?'"

She stood up and put her sunglasses back on. "Goodbye, Titus."

"Oh, come on," I said. "I was joking. I know you have no white suits with the sleeves rolled up to the elbows."

She frowned. "You know, asshole, I did you a favor the night you drove into town by preventing you from committing a felony. I don't know why. I should have just busted you. That doesn't make us friends. My official advice: drop this."

"Or what?"

"Or next time I see you, I *will* arrest you."

"You keep saying that, but when are you really going to mean it? Sounds like fun. Do you have cuffs with zebra stripes?

Those are my favorite."

She shot me the finger, turned, and strutted off. I stared at her rear under the black polyester as it sashayed away. Lucky polyester.

I stood up, walked to the trash bin, threw my cup in, and was about to leave, but Sofia had walked back. Her eyes were invisible behind the big black frames. She sat back down and so did I.

"I shouldn't tell you this," she said, "because you're a dickhead and you're going to screw it up anyway and it's going to come back and bite me, but you might want to talk to the Reverend."

"Who, pray tell, is the Reverend?" I said.

"He's a, uh, self-styled savior of lost young souls. He runs the Apostolic Rescue Mission Church of Miami Beach."

I chuckled. "A preacher? In South Beach? They have those here?"

"He's—more than a preacher."

"Okay. Do you think he might know where Allie is? I don't picture her at Tuesday evening Bible Study class."

"He might be able to help. That's all I'm going to say. Just talk to him."

"Maybe I'll talk to him."

She stood up again.

"Oh, and you, uh, may not want to use my name," she said. "The Reverend and I, uh, have had some conflicts of interest from time to time."

"Sounds like a reasonable fellow," I said. "Where is this church?" She told me. I scratched my chin. "Walked by there a few times. Never seen a church."

"Look closer."

She walked away and I stared again until her rear was out of sight.

Not a bad day so far. Not bad at all.

7

I TRIED THE big old department store first. The guy working men's suits was named Bernie and looked maybe a hundred and fifty. While I'm sure Bernie was a fantastic guy, I feared the last time he went to a club, Tommy Dorsey and His Orchestra were the headliners.

So, I drifted over to a place across the way that resembled a glass spaceship about to blast off. The skinny salesperson over here was a blue-haired boy in a three-sizes-too-small peach suit that rode halfway up his leg. His name was David (pronounced *Da-veed*) and was perhaps a tad too excited to help me.

"I want to look cooler than Don Johnson," I said.

"Who's that?" he said.

"Never mind."

While he showed me the latest styles, a girl in a black cocktail dress arrived to offer me champagne, which I declined. Nice to live on the other side, if only briefly.

David tried selling me a bright purple suit that looked like it could signal low-flying aircraft, but I went with a more traditional navy blue linen, black silk shirt, and black Oxfords. I thought David might have a stroke when I opened the manila envelope to pay in cash. Maybe he's never actually seen cash.

The tailoring was going to take a couple of hours, so I figured I'd grab a bite to eat and then visit Sofia's mysterious "Reverend." Should be interesting, if only to see why she thinks he's worth talking to.

I walked past my bank and thought maybe I should put the money in my account, but an alarm bell in my head told me not to. Not sure why.

As I walked down Washington Ave, I came to the Art Deco Supermarket, which I can never pass without going in to buy a hot Dominican meal. Today I selected pork ribs, rice, and *maduros* for five dollars. Can't beat it.

I know only bits of Spanish, but I got enough of the conversation between the cashier and the sixteen-ish girl ahead of me in line to understand that the girl was short a few dollars. She told the cashier to take the chicken off her order, but I stepped in with a five-dollar bill.

"No, no," said the girl, and then something in Spanish too fast for me to follow. She was clearly embarrassed, almost in tears.

"It's okay," I said. "I just had a huge payday. Really."

"No," she said, "I no take your money. It's my stupid fault."

"Hey! Take it. It's all good. I'm serious. I made some extra this week."

She flashed a beautiful but shy smile at me and said, "Thank you. Give your phone number to me. I make sure you get paid back."

"No, it's a gift. I insist."

She touched my arm. "You are good man. Thank you. *Dios te bendiga*. I mean, God bless you."

Ah Titus, you superhero you. Captain Cash to the rescue.

Slayer of financial dragons, savior of young girls everywhere. Got to admit, it felt good. I haven't been able to do anything even close to that in a long time, and it was only five bucks. Take that, Pam Hayes.

I paid for my own meal, walked to my apartment, stuffed the manila envelope into my stash spot, and ate the meal. Right on cue, my upstairs neighbors kicked into Act One. Time of day be damned, Titus must be annoyed at all hours. Thankfully, the meal was so delicious I was able to ignore them. The final stabs of my hangover dissolved.

I thought about skipping Sofia's advice and was about to walk back up to the suit store, but as always, my curiosity got the better of me. I walked the short distance to the address she had given me.

8

IF THERE'S ONE type of building that looks out of place in South Beach, it's a church. If there's one actual building that looks more out of place than any other building in South Beach, it's the Apostolic Rescue Mission Church.

God must be on its side, that's for sure. Meaning it's made of wood, a rare building material down here due to frequent hurricanes. Looks like it's survived maybe one or ten, some older panels replaced with newer-looking ones.

Peeling white paint, a high pointy roof with fancy Gothic bargeboard, and rotting front steps led up to a big oak door. A relatively new sign in block letters read:

YOU'LL NEVER FIND ANOTHER LOVE LIKE THE LORD

ALL WELCOME SUN 10:00 AM

THE REV LUTHER WIL I AMS

A voice in my head told me to forget about this side trip and I was about to walk away when a loud crashing sound drew my attention to the right of the building, followed by several obscenities.

I crossed the tiny yard and over to the side to see a gargantuan bald black man in white coveralls and a black boy about fifteen in an oversized T-shirt and basketball shorts. The boy had a tall red afro. I recognized him.

"I'm sorry," said the boy to the man. "I didn't mean to do it."

"It's all right, son," said the large man in a deep voice that would make James Earl Jones jealous. "It's just one gallon of paint. It can be replaced."

"I told you I'm no good at this. I suck at painting. This is bullshit."

"Stop cursing on God's property and listen to me. We all God's children. We all make mistakes. Now, keep on painting the shutters with the green and tomorrow I get a fresh can of white. Remember what Jesus said, 'Go and sin no more.' That means we all make mistakes, but mistakes can be forgiven."

The boy nodded and walked over to where he had been working. He picked up the spilled can of white paint, which had apparently fallen from a ladder.

The large man returned to his own gallon of white and removed the brush. He half-turned, spotted me, and gave me a once-over that sent a twitch through my spine. Then, he resumed painting.

"Can I help you?" he said as he brushed.

"Why aren't you using a sprayer?" I said.

He glared at me. There was something off with his eyes. My nerves triggered a silent alarm way down inside me somewhere.

"You from OSHA or something?"

"No, it's just rather a large building and I used to do some paint work. Going to take a long time that way."

He painted some more.

"Teaching the boy skills," he said. "Young 'uns need to learn how to work with their hands. All hard work brings a profit, but mere talk leads only to poverty. Proverbs chapter fourteen, verse twenty-three."

"Right," I said.

The voice in my head telling me to leave got louder and I felt myself turning.

"Aren't you going to ask me the question you came here to ask?" said the man, focused on his brush strokes.

I scratched the back of my neck and turned to look at him. "Never mind," I said. "I was just looking for the Reverend—well, I guess the Reverend Luther Wil-I-Ams according to the sign, but forget it."

He stopped painting, put the brush down, and turned to me. He took a step forward to stare directly at me. I felt myself involuntarily moving backward a little.

I'm six-one, but this guy loomed over me. I'm not used to that. Six-four, at least. Forty or so. His right eye was grayish-white and slightly off-center, which only added to the menace of his size. Shoulders out to the West Coast. Trapezius muscles glistening in the sun like steps carved from onyx. A neck that could deflect a tire iron. Forearms as thick as my legs covered in tattoos.

While I could handle myself in most situations, I decided it would be best to distract and run if ever I had to go up against him. Some fights are better left avoided.

"What you want with the Reverend?" he said.

"Nothing," I said as I moved to go, "never mind. I'm just going to—"

"Wait. Maybe he in. I'll check for you."

"Nah, s'okay. I'll come back."

Ignoring me, he walked up the steps to the main entrance and waved me to follow.

Wondering why I blindly obeyed his commanding gesture, I soon found myself inside. First church I'd been in since Ariel's funeral. My chest tightened and I took a deep breath.

The pews were ancient, but recently restored. Sandpapered and varnished with care. The fresh smells of furniture polish and incense filled the space with a sense of hope. The sunlight from high windows beamed shafts of light in a warm glow that made the white rafters gleam. A new deep maroon carpet led up the main aisle to the plain altar.

"Wait here," said the large black man, his voice even deeper and more resonant indoors, and disappeared around to the right of the altar through a door.

I waited, sitting in the front pew gazing up at the plain white cross. Simple. Unadorned. Humble. No stained glass, no chalices. Everything white except for the pews, the carpet, and the floor.

I noticed I was sweating and my breathing had become heavy. I felt an urge to run.

A movement caught my eye from the right. I looked over and saw the boy outside, peeking in at me through a high window. After meeting my eye for a split second, he vanished. I wondered if he recognizes the man who knocked him off the bike he was trying to steal and didn't turn him in.

I was about to leave when the black man returned, his hand again motioning me to follow. "Reverend is in," he said. "Office back here."

I hesitated, patting the gun in its holster on my belt. I stood up, then turned and looked back at the door.

"Well, come on!" he said.

I walked up the steps and followed him back to a tiny office. Like everything else here, very plain. One small bookcase with several Bibles. One high narrow window. A wooden desk with two wooden chairs. Everything seemed handmade.

He walked behind the desk and smiled broadly.

"The Reverend Luther Williams," he said. "At your service."

"You?" I said.

"You surprised? Don't I look like a Reverend?"

I folded my arms and looked at the window. "Well, I just thought, uh—"

He stuck out his hand. "Pleasure to meet you, brother—"

"Titus," I said, staring at his giant tattooed hand for a long moment. I relented and shook it, feeling vulnerable for a heartbeat as it completely surrounded mine.

He sat down behind the desk and motioned to the chair on the other side. "Sit."

I sat down cautiously. His smile vanished as his left eyeball bore into me. The gray-white one on his right seemed to be looking at something else very far away.

We stayed that way for an uncomfortably long silence, staring at each other. I wasn't sure if he was looking into my soul or planning to kill me.

"I see only shadows with that one," he said. "Enough to know someone sneaking up on me."

"Excuse me?" I said.

"You were wondering about my eye. You were also thinking that if you had to make a tactical move, it would be best to create a distraction to my right and then back out the door."

"And you know this how?"

"The way you sitting, like a big cat, all silent and still, eyes peeled waiting for that right moment to pounce. Ready for action. I'd say you used to be a cop, but ain't no cop no more. You ain't a criminal, but you had some run-ins with the law yourself. You undisciplined, rebellious, don't function well on teams. Gets you in trouble. You also passionate and dedicated. Like to help people. But you impulsive, even a little unhinged, sometimes your heart takes over and makes your brain all scrambled. And let me guess. That bulge on your hip is a

Beretta, maybe a Sig."

I laughed.

"Oh, yeah?" I said. "Two can play that game. First, those aren't ordinary tattoos. They're the prison kind. The one on your right hand between your thumb and forefinger signifies serious time. I'd guess ten, maybe fifteen years served. Manslaughter— probably because that's all they could pin on you. Lost your right eye in a prison fight. The Jesus tattoos are more recent, some sort of a conversion while you were inside. You struggle with your old violent ways, especially when you see kids like you when you were their age. Oh, and the reason you came back here alone first was to get your gun out of its hiding place and put it in the top right-hand drawer of your desk there. I'd bet a Colt .45 long barrel."

The Reverend laughed, a big hearty laugh that filled the tiny office.

"Python .357," he said. "You?"

"Smith & Wesson Shield," I said. "Although I do own a Sig for formal occasions, so you were close. Python, huh? Big gun."

"I a big man. Big man look silly without a big gun."

"Fair point. How'd I do with you?"

"You right about almost everything, 'cept for the eye. That was an incident when I was a young 'un. And it was armed robbery, not manslaughter. I did eight, out on parole. How long *you* in for?"

"How'd you know?"

"Prison eyes be prison eyes. They never go back to normal."

I gritted my teeth. "Ten months. Attempted murder. Cleared by new evidence and expunged."

"Must be nice to carry legally again. I knew you was trouble when I saw you staring at the sign."

"Is your name really spelled Wil I Ams like the rapper?"

"No," he said as he moved his hand in front of his face with an irritated wave. "I just run out of L's."

"I know a guy can get you some," I said. "Good quality."

"You think you funny, don't you? Hide behind humor. Mr. Tough Guy, nothing affects you. Make a sarcastic comment, brush everything off."

I glanced over at the window with a view of a rotting fence.

"Been told that," I said.

"You ain't a God-fearing man, are you?" he said.

"Not since about fourteen."

"Life can do that. But it up to you to get your soul back. Redemption is possible. Ask, and it will be given you. Seek, and you will find. Knock, and it will be opened for you. Matthew, chapter seven, verse seven."

"I'm looking for a missing girl," I said. Anything to change the subject.

"Relative?" he said.

"No, client."

His eyebrows went up. "Someone hired you? You a private investigator?"

"No, not really. Although, informally I guess that's what I'm doing. Woman hired me to find her daughter."

"Why you come to me?"

"A, uh, mutual friend, said you would be good to talk to. Not quite sure why."

His face dropped. "This mutual friend wouldn't happen to be a police officer, would *she?*" His accent had traveled from from the backwoods of Georgia to West 125th Street.

I smiled.

"Maybe I shouldn't say," I said. "I'm not even sure why this person sent me to you. The girl I'm looking for isn't the church-going type."

"Police officer I'm thinking of got a chip on her shoulder," he said. "Maybe both shoulders."

"Sounds like her."

"You be careful with that one. She toss you in and throw away the key, never lose any sleep over it."

"I gather you two are close."

His hand waved sharply in front of his face again, as if he was swatting away an annoying fly.

"She busted me for trespassing when I got out," he said. "Then again for something else."

"What was the second time for?" I said.

"Preaching without permission."

I laughed. "That a big crime in Miami?"

"I went into this church, see. Not this one, a different one. Moved by the Holy Spirit. It flowed through me and the words came out, but—", he caught himself, "—why am I telling you this?"

I laughed again. "I can see her doing that. She's all about permission. Licensing, authentication—everything stamped, sealed, and approved. Don't let her find your Python."

"How you know Officer Jezebel?"

I again felt my hands all clammy on the steering wheel of the rental car the night Sofia pulled me over. The sinking feeling in the pit of my stomach returned to me, my hands lit by blue-and-red flashing lights as I gripped the steering wheel and looked over at the graffiti art that said *Welcome to Miami Beach*.

"I caught her at a low moment," I said. "Or maybe she caught me at a low moment. Prevented me from doing something."

Luther's bad eye seemed veered from its faraway gaze and directly onto me, which rekindled my desire to run.

"Tell me more about this missing girl," he said.

I gave him the bare facts about Allie Hayes, leaving out some details.

"Rich college girl," he said. "Messed-up rich club boy. Find him, you find her."

"Exactly," I said.

I showed him the pictures of Allie and Jake.

"He no pimp," said Luther. "Wouldn't last ten minutes on the street. My instinct tell me they into something high-end. If she into hooking, she going to run into Royce de la Vega. He run most girls in Miami Beach."

"You know this how?" I said.

"I save children from the street. I know the players. If it be drugs, she going to run into Frank Terillo or Andres Vasquez-Ruiz, 'El Carnicero.' Tommy Nero maybe, but Tommy strictly top shelf. Protection and money laundering."

"What about porn?" I said. "I know there used to be a couple big distributors here."

"Not no more. Back in the day, girls come to Miami from Podunk, Iowa, walk out on the beach, and ten porn producers be there saying 'Hey girl, where you from? I make you a star.' First, everything moved to San Fernando Valley, but now the entire industry in decline because every girl from sea to shining sea be 'videoing' theyselves on their iPhones, twenty-four-seven. They perform a lewd act, stream it live on PornHub. Look, ma and pa, I got mad skillz."

"Yeah," I said. "What about human trafficking?"

"Happens all over too. Same sales pitch. Come with me, I pay for everything, and girls find themselves trapped in a harem."

"Yeah," I said, thinking of the documentary Trina had been watching.

We were both silent for a long pause.

"What you going to do?" he said.

"I don't know," I said as I stood up with my hand out. "Well, thanks for your time."

He stood and shook my hand. "Good luck, brother Titus."

I took a step out of the tiny office, but turned back.

"One more thing," I said. "You'll never find another love like the Lord? Really?"

The Reverend beamed a big smile that became another hearty laugh.

"Bet you didn't know God a big Lou Rawls fan," he said.

I chuckled and headed down the aisle to the door. I was

almost out when I heard his big booming voice behind me.

"Brother Titus," he said, standing on the pulpit, his voice echoing in the rafters. The big serious stare was back. "Before you leave, I have a message for you."

My heart fluttered as I looked back at him, unsure of how to respond.

"Let go of your resentment," he said.

I froze, neck muscles clamped.

"What are you talking about?" I said.

He took a step closer, his wonky eye piercing through me, sending shivers up my spine.

"Resentment coming out your ears," he said. "You angry at someone. I sense it, I feel it. Eating you alive, burning a hole in your soul. If you let it, it will be your undoing. Resist, my brother. Don't let it consume you. Give your resentment to God and accept His blessing."

I trembled, tried to say something, but all I could do was turn and walk out.

I walked a full block until I realized I was headed in the wrong direction. I turned back, passed the church again, and picked up my new suit.

9

OCEAN DRIVE AT night is a hot and sticky Hollywood East. Celebrities with bodyguards and limousines, an endless parade of "look-at-me-I'm-rich" exotic cars, and a nonstop *thump-thump-thumping* bass beat pulsing everywhere. Rappers in chains and top hats with entourages of wannabes. Young guys with ridiculous multi-colored haircuts, standing up straight and long on the top and shaved on the sides. Some in five-sizes-too-small suits, others in outfits like the circus was in town. Unbelievably sexy girls in tight bright dresses with maybe a tenth of an ounce of fabric, each vying to win the velvet rope beauty contest that grants access to a pill-and-alcohol fueled nirvana of loud music and strobe lights.

Leaning on the low stone wall in the park across the street in my new suit with my hair slicked back, the dark Atlantic behind me, I smoked a cigarette and took in the dazzling show. I dreaded the moment I had to enter it. I had always hated the late-night club game, everyone trying to outdo each other in arrogant assholery. I never got the whole status-seeking thing—the self-absorbed need to be watched, admired, and adored. You see it everywhere from the L.A. celebrity crowd to Ivy League country clubs to the Washington, D.C. power junkies. Everybody trying to one-up everybody else. Silly popularity contests, just like high school. And for what? We all end up in the same place. I thank my lucky stars that I was born blessed with the apparently rare ability to be happy without any approval from another human being.

I tossed my cigarette into the nearest bin and crossed the street, nearly hit by a black Maserati outfitted to be part-Batmobile. I glared at the kid driving it, who appeared mesmerized by the tantalizing waves of round bosoms and bottoms bouncing to-and-fro along Ocean Drive.

I sauntered up to Sinz. The line was around the corner, just like Paulie said. Also just like Paulie said, I felt ancient as I walked up to the doorman. He was a big black guy who looked at me with an expression that said, *You're kidding, right?*

He was about to shake his head no when I said Tony V's secret code-phrase. He looked me up and down incredulously, chuckled, and said something into his lapel microphone. We waited for an uncomfortable moment while the person on the other end spoke. The doorman rolled his eyes, shook his head, and opened the velvet rope.

A twenty-two-ish kid with a dyed red pompadour in a shiny maroon suit and little round red glasses at the head of the line said, "Well done, my man!" with a thumbs-up sign. Six glittery girls surrounded him.

I passed the metal detector, having reluctantly left my gun secured at home in the stash spot. Once fully inside, the music hit me with an eardrum-piercing barrage of noise. Then I remembered the other reason I hate these places. They destroy your senses while placing you in a crowded uncontrollable environment. Too many variables. Too many people stuffed into too small a space, senses violently assaulted by music and strobe lights. Not to mention everyone's ingesting copious amounts of reality-bending substances that inhibit thinking skills.

Without a gun, I felt naked as I walked around the perimeter, getting a feel for the layout and the exit locations. Always good to know.

As I looked for how to get up to the VIP area, a big bald white guy with a black beard in a black suit stood in front of me, blocking my way. He was built like a tank, only sturdier.

"Mr. Titus," he said, barely audible above the pounding music.

"Just Titus," I said, not even hearing my own voice.

"My name is Axel. I'm with Tony V. Do you have a crew?"

"A what?"

"Never mind. We'll get you one. Follow me." He had a voice like gravel in a food processor on pulse.

Axel led me to a staircase with another velvet rope. On either side of the staircase was a set of three beautiful girls of various heights and skin colors. They looked like they were auditioning for a pageant, hands on hips, glossy lips in photo-shoot pouts.

Axel gave them a hand signal and they surrounded me, two of them taking me by the arms. My guess is it looks bad to be in the VIP area without a bevy of attractive women and in cases like mine where I didn't bring my own entourage and I'm a guest of the house, Tony V supplies one. Nice gig.

Together, we walked up to a skybox of sorts, looking down on the center of the club over a glass railing. There was a clear view of the dance floor below and a series of alcoves with little round tables surrounding it.

Nearly-naked girls in either angel wings or devil horns were raised and lowered on cables Peter Pan-style to retrieve bottles from a glowing structure that protruded from the ceiling and was stocked with every variety of liquor imaginable, suspended high above the mass of writhing bodies below. As if that wasn't enough spectacle, the flying girls were bombarded by laser-lights that flashed words on their bodies as they flew up and down.

The skybox itself was a mini-living room with a low glass coffee table surrounded by a plush black wraparound couch. On the table was a bucket of ice and a variety of sodas. Each skybox was separated by a low diagonal wall with a tiny latched door on either side. Separate, but if you wanted to invite your neighbors over, all you had to do was flip it open.

The girls piled onto the couch just as an angel floated down from the sky and hovered directly in front of me like a blonde hummingbird. The words DIRTY and YES flashed intermittently on her tiny body in pink and violet laser-light.

"Hi, I'm Ariel," she said, reaching out to touch my face. "I'm your bottle girl. What can I get for you and your party?"

At the name, I was momentarily transported to another time and another place. A winter morning far from here and long ago, the smell of perfume and soft skin as a much different Ariel turned in bed, flipping her red hair over my face.

"Are you okay?" said the floating girl.

"Yeah," I said, shaking off the memory. "Uh, what do you recommend?"

"Swarovski is always a crowd-pleaser."

"Sure."

Trying to figure out how the signaling for the rig worked, I watched her float up to the bottles, which were all tucked into glowing beehive-like cubbyholes. The whole thing looked like something right out of *Star Wars*. Quite impressive. Must have some sort of safety system built in, plus controllers working the lines somewhere.

Ariel flew back down and handed me the bottle.

"If you need anything else," she said, "just wave to me and I'll come."

"Sure," I said.

She pushed off and floated backward, performed a midair somersault, and dove to another table far below where a group had just sat down.

I turned to my "crew" and placed the bottle on the low table with a hand gesture for them to fill their glasses, which they happily did.

I sat between a curly-haired blonde in a tight fluorescent green dress and a straight-haired brunette in a tight fluorescent blue dress. The blonde licked the edge of her glass, which was full of vodka and something fizzy, and handed it to me. I had sworn to myself not to give in to temptation of any kind, but her green eyes held mine and my hand took the drink. I sipped. Smooth and strong with a hint of lime. She made another one for herself. Both girls pressed themselves into me on both sides, their hands on my thighs. For a moment, I felt like the King of Siam. This part of the club scene wasn't all bad.

"So what's your name?" said the blonde.

"Ti—", I said with a cough as she squeezed my upper thigh, digging her nails in. I cleared my throat. "Titus."

"What?"

"Titus!"

"Yeah, right. What's your real name?" Another squeeze, this one closer to my crotch.

"That's my real name, darlin'."

"I'm Bri. That's Sash."

"Hi, Bri." I turned to the girl on my right. "Hi, Sash."

"Hi," said Sash with a big smile.

"Short for Sasha?" I said.

She shrugged her shoulders. "Sure."

Bri sipped some vodka and squinted at me.

"You're old," she said. "You're like what, thirty?"

"Something like that," I said.

"Just decided to go out tonight and pick up a hot young chick, huh?"

"Sure."

"Am I a hot young chick?"

I took another swig, finishing my drink. "Of course you are."

And with that, her tongue was in my mouth. I reeled back, spilling some ice.

She pulled back, perplexed.

"What?" she said.

I grabbed a napkin and wiped my mouth. "Sorry," I said. I made another drink.

"You don't like me?" she said, her lips in a sad pout.

I patted the hand on my thigh and moved it away from my crotch.

"You're sweet," I said.

As she twirled her blonde curls, a devious smile spread across her face.

"You know what I like to do?" she said.

"I can't imagine," I said.

She leaned to whisper in my ear and told me. I nearly spilled my drink.

"Good to have hobbies," I said.

"We could do it now," she said. "The bathrooms are real private up here. Or I could just blow you."

A tall black man in a dark suit had entered the skybox. Lean, thirty-five or so, a carved part in his hair, and a pencil-thin mustache.

"Excuse me," I said, disentangling myself from the girls.

"Sure," said Bri.

I stood up and crossed to the railing, where the man smiled at me with an outstretched hand.

"Titus," he said, "I'm Tony V."

"Nice to meet you," I said as I shook his hand and got pulled into one of those ridiculous bro-hugs, which have always felt forced and showy to me. Tony V looked like a million bucks, his baby blue silk tie clipped to his baby blue silk shirt with a diamond-studded bar.

"Is there anything I can do to make you more comfortable?" he said.

"Move me to a nice quiet beach with moonlight?" I said.

"I'm sorry?"

"Just kidding. This place is amazing."

"Anything for Paulie. Anything."

I took out my phone and scrolled to the montage of Allie Hayes.

"Have you seen this girl?" I said.

He took the phone and studied the pictures.

"I don't think so," he said.

I scrolled to the photo of Jake Preston.

"How about him?" I said.

"Yes," he said. "He's here quite often, but I haven't seen him tonight. You want me to send him up if he comes in?"

"No, but thanks."

"Not a problem. Just let me know if you need anything. Wave to Axel or Ariel and I'll be here fast."

"Thanks, Tony."

He smiled, forcing another silly bro-hug, and then he was gone.

I felt a hand on my midsection as Sash slinked up beside me and ran her hand up my back. She smiled up at me and licked her lower lip. I nodded and smiled back, momentarily lost in her deep blue eyes. Shards of blue glitter on her face perfectly matched her fluorescent eye-shadow and dress, making her skin seem darker than it was. She flicked her black hair up to my neck to fill my lungs with an intoxicating aroma of floral essence, balanced and enhanced by nature's irresistible narcotic of young woman.

"I don't know what Bri told you," Sash said, "but I do everything she does, and I do it a lot better."

"Good to know," I said.

I smiled again, took another sip, and forced myself to look down at the dance floor for clues.

Bri must have noticed Sash moving in on me because she was soon attached to my left side again. Down on the main floor, Dyed-Red-Pompadour from outside entered. He and his "crew" had finally made it in. He walked with an air of total confidence, like he owned the place. He looked up deliberately as if searching for someone. His gaze fell on me and he threw me a salute. I saluted back and motioned him to come up. He shot me a thumbs-up, not too eager, gently nudging his shapely companions to the VIP area. I glanced at Axel, who nodded.

This could help. I'm somewhat lost here and could use an insider to help me navigate the scene. This kid looked like he might fit the bill. He had sized me up outside, saw from my interaction with the doorman that I had some clout—no matter how out of place I appeared—and he wanted in on that. Maybe we could help each other out.

"Friend of yours?" said Bri as the kid and six girls swayed up the stairs into our skybox.

"Sure," I said.

"He's kinda cute."

I was about to comment, but decided against it. Dyed-Red-Pompadour walked up to me.

"Titus," I said with an outstretched hand.

"Jason Stark," he said, took my hand, and pulled me into another bro hug

"Drink?" I turned to the bottle on the table but it was empty. Like magic, Ariel the bottle girl was next to me in midair on the other side of the railing holding out another. I took it and she blew me a kiss as she drifted away.

Am I dreaming all this?

Jason fixed himself a drink and introductions went all around—Bri, Sash, Amber, Lexi, Brooke, Jenna, Katie, and several others.

"Place is hot tonight," said Jason in a deep voice that sounded like he practiced it to sound more manly.

"Yeah," I said.

"Haven't seen you before. You're a friend of Tony V's." He said it as a statement, not a question.

"Yeah." I sipped some more, finishing my second drink. I

poured another. "You know him?"

"Naw, but he'd be good to meet. How do you know him?"

"Friend of a friend."

"You new in town?" he said.

"Sort of," I said.

Jason smiled. "You're not a big talker, are you?"

I must have accidentally given him one of the deadpan stares I use at Cap'n Jack's because he leaned back and put his hands up.

"That's cool, dude," Jason said. "That's cool. Thanks for having me and my crew up."

I relaxed my shoulders and smiled.

"You're good," I said.

"What do you mean?" he said.

"That thing you did at the front door. That how you always get into VIP?"

"Hey, whoa, I didn't mean anything by that."

"Relax. It's a compliment. You can also probably see that I'm a little out of my element."

He laughed.

"You do seem a bit mature for this place," he said. "Don't get me wrong, that's a good thing."

"Yeah," I said. "So, maybe we can help each other."

"You name it, dude."

I pulled out my phone and again dialed up the montage of Allie. "Seen her?"

"Looks familiar," Jason said, "but dude, my cock is in so many girls' mouths, it's hard to remember."

I resisted the urge to throw him over the balcony. I scrolled to Jake Preston's picture.

"How about this guy?" I said.

"Aw, fuck, man," he said. "That's Testarossa."

"Testarossa?"

"That's what we call him, 'cause that's his sweet ride. Plus, it's a symbol of his mindset. He thinks he's a Ferrari. Model pick-up artist. That's how he gets all the girls. See, bro, the human mind can be programmed to do astonishing things. If you think you're a Ferrari, really believe you're a Ferrari—*boom!*—you're a Ferrari. A Testarossa, in his case."

I tried not to roll my eyes.

"You know this Testarossa?" I said.

"Not well," he said. "Only met him once. But I'd love to party with him. He's on Hinraker's A-list."

"What's Hinraker's?"

"Not what. Who. Hinraker is an old rich dude. Sick motherfucking house on the water. The craziest shit happens at his parties. I mean the craziest motherfucking shit. Or so I've heard. I don't have the cred to get in yet, but I'm getting there."

"You don't have the what yet?" I said.

"The cred," he said. "You know. The status. Being in with the celebrities, the top tier social circles, the biggest parties. Life is all being about being high status, attracting attention."

"It is?"

"Fuck yeah! Once you reach the highest rung of status, you get to party with Justin Bieber and Ariana Grande."

"Is that good?"

"Dude, seriously?" He looked at me as if I had asked a blasphemous question, like it was pathetic that he even had to answer it. I shook my head.

"So who's this Hinraker?" I said.

"I told you," said Jason. "Some old rich guy."

"No, I mean what's he do?"

"Fuck, man, I don't know. Sits around and counts his money, I guess. All I know is the hottest girls party there. I'm talking super-hot, hotter than all these girls here. And they do anything and everything, right there. From what I hear, he doesn't care what you do or where you do it. Probably hires a cleaning crew to hose the whole place down afterward."

"Drugs?" I said.

Jason froze, leaning back and squinting at me. "Are you a

cop?"

"Do I look like a cop?"

Jason paused and bit his upper lip while staring at me. "No, I guess not. Yeah, I've heard Hinraker has anything you need, always there."

"Gotta be expensive."

"Hinraker can afford it, dude."

"And this guy Testarossa hangs there?" I said.

"All the time," he said. "He brings a boatload—I mean a fucking boatload—of pussy with him."

I glared at him, trying to figure out if there's anybody authentic inside Jason Stark. He's observant, perceptive, and takes action—positive skills which have helped him become a dominant up-and-coming leader in this fabricated nighttime empire. But I suspected it's all show. He'd probably be useless out in the real world.

"Speak of the devil," said Jason, "here is the man Testarossa himself now."

Down below, in walked Jake Preston surrounded by girls. White puffy shirt open to his waist. Black shiny pants like a rockstar. Swaying with two girls as the sea of dancers parted for them. None of the girls looked like Allie, although it was hard to tell from up here.

"Like I said," said Jason. "Act like a Ferrari, be a Ferrari."

"Uh-huh." I finished my drink.

I watched Jake Preston as he paraded through the center of the club. Everyone seemed to know him, waving as he passed like he's a celebrity. Fist bumps from guys. Smiles and waves from girls who paused bopping just to witness a god walking among mortals. The fable of the emperor with no clothes came to mind and I chuckled to myself. There were also some guys at the end of his entourage, trying to be as cool as their imperious leader but coming across as Toyotas instead of Testarossas.

Jason turned and looked hard at me from the side with a curious squint.

"You're not impressed with any of this, are you?" he said.

"Shows, huh?" I said.

He was perplexed. Must be a huge mystery to him why any guy wouldn't want all this. Bet he couldn't even stomach the thought that right now I'd even choose my two-room hovel with its broken air conditioner and lizard buddy over one minute more than absolutely necessary here.

"You sure you're not a cop?" Jason said.

"I'm not a cop," I said.

"What's with the pictures of the girl then? Why do you want to find her?"

I looked directly at him, wondering how to play this.

"I'm a hired gun," I said.

"No shit?" he said. "You work for the club?"

"No, private. Woman hired me to find her daughter."

"Duuuuude! That's awesome! A real life private eye. Just like in the movies."

"Well, I'm not really a—"

"I've often thought about getting into that kind of work myself."

"Bet you'd call yourself Jason Stark. How'd you come up with that name anyway?"

His eyes went wide and then he laughed.

"You said I was good," he said, "but you're sharp, too. Hey, what can I say? It's my business-name-slash-club-name. Kind of a combination of Jason Bourne and Tony Stark."

"Who's Tony Stark?" I said.

He shot me another look like I'm from a different planet.

"Seriously, dude?" he said. "*Iron Man*."

"Oh," I said. "That's a comic book, right?"

"Man, you got to get out more."

"So I've been told. What's your real name?"

He hesitated, then looked down. "Aaron Silverstein."

"I'll just call you Jason Stark."

"You da man."

He held his fist up for me to bump, which I reluctantly did.

"What do you do?" I said.

"Hang out, go to clubs," he said.

"No, I mean for work."

"Oh. I teach rich dorky dudes how to pick up girls."

"You're kidding."

He laughed, like he was letting me in on a secret. "No, I make a metric shit ton of money doing it."

"Does it work?"

"Naw, the guys that hire me are pathetic. But they're loaded so who am I to stop them from throwing wads of green at me? I usually just end up having one or two of my crew blow them and they feel all top dog, like they earned it themselves and got their money's worth."

Jake Preston, a.k.a. Testarossa, entered the skybox of another guest on the other side of the club, a large guy with long curly hair. A very large guy. Maybe too large for the skybox.

"Who's that?" I said.

"Aw, man, you shitting me?" said Jason. "Didn't you ever see the TV show *Gone* about all those people stranded on a distant planet and all the weird shit that happened to them?"

"No."

"JoJo Burley was the star. Well, one of the stars anyway. He played the fat goof who always got into trouble."

"Looks like a stretch for him."

"JoJo is cool. He's tight with Testarossa."

"You know JoJo?" I said.

"Met him once or twice," he said.

Time to drop a challenge. "You're a big enough name around here to introduce me, right? How about a little reconnaissance mission, Agent Stark?"

Jason's eyes lit up and put his fist up for another bump.

"Lock and load, brother," he said and led the way.

10

I HAD TO hand it to Jason Stark—authentic or not, he had the testosterone-infused swagger required for this place. As we walked through the throng of girls over to the other side, we both caught the attention of several of them.

"JoJo, my man!" said Jason as we reached the entrance to the large man's skybox.

JoJo waved to his security guy, who allowed us in. More bro-hugs as Jason introduced me.

"Drinks here," said JoJo. "Good stuff is out back."

JoJo Burley was at least three hundred pounds. He had tightly-curled hair that spread out from the top of his large oval-shaped head in long waves. I wondered if it could provide shelter from the elements.

I glanced toward the spot where JoJo had gestured. The skyboxes on this side were not only twice the size, but also had a private suite in behind. I saw leather couches and a big-screen TV back there, as well as a glass table surrounded by people.

They all seemed to be taking turns bending down. I couldn't see, but I'd guess doing lines of coke.

"Thanks," I said. "But I'm fine. Jason tells me you're quite the TV star."

"You a *Gone* fan?" JoJo said.

"Can't say I ever saw it."

"I respect you for that. Show sucked. It never allowed me to reach my true acting depth. I've been trying to get back on TV. I'm moving into producing. I have an idea for a reality show here in Miami."

"Oh yeah?"

Jason appeared at my side, handed me a drink, and moved away. I took it and sipped. Pure vodka. Ouch, I'm headed for trouble.

"Yeah," said JoJo. "It's kind of like *South Beach Tow* meets *The Apprentice* meets *The Bachelor*. Twelve hot girls in skimpy outfits need to impress a billionaire by starting their own streetwise business—all while helping underprivileged children from the inner city. Winner gets to fuck the guy and save the kids. And get this—I'm calling it *Miami Hotties*. Yeah? You like it?"

I forced my eyebrows to rise like I was impressed.

"Interesting," I said.

"You get it, right?" said JoJo. "'Cause, you know, you've got Miami Heat. This would be *Miami Hotties*. Get it?"

"I get it. It's brilliant. High concept."

"Thanks, man." He patted me on the back.

I caught the eye of a guy staring at me. Latino, in a shiny red shirt. Everything about him was shiny. His skin, his eyes, his thick black hair that looked like a bike helmet.

Over to my right was Jake Preston making out with a blonde in a white dress on his right. Then, he turned to make out with a black girl in a red dress on his left.

"He's doing well," I said, hoping JoJo would take the bait.

"Aw, he always does well," he said. "That's my man T,

short for Testarossa. Mango-Wango!"

I turned. Apparently the short black guy with bright green hair in a white pinstripe suit now entering the skybox was named Mango-Wango because he and JoJo bro-hugged while I took the opportunity to work my way over to Jake Preston.

I was halfway there when Shiny-Red-Shirt stood in my way.

"I know you," he said.

My brain scanned its database. He looked familiar, but I couldn't exactly place the face.

"Titus," I said with an outstretched hand.

"The bartender at that shit bar," he said without shaking my hand. Then, he turned to his right and spit.

Ah, now I remembered. He came into Cap'n Jack's one night with some friends and harassed some girls from Ohio. I had interceded, ending up punching his friend in the face.

"What you doing here?" he said.

"Enjoying the SoBe nightlife," I said and raised my glass, which only seemed to intensify his stare.

He glanced over at JoJo and Mango-Wango. "You friends with JoJo?"

"We just met. Seems like a great guy."

"You no belong here. You too old for this place."

I had a flash of the joy I would feel as my fist met his chin, but I filled my head with more serene thoughts.

"I remember that night," I said. "You guys were rude to my customers."

"You are son of a whore," he said.

"Eddie!" said Jason, appearing out of nowhere. "Eddie, meet Titus. Titus, this is Eddie Corrado. Eddie, this is my man Titus."

"We already meet," said Eddie Corrado. "You friends with this *mama pinga?*"

"Titus is cool, man," said Jason, massaging Eddie's shoulders. "He's cool."

"No, he is not cool. He a *hijo de puta.*"

Another turn and spit. His signature move, apparently.

"Hey, Eddie," Jason said, shooting me a shared look. "Come on, man. Is Martika here? The one you were telling me about? The one with the fine ass?"

He eased Eddie away from me with a wink. I sipped my drink and continued toward Jake Preston.

Jake was mid-makeout, his tongue deep down a new girl's throat, another one waiting her turn on his other side, when I approached him.

"Jake Preston," I said.

He shook his head like he needed to clear some clouds away just to hear me.

Then he regained his sense of place and looked at me. Up close, he was picture perfect cool. Longish wavy auburn hair with expensively foiled blond streaks. A shark-tooth pendant and another one with some numbers on it hung over his skimpy hairless chest.

"Have we met?" he said in a slow voice that intoned supreme control, yet stoned and high at the same time. So suave, so cool, so the man. The girls ignored me, one taking to his neck and the other nibbling on his ear.

"My name's Titus," I said. "I'm looking for Allie Hayes."

He froze, expressionless, and stayed like that for what felt like a century as the girls kept up their work. His eyes flickered.

"Who?" he said.

"Allie Hayes," I said. "I'm looking for Allie Hayes."

After another pause he relaxed even more, so much that I thought he might dissolve completely.

"I don't know any Allie whatever," he said. "Do you know Allie whatever?" he said to the girl on his right. She shook her head and kissed him. He turned to the girl on his left and said, "Do you know Allie whatever?"

"No," she said, shooting me a dirty look before she turned to suck on his tongue.

I turned to see Eddie Corrado talking with JoJo Burley. He

72

was gesturing with his hands.

"Well," I said, "Jake, we may have a problem. I know you know Allie Hayes and I'm going to find her."

There was a long pause, and then he laughed.

"It's a free country, man," he said. "Do whatever makes you happy. Good luck. I wish you the best."

This was obviously getting me nowhere. I felt the buzz of the drinks.

"I'll find her," I said.

He pretended not to hear me as he chomped on the blonde. I walked away and headed out back, past the cokeheads, and into the men's room. There was an empty stall on the far left where I unzipped.

I had finished and was about to flush when I felt a presence behind me. Before I knew it, there was the feel of cold steel at my neck.

"Hola, mama pinga," said Eddie Corrado and spat in my ear. "I not know what you up to, but I kill you if you show your face anywhere near my friend JoJo again. You leave now."

I've handled guys like Eddie Corrado hundreds of times, but it's been a while. I was unprepared. I should have known he would try this. I must be getting soft to allow him to get this close to me in the men's room with a knife in his right hand at my throat.

No biggie, though. Guys like Eddie think they know what they're doing but most don't go up against pros with a lot of experience.

With both hands, I grabbed his right forearm and forced it downward from my throat to my chest, keeping it pressed tight against me. At the same time, I crouched forward and spun right, knocking him off balance as I ducked under his arm and turned around to face the other direction. His right arm was now twisted out in front of me, both my hands clasped tight onto it like a vise, the knife pointing off to the side on my left. I could have easily broken his arm, but thought I'd be nice to a lesser foe. I kept my grip on his wrist with my left hand as I punched him in the throat with my right. His right hand released the knife and it clattered onto the floor. He made a gurgling sound and gasped for air. I pushed him gently against the wall and he went down, ending up in a seated position on the floor under the paper towel dispenser. He breathed hard, trying to get air back into his windpipe.

"Dropped something," I said as I picked up the knife, folded it, and tossed it near him. I got some paper towel out of the dispenser and walked to the sink.

"Eddie," I said as I wet the paper towel and cleaned out my ear, "if you're going to use a knife, learn some proper technique, okay? You might hurt yourself."

He wheezed some more, holding onto the floor like he was going to fall off it.

I washed my hands and checked my hair in the mirror. I walked over to the dispenser, took some more paper towel, and dried my hands. I walked back to the mirror, threw the paper towel in the trash, and straightened my collar.

Eddie continued his gasping and gurgling.

"Have a nice night now," I said and walked out.

When I re-emerged onto JoJo's skybox, some kind of shit had hit the fan. JoJo was talking to Tony V with a serious look on his face. Jason Stark was off to the side with Bri, who waved at me with a smile. Jason shrugged and gave me a look that said *I-don't-know-what-happened, dude.*

Sash, ever determined, clamped herself onto my right arm.

"We found you," she said.

"Can't fool you," I said.

Tony V and JoJo turned to face me as we approached. JoJo gave me a hard look that he had likely used on TV. I don't sense another bro-hug coming from him.

Tony V put his arm around me, steering me and my attached glittery blue shadow toward the back room.

"Titus," he said, "I have no idea what's going on up here,

74

nor do I need to know. But I have to ask you to—"

"It's okay, Tony," I said. "I'm leaving."

"I appreciate that, man. Some people around here are a little sensitive. It's not your fault. I respect the shit out of Paulie."

"It's all good. You did me a favor. Thanks."

I looked back at Jason Stark, now busy making out with Bri. Axel appeared out of nowhere.

"Axel will escort you out the back," said Tony V.

"Okay," I said.

I turned to see Eddie Corrado, still breathing with difficulty. He glared at me and I met his stare.

"Please," said Axel, motioning toward the exit.

I started walking, and then remembered I still have a girl hitched to me. I tried removing her, but both her arms clung mine like a serpent wrapped around a tree trunk.

"I'm going with you," Sash said.

"Now, Sash," I said, "I don't think that such a—"

"I'm going with you!"

Okay, fine. I figured I'd get her tucked into a cab outside to take her away and home. We walked out a door, down a set of stairs, and out a side door into the hot night.

Somehow, the relief of being away from the over-the-top world of Sinz caused the vodka to hit me full force. As we walked, I silently cursed myself for not getting to Jake Preston. But I did find out some valuable information, maybe something I can use.

I rolled this over and over in my head as I walked home, completely forgetting to tuck Sash into a cab. Then I rolled everything over and over in my head again on my airbed in my dinky little apartment with her.

11

MY EYES SHOT open at a scuffling sound. I was face-to-face with my tiny lizard buddy. The sky was light, but the sun wasn't up yet. My head pounded.

My buddy lingered a tad longer than usual today, seemingly dumbstruck at the naked girl asleep on my airbed.

Don't blame him.

Shit. Did I? I did, didn't I? Oh God, how could I have let this happen?

I leaned up and reached for my phone to check the time. 6:15 a.m. The room took a spin. Still somewhat drunk. Great.

Things got hazy after leaving Sinz. There was some walking, some talking, and a whole lot of soft and warm sweaty wonderfulness here afterward.

I quietly got up, steadying myself as the room twirled again. It stopped. I picked up Sash's flimsy blue dress and panties from the floor and hung them on the plastic chair. Then I showered and dressed, being careful not to stare at the naked girl. Which I did anyway.

Shit.

I went to the coffeemaker and opened up the coffee container only to discover I was out. Forgot to get some yesterday.

Shit shit shit.

I threw on some clothes, retrieved my day gun from the stash spot, and quietly went out.

I considered walking to Dunkin' Donuts over on Alton Road, but I wasn't sure I'd live that long. I headed to my emergency Starbucks on Washington Ave at 12th Street. Much closer.

I bought two large iced coffees and immediately downed the first one. Not as toxic with ice. The second was for Sash, but she'd probably be asleep for a while and I needed some time to think so I stuck the straw in it and walked two blocks to the beach.

Ocean Drive in the morning is unrecognizable from Ocean Drive at night. Elderly women with fanny packs speed-walked the pink sidewalk. The smell of bagels, muffins, and bacon swirled with the salty air. Bicyclists leisurely pedaled by. No exotic cars. No thumping bass. No long lines.

I almost liked it.

I crossed the park, passing several homeless people sleeping in the shadows of palm trees. I sat on the same stone wall that I leaned on just a few hours ago, only a few blocks south.

I fired up a cigarette and sipped my coffee, trying to kick-start my brain while staring at the iconic Art Deco buildings. One of them was where Al Pacino carved a guy up with a chainsaw in *Scarface*, but I forget which one.

I forced myself to slowly replay the events from Sinz. My thoughts drifted from Tony V to Jason Stark to JoJo Burley to Eddie Corrado, but they all blended together to form a confusing vodka-tinged swamp.

I blanked my mind and sipped some coffee.

In the meantime, what do I do about the naked girl in my bed? Most guys my age would consider themselves lucky, but I felt like a dirty old man. How I allowed that to happen was beyond me. No idea how to handle this. Will she want breakfast? It's been years since I've been in this situation. I really fucked up. What would Ariel say? Truth is, I haven't touched another woman since she died. It's almost like the thought hadn't even occurred to me.

No, that's wrong. The night I arrived here in Miami, Sofia's face above her badge and uniform lit by flashing lights as she peered down into my driver's side window. Yeah, I thought about it that night.

I shook my head, stubbed out my cigarette, and lit another one. I closed my eyes and listened to the sounds of the ocean behind me. Then, I heard footsteps approaching. I opened my eyes and looked in the direction of the sound.

Like he heard my need to confess, there was the Reverend Luther Williams. Running toward me in a black skull cap, blue running shorts, a white tank top, and incredibly large fluorescent green and white Nikes, his carved trapezius muscles glistening in the sunrise glow. He slowed as he saw me sitting on the wall, his good eye expanding wide.

"Well, I'll be," he said as he slowed to stop and placed his hands on his hips. "You following me?"

"You following *me?*" I said.

"Now why in hell I be following you?"

I sipped and smoked, my head still pounding.

"It's a sign," he said. "Meet a traveler on the road, and if his heart is true in his quest for light, you will meet again before the sun sets twice."

I blew out some smoke. "That's in the Bible?"

"No, Book of Luther, chapter five, verse ten. Translates to 'there ain't no coincidences.'"

"Yeah, whatever," I said, holding up the half-empty cup. "Coffee?"

"Devil's juice," he said, shaking his head. "So what you up to this fine morning, Brother Titus?"

"Trying to remember which building was the one in *Scarface*."

Luther turned and pointed. "CVS over there."

"You're shitting me," I said. "It's a fucking drugstore now?"

"Tony Montana be proud. Want to run with me?"

I exhaled a plume of smoke. "Do I look like I'm in any condition to run? It's painful to even look at you."

"You do somewhat resemble a rodent been dragged through a sewer."

"'Bout right," I said. "Needed to walk, think. Went to Sinz last night."

His eyebrows rose. "Kiddie Land let you in? You too tall for those rides."

"I was a special guest of Tony V, the owner, friend of a friend. Found out some info. Jake Preston likes to party at Hinraker's."

"Morton Hinraker," said Luther as he leaned back and folded his arms.

"Is there anybody in Miami Beach you don't know?"

"No. Go on."

"So apparently," I said, "this Hinraker owns a big mansion and has sex parties there. My question is, where does Allie Hayes fit in with all this?"

"You asked me about porn yesterday," Luther said. "That's how Hinraker made his fortune. Backed several companies then got out before it went sour. Now he an upstanding Miami citizen, a noble humanitarian who runs charitable organizations and dines with politicians while smoking big cigars at thousand-dollar-a-plate fundraisers."

"Politicians, huh? Did I mention Allie's dad is running for Senate?"

His head tilted. "Her dad is that bozo? The plot thickens."

"Gets better," I said. "I had a run-in with a lowlife named Eddie Corrado. Don't know if he's involved in all this, but he's in with all the players. Plus, he threatened me and I had to— ah—reason with him."

"Be careful," said Luther. "Eddie Corrado be nothing, but he work for Tommy Nero who I told you 'bout yesterday. You get on Tommy Nero's bad side and I be reading how they find pieces of your shark-eaten bones washing up by Pompano."

"Eddie Corrado works for Tommy Nero?" I said. "Interesting."

I blew some smoke away from him and stubbed out the cigarette. Then, I lit another one.

"When you going to give up the Satan stick," Luther said, "treat your body with respect?"

"When I finish my task," I said. "Then, I'm pretty much giving up everything."

"Your task of finding this rich college girl?"

"No, something else."

"Thought so." There was a long pause. "The same something else Officer Jezebel prevented you from doing, right?"

I nodded.

"At this very moment, though," I said, "I have another pressing problem. I could use a confession, maybe some penance, bless-me-father-for-I-have-sinned, couple rosaries or something, that kind of thing."

"Can't help you there," he said. "I non-denominational. Plus, only God Hisself can forgive sins. What sin did you commit, brother Titus?"

I turned and looked directly at him, wondering why I trust him enough to open up.

"There's a naked twenty-one year old girl in my bed," I said. "Well, *on* my bed. It's just an inflatable mattress on the floor. Surprised she didn't run when she saw where I live, but she was likely in no condition to judge. I don't know if I'm twenty-one or a hundred myself, because I feel like both this morning."

Luther folded his arms and frowned.

"You need to take a good long hard look in the mirror," he said. "Look at yourself—smoking, drinking, fornicating. I told you yesterday. Whatever burning you up inside is coming to your outside, setting fire to your soul. If you don't let it go, you going to flame out and there be nothing left of you but a pile of ashes."

I blew out some smoke. "Yeah, yeah."

"Start with your body," he said. "Strong mind fueled by a strong body. I run at sunrise every morning. Start down by 5th Street at the bottom of the park and then up to 25th and back, greet the Lord's gift of a new day by thanking Him for my health, my blessings, and the magnificence of his vast ocean. Meet me there and we run together. Soon you won't need no devil's juice or Satan sticks or be corrupting girls almost half your age."

"I'll think about it," I said, my stomach rolling at the thought. "But right now, what do I do about what's waiting for me back at my place?"

"Pray to God for forgiveness," he said, "then go and sin no more."

I exhaled and stubbed out the cigarette. "You're a big help, you know that?"

He shook his head and resumed his run.

"Sunrise," he shouted as he ran, "every morning, 5th Street, bottom of the park."

"Yeah, yeah," I said and he was gone.

I had consumed both coffees, so I stopped at Starbucks again on the way back and bought two more. I fought a street kid with a knife just hours ago without breaking a sweat, but as I neared my apartment my heart pounded out of my chest. I took a deep breath, opened the door, and walked in.

No girl. No purse. No slinky little dress and panties. Just

me and my lizard buddy.

There was a note written in lipstick on the countertop. It read:

Had a great time! Text me. =)

With a phone number and a sprinkle of glitter.

My heart calmed down. I sat at the table and sipped my coffee.

Well, that was easy.

I lay back down on the bed and went to sleep.

12

I WOKE UP at ten, the morning bright now. The flowery smell of Sash still lingered in the air, stinging the gaping chink in my armor.

I lit a cigarette and lay there, flicking ashes on the linoleum while reviewing the players. Eddie Corrado, who works for some gangster named Tommy Nero. Jake Preston, living arrangements unknown, royal prick-and-a-half. Morton Hinraker, one-time porn producer turned politician pal, hosts sex parties at his mansion. JoJo Burley, fading TV star. Jason Stark, SoBe club set social-climber.

Is there a connection between Eddie Corrado and Allie Hayes? If so, where does Jake Preston fit? He appears to have sex with several girls a day, maybe even an hour. Is Allie one of them? Is she okay with that? She can't possibly still be with him. Pam Hayes must be wrong about that.

If Pam Hayes is wrong about that, then this entire line of investigation is a waste of my time. But I know it's not. I saw it in Jake Preston's eyes when I said Allie's name. My gut told me he knew something.

Unfortunately, my gut has a spotty track record. But I'd bet on this one. Lieutenant Randall always used to chide me for leaping to conclusions without evidence, always made a show of throwing it in my face when I was wrong. Thing is, I was right more than I was wrong.

The next step was to get into a Hinraker party. Something told me I'd find my next clue there. Not sure what it will be nor how to go about getting it, but showing up is the first step. Then, I'll shake the tree and see what falls out. That's what I do.

But how do I get into Hinraker's party? Jason said he doesn't have the "cred" to get in. Jake Preston isn't going to get me in, that's for damn sure. Who can get me in? JoJo Burley?

I puffed out a ring of smoke around the rather large oval portrait of JoJo Burley in my mind. If there was a way to get to him, maybe wrangle an invite . . .

I booted up my Chromebook and ran an online search for 'JoJo Burley.' There he was, along with pictures from the TV show *Gone*. I found interviews, an IMDb profile, and a Wikipedia page. Looks like he grew up here in the Wynwood section of Miami, but now lives in a big house in L.A.

An idea began to percolate in my head. I looked at the time on my phone. 10:25 a.m. I searched for Jason Stark on Facebook Messenger and found him quick. I sent a friend request and a message:

You up?

No response. I waited a few minutes and messaged again with my phone number:

Want to party at
Hinraker's? Call me.

My phone rang in two minutes flat.

"Duuuuuuude," said Jason.

"Thought that would get you up," I said. "I figured you probably rise in the late afternoon."

"Close. What time is it anyway?"

"Ten-thirty."

"Shit." He yawned. "You serious about Hinraker's?"

"Dead serious."

"Dude," he said, "what happened last night with you and Eddie Corrado?"

"What did JoJo and Eddie tell you?"

Jason started talking but I couldn't hear him. The couple upstairs had begun Act One. They probably sensed I was on the phone and needed to be bothered.

"Hang on, Jason," I said.

I walked outside to the drab little courtyard and lit a cigarette under the sea grape tree. The heat was on High Inferno today. Not that it ever wasn't.

"Okay," I said, "say that again."

"I was just saying that Eddie Corrado hates you, dude," Jason said. "I mean, he really fucking hates you. I'm not even sure I should be talking to you. If anyone finds out, it could hurt my cred."

"I threw him out of a bar once. No big deal. So Hinraker's? You. Me."

"Dude, how?"

I blew out some smoke.

"Stop calling me dude," I said. "JoJo Burley. Ask him for an invite."

"Aw, dude—I mean, man—I can't, especially not after last night." There was a rustling sound on his end of the line. His voice went a couple of notches lower. "Hey, that girl Bri—thanks for hooking me up with her, man. You wouldn't believe what she likes to do."

"She told me," I said.

"Oh man, first she stuck her tongue in my—"

"Hey!" I said in my *shut-up* tone, cutting him off. "Discretion. So, I need to speak with JoJo, maybe mend things up. You know where he's staying?"

"JoJo's got a condo over at South Deluxe Towers. Multi-fucking-million dollar view of the ocean high up there. Owns like a whole goddamned floor. What are you thinking, man?"

I finished my cigarette, stubbed it out, and walked back inside.

"I'm thinking I go over and pay him a visit," I said.

"You can't just walk up," Jason said. "They've got massive security there. I mean fucking massive, man."

"Is there anything you can tell me about JoJo Burley that might help?"

"Help? What do you mean? Like how help?"

I sat down at my little table and stared at my empty airbed.

"I mean," I said, "think like a private investigator, Agent Stark. Who goes up there? How do they get in?"

"Hm, let me think," he said. "JoJo's got family. They're local somewhere. Don't know if that helps. I do know he gets a massage every day."

"Every day?"

"Yeah, guy named Guido. I met him once. Every day at two on the dot. Guido told me sometimes he has to kick JoJo to wake him up."

"Guido, huh? Is he independent or does he work through an agency?"

"No idea, man," said Jason. "Sorry."

While I was talking and smoking, I turned to my Chromebook and did an online search for 'Guido' + 'massage' + 'Miami.'

And there he was. Guido Lazzarone. Massage specialist. Miami Holistic Rejuvenation LLC. Full website with his picture

"Thanks, Jason," I said. "I think that will work."

"What will work?" he said.

"I've got a plan to get JoJo Burley to invite you and me to party at Hinraker's."

"If you accomplish this, man, you have forever earned my total respect and devotion."

"Good to know."

My little lizard buddy scattered out onto the linoleum looked around for the naked girl, saw she wasn't here, and then left.

Don't blame him.

"This is going to be epic," said Jason.

"What about your cred?" I said. "Being seen with me and all?"

"Get me into Hinraker's and my cred is golden. My social status automatically goes up ten notches." There was another rustling sound. "Hey, someone wants to say hi."

Before I could ask who, a soft female voice said, "Hi, Titus."

Shit.

"Hi, Bri," I said.

"I hope you're not mad I left with your friend," said Bri.

"No, not at all."

"Sash texted me. She said you have mad skills. She was very impressed. I mean, like, very *very* impressed, if you know what I mean." She giggled.

"Yeah," I said, unsure of how to respond to that, wishing a meteor would hit me.

"I got your number from her. You and I should hook up sometime."

"Now, Bri, I don't think—"

"Hey, man," said Jason, back on the phone. "So look, when are you hitting up JoJo Burley?"

"What time did you say he gets his daily massage?" I said.

"Two in the afternoon."

"Two in the afternoon, then."

13

MIAMI HOLISTIC REJUVENATION LLC was registered to an address on Jefferson Ave, a two-story apartment building that looked like it might be owned by the same guy that owned mine, if the rotting lime green stucco was any indication. The ten-year-old baby blue SUV out front had the business name stamped on its side with an ethereal New Age logo that looked like it might peel off at any moment.

Miami Holistic Rejuvenation LLC wasn't rolling in cash, that's for sure. As I smoked a cigarette while leaning on a telephone pole, I watched Guido Lazzarone exit a door on the second floor. He carried what must be a folded massage table, and walked down the steps to the SUV. Small guy, maybe five-foot-four. Lean, fit, thick black hair, a face that could be anywhere from twenty to fifty. Blue polo shirt, khaki pants, boat shoes.

Timing is everything in these situations. As Guido loaded the massage table into the back of the SUV, I counted down from ten-to-one as I pushed myself off the telephone pole, pulled my gun from its holster, and strolled across the street.

There was probably a better way to do this. In fact, I was certain there was a better way to do this—but I was hung-over, cranky, and impatient. I wanted to solve this sooner rather than later, so I was taking things to a level that could be termed extreme.

I approached the rear right of the SUV just as Guido sat in the driver's seat. As soon as the door shut, I opened the passenger-side and slithered into the seat, pointing the gun directly at Guido's face—a face definitely closer to fifty than twenty.

"Hi, Guido," I said.

He made a whimpering sound like he was going to cry.

"Guido," I said. "This has nothing to do with you. I need to speak with JoJo Burley. That's where you're headed, right?"

His face was locked in an odd frozen expression. I sincerely hoped he wasn't shitting his pants right now. Maybe I'm coming on too strong. Damn, I'm coming on too strong, aren't I? I should have thought this through. Too late now.

What was it Luther said? Impulsive, even a little unhinged. Maybe he's right.

"Guido," I said, "it's okay to nod."

Guido made a tiny up-and-down gesture, his eyes so wide I thought one might fall out.

"Now drive," I said.

He made a mouse-like sound and started the SUV.

We followed Jefferson Ave south all the way to 2nd Street, where we turned right and then left onto Alton Road, which became South Pointe Drive.

South Deluxe Towers is one of the latest condo developments on the south tip of the south end of South Beach. A zillion stories high, it's a "monument to modern architecture", or some bullshit that makes the Chamber of Commerce wet its collective pants. To me, it looked like a giant penis with wings.

The security guard at the garage entrance was a kid in a khaki outfit with a ponytail and a long beard. He reclined in a tall chair with his feet up, absorbed in his phone. Not the "maximum security" I had been expecting based on Jason's description.

He recognized Guido's SUV and waved him through without even noticing me. Guido tried to get his attention, but whatever the kid was doing on his phone was far more engrossing.

"I'm sorry, Guido," I said as he parked the SUV. "I know you're a good guy and I don't want to hurt you. I don't want to hurt JoJo either. I just need to talk to him and I could think of no other way to get in here. I'm a private investigator. Shit. No, I'm not. Although, I have been hired privately to investigate something. So that sort of qualifies, right? I mean, sure I'm not sealed and stamped and certified and all that shit like Sofia says, but by the definition of the phrase private investigator, that counts, right?"

Guido nodded. I think Guido would have nodded if I said I was Luke Skywalker.

"Let's do everything just the way you always do it normally," I said. "Okay, Guido?" He nodded again. "Say okay."

"Okay," he said. He sounded like his mouth was full of apple pie.

We exited the SUV and Guido got the folding massage table out of the back. We walked over to a bank of elevators. Guido inserted a keycard with a shaky hand and the doors opened. Once inside, he pressed "24." I tucked the gun behind my back for the security cameras and up we went.

I looked over at Guido and smiled. He didn't smile back. I felt bad for him. Just a guy doing his job and here I am playing the part of some thug with a gun scaring the shit out of him.

Fuck, I'll have to make it up to him somehow. Why do I put myself in these situations? Why?

Ding! The doors opened.

We stepped into an anteroom with a spectacular view of the Port of Miami. Bug-like dots moved to-and-fro down there, dockworkers loading and unloading brightly colored shipping containers. I looked straight down. Directly beneath us close to the building, a sailboat gracefully drifted into Government Cut.

To my right was a door. The decor was modern fluorescent blue glass with lots of marble. There was a mirror over a stand with a vase of flowers by the door. A numbered keypad glowed with a red light.

"What now?" I said.

"N-now I en-enter the code," Guido said.

"Breathe, Guido, just breathe. Everything is going to be okay. Just enter the code."

He entered the code. The red light turned green and there was a click. He reached for the handle and turned it.

The door opened into possibly the largest living room I have ever seen. The walls and floor were a brilliant white. Funky modern chandeliers with glass squares dangled artfully. A white shag rug lay under a large round glass coffee table in the epicenter of the large space surrounded by two white sofas that faced each other. The rest of the furniture was all black—black chairs, black dining set, black TV cabinet.

Brilliant light streamed from floor-to-ceiling windows that stretched up at least three stories to a point, presumably the top of the building. Downtown Miami bustled on one side and the turquoise Atlantic glistened on the other. Several large glass doors opened out onto a wraparound deck.

That TV show *Gone* must have made a lot of money.

Guido and I stood there on the white marble floor for what seemed far too long. White marble steps led up to the entrance to a room that from here looked like it had an even higher ceiling, kind of like an airplane hangar.

"What do you usually do now?" I said.

"I wake him up," said Guido. "Or try to. S-some days it's h-harder than others."

"Breathe and relax, breathe and relax. Start by calling him."

"H-hey," said Guido in a soft voice and coughed.

"Little louder maybe," I said.

He nodded and cleared his throat. "Hey! JoJo! Hey-yo-hey! Massage time! Wake up!"

He looked up at me with an expression that said, *Was that good?*

I smiled and nodded, feeling like the worst bully on a school playground. This was definitely not the way to do this. I should have thought it out better. But whatever. We're here and we need to make the best of it.

"Again," I said.

"JoJo!" said Guido. "Massage! It's Guido. Massage!"

"Just a minute," said a muffled male voice from the airplane hanger.

"Is that his bedroom?" I said.

"Yeah," said Guido.

"It's huge."

"Coming," said a voice I recognized as JoJo Burley from last night. "Just a sec."

Next, I witnessed one of the strangest sights I had ever seen. JoJo Burley, in a bright pink silk robe, emerged from the bedroom. The robe was open, his rolls of fat jiggling to and fro above what looked like a vast black patch of forest that started at his chest and continued all the way down to his knees.

Even though he was exposing himself completely, the thick forest of pubic hair covered everything. If I didn't know he was male, there was nothing visible to confirm that.

"God," said JoJo, yawning and scratching his head as he walked down the steps, talking to nobody in particular, "what a fucking night. Don't know what the fuck time it is or who the fuck I am or who the fuck I fucked."

He stopped, pounded his fist on his chest, and let out a belch that echoed all the way to Cleveland.

Then he waddled past us into the kitchen, not even

registering me or my gun. He opened up a refrigerator the size of my apartment and removed a gallon of orange juice. He chugged from the plastic bottle, consuming three quarters of it.

I glanced at Guido, who almost smiled.

"Man, that shit hit the spot," said JoJo as he replaced the container and wobbled back out into the living room. "Guido, my man, how you doing?"

JoJo went in for the bro-hug, suddenly realizing Guido wasn't alone.

"Holy fuck," said JoJo, eyes popping at me. "It's you. The guy from Sinz."

"No noise," I said. "No sudden moves. I just want to talk, JoJo."

He finally saw the gun and wavered like he was going to throw up. He made a gurgling sound and turned to run.

I leaned forward a foot and tripped him. He went down hard onto the rug. I swear the entire building shook. Then, he vomited all over the white shag.

Guido made a run for the door. I got to him halfway and grabbed him by the shirt collar, dragging him back.

"Ow! Ow!" he said. "You're hurting me."

"Sorry," I said, as I dragged him to the couch and threw him down on it.

Guido landed all slumped, hitting his elbow on the armrest with another "Ow!"

I grabbed JoJo by the hair at the back of his head. It felt slimy.

"Ahhhh!" he said and rose, allowing me to lead him to the facing sofa, where I pushed him down to sit across from Guido, who was nursing his elbow.

"JoJo," I said. "Sorry about this, but I need to talk to you. I couldn't think of any other way. I'm not a bad guy, probably not what anybody told you last night. I just need to talk. In fact, I need your help."

Both of them just stared at me incredulously.

"Is there anyone else here?" I said.

JoJo thought for a good long time and then finally said, "Two girls. No, wait—" He counted on his fingers. "—three girls."

"Where?"

"Bedroom," he said, motioning toward the airplane hangar with his finger.

Keeping the gun raised and pointed at a space between them, I circled the couch and moved up the steps backward to the entrance to the bedroom.

On a sinfully large round silky bed lay a variety of legs, breasts, and buttocks with no beginning and no end, like an M.C. Escher porn shoot.

"I count eight legs," I said, circling back to the guys who hadn't moved.

JoJo closed his eyes and counted again on his fingers.

"Oh, right," he said. "Four girls. I forgot Amanda."

I centered myself between them and the door, tucked the gun away in its holster, and spread my hands. Warm. Open. Mr. Friendly.

"JoJo", I said with a big smile.

"That's my name," said JoJo.

"Good. We're making progress already. This won't take long. I need you to answer just a couple of questions for me."

I could see JoJo in his mind changing character, like he was propping himself up for a scene. He raised his head and looked at me deadpan, not caring that the robe was wide open.

In a thick Western twang, he said, "I ain't telling you shit."

"You forgot to spit," I said.

His face lost the façade. "Huh?"

"The spit. When you say 'I ain't telling you shit' like John Wayne, you're supposed to turn and spit. Your buddy Eddie Corrado has it down pat."

JoJo's face went from frozen to a tiny laugh. Then, he started laughing hard, almost doubling over. He continued to laugh for much too long.

"What's he on?" I said to Guido.

"Everything," said Guido with rolling eyes and jazz hands.

"JoJo!" I said in my *toss-drunks-out-of-Cap'n-Jack's* voice. "Listen up!"

JoJo snorted and sat up, a huge chunk of something falling out of his nose and landing splat on the coffee table. He didn't seem to notice.

"There's nothing you can say or do to make me help you," he said, again trying to sound like a gunslinger, "so get off my property, pardner."

This time he turned and spit to his right, then turned his head to meet me with hard eyes.

"Better," I said. "Much more convincing."

He broke character to say, "Yeah, you like that?"

I looked over at Guido, who rolled his eyes again.

"Yeah," I said. "But we've got a problem, JoJo. Those hard eyes, that gravelly voice. You've probably practiced that in front of a mirror a hundred times for some scene where you had to pretend to be a tough guy. I, on the other hand, have never had to pretend to be a tough guy, because I actually *am* a tough guy."

He stood up, the actor's stare focused on me, his thumbs looped on an invisible gun belt. "I'd like to see you back that up," he said.

I leaned forward and tapped JoJo Burley in the chin with the back of my hand. Well, to me it was a tap. To an out-of-shape Hollywood actor who had never been in a real fight, it was a heavy blow.

JoJo Burley buckled down into a fetal position on the floor. Oh God, now he was crying. I looked at Guido, who was about to burst into either tears or laughter.

"JoJo," I said, "pull yourself together." I kicked his large rear.

"I've never had a gun pointed at me before, man," he said. "Please."

"I already put the gun away, JoJo. Just tell me what I need to know, I'll go, and everything will be fine."

He put his hands up. "Okay, man. Okay. Okay."

He got up and sat on the couch, finally realizing his robe was open. He wrapped it around himself.

A yellow puddle had formed on the floor where he had been. I felt bad for his cleaning staff.

"Now," I said, "listen to me. I have been hired to find a missing girl. Her name is Allie Hayes." I took out my phone. "Now, I'm going to hold up a picture of her and you're going to take a good long look at it and tell me if you've ever seen her before."

I held up the phone and JoJo looked.

"Uh-uh," he said.

"Uh-uh what?" I said.

"Uh-uh, no. I've never seen her before."

"Okay." I turned to Guido. "While we're here, not that you frequent the same stations in life that JoJo here does, have *you* seen this girl?"

Guido leaned forward and looked at the picture. He shook his head.

"Okay," I said. "She hangs around with Jake Preston. Jake Preston goes to Morton Hinraker's sex parties at his house. You go to Morton Hinraker's sex parties at his house. I want to go to one of Morton Hinraker's sex parties at his house. It's that simple. See, I'm a good guy, JoJo. Just like you. Your buddy Eddie Corrado doesn't like me. Although if I were you, I'd question *his* intentions, not mine. I'm a good guy trying to find a missing girl for her mom who misses her dearly. Sounds like a movie, doesn't it? Or maybe the pilot of a TV show you could star in, kind of like a new version of *Miami Vice*, only darker and more modern. Made for today."

At that, JoJo's eyes lit up and his face expanded like a balloon inflating slowly, stretching into a big wide smile.

"Kind of like the good guys aren't all good and the bad

guys aren't all bad," he said. "The cops are part-criminal, and the criminals are part-cop."

"I like your thinking, JoJo," I said.

"Dude, this is a great idea! This is the idea I've been waiting for. I can see it now. You're never too sure who the good guys are and you think the crime is solved and—*bammo!*"–he slammed his fists together— "the season is over and everyone watching on Netflix is like 'what the fuck just happened?' Brilliant, man, brilliant!"

One of the girls appeared at the doorway stark naked.

"Oh," she said, scratching her blonde head. "I didn't mean to interrupt your meeting. Sorry. Where's the bathroom?"

"Other side of the bedroom," said JoJo.

"Okay," she said while yawning. She turned and disappeared.

"Then," said JoJo, "we could have a guy who looks just like Edward James Olmos to play the old grizzled police commander. In fact, maybe we could get Edward James Olmos himself. What's he doing now since *Battlestar Galactica?*"

"JoJo", I said, "back to here and now."

"Huh? Oh, sure man. No problem. Look, man, this is brilliant. I'll cut you in. This was your idea."

"Just get me into one of Hinraker's parties."

"That's it? That's all you want?"

"That and fifty percent."

"Eighty twenty."

"Seventy thirty."

JoJo stared at me and said, "Fine." There was a long pause. "So this pretty girl? Her mom misses her, huh? Thinks something bad happened to her, huh?"

"Yes," I said.

"Her mom thinks she may go to Hinraker's parties?"

"Yes."

"I can see that." He scratched his chin, trying to play the part of a deep thinker. "Okay, I'll get you access. Next one is

Tuesday night. Shit, I won't be here. I have to fly to L.A. I have pitch meetings all next week out there. Got to catch a flight at four today. Hey, what time is it?"

"Two."

"Shit. I've got to go. No massage today, Guido. Sorry."

"Can you call Hinraker before you go?" I said. "Get me in?"

"No, man," JoJo said, "that's not how it works. Wait a sec. I'll give you my Sapphire Key, but you've got to promise to give it back to me."

"I promise."

He got up and wobbled up the steps to the bedroom.

I smiled at Guido. He didn't smile back. I took out my wallet, peeled out two hundred dollar bills of Pam Hayes' money, and handed them to him. He took them and looked at me incredulously.

"For the trouble." I said. "No massage, having a gun pointed at you, shit like that. No hard feelings, I hope."

"Sure," said Guido, still jumpy.

I felt bad so I handed him two more hundred dollar bills.

"Thanks," he said, less jumpy.

Rummaging sounds emerged from the bedroom. Then, JoJo appeared in the doorway holding what looked like a purple leather box.

He set it down on the glass coffee table and opened it. Inside, encased in purple velvet, was a huge old-fashioned key with a sapphire embedded into it.

"This will get you and a guest into Hinraker's," said JoJo. "Just show it to the guys at the door. But you've got to really really seriously promise to bring it back to me. I mean really really really seriously, no shit."

"You'll get it back, JoJo," I said. "I really really really seriously promise. I'm a man of my word. Thank you. I appreciate it. Mrs. Hayes appreciates it. See, I told you. You're a good guy, I'm a good guy. We're friends now."

I heard Guido breathe a sigh of relief as JoJo stood up with both arms extended, going for a bro-hug. The silky robe flew open.

"Let's just fist bump," I said.

He smiled and held out his fist, which looked slimy.

"Later," I said. "When I return the key."

"Okay, man," said JoJo. "Later. But we are going to make a fortune with this new updated darker *Miami Vice* reboot idea!"

"Of course we are. But hey, if you run into Vin Diesel out there in L.A., you might not want to mention it to him. Now I'm going to leave and everything is going to be cool, right?"

"So cool," said JoJo.

Guido nodded emphatically.

I backed out of the apartment and got the hell out of the building as fast as I could.

14

BACK AT MY place, I placed the "Sapphire Key" in my stash spot between Pam Hayes' envelope and my Sig. The JoJo's condo incident made me want to shower again, so I did. Once done, it hit me that I hadn't eaten since yesterday.

I considered another five-dollar Dominican dinner from the Art Deco Supermarket, but instead walked to Puerto Sagua at 7th and Collins, where I had a Cuban sandwich with a side of deep-fried yuca sticks. As I ate while watching tourists scream and run for cover as the daily summer storm rolled through, I thought about Allie Hayes, Eddie Corrado, Jake Preston, and JoJo Burley. Nothing new came to me.

I looked at my watch. 4:00 p.m. Shit, what do I do now? I'm not used to two days off in a row. Maybe I should go buy a car with Pam Hayes' money.

Itchy and restless, I walked to Alton Road, picked up a large iced coffee at Dunkin' Donuts, and headed back the long way around. Everywhere, sunshine twinkled rainbows through post-storm steam. I passed Cap'n Jack's and thought about stepping in to check on Bruno. No, I needed to think some more. I crossed at 1st Street and lit a cigarette. As I rounded the corner up Meridian, I decided Luther was right. I'm unhinged—smoking, drinking, bedding club girls, pointing guns at people's faces. I needed to change, get my edge back.

Maybe if I hadn't been so unhinged, I would have noticed the man in a baby blue sport coat walking a hundred yards ahead of me and how he maintained the distance between us. By the time I spotted him and another guy on the other side of the street in a tan sport coat, it was too late. Classic mistake, and I walked right into it.

I turned and looked behind me, knowing what I would see. Yep, a third guy. In a red plaid sport coat. Do they call each other in the morning to color coordinate?

The guy across the street crossed, moving parallel to me. A car glided up on my left just as I reached for my gun.

"Think again," said a deep voice behind me. I turned to see a guy with thinning red hair, a gun in his hand.

Shit.

The guy ahead of me had turned around and was walking toward me, also with a gun out. Thinning-Red-Hair opened the door to the back of the car and put his hand out.

"Tommy Nero would like to see you," he said. "Gun, please."

"You think I'm just going to hand you my sidearm and get in the car?" I said.

"You will. One way or another."

"Who's Tommy Nero? What's he want to talk to me about? I got no business with any Tommy Nero."

"Look, pal, Tommy Nero says to get you and bring you to him. I do what I'm told. I'm not his fucking therapist, okay? Now, can we play this civil, please? I've got a headache and you're not helping it any."

Rage boiled up inside me—not at these goons but at my own stupidity. I walked right into this. The only people in sport coats in the summer in South Beach are morons with guns.

I could flame out now, hit the "full unhinged" button, go out in a blaze of glory. Pull, shoot, and die right here a block from my place. Why not? What's the point of going on? What do I really have to live for?

But something inside kept me steady and said to play along. Fine, whatever.

I took out my gun, butt up, and handed it to Thinning-Red-Hair. He dropped it in the right front pocket of his sport coat.

"Lose the coffee and the smoke," he said.

"Aw man, really?" I said. "It's Dunkin' Donuts. This is the good stuff."

"Lose it."

I sipped a huge gulp while staring into his dead eyes. I placed the still half-full plastic container at the foot of a No Parking sign, threw the cigarette on the pavement, stepped it out, and got in the back. Thinning-Red-Hair joined me. The other two guys piled in, one on my left and one in front next to the driver. There was a heavy smell of garlic.

"You forced me to litter," I said to Thinning-Red-Hair. "That's against the law, you know."

"My trigger-finger is itchy," he said and shoved his gun into my side. "I'd hate to have the urge to scratch it."

"You've been watching too many gangster movies. The New York accent is good, but you've got to frown and smile at the same time if you want to really sound like Robert DeNiro. Not to mention calling someone who's obviously not a pal 'pal' is so outdated."

He laughed. "Boys, we got ourselves a real comedian here. Thinks he's hilarious."

Nobody said anything. The driver took the car right past my apartment. We turned right and then left onto Collins, going north.

We rode in silence all the way up to where endless rows of condos on both sides of the street block the sun, creating a wide dark tunnel.

As we pulled into a building on the right, I saw the same large Latina woman from two nights ago standing in the middle of traffic on a divider way up here. Still holding up the same sign. Still braving the elements to find her missing daughter. Damn. What was it Luther had said about no coincidences?

The condo complex reeked of Miami Beach circa 1961, that Fontainebleau-Jack Kennedy-Frank Sinatra era. Framing the big outdoor space in front of the lobby were several oblong concrete rings that once may have passed as modern architecture, but were now high-maintenance kitsch. Some plucky weeds had climbed the side of one over the years. Nobody seemed to care.

We got out of the car in the first-level parking garage. Thinning-Red-Hair pointed me toward a bank of elevators, his gun still in my ribs.

"Aren't you going to say 'No funny business, now'?" I said.

"Keep it up, smartass," said Thinning-Red-Hair. "Just keep it up, see what happens to you."

"That's a good line, too. I knew you were a pro."

We rode up to the tenth floor and stepped out into a hallway. The building was clean but the air was thick with that unique Florida decades-of-mildew-buildup aroma. Thinning-Red-Hair opened a door and we entered a suite. It was an office waiting room. Couch, two chairs, coffee table, bland art on the walls. A large black man in dreadlocks and a black suit with a white shirt open at the neck stood guard. He was as big as Luther but more fat than muscle. The bulge of a large gun protruded from its holster under his right lapel. Must be left-handed. Thinning-Red-Hair moved past him and knocked on the office door.

"Yeah," said a voice from inside. Thinning-Red-Hair opened the door and motioned me in with a head nod. I entered a sparse office with a stunning view of the Atlantic. He and the large black man followed me in.

Sitting behind a plain desk was one of the strangest looking men I'd ever seen. He was almost perfectly round, except for the top of his pale bald head which was flat, almost like a crater. It reminded me of a big white dormant volcano. His face looked like it had been mashed together from pounded clay. His rotund but hearty body was a messy mix of fat and muscle that filled the space behind the desk with equal parts beach-ball and granite. He wore a white suit, a pale blue shirt, and a white tie. A gold chain fell inside from one lapel to the other. He had the whitest skin I've ever seen on a human being, nearly translucent. That, combined with not one follicle of hair anywhere, made him look like a tough mutant baby.

"Close the door," he said to Thinning-Red-Hair, who placed my gun and magazine on the desk, and closed the door. The big black man stood next to me, hands clasped in front, staring straight ahead. My only way out was either through him or a leap out the window ten stories down. Bad odds, either way.

The mutant baby motioned me to sit in the swivel office chair on the opposite side of the desk. I sat. We stared at each other for a good long beat before he said my full name in a deep voice with what could have been a New York accent.

I shrugged. His stare told me he didn't like shrugs. Most people probably beg him for mercy at this point. He wasn't used to shrugs and it irked him.

"My name is Tommy Nero," he said. "I'm sorry for the abrupt manner in which I called this meeting, but I got the impression that you wouldn't respond to a handwritten invitation on linen stationery. Plus, it's faster this way. I like to get things done. Money loves speed."

I shrugged again. We stared at each other for a good long beat. Yep, definitely irked.

"You're a former police officer," he said, studying a paper on his desk. "Discharged for a series of offenses including failure to follow proper interrogation procedure, witness intimidation, insubordination, and assault on a Federal agent. Did time for conspiracy to commit murder. Sentenced to fifteen years. Yikes. Only did ten months. Case was expunged when a grand jury allowed new evidence that cleared you. Sorry about your time in the stink. I've never been."

I shrugged. He laughed. A vein pulsed near his temple.

"Do you know who I am?" he said.

"I think you said Tommy something," I said, "but I wasn't really paying attention. Why, do you have memory issues? They have supplements for that now, you know."

He slowly turned red. I thought he might burst, which would be messy. He closed his eyes, inhaled a couple of deep breaths, and returned to his normal Arctic pallor.

"Okay, Titus, you're a funny guy," he said. "I get it. Ha ha. But help me out here. What brings a former police detective all the way from Boston to Miami to work at a run-down bar that caters to local drunks? Doesn't make any sense to me."

"I like the ambience," I said.

"You like the ambience. At Cap'n Jacks."

"Okay, you're right. The real reason I'm here is to audition for the new *Miami Vice* reboot with JoJo Burley, the guy from *Gone*. I think I've got a shot at Crockett."

"Well, you see Titus, I've got a problem. I hate problems. All I want to do is make money, but all I seem to get is problems. I like money. Money is what I do. It's my passion. I grew up on the streets in Camden, New Jersey. Ever been to Camden, New Jersey?"

"Only passing through on Amtrak."

"Do you have any idea what it's like for a guy as white as me to grow up in Camden, New Jersey?"

"Probably not a hell of a lot of fun," I said.

"Exactly," he said. "And yet, I came out on top. Ran a successful business, and then realized maybe it's best to go somewhere warm, someplace maybe I wouldn't stand out so much. So I come here to sunny South Florida, vacationland, endless sun and beaches, and guess what? I still stand out like a sore thumb. Everybody here is tan as fuck. I can't go anywhere near the sun. But it's okay. It's nice and warm. I like Miami. Coming from Camden, it's a piece of cake, 'cept maybe for the Cubans. They don't seem to appreciate me."

"Shame. And you such a lovable fuzzball and all."

"I'm a straight-shooter, Titus. I'm—what's that fancy word?—guileless. Got no guile, not an ounce. I tell it like it is. I'm a businessman. My word is good. If I say something is going to happen, then you can bet your ass it's going to happen. Got it?"

"I think I got it."

"If I say I'm going to kill you, you can kiss your ass goodbye because it's a guarantee. I'm *not* going to kill you, Titus. You're not worth it to me. I just need to know what's your beef with Eddie Corrado."

"Look, Tommy," I said, "this has been a great show. Way better than *The Godfather Part Three*, but I've got to hit the road. Time waits for no man. Bet you don't know who said that."

"Chaucer," he said.

I raised my eyebrows. "Impressive. A literate gangster."

"Titus, don't make me prove my credentials to you. Truth is, I don't like using my credentials unless I absolutely have to."

"Your credentials being Bubbly Bob Marley here?"

"His name is Arnaud, and I seriously doubt you would be able to prevent him from showing you my credentials."

I sat back in the chair. "Tommy, let's stop the dick-waving and get right down to it. If I was really in the way of something, you wouldn't bother to cart me here to your office. I'd be shark food. I know Eddie Corrado works for you, not you for him. You wouldn't cart me here to chide me for bruising your boy. You're trying to find something out *about* your boy."

Tommy Nero shot me with his finger.

"You're good," he said. "You think. You quote Chaucer. I may hire you."

"No thanks," I said.

"Pays better than Cap'n Jack's."

"Most things do."

He shrugged.

"The way things look to me," I said, "you suspect Eddie Corrado of something. In your business, everything is about money, so it's something to do with money. Skimming, maybe?"

"Go on," he said.

I sat forward, a plan forming in my head.

"Fine," I said. "I'll tell you what I'm doing. I was hired to find a girl."

"What girl?" he said.

"I'm going to reach into my pocket and take out my phone to show you a picture, okay?"

He nodded. I got my phone, scrolled to Allie's pictures, and turned it to show him.

"Her name is Allie Hayes," I said. "Know her?"

"No," Tommy Nero said. "What does she have to do with Eddie Corrado?"

"Don't know. I'm still detecting. Maybe nothing."

"So your connection with Eddie was just that he was there at Sinz? Nothing else?"

"As far as I know. Besides the fact I threw him and his buds out of Cap'n Jack's one night and Eddie holds a grudge over it. But that's it."

We stared at each other for a solid minute. Way offshore behind Tommy's head, a tanker plodded its way across the bright aqua waves toward Port Everglades.

"Titus, I believe you," he said. "You're a straight-shooter, too. I recognize my own kind."

"I'm nothing like you, Tommy," I said.

"Maybe not, but your word is your word. I like that."

I nodded.

"Okay," he said, "so somebody hires you to find a girl. Why they would hire *you* is questionable. If I were you, I'd watch my back."

"Thanks for the loving concern," I said. "Bottom line, Tommy—I have no idea what Eddie Corrado is up to with you."

"Which is what worries me. Eddie doesn't act on his own, most times."

"Until now."

"Until now. Titus, I would appreciate your help."

"To flush someone out? So you can find out how much he knows, how deep he's in, so you can feed him to the gators? No thanks. I'm no accessory."

Tommy Nero templed his hands and stared at me for an uncomfortably long beat. My plan took full shape. It was going to require turning up the unhinged knob, which of course would be no problem for me.

"I could hurt you," he said.

"You could fucking kill me," I said. "Go right the fuck ahead. You'd be putting me out of my misery."

There was another long pause.

"Well, come on, man, go!" I said, turning on the crazy. "What the fuck are you waiting for? Kill me! Because I'll tell you, son of a bitch, if you stand in my way, I wouldn't hesitate for a second to kill you."

We stayed that way some more—one crazy set of eyes staring into another crazy set of eyes.

He broke the stare first, and then laughed.

"You're something else, Titus," he said. "Fine. Let's just leave it at me telling you to stay away from Eddie Corrado."

"I don't take marching orders from you or any man," I said. "If Eddie is involved in my case, then I won't be able to do that."

"Why play it hard, Titus? I could use someone like you to handle things on the outside, make sure my team is clean."

"I'd rather eat fire ants."

"That can be arranged."

"So, are we done here? Can I get my gun back?"

"Phil will give it to you when he drops you back at your place."

I shook my head, reaching for my gun on the desk with my right hand. I felt the breeze of Armaud's arm as it came down to prevent me as I knew it would, but I swiveled to my left in the office chair and, in one swift motion, I slid the office chair right, my right foot stomping Armaud's left foot as my right elbow smashed into his groin. As he doubled over, my left hand went up under his sport coat and yanked his gun out of its holster under his right lapel.

Tommy had opened a drawer in the desk, his hand on a Browning 9mm, but I had Armaud's Ruger Super Redhawk pointed at his large head before he could get it out.

"Take it out and hand it to me, butt up," I said. "Or find out how crazy I really am."

Tommy hesitated, but realized he had no choice. I took the Browning, put it in my left pocket, and shifted the Ruger to my left hand.

With my right, I reached over and snapped the magazine back into my own Smith & Wesson, never taking my eyes away from Tommy's. I pointed it at Tommy, and stuffed Armaud's Ruger in my belt with my left hand. Three guns. Talk about armed and dangerous.

"Now Thinning-Red-Hair," I said.

Tommy nodded and said, "Phil."

"Son of a bitch," said Phil as he tossed his own Browning 9mm onto the desk. I took it with my left and just held it. I was running out of space for guns.

"Nice meeting you, Tommy," I said.

"The pleasure was all mine, Titus," he said.

"I'm going to leave now. I'll place everybody's guns on the coffee table in the waiting room. If you want to send your boys down the hall to kill me, that's your choice. Go right the fuck ahead. But you said you weren't going to kill me and you're a man of your word. You wouldn't want to be called a liar now,

110

would you? Thanks for the offer of a ride, but that car stinks. You might want to get it cleaned, seriously."

Tommy made a silent gesture to Armaud to let me go. I slinked backward and out the door, leaving their guns on the table as promised and closed the door to the suite behind me.

I took my time walking out. Like Tommy said, they had no reason to kill me. Tommy would do it, but only if absolutely necessary. He's a criminal, but he's also a practical businessman. Probably why he never did time. Wish I could say the same.

Out in the hot sun, I crossed Collins and over to the big Latina woman with the sign in the divider.

I approached her and studied the picture of a pig-tailed teenager with big pretty eyes and a sweet smile. It was a school portrait, 9" x 16" with a white border. Middle school graduation picture, I'd guess.

"You see her?" said the woman. "You see my Marisol?"

"No," I said. "When did she go missing?"

"I sorry, not good English."

I tried to dig up the little Spanish I knew from the back of my brain. *"Cuanto tiempo desde . . ."*

"Oh, sí, sí! Hace una semana. Siete días."

A week. Not good. A lot can happen in a week. I stared at the picture of the girl. She looked familiar. Stunning eyes. Where have I seen that face before?

I took out my phone and snapped a picture of the picture. *"Cuál es . . . uh . . . su número de teléfono?"* I said.

She gave me her name and number and I programmed it into my phone.

"If I see her, I'll call you." She frowned, not understanding. *"Si la veo, voy a llamar a usted por teléfono."*

I hoped that came out right.

"Sí, sí!" she said. *"Gracias, gracias, gracias! Sólo quiero saber que Marisol está a salvo."*

I nodded, not exactly sure what that meant, and crossed to the sidewalk. Then, I thought of something and crossed back.

I pulled two hundred dollar bills of Pam Hayes' money and handed them to her.

"For you," I said.

"No," she said. "No, no, no. I no take."

"You need food and rest. Are you eating? Where do you sleep?"

"*No puedo tener su dinero,*" she said. "I no do this to take money. *Soy cubana. Los cubanos trabajamos por nuestro dinero. Solo necesito mi Marisol.*"

The fire in her eyes was palpable. She was serious. Her hard-edged 'I-can-take-care-of-myself' tone reminded me of my own mother.

"I can tell you're not doing this for money," I said, shoving the bills into her hand. "But I insist."

"You good man," she said with tears in her eyes and wrapped her hands around mine. "*Dios te bendiga!*"

I nodded. I knew that means 'God Bless You.'

I turned and crossed to the southbound side of Collins. Several cabs passed. I could have easily hailed one, but I didn't. I didn't have to work tonight and if I was going to join Luther on an early morning run one of these days, I'd better start getting in shape.

Plus, I needed to shake off the jitters from Tommy Nero and company. I put one foot in front of the other and headed south past the Fontainebleau.

I noticed a black SUV with its engine running parked at the corner of 41st Street, but it pulled out into traffic before I neared it.

15

I PASSED ALVIN'S Island at Lincoln Road and tried not to look at the I Love Liquor superstore coming up on my right. But one glance and I was inside paying for another 750ml bottle of Rebel Yell, the idiot voice in my head telling me it had been a stressful day—naked girls and TV stars and gangsters and guns and all—and how much I deserved it.

As I neared my building, I saw a gold Cadillac Escalade with tinted windows parked out front. I tensed up, my hand on my gun. The window rolled down and I relaxed when I saw who it was. I recognized him from the pictures on FoxNews and CNN.

He was sixtyish, big and soft, jowly cheeks, large pudgy nose going to rosacea.

"Titus?" he said.

"Yeah," I said.

He opened the door and got out. Our eyes met for a moment, two predators from two different worlds sizing each other up. A smile spread across his vast face.

"I'm Rexford J. Hayes," he said in a molasses-thick Southern drawl with a smile and an outstretched hand. "Pleasure to meet you."

I shook his hand. It was slimy and soft.

His face was more lined and bloated than the pictures let on. He was golf casual today, a size 2XXL yellow-and-blue striped polo shirt tucked into large baby blue Bermuda shorts, brown leather belt barely visible under a drooping mid-section. His silver hair was thick and recently trimmed, parted on the side. Top-Siders, no socks.

"I'm Allie's dad," he said. "Mind if I come in? I'd like to talk with you about my daughter."

I opened my door and motioned him in. A puff of cigar smoke hit me, lighting up my lungs.

"Much obliged," he said with a big smile.

I stepped in and closed the door behind him. He looked around and made no reference to the shabby state of my existence.

"Oh," he said, "do you mind if I smoke? I'll put this out if you like."

"It's okay," I said.

I made a silent bet with myself. I opened the cabinet and took out two plastic cups. I removed the bourbon from the bag and poured a thick finger into each cup. I placed one in front of him on the countertop.

He glanced at the cup, then at me, and then at the bottle. He wanted to say no, but something told me he never says no.

"Well," he said as he took the cup, "I suppose it's late enough in the day. Thank you kindly."

I win.

He downed half of it. I raised my cup and sipped, smiling at him full force. Eager beaver. Willing prospect. Persuade me, you master politician you.

I motioned toward one of the plastic chairs. He studied

them, and then said, "No, this won't take long. Mr.—"

"Just Titus," I said.

"Titus, I want to thank you for your hard work, all you've done to find Allie. I heard my wife hired you and I'm sorry for wasting your time with that, but I want you to know that Allie is fine. In fact, I just saw her earlier today. We had lunch together."

Alarm bells went off in my head. "You just had lunch with your daughter Allie?"

"I did, and she's fine. Now, I'm sure you're wondering what's going on, so I'll explain. Allie is living with a boy that my wife Pam doesn't like." He puffed on the cigar and his voice went lower. "Tell you the truth, I don't like him either. But what's a dad to do? Tell his daughter she can't live her life the way she wants? That only works for so long."

"Where is she living?"

"Now, that's not really important."

"It's important to Mrs. Hayes."

He looked out the window and sighed.

"Titus," he said, "do you have kids?"

I had a flashback to the ultrasound, the tiny heartbeat five days before Ariel died.

"No," I said.

"It's a complicated business," he said. "Mothers and daughters, fathers and daughters. They all get up in each other's hair and there are—how do I phrase this?—certain misunderstandings."

"Misunderstandings?"

"Titus, my wife Pam is a good woman. A strong woman. She wants the best for everyone—for me, for Allie. But she also doesn't understand that Allie and I have a special father-daughter relationship."

"Special?"

"I'm sorry, that came out wrong. Makes me sound like I was having an affair with my own daughter." He laughed a big uncomfortable laugh and turned beet red, then downed the rest of his drink. "That's not how I meant that. Allie is a Daddy's Girl and I'm her big daddy. She and my wife, Pam, well, they both love each other, naturally—"

"Naturally."

"—but Allie and Pam don't get along all that well."

Hm, Pam Hayes said just the same thing in reverse. Which one of them is lying?

"Go on," I said and poured another shot into his cup. He didn't stop me.

"So", he said, "when sweet little Allie does something bad, makes a mistake, or gets into trouble, who do you suppose she runs to? *Mommy?* No, she runs to her Big Daddy, who loves his little girl and bails her out. He tells her not to do it again, but he knows full well she's going to do it again. And, of course, part of the deal is that *mommy* doesn't find out."

I didn't like the way he emphasized the word *mommy*. Something was off there.

"So," I said, "you've known all along that Allie vanished from school and moved in with Jake Preston?"

He paused, contemplating something.

"Hell, Titus," he said, "I shouldn't tell you this but I'm the one who writes the damn check for their rent. But Pam doesn't know because she'd be completely against it and there's no reasoning with Pam." He laughed yet another big fake laugh. Then, he stared at the floor. "Now I find out she's hired you to find Allie. What for, I don't know. So she can go yell at her? Tell her to grow up or something? Bottom line, Titus, we no longer need your services. Allie is safe and fine, and I'm here to pay you whatever we owe you."

"Who told you that your wife hired me?" I said.

He put the cigar to his mouth and stared at me like I was a fly that needed a swat.

"I figured that one out on my own," he said and sipped his new drink.

"That was you yesterday parked around the corner in the

black SUV with the engine running, wasn't it?" I said.

He squinted and puffed again, looking directly at me with genuine confusion. No, that wasn't him.

"Excuse me?" he said.

"Never mind. Next question. When were you planning on telling your wife you're putting Allie up with Jake Preston?"

He sipped and puffed some more.

"I've been working up to that," he said. "Pam is not easy to break news to. My fault. I take the blame for that. I need to sit Pam down this very evening and have that talk."

"So," I said, "you came here today just to make sure I'm going to stop snooping."

He laughed again. "Not at all, Titus. I'm only here to make sure you get paid for a job well done. I'm an honorable man. I'm sure you know I'm running for the Senate."

"So are they all, all honorable men."

"Well, not all of them," he said, not recognizing the quote, "but I certainly am. And our country needs someone who is going to best stand up for the values of the people of South Florida."

"Wouldn't it be damaging to your election efforts to have a daughter who frequents SoBe clubs and lives with a lowlife rat like Jake Preston?"

"Well, you got me dead to rights there, Titus. But what can I do? Allie is Allie. She's miserable at college. I mean, I'd love for her to graduate, but I don't think that's going to happen and she just loves this Jake."

I thought about telling him that Jake's tongue seems to be inside every girl in Miami *except* for Allie, but decided to hold that card.

"I figure I'll set them up in a nice condo," he said, "and then set Jake up in a nice clean business somewhere. Make them happy. If they're happy, then what can the press say, right?"

"Press can be vicious," I said.

"Then let them be vicious. I love my daughter and I

support her decision. Now, let me pay you so we can part as friends."

He scoffed down the rest of the second drink and placed the cup on my counter. He reached into his large side pocket and took out one of those big leather-bound checkbooks full of oversized checks that shout 'I'm-a-bigshot.' He placed it down and flipped it open with showmanship. He removed a fancy gold pen from the chest pocket of his polo shirt and wrote as he chewed on the cigar.

"I think this should cover your final expenses," he said mid-puff.

"I don't need it," I said. "I've barely used what your wife gave me."

"Oh, I'm certain that's long gone. I know you've been working hard. Now, please Titus, I'd appreciate it if you wouldn't contact my wife anymore. Just consider your case solved and closed. I'd love for us to just handle everything 'in-house' from here, so to speak."

A stab of anger boiled up in my gut.

"I can't do that, Mr. Hayes," I said. "I was hired by Mrs. Hayes, not you. She needs a report from me when I find Allie, but I haven't found Allie yet, and you don't want to tell me where she is. Of course, I *will* find Allie. And when I do, I will do what I was hired to do: report her location to Mrs. Hayes."

There was a long pause as predator and prey sized each other up again, although who's who was yet to be determined. I'd bet on me.

"Now, Titus, really," he said with a smile, the Southern-boy charm turned up to high. "We both hired you. We are a team. Rex, Pam, and Allie. Together always, through thick and thin. This is a family matter and I apologize to you from the bottom of my heart for wasting your time, getting you involved in all this. Please, Titus, accept this as a bonus. Everything I do is big. Let me make this big gesture to you as a way of thanks. Take a vacation."

"No," I said.

"You know what? You're a good man, I can tell. You cross your t's and dot your i's. I respect that. In fact, I respect the hell out of that. Look, I'm just going to leave this check on the countertop here. Put it aside until the morning and then I'm sure you'll see things in a new light."

He tore out the check and placed it on the counter. He stuffed the checkbook back in his shorts, and turned to the door.

"Well," he said, "I'm going to mosey on along now."

"Mosey on along now?" I said. "I haven't heard anyone say that since I was a kid, and he was eighty. Or was it Festus on a *Gunsmoke* rerun?"

He turned to look back at me. His eyes narrowed. The good ol' boy was gone, replaced by dead cold eyes.

"Titus," he said, in a lower voice with less accent, "you're a hard man. I respect that. I certainly do. But you think about what I've said now. Things could turn sour, and I'd hate for that to happen."

"Huh," I said. "That sounds like a threat."

He met my eyes squarely, not blinking. For a flash, I saw it. The willingness to kill. I knew it. I've seen it enough times.

"No threat, Titus," he said. "Just concern for my daughter."

He turned away and walked out the door.

"I'm not done, Rex," I said. "I don't know that Allie is safe. I'll ask you again. Where is she so I can talk to her and confirm everything you say?"

Rexford J. Hayes didn't like me calling him Rex. Nor question his version of how things should proceed. The stare when he turned back to face me said so.

"We'll see, Titus," he said without inflection, "we'll see."

His tone was dismissive now, like he's firing the gardener.

I watched him walk to the gold Escalade. He got in and slowly drove away. I drank the rest of my drink. Then, I poured another.

Shit, something is off here, way off. The lies are swirling

around, circling for a place to land. Seems like everybody in Miami is lying. And they all want me to stop looking for Allie Hayes.

I picked up the check and looked at it.

Holy fuck.

It's double what Pam Hayes gave me, which is double what I originally asked for.

A sinking sensation surrounded me again. I felt buried. Is this how it feels when you know you're about to be killed? I downed my drink and poured another, getting the feeling I wouldn't be joining Luther for a run in the morning.

I grabbed a plastic chair, brought it outside to the dank little courtyard, and placed it under the sea grape tree. Surrounded by once-white blocks laid in a perforated pattern, the space was a square of dirt filled with years of fallen leaves and a handful of soda cans. I sat, cradling my plastic cup, the world taking on that warm bourbon-infused glow. I looked around, wondering where my little lizard buddy lives.

I took the check out and stared at the amount again. I should just cash this. Really, why not? That's a freighter-load of money. More than I've ever made in a year. More than I've ever even considered to be mine, all mine. How can I ignore that?

I got a flash of myself on a beach, surrounded by a group of bikini-clad girls. Maybe I'll buy a home in Costa Rica and sip mojitos all day. Or maybe I'll buy a whole island, what the hell.

Why go on playing these games? They all lead to the same place. To misery, to death. Why not just get out? Why not just escape? Go, Titus, go. Get the fuck out. Forget everything. Just enjoy what remaining days you have left. Move to an island, live with some island girls, have island babies, forget the past.

I sipped my bourbon, remembering Mel Gibson as Fletcher Christian in the movie *The Bounty*. He threw away his ship, his command, and his life—just so he could live in paradise with a girl who wore flowers in her hair and little else.

I held the check up and gave it a long loving look.

Then, I tore it in half.

No, I can't live on blood money. I'd never be able to look at myself in the mirror again. Plus, an amount like that tells me I'm getting close. Too close for somebody. Having come this far, I can't not figure it out. I *will* figure it out. I *need* to figure it out.

Not to mention that fat mutant baby really pissed me off. Tommy Nero thinks he can order me around. He didn't tell me the whole story. He's in deeper here. If it were only a matter of catching his boy Eddie Corrado skimming, he wouldn't watch him walk around and bring people in to ask about him. Eddie would already be digested by swamp gators.

I sipped some more.

And this fat fuck Rexford J. Hayes. Fuck him. Nobody pays me off. Nobody pays me to snitch. Nobody pays me to look the other way. Nobody pays me to *not* do my job, ever.

If I don't have me, then what's it all worth anyway? If I'm living, then I'm living for who I am, what I stand for, what I believe. Not to get paid to deny my very existence. If I gave in, I wouldn't be an authentic man. I'd be a dead man.

So what is an authentic man? A man who lives by his own beliefs and his own rules. A man who respects life and liberty. A man who sits in dank courtyards drinking bourbon while looking for little lizards.

I was about to tear the check into smaller pieces when I saw the name on it. I held the two halves of the check together to read it.

A business name. Foundation Investments LLC with a downtown Miami address. Hm. If there's one lesson that led to more arrests than any other when I was a cop, it was *Follow the money.*

At that moment, the upstairs couple kicked into Act One, derailing my train of thought.

That's it. That's fucking it.

I went up the outside stairs to their door and knocked.

Everything went silent. I waited. And waited. Then, I knocked again. Nothing.

"Hey!" I shouted. "Open up!"

More silence.

"Hey!" I said, knocking harder. "I'm your downstairs neighbor."

The door opened with the chain attached. I thought about busting it, but I retained enough self-control to look at the short Latino kid grimacing at me in the three-inch space. He was shirtless and covered in tattoos. Muscular for his small frame. Probably eighteen years old, maybe a little younger.

"I've had enough," I said. "The two of you need to quiet the fuck down."

"Nobody here but me, *señor*," he said with a challenging smile.

"Look," I said, my fists itching to beat him, "I know it's a huge turn-on to argue and then fuck, but the two of you need to once—just once—make sweet love like humans, not wildebeests. Soft and gentle. Try it, you might like it. Or even take a break for a few hours. You're going to wear it out."

"Nobody here but me, *señor*," he said again, a bigger smile this time. He spouted off something in fast Spanish that sailed right past me, although I did pick out the phrase *mama pinga*.

People love calling me that, don't they?

"You've been warned, asshole," I said.

He pulled a knife.

Oh, not again. No, I can't do this here. This is where I sleep. Or try to, anyway.

"Hey," I said with my hands up, "I don't want to fight you. I'm your neighbor. I sleep downstairs from you. We live here together. All I'm asking for is just a little quiet. You respect me and I respect you, okay? No trouble, okay?"

His eyes held mine as he streamed another flow of Spanish.

I turned and headed down the steps, attempting to talk myself into forgetting about it, but the bourbon sparked a fire that burned up within me and I marched back up, occupying the space an inch from his face.

"No, I talk to you, motherfucker!" I said. "You! I'm giving you one warning. Keep it down, or you will regret it. *Entiendo?*"

He glared at me, breathing hard. This time, I could see that, even though he was holding the knife, he was the scared one. He saw the crazy in me. Good. That's how I wanted it. I went down the stairs and inside to my kitchen counter.

I poured another drink and went back outside to my plastic chair. I sat down and lit a cigarette. The air was so thick I felt like I could reach out and grab a handful of it.

Now, where was I?

Something about lizards and money. I looked around for my lizard buddy. Maybe he'll remember.

That's when into my field of vision walked painted turquoise toenails in glittery sandals. I looked up, a Barry White song firing up in my crotch at the sight of a blonde tanned girl in white shorts and a turquoise tank top, neither of which covered much of anything.

Oh, fuck, no. No, no, no.

"Hi," said Bri, stretching *hi* into two syllables and posing with a hand on her hip.

Her blonde curls glowed in the setting sun. The glitter she had sprinkled all over herself was turquoise to match the tank top, the toenails, and the glowing lipstick. Fantastic choices all. I smelled something coconutty. Also fantastic.

"Whatthefuckareyoudoinghere?" I said, fully aware that my words had no spaces between them.

"Shhhhhh," she said with a finger over her glowing lips, taking full advantage of my bourbon-induced vulnerability. She took a step toward me and straddled my lap.

I thought about protesting, but couldn't remember any protest words, especially with her tongue in my mouth and her crotch grinding on mine.

We finished the bourbon together.

16

"YOU'RE REALLY PISSING me off!" said Sofia behind the wheel of the unmarked SUV.

"Take a number," I said, hung over again, in the passenger seat sipping an iced coffee. "I'm tired of my bullshit, too."

We were speeding along the MacArthur Causeway past the big loaders, the rumble of the tires on the blinding asphalt twirling my brain into a vortex of pain.

Sofia had called me when I was at my emergency Starbucks yet again, picking up iced coffee for yet another twenty-one year old girl who landed on my airbed. Sofia said she needed to talk to me and picked me up about a minute later. Now we seem to be on some surreal joyride that's bending reality into a haze of nausea.

"Why are we speeding, officer?" I said.

"Because I'm fucking aggravated," Sofia said.

"Do you always take your aggressions out with speed?"

"Fuck you."

"I'll take that as a yes."

I gripped the hand rests, the equilibrium of the SUV way off, like the sensation of floating on a sea. The water on both sides of the highway only added to the sickly illusion.

Sofia buzzed an old lady in a Chrysler Sebring who was obeying the speed limit like a good citizen. The Sebring slowly moved right and we leaped past it.

"You are causing a problem," said Sofia.

"I was born causing a problem," I said, attempting to sip my iced coffee but continually missing the straw due to the rollicking lane-shifts.

"I was called into the lieutenant's office this morning. She wanted to know about you."

"Who is your lieutenant?"

"You don't want to know!" The fury of her voice exploded in my head. A vein may have burst somewhere up there.

"Okay," I said. "Why does the OCS lieutenant want to know about me?"

"Exactly my question. I told her I pulled you over a few weeks ago when I was on uniform probation."

"Which you did."

"I told her I wrote you a ticket for a busted taillight."

"Which you did."

"I didn't tell her anything else about that night."

"Well, good. Thank you. Because you and I are the only two people who know what went down that night."

She turned to sneer at me with squinted eyes.

"That better be fucking true," she said.

She shifted lanes again, cutting off a semi-trailer who leaned on his horn. She flashed the lights and siren to tell him to shut up. We sped up, zipping past Parrot Jungle in a flash.

"Why is my boss asking about you?" she said.

"Fantastic question," I said as we hit eighty. "How the fuck would I know?"

"Because, asshole, you're up to something."

We pulled off at the Biscayne ramp, immediately hitting traffic. She went full lights and siren, the sea of cars meekly parting for us.

"Did you ask her?" I said.

"You don't ask the lieutenant why she wants to know something," she said.

"Sounds like my old captain."

"Fuck you. Stop trying to be my friend. Look, I don't need this. I'm working a huge case and I don't need aggravation from some *cabron* from North Bumfuck to get in my way."

"*Cabron* from North Bumfuck? Classy."

"I was up for promotion before I got probation."

"You were on probation when I got here. That had nothing to do with me."

She shot me a dirty look and turned us north onto Bayshore. She left the lights and sirens on. My hands clenched as we sped up again, blasting through red lights. We didn't say anything all the way to 36th Street, where she banked hard right with screeching tires. I caught the horrified stare of a woman whose bumper we cleared by about an inch.

"I need you off my lieutenant's radar," said Sofia.

"I don't even know how I'm on her radar," I said.

"The fuck you do. You've taken this missing girl bullshit to a level that is getting you noticed. Trust me, you do not want to get noticed by my lieutenant. If she finds out—"

"If she finds out what? That I'm a legal citizen working at a bar? I haven't broken any laws."

"The fuck you have."

We were up on the I-195 ramp, heading back to the beach on the Tuttle.

"You are acting as a private investigator without a license," she said.

"I'm looking for a missing girl," I said. "I'm showing some pictures around, hanging around lowlifes, just looking. That's all. No laws broken."

"Well, you need to stop."

"Why? Because your boss is pissed off and it could ruin your promotion?"

"Fuck you!"

"If you were so hell-bent on my not doing this, why did you send me to The Rock?"

"Send you where?"

"To the big bald black priest who belongs on *WWE SmackDown*."

"Luther knows shit," she said. "I thought he'd talk you out of it."

"So you don't care that a young girl is missing?" I said. "Maybe she's being tied up and raped right now. Maybe she's being sold into human slavery. Oh, but wait. None of that fucking matters. Because Sofia's lieutenant is mad at her."

She pushed the SUV past ninety.

I looked over at her and saw it. The same thing I saw in Tommy Nero's eyes. The same thing I see in my own eyes in the mirror every morning. *Impulsive, even a little unhinged.* Then, another thought hit me and I smiled.

"No," I said with a laugh. "I just figured it out. That's not why you sent me to Luther. There's another reason. You know that Luther can handle himself. You know that Luther can give me a hand in places where I might need a hand."

"You need to stop," she said as we hit lightspeed and started to go back in time. "That's all. This is way over your head. You just need to fucking stop."

I laughed.

"Oh my God," I said. "I'm right, aren't I? You give a shit."

She launched into a stream of Spanish. I think I heard *mama pinga* again, but maybe not.

"People really need to stop doing that," I said. "You know what? From now on, whenever I get pissed off, I'm just going to launch into a fiery diatribe in a language the other person doesn't understand. Maybe Klingon."

She swerved into the right hand lane, cutting three people off and slammed on the brakes, screeching us to a stop in the breakdown lane. The smell of burnt rubber filled the SUV.

"Get out!" she said. We were at the beginning of the strip of land right before the Alton Road exit.

"But we're—"

"Get out!"

"Sofia, I—"

"Get the fuck out!"

I got out, making a point to not close the door as I backed away from the SUV onto the hammock, my hands up in a surrender gesture.

"Drop this case!" she said.

She gunned it, the door still open. The sudden acceleration forced it shut as the SUV sped away, leaving me to walk along the shoulder back home.

Well, that went well.

My head pounding and my vision skewed, I realized I had left my iced coffee with her.

Fuck.

I started walking. Looks like I'm going to be late for work.

Somehow, I didn't mind. Sofia gives a shit.

Hot damn.

17

"YOU'RE REALLY PISSING me off!" said Jenny as she slammed down a tray of clean highball glasses.

"Take a number," I said, filling the cocktail mixes with a sense of *déjà vu*. "I'm first in line."

I think I've already had this conversation today.

Jenny finished loading the glasses and tore out the tray, nearly hitting me with it.

"You're going to owe me so so much, asshole," she said.

Everybody just loves me today.

It was four o'clock. I was an hour late for my shift at Cap'n Jack's Seafood & Bar due to the long hot walk home courtesy of Sofia. My head felt like a bloated pufferfish and I could hear every damned beat of my pulse.

Jenny turned to me with a long string of words, but I couldn't hear any of them. I was momentarily lost in her big beautiful blue eyes—which became Bri's eyes—which became Sash's eyes—which became Sofia's eyes. I squeezed my eyes shut, put my hands to my temples and pressed, and opened them again.

"Hello," Jenny said. "Hello. Earth to Titus. Did you even hear me?"

Jenny's hand was on her hip, tapping.

"No, sorry," I said. "I was thinking."

"Well, don't do that," she said. "You're so *not* sexy when you do that."

"Note to self, think more often." I put on my apron and took out some lemons to slice.

"Hardy har har. Okay, I'm leaving. Matt's going to kill me."

"Hey, can I ask you a question?"

She slid up to me, her hip against my leg. "The answer is yes. When?"

"Shut up. Are you close with your parents?"

"They'll never know," she said, her hand finding my back pocket. The devil in me pushed for a hat trick, but I resisted. I removed her hand and slapped it away.

"Hey," I said, "that's sexual harassment."

"Oh, don't bullshit me. You love it."

"Listen to me, seriously."

She rolled her eyes, sighed, and folded her arms.

"You get along with your parents, right?" I said.

"Yeah," she said.

"And you're an only child, right?"

"Yeah."

"Do you get along better with your mom or your dad?"

"Oh God, that's easy. My dad. I'm a total Daddy's girl."

"He'd help you out if you were in trouble, maybe hide it from your mom, right?"

"In a heartbeat."

"What if you moved in with Matt?"

She rolled her eyes.

"Matt and I broke up," she said.

"I thought you just said he's going to be mad because

130

you're late," I said.

"Oh, we broke up—but we still hook up."

I shook my head. "I don't get your generation at all. Let's just say you move in with another guy."

"Like you."

"No, not me. Some dirtbag."

"Like you."

"Fine. Let's say, for example, you moved in with me."

"Oooh, I like where this is going. Go on."

"Wait, I didn't finish. You move in with me, but obviously I'm bad for you."

"Obviously." Her eyes glowed and her smile expanded.

"Would your dad let that go on, even buy us a house because he wouldn't want it to get out?"

"Hell no. He'd fucking kill you."

"Exactly what I thought."

"Exactly what you thought what?"

"Nothing. Something I'm working out in my head. Never mind."

"If I can help," she said as her hand reached across my chest, "just let me know."

I slapped her hand away again. She giggled.

Jenny went home and another average night ensued. More artery-clogging fried seafood, more beer, nobody too rowdy. Paulie and Trina were visiting relatives in Fort Lauderdale, so after the dinner surge I handwrote a note:

Paulie,

Gotta give my two weeks. Time for me to go. Bruno can handle it. My last day will be Sat July 22.

Thanks for everything.

Titus

It's time. It really is time.

After cleaning up, I said good night to Marty from Jersey and locked the door behind him. I went back to the office and stuffed the note inside the top of Paulie's locked desk. I took out a cigarette and balanced it on my lip without lighting it. I shut the lights, typed in the security code on the ancient alarm system, grabbed the big bag of trash, walked out, and locked the door.

It was raining, steady but not heavy. Just a constant steamy dribble, simmering on low. I lit my cigarette.

I walked down the three steps to the tiny dumpster area on the side of the bar and opened the gate. I flipped up the big plastic lid and tossed in the trash bag. A bundle of nerves fluttered in my neck. Sometimes it's a twitch in my toes. Sometimes it's a tightening in my shoulders. Tonight it was nerves in my neck.

They say there's no such thing as extra-sensory perception, but any experienced cop or criminal knows we develop a sixth sense that warns us of danger. It can grow stale. Mine failed me the other day with Tommy Nero's boys, but it was on tonight. Still sluggish, but on.

I dove to my left as a crowbar slammed into the metal rim of the dumpster with a loud clang. The lid crashed down onto it as I aimed my left elbow at the spot where my instinct told me a head would be and threw all my weight backward into it.

I heard the sickly cracking noise of bone against bone. I spun, my hand reaching for my gun.

My sixth sense didn't help me with the next one. Before I could get my gun, a fist fell from the sky and smashed into the right side of my face, knocking my left shoulder hard into the dumpster. Another fist pounded my kidney from the side and then something struck the back of my neck and I was on the ground. The blows came from multiple sources.

My head on the wet pavement, I saw three sets of boot

silhouettes in the dim streetlights walking toward me. One grew big and slammed into my nose. I heard the bone crack and felt a stream of hot wetness trickling down my face. Everything went dark.

As I lay there wheezing, head spinning, stars popping, it occurred to me this is *not* what I came to Miami for.

I came to this steaming hellhole full of vengeance to kill a blond man who wears five-thousand dollar suits and lives in a big bayfront house on West Lido Drive. One goal, one objective. Point, shoot, done.

How the hell did I get side-tracked into *this* mess?

It was my damned curiosity that got me into this trouble, that's what it was.

In fact, it all started right here on this very spot. Right in front of this dumpster. This was exactly where I stood three days ago, smoking a cigarette when I first saw Pam Hayes standing outside the bar as she pondered walking in.

"Hola, *mama pinga!*" said a voice I recognize.

It was almost a relief to hear it. Now I knew I was going to get out of this. Bruised maybe, but out.

I looked up at the three faces staring down at me. Eddie Corrado and two kids, neither of whom looked older than twenty. All Latino. The one on the left bled profusely from his nose and mouth.

"Eddie," I said, spitting out some blood of my own. "Nice to see you. How've you been? How are the kids?"

One of Eddie's boots got big again. As it flew toward me, I rolled and it smashed into the hard metal of the dumpster. At the same time, I reached up with my right hand and grabbed a bunch of the fabric on Eddie's jeans near his knee and rolled to my right, twisting as hard as I could.

Eddie lost his balance and went down, arms flailing. I saw a kick coming from the bleeding kid and rolled back the other way, catching it in my left ribs. It hurt, but it was better than taking it in the face.

Now in a push-up position, I launched myself off the ground while catching another kick in the solar plexus from Eddie, who had gotten back to his feet quick. I retched, a spurt of bile projecting from my stomach outward with a splash onto the ground. That's when a switch flipped inside me.

Something else cops and soldiers will tell you—and maybe even doctors—is that the human can become a "survival beast", able to perform amazing feats when threatened. Some have a stronger inner "survival beast" than others. The only way to know is to be in a situation where there is a real threat of death.

It runs strong in my family. When my grandmother was seventy-five, a thief grabbed her purse. This was a woman who had never had any fight training her entire life, but she refused to let go of the purse. The thief was much bigger and stronger than her, but she beat the guy silly and he ran off. Later, she had no memory of how she did it.

I must have been channeling my grandmother because everything became a blur. Fists and feet slammed into me, but I didn't even feel them. My own fists and elbows pounded in a frenzy to my right and left, not even sure what I was hitting, running on raw animal instinct and the experience of growing up on the street. I felt like I had the power of ten men, throwing Eddie Corrado and the two kids around like toys.

As I came out of it, I noticed that every sound and shard of light on the street had become enhanced as if the picture brightness and sound knobs had been turned up on a video screen. The blood on the ground was bright red. The footsteps from Eddie's friends running away in slow-motion echoed with a crystal clarity.

Eddie himself was on the ground, face puffy, one eye completely closed. His knife was in his hand, but apparently I never gave him the chance to use it.

My breathing was deep and hard. I tried to get it under control. I heard a loud noise like a waterfall closing in on me and looked around for the source, then realized it was the blood rushing past my ears.

My hands shook, still twitching around for someone to hit, but there were no volunteers. I leaned on the dumpster, waiting for the colors and brightness to return to normal. I felt no pain, but I knew that would change soon.

Two minutes later—or was it a year?—the world righted itself. The first twinges of pain hit me. No location. It was everywhere.

I pushed myself off the dumpster and looked down at Eddie Corrado, all shiny again in the rain. A steady stream of red ran from the dumpster area down to the rain gutter on the corner. Other than that, there was no sound.

I reached down, took Eddie's knife from his hand, folded it, and stuffed it in my pocket.

My half-smoked cigarette lay in a pool of thinning blood by the dumpster. I picked it up, opened the dumpster, and tossed it in. I grabbed the crowbar, closed the lid, and was about to close the gate when I walked back, took out the pack of cigarettes, opened the dumpster, and tossed that in too. Then, I closed the gate and locked the padlock.

"Night, Eddie," I said, tapping his leg gently with the crowbar. "Thanks for the fun time. Stop by again now, y'hear?"

He groaned and began to move.

I walked up the street, heading home. A block away, I looked back. Eddie was on his knees, throwing up in the rain gutter.

18

JASON STARK PICKED me up in a black Lamborghini. I carefully climbed in, every part of my body aching even though it had been two days since my night encounter in the rain with Eddie Corrado and *amigos*.

"What the fuck happened to you?" Jason said.

"You don't want to know," I said.

He drove us to Hinraker's house, making sure to rev the engine in neutral at every stoplight.

"This your car?" I said.

"Of course it is," he said. I shot him a dubious look. "Okay, no, it isn't, all right? But I can't show up to Hinraker's in my 2002 green Honda Accord with peeling paint now, can I?"

"I thought you made a metric shit-ton of money doing that teach-guys-to-pick-up girls shit."

He gave me the finger. I grinned.

"Where'd you get it?" I said.

"You don't want to know," he said. "Don't worry. I didn't

steal it, just borrowed it from a friend."

"You're right. I don't want to know."

Morton Hinraker's house was on Star Island, an enclave of Miami's ultra-rich and ultra-famous. Ordinary rich and famous need not apply.

I'm not sure if mega-mansion or giga-mansion is the right term for the marble and glass travesty that appeared to be Hinraker's residence. It had all the charm of an office building—hell, an entire office park.

Rows of palm trees lit by in-ground lights surrounded a fancy drive paved with shiny black bricks. Large steps led up to wide glass doors under a portico that looked like the entrance to an airport gate with a line of well-dressed people moving through a security checkpoint.

I've never understood why people who have money need to own big things. Big things are hard to clean.

"Ready?" I said.

"So ready, dude—I mean, man," said Jason.

"Go back to dude. Dude is okay again."

Jason pulled the Lamborghini up to the valet and handed him a hundred-dollar bill. I carefully climbed out, trying not to move like an old man recovering from triple-bypass surgery. The valet drove off and I joined Jason on the pathway.

"You sure you're up for this?" Jason said. "You look like a freight train ran over you and then backed up just to make sure."

"I'm fine," I said. "Let's go."

Luckily, Eddie and his boys broke no major bones. I had a shiner on my left eye and my nose was the color of a Concord grape, as well as a new shape. Under my suit, the rest of my body looked like a weather radar map displaying outbursts of storms. If Jason noticed it's the same suit I wore to Sinz, he hadn't said so.

Jason Stark was in a bright orange suit with a white shirt and brown cordovans. The suit may or may not have had an intensity control. I wondered if he had gotten it from Da-veed at the spaceship.

Jason was alone. Apparently, you don't need a "crew" for Hinraker's. We walked down a stone path lined on both sides by futuristic cubes displaying 3D videos of genderless people in multi-colored tight costumes performing interpretative dance. Classical music emanated from hidden speakers.

"Puccini," I said.

"Huh?" said Jason.

"The music. Puccini. Opera."

"Oh, yeah. Of course."

"Not what I expected."

"Me neither. I'd be dropping some Kendrick Lamar and Chance the Rapper, but it's his house. Man can do what he wants."

I scanned the crowd for Allie Hayes. Nothing. I did see two very famous Hollywood celebrities whose presence surprised me.

The security here would make the TSA blush. Five young big-shouldered guys in light gray suits, shaved heads, dark sunglasses, and earpieces with those little coiled cords.

As we waited to pass through the metal detector, I said, "Why do they still have those earpieces with the little coiled cords? Hasn't technology evolved beyond little coiled cords?"

"They're cool," said Jason. "They make you look like Secret Service or something. I tell my clients to wear fake ones. Hot girls love security dudes."

I turned and looked at Jason, wondering if he's real or a figment of my imagination.

"What?" he said, responding to my stare.

I just shook my head.

I held out JoJo Burley's Sapphire Key. The lead guard placed it in a device that scanned it and handed it back to me without a word. Then, we moved through security. I evaluated the guards. They had an air of quality training. These were not Eddie Corrado-types.

As they patted me down after I set off the metal detector with my belt buckle, I noticed a light glow behind the glasses. There was some sort of a display visible only to the wearer. These guys were seeing something we weren't. They didn't like me. I was frisked, prodded, and probed. I figured I would be, so I left my gun at home, again the sensation of nakedness.

We emerged into a series of interconnected living rooms with spectacular views of the twinkling Miami skyline across the bay. Each had a slightly different style but nothing too garish, a subtle unifying theme likely created by an interior decorator who charges a thousand dollars an hour. Couches everywhere. Sculptures looming like demonic stick-figures. Paintings of human body parts tangled in odd ways. The soft classical music followed us from room to room.

The men here skewed older and richer than Sinz—much older. Tonight was Jason's turn to feel out of place, age-wise. There was even a smattering of middle-aged couples with wedding rings. I hadn't expected that.

Jason Stark was right about the women, though. I've never seen a collection of so many stunners all in one place.

But not like the Sinz girls. No Bris or Sashes in glitter and sprayed-on neon dresses. This was a different planet—top-shelf designer clothes that exposed just enough skin and curves with flair and mystery. The women here were subdued and elegant, sipping champagne from long flutes, eyes down, respectful, controlled. Like they had been bred on an island, trained to serve, and imported. If I had to guess, I'd bet Morton Hinraker had graduated from collecting drug-addled porn girls to carefully cultivated slave girls. I felt suddenly sick.

I scanned the crowd again for Allie. Still nothing. More celebrities, though. One famous musician whose albums I collected as a kid.

"Man, these girls are hot," said Jason. "Hotter than even I expected, and so elegant."

"Yeah," I said.

"Hello," said a stunning girl with auburn hair, blue eyes, and bright red lips. "My name is Aleksandra." Her accent was thick Eastern European. "I will be private hostess for you this evening, yes? May I get for you something to drink?"

"Sure," said Jason.

"We have celebrity bartender Daniel Deschamps from famous restaurant La Glace in Paris. His specialty is martini made from cucumber vodka, eucalyptus leaves, and Himalayan Goji berries."

"Oooh," said Jason, "that sounds good. I'll have one of those."

Aleksandra turned to me. "And for you?"

"Is that what you drink in Ukraine?" I said.

"Excuse me?" she said.

"Ukraine. That's where you're from, right?"

Fear appeared in her eyes for a brief beat, but she pushed it away with a forced smile.

"No," she said, "you are mistaken. I am from Czech Republic."

"My apologies," I said.

"No, I apologize to you. Would you prefer Ukrainian girl to serve you?"

"No, that's okay. You're wonderful."

"Thank you. You are much kind. What would you like for to drink?"

"Nothing, thanks."

She smiled with a hint of a bow and walked away.

"Dude," said Jason, "this is amazing. This whole place is amazing."

"Dude," I said, "stop thinking with your dick and open your eyes. This is fucking creepy."

He shook his head and we both returned to scanning the crowd.

I listened to a nearby conversation. A famous New York

fashion designer in an outfit that looked like something out of a Doctor Seuss book was emphatically talking to two young men in matching plaid pink-and-blue suits with bright blue neckties about the upcoming fall season, gesturing wildly with his hands.

"So, I heard you fucked Bri," Jason said.

I coughed.

"Who told you that?" I said.

"She told me herself."

I reeled back a little, surprised. "Sorry. She showed up and it just happened. Won't happen again, I promise."

"Relax, man. It's okay. We all fuck. No biggie.'

I had a sudden urge to punch him, but I controlled myself I turned to face him directly.

"Bri is not a notch on a bedpost," I said, maybe a little too harshly. "Neither is Sash. They are human beings, not Fleshlights."

"Dude," Jason said with his hands up, "why are you freaking out? I pretty much stole Bri from you, so you had first dibs. You fuck her, I fuck her, they fuck each other, we all fuck, it's all good. Fucking is fun. It's normal. Relax."

I stared hard at him.

"I'm not sure I understand your generation," I said.

"That's okay, dude," Jason said. "I'm not sure I understand yours."

"I mean, do you feel anything at all? Or are people just interchangeable holes?"

Aleksandra arrived with his drink. He thanked her and sipped it.

"Oh my God!" he said. "This is amazing. I don't know what your problem is, dude. I'm liking this place."

A gong sounded and the lights dimmed three times.

"What's that?" Jason said.

People began to drift to one side of the house.

"Must be show time," I said.

He nodded and we followed the crowd. We passed the

living rooms into a hallway area that ended at three large doors with more security guards.

On my left along a bank of floor-to-ceiling windows was a sixty-ish man with long white hair in a ponytail and a white beard, smiling and nodding at everyone as they passed. He was dressed in a loose flowing all-white outfit that could have been a suit, a dress, or a robe. It hid the shape of his body well. He could have been moderately heavy or approaching obese. I'd put money on approaching obese.

On either arm was a cover-girl quality model. I recognized this man from the pictures I had found online. So this is what a former porn producer turned philanthropist looks like. All I could think was Jake Preston in about forty years.

"Titus," said the man, singling me out of the crowd as Jason and I passed, steely silver eyes locked with mine, "I'm Morton Hinraker. Welcome to my home."

His voice was deep and theatrical. I held his gaze as we moved forward and stayed silent. I saw nothing behind his eyes, just a vast emptiness.

He laughed and said, "Enjoy the show."

"Oh, I intend to," I said, finally breaking the eye contact.

We neared the doors, which opened into a room that looked like a theater of sorts. Jason turned to me, slapped his arm around my back, and massaged my neck like a coach to a fighter.

"Dude," he said, "that was a Batman moment."

The large room had no windows. It didn't match the decor of the previous rooms, as if we had been transported to a three-hundred year old château just outside of Paris—gilded wallpaper in a gold and maroon floral pattern over a white chair rail and dado with white panel molding, carpeting with an intricate Persian pattern, three rows of elegant Louis XVI white chairs with maroon silk padding and gold trim arranged around an empty space in the center. All the room needed was Marie Antoinette and a guillotine.

I scanned for exits. There was one large opening on the other side of the room with no door. There appeared to be a hallway running behind it.

I picked a seat at the end of a row and motioned for Jason to take the second one in.

"Mind if I sit on the end?" he said. "I like to sit on the end."

I shot him a look I use at Cap'n Jack's.

"Naw," he said, "on second thought, I'll just sit here and let you have the end."

I grinned. We sat.

I scanned the crowd for Allie. Lots of beautiful young women, but no sign of her. Four security guards lined up with folded arms behind us at the entrance.

The crowd seemed collectively under the spell of a substance. Or maybe so enthralled to be there that they couldn't speak. No soft conversation. Just an ever-building tension and excitement of whatever it was we were about to see.

In glided Morton Hinraker, the long-gowned cover-girl models still on each arm slow-stepping with him. They paraded him to a throne-like chair on a raised dais on the right side of the room. He paused to wave to the audience, who responded with applause. All hail Caesar.

He sat, but the two models remained standing on either side of him. The doors shut behind us and the lights dimmed. I missed my gun terribly.

Two almost naked and very muscular men in black leather masks and straps chain-linked to black leather shorts walked into the room. Metal studs protruded from the straps and shorts. Combat boots completed the ensemble. Each man dragged behind him a large cage on rollers.

Inside each cage was a naked girl wearing a black leather gag with a bright red ball in her mouth. My muscles tightened. I felt the urge to retch, but I forced myself to control it by looking at the girls' faces. Neither was Allie.

"Fuck, this is weird," said Jason, his eyes perplexed but fascinated. The couple in front of us turned and gave him a *be-silent* look. He nodded, looked at me, and shrugged.

Another gong sounded and the room filled with some sort of confetti. Or so it seemed. Nothing actually landed on the floor. An illusion of some sort.

I was sweating now, trying not to picture my hands around Hinraker's throat. Another part of me was planning an escape. Through the guards behind us wasn't the best idea, maybe ahead through the big door and down the hallway.

Although I'm sure there were guards over there too. Shit, I was trapped. My breathing got heavy and I felt a trickle of sweat down my back.

A young woman carrying a silver whip walked into the room. A spotlight appeared on her and the crowd "ooh"-ed. She wore a bright shiny purple wig in a long pageboy cut with straight bangs, heavy blue eye shadow over thick black lashes. Her eyes glowed with blue contact lenses and her lips glistened with fluorescent blue lipstick. She was in a silver space outfit right out of an old science-fiction TV show I remember watching as a kid but forgot the title, something with a moonbase. A glistening metal collar wrapped around her neck and connected down to a ridiculously short metallic skirt with flared sides. Her firm breasts and tiny waist hid under a tight fabric that looked like chain mail. Shiny knee-length metallic boots reflected the spotlight like tinfoil. From under the rear of the skirt swung a long silver tail with a silver arrow at the end. She cracked the whip above everyone's heads as she walked, the tail slapping the carpet from side-to-side with the swinging of her hips.

"Good evening," she said, her voice filling the room with an air of authority, even though she couldn't be more than twenty. "Welcome to the Cage Girl Show. Before we begin, let me introduce the Cage Girls. Tori!"

A spotlight shone on one of the girls, sharply defining her

naked body. Music softly rose. I recognized it. "Also Sprach Zarathustra" by Richard Strauss.

"Tori," said the silver space girl, "are you here of your own free will?"

Tori nodded yes.

"And are you of legal age?"

Tori nodded yes again.

She repeated this procedure with the other girl, who was named Anya, timing the answer to coincide with the first crescendo of "Also Sprach Zarathustra."

"Now let me introduce the Slave Boys," she said, going through the same procedure with the two muscular young men who dropped to their knees with their heads bowed. When the music reached its second crescendo, she slapped her whip across their backs.

Then, in time with the music, she walked to the center of the room as the spotlight narrowed on her face. "I am your domme, Mistress Tiffany. All rise to me!" Everyone in the room stood up except for me as the music reached its big climax. Massive applause greeted another whip display over our heads.

I glanced at Hinraker, who was motionless, staring at me with a smile. My blood boiled. Sick fuck. I turned to look at Jason, who looked at me like I was a bomb about to go off.

For a moment, I seriously considered walking over to Hinraker and slamming his head to the floor. But that won't end well. I'd probably end up living in his basement in a box with my arms and legs cut off, fed by tubes with stimulants to keep me alive.

So I should leave. Allie is not here. Why am I staying? If I stay, I'm going to end up busting some heads.

The room went quiet, the spotlight vanished, and subtle lighting surrounded the cages.

"Slave boys!" said Mistress Tiffany. "Open the cages." The two men rose. Each lifted one side of each cage. "Crawl to me, slave girls!"

The girls crawled out of the cages. "Heads down!" shouted Mistress Tiffany as she cracked the whip over the girls' backs.

I slammed my right fist into my left palm. I had to get out of here soon. I looked behind me at the nearest door, catching the gaze of one of the security guys.

I was about to get up when Mistress Tiffany, posing and gazing into the audience's eyes in a slow arc, whip at her hip, looked directly at me. I froze in place, meeting her glare. Big hypnotic eyes, even behind the contact lenses. She passed me and continued around the room, but I had peered into them long enough to know.

Oh, definitely. I knew those eyes. That face. Those lips. Staring at me from the home page on my Chromebook.

Shit.

I just found Allie Hayes.

19

THE "SHOW" DEVOLVED into a vile spectacle that would make the Marquis de Sade proud. As I sat through the depravity, I wondered how Allie had been corrupted into this. How did Morton Hinraker get her into this? Or was it Allie's own father, the honorable Rexford J. Hayes? Was it abuse she suffered at his hand that drove her to this?

There are some people who are wired to equate sexual pleasure with pain, but I've never understood it. In my experience as a cop, most of them learned the link from abuse at a young age.

At each insertion of an object and every other perversion at the command of Mistress Tiffany, a bile rose in my stomach. I wondered if this is how people felt when Rome was in its final hedonistic nosedive into oblivion.

Thankfully, it ended. The five participants inexplicably stood up with big smiles to a roomful of applause. They held hands and took a collective bow as the audience rose for a standing ovation. Then, they hugged and laughed like they had just performed a school play. I hadn't expected that. It was unnerving.

I turned to look at Jason, who sat with his mouth open, not applauding like me. He was somewhat pale.

"Okay, dude," he said, "I'll admit. That was fucked."

"There's hope for you yet," I said.

The "performers" went through the big door and out. The crowd moved toward the exits. Jason and I joined them.

More drinks were served. More mingling. The mood had shifted, though. People were making out all around. Further on up the hall, on a couch, a young naked couple had sex while a group watched.

Jason was oddly quiet, barely touching his new drink.

I milled about, looking for Mistress Tiffany. The performers finally emerged, the Cage Girls still naked but nonchalant about it.

I saw Mistress Tiffany hug Hinraker and his two gown girls. She appeared to be thanking him. What the fuck?

The Cage Girls laughed and clasped hands with an older couple, who appeared to be congratulating them on their "art." I shook my head. Each of them had just been violated in every way possible by each other in front of a live audience, but now acted like it was just another day at the office.

I moved directly toward them.

"Did you enjoy the show?" said Morton Hinraker, coming at me from the side with a big smile.

"You're a sick fuck," I said.

He laughed. "I thought so. Give it some time. Your initial repulsion will give way to an acceptance—then a curiosity—then an arousal. Then, the fun begins."

"I'd rather eat smoldering charcoal."

"Well, to each his own. I have nothing to hide. No laws have been broken, Inspector. Everything is consensual. You are free to leave—or stay. Be yourself pleased."

He smiled and walked away. It was all I could do to hold myself together enough not to knock him down. I drifted over to Mistress Tiffany, who was chatting with a couple in their twenties, gushing over her "talent." She met my eye. I waited for a break in the conversation.

"Hello," she said with her hand out and a smile, turning to me as if I was just another raving fan.

"Hi, Allie," I said.

She froze, statue-like, then shook her head. "I'm sorry?"

"My name is Titus. Your mom hired me to find you. Looks like I found you. I need to know that you're safe and to ask you to call her."

The small group turned to throw eye-daggers at me. Mistress Tiffany touched my arm and smiled.

"Excuse us, please," she said as she led me away. We walked off to the side into a less crowded area overlooking a patio. A large sculpture of a ram's head stood on a marble block. We moved to the other side of it. There were no people here.

She looked at me head-on. The smile was gone, replaced by a nasty petulant expression.

"Who the fuck did you say you are?" she said.

Nice.

"My name is Titus," I said. "Your mother hired me to find you. She wants to know that you're safe."

She laughed. "You're full of shit. She did not. My 'mother' doesn't give a shit whether I'm alive or not as long as she gets her check. Wait, *who* did you say hired you?"

The mistress voice was gone, replaced by the unmistakable coarseness of a streetwise kid. I could swear I heard a faint New York accent, but that was impossible.

"I told you," I said. "Pam Hayes."

"Ha!" she said with a victorious laugh. "That woman wants me dead. She's insane. She tried to fucking kill me. I'll be damned if she'll come anywhere near me again."

My mind raced in several different directions, trying to

regroup. This is not the reaction I had expected. Maybe a little mother-daughter tension, but not this.

"Allie," I said, "what's going on?"

"You a cop?" she said.

"No. I'm, uh, private."

"Do you have a badge?"

"No, I'm, uh, super-private."

"Listen to me, Titus—if that's your real name, which I doubt—it's none of your fucking business. I don't need you to goddamned save me. I'm fucking fine."

"Doing this?" I said. "Being forced to perform this sick show every night?"

"Nobody's forcing me to do a goddamned thing. I choose to be here. I actually like this. I came here to get away from that sick world of yachts and country clubs and bullshit fakery. *That's* what I was forced to do."

"Don't blame you there. But why this?"

"Because I'm real here. I'm free here. I can let loose and be the real me here. This is what I love."

"This?" I said. *"This* is the real Allie? That freak show?"

"Look, I don't expect you to understand. You're obviously vanilla. This is the BDSM lifestyle. Didn't you ever fucking read *Fifty Shades of Grey*? It's completely consensual. You have no right to judge, and I'm a perfectly legal adult. Go fuck yourself."

I winced and glanced down at the outdoor patio. Four people were having sex next to the pool.

"Fine," I said. "I told your mother when she hired me—"

"That woman is—" she said.

"That woman is what?"

"Nothing."

"When your mother hired me, I told her I couldn't bring you back. But I will tell her where you are, because that's what she hired me to do. The rest is up to her and to you."

"Then if I die," she said, "it will be your fucking fault, dickwad."

In that moment. I realized this is one sick family. I felt bad for Pam Hayes. Not only does she have to put up with her ridiculous husband, but now I had serious doubts about the sanity of her own daughter.

I started away but turned back, moved by something beyond me.

"You think you've figured life out, Allie, but you don't know a goddamned thing," I said. "This is a dark world you're in and it will burn you eventually. You're only nineteen. You don't know. They will chew you up, spit you out, and ditch the rest in the 'Glades. Please talk with your mother."

"My 'mother' is none of your goddamned business," she said through gritted teeth, emphasizing the word *mother* in an odd way. "Now if you'd be so fucking kind, dear fucking sir, I'd like you to fucking fuck off and leave."

I nodded and turned. Morton Hinraker had appeared, still smiling. Is he always smiling? Two large security guards were with him.

"I hope you had a nice night, Inspector," he said. "But I think everyone will agree, including yourself, that you don't belong here."

A row of expletive-laced insults came to mind, but I held it.

"Call your mother, Allie," I said while looking into Hinraker's empty eyes and strode to the door, the guards in lockstep with me.

At the security checkpoint, Jason stood with two other guards. His arms were folded and the look on his face was dour.

We walked out in silence. The Lamborghini had been brought up and the valet held the door open. I didn't say anything and got in. Jason did the same. No tip this time.

He revved the engine, burned rubber, and slammed us out onto West Star Island Drive.

"You are destroying everything I've worked to build," he said as we crossed the bridge to the MacArthur. "Now I'm on a fucking blacklist 'cause of you."

151

"Sorry, dude," I said.

He gunned the car left into the merge lane of the causeway, cutting off a semi-trailer who barely missed us and blasted his horn. We accelerated obscenely and were back at my place in two minutes.

"You're better off," I said as I got out.

"Fuck you," he said. I closed the door and he screeched off.

I sure know how to make friends, don't I?

20

MY ARMS SHOOK as I exhaled hard and pushed the bar up for my fourth rep.

"One more," said Luther, his face upside down above me. "You can do one more."

I inhaled, letting the bar down slow and then exhaled on a push with all my might to get it back up. I felt it float away as Luther guided it to the rests.

I was breathing heavily, which triggered a coughing fit. Luther tossed a towel around my neck and handed me a water bottle.

"Good," he said looking at the two 45-pounders on each side of the 25-pound barbell.

I took a swig of water.

"Not good," I said. "Not good at all. I used to be able to do twice that much in my sleep."

"First time back, got to be easy on yourself."

We were at South Beach Boxing on Washington Ave. I

hadn't been in a real gym since Ariel died. It was good to be back. I had never been to this place, but all gyms feel like home.

"One more set," I said.

"No," said Luther, "you done for the day. Need to cough up some of that cancer in your lungs, get it out of your system." On cue, I went into another coughing fit. "How long since your last smoke?"

"Three days. You wouldn't believe some of the things I've coughed up. Even so, my cravings are out of control. Last night I had a dream I was climbing up the outside of a giant cigarette on top of a big hill, trying to light it with a torch."

"Resist the devil and he will flee from you. James, chapter four, verse seven."

"He who fears being conquered is sure of defeat."

Luther scowled. "Who said that?"

"I don't know, it's up there." I pointed up at one of the blue steel beams on the ceiling and Luther looked. Each one had an inspirational quote on both sides in yellow block letters. "I just figured I needed a quote too seeing as it's Quoty-McQuote day."

"Jackass."

We moved over to the squat rack. Luther put three hundred pounds on his shoulders and did four sets of twelve reps. If he struggled at all, I couldn't tell. He didn't grunt nor breathe heavily. No movement was wasted, no extra effort expended. Easy as buttering bread.

"I normally do more weight," he said as we took the plates off, "but today is my day off."

I flipped him off and stood in the squat rack.

Again, I stuck with two 45-pounders. Again, I wheezed and struggled. Luther helped me up on the last rep of each set, racking the bar with about as much effort as if it were made of foam.

"Good job," he said. "Next time, you do a little more."

"Thanks, coach," I said. "Maybe I'll make the team this

year."

"My my, aren't we sensitive." He broke up the word *sen-si-tive* into three syllables.

"I've lifted before, you know."

"I know, but you been letting whatever burning you up inside feast on you for too long."

I nodded and drank some more water.

We moved over to the heavy bags. Legs spent, I felt like I was wading through wet concrete.

I started in with a handful of combinations, but quickly had to stop. I ended up sitting on the floor against the wall feeling like a dying mule while Luther made the heavy bag dance as if it was a balloon.

"You fight pro?" I said.

"Long time ago," he said.

"What happened?"

"My career cut short by extenuating circumstances."

"Ah."

Three young guys had paused their workout on the other side of the room to watch Luther. Damn, he wasn't even sweating. He whistled a tune in time to the punches.

"Are you seriously whistling?" I said.

He turned it up, jabbing left and right, footwork perfect. I recognized "Proud Mary."

"Holy shit," said one of the guys watching.

I couldn't help but laugh.

When Luther was done, he turned to me and said, "Lunch?"

"Hell, yeah," I said.

We showered and walked over to the News Cafe on Ocean Drive and sat at an outdoor table. I had steak, scrambled eggs, and toast. Luther had eggs Benedict. We both drank orange juice, but I was alone with my two cups of coffee.

"Devil's juice," he said.

"Coffee is good for you," I said. "Studies show people who

drink coffee are less likely to get Alzheimer's."

"Touch not the unclean thing. Second Corinthians, chapter six, verse seventeen."

"Hello darkness, my old friend. Simon and Garfunkel, 'The Sound of Silence.'"

We finished our meal. I checked my phone. Still no response from Pam Hayes. I had called and texted several times this morning, but no answer.

"So what spirit move you, brother Titus?" Luther said. "Last time I saw you, you look like you trying to kill yourself."

"Since that morning," I said, "someone stepped up to offer to do it for me."

"And you saw the light? Just like that?"

"Don't know. Maybe I've changed, found a reason for living."

"Not that girl from the club, I hope."

"No, not her."

I hadn't told him about the second girl and wasn't planning to. I also hadn't told him about the roused sensation of life I felt whenever I'm near Sofia, seeing as she isn't his favorite person.

"How go finding the rich college girl?" he said.

"Oh, didn't I tell you?" I said. "I located her last night."

"You don't say."

"Yep. My Super-Sleuth Club membership card should be arriving in the mail any day now."

"Where was she?"

"At Hinraker's. Puts on a sick show. She's a dominatrix who likes space costumes. Oh, and tails up her ass."

"What you think of our boy Morton?"

"Smart but sick," I said. "He's fashioning his own private permanent orgy. Thinks he's Caligula. Makes Hugh Hefner look like a wide-eyed virgin."

"You rescue the fair maiden from the dark castle?"

"The fair maiden doesn't want to be rescued. She escaped a different castle and likes this one better. No yachts and tennis here. The lifestyle she seems to want is this one—whips, chains, pain, that shit."

"You believe her?"

I mulled that over.

"Strangely," I said, "I do. Even though I think people who get involved in that shit are running from something. Usually can't have normal relationships. Usually suffered some sort of sexual abuse."

"Didn't know you were a trained psychologist," he said.

"When I was a cop, I saw some shit."

"So anyone who into BDSM is mentally ill?"

"We're all mentally ill, just some more than others. There is no normal."

"God disagree with you there."

"He's free to do so."

I sipped some coffee.

"Strange thing is Allie seems wise beyond her years," I said. "And when I say wise, I mean streetwise. I heard it in her voice, the way she looked at me. Where'd she learn that growing up in the lap of luxury?"

"Movies and TV shows," Luther said.

"No, this was real. You can't learn it from TV. Comes from hustling in person."

He nodded. "What you going to do next?"

"Don't know. Pam Hayes is not responding to me."

"Odd. She be your boss lady, so to speak."

"She be. And she put on quite the act that she was concerned about her daughter, but—"

"But what?"

"There was something off about her too. Her words felt, I don't know, scripted."

"Now you find dear sweet Allie, but mommy seem to be done with you. Maybe she found her herself."

"Maybe. Or maybe something happened to her. Maybe Rex got to her, silenced her somehow."

"Rex Hayes is a scuzzbucket."

"Yes, he is."

"Maybe you should drop in on ol' Pam. See what reaction you get."

"Yeah. I was hired to find Allie Hayes. I found Allie Hayes. I need to report my findings to my client and return the money I didn't use. Time for a visit to Coral Gables. Gables Estates, actually. Arvida Parkway was the address, I believe she said."

"Oh my," Luther said in a marble-mouthed voice straight from the Hamptons, "my dear boy, I do believe one needs to be worth ten million just to drive on the pavement over there. Only Rolls-Royces and Mercedes-Benzes allowed."

I laughed so hard I slapped my hands together in applause, the Brahmin voice so out of place coming out of Luther's bald head.

"Place back home called Manchester-by-the-Sea," I said. "That's exactly how they talk."

"My dear boy," he continued in the accent, "don't insult me. Buffy and I sail our yacht there every year. Perhaps you've seen it at the club—the S.S. *Overbearing*."

"That's twice you've sent me into hysterical laughter today. I forget the last person who was able to make me do that."

He stared at me for a long moment. "Bet she was something."

The world stopped. Her scent flowed around me, the intoxicating aroma of red-headed bliss as she touched my face and leaned into me.

"What was her name?" he said.

Bastard. He got me to drop my guard and pounced on the moment of weakness he created, fully aware he had struck a nerve that sent me right back into her arms.

"Ariel," I said, the word echoing into the sky of a thousand lost horizons in my memory.

"What happened to her?" he said.

I forced myself back to the here and now. Staying on that

road, even for a few moments, only leads to darkness. I sat up and sipped my coffee.

"I'll tell you sometime, but right now I've got to get over to Coral Gables," I said.

"I'll be painting with DaShawn this afternoon," Luther said, "so if you want, you can borrow the official Apostolic Rescue Mission Church truck, seeing as you be in a automobile-inhibited place in your life."

"Me? Driving a vehicle of God? What if I get in an accident?"

"Then you go to hell instantly, no wait."

We walked to the church and went inside. On the left side of the altar, a plump black girl in her mid-twenties with tight braids played an old upright piano that hadn't been there last time. Based on its condition, I suspected it was much older than me. Maybe older than Miami.

Two black boys, a black girl, and a Latina girl—all high-school age—rehearsed "Oh Happy Day." They and the piano were both horribly off-key. Thankfully, they stopped when we walked in.

I followed Luther over to them, the fear on one of the boy's faces intense as he looked at me. I hadn't told Luther about his bike-thieving and I didn't intend to—but DaShawn didn't know that.

"Brother Titus," said Luther, "this is Sister Candace. She's putting together this motley crew for some Sunday hymns. We just rescued this brand spanking new piano from an elementary school in decline."

"Brand spanking new?" said Candace. "This piano is a piece of, uh, well let's just say it needs some TLC. My apologies, Mr. Titus. Nice to meet you."

"No apologies necessary," I said. "And it's just Titus."

She gave me a lovely smile.

"Titus," said Luther, "this is DaShawn, Bobby, Shardene, and Rosa. Say hello to brother Titus."

"Hello, brother Titus," they all said together except for DaShawn, his mouth hanging open.

"Hello," I said.

"You should come to service on Sunday," said Luther. "Candace here going to whip this quartet into shape till they put the Mormon Tabernacle Choir to shame. Going to be quite a sermon, too."

"Maybe," I lied. "Keys?"

Luther frowned.

"Candace," he said, "you still got the keys to the truck?"

"Oh, sure," Candace said and fumbled in her purse. She took out a single key on a rubber keychain in the shape of the number one. Luther took it and handed it to me. It read A-1 Tire Repair with a cartoon of a coyote pushing a big tire uphill. I felt his pain.

"Thanks," I said.

"Put some gas in if you feel so inclined," said Luther with a big grin.

21

I DROVE LUTHER'S ten-year old navy blue Ford Ranger across the MacArthur to I-95 South, then followed that until it dissolved into U.S. Route One, known locally as Dixie Highway. There was a profusion of strip malls and billboards, a concrete jungle similar to the same U.S. Route One back home in Boston. Is there a law that Route One must be endless strip malls and billboards from north to south?

Following Google Maps directions, I turned left onto Riviera Drive, then past Cocoplum Circle onto Old Cutler Road. It was as if I had been transported to a South American jungle in a previous century. The ancient banyan trees were breathtaking in their panoramic splendor. Timeworn but muscular trunks, some as wide as stretch limos, fired barrages of hearty branches skyward. Stately limbs tangled with their counterparts across the road, forming a canopy of succulent green that dangled overhead like a cloistered tunnel of protection from the modern world.

All that ended when I crossed yet another magical line in

time and space and entered Gables Estates, a modern playground for the most wealthy of the wealthy. I thought Hinraker's house and its contemporaries were over-the-top, but it was more showy celebrity rich. Gables Estates was old boys' club rich—mansions big enough to house the population of a small city, meticulously maintained rolling lawns with mile-long driveways, high stone walls with colorful vines in artful patterns, and a white mega-yacht at every dock.

I didn't blame Allie for wanting to escape. This world is beautiful on the outside but must have been dark and confining for the only child of a power-broker Senator-wannabe who needs to live a public life with zero tolerance for mistakes. As a cop, I had run into a couple of "trust fund junkies" who ended up on the street because they needed drugs to escape their callous parents' obsession with being the hoity-toitiest of the hoity-toity. The pressure had been too much—the right schools must be attended, the right grades achieved, the highest awards granted, the right club memberships attained. And for what? So they can spend the rest of their lives playing golf and tennis with other "approved" elites all trying to out-blue-blood each other?

It almost made me ill thinking about it as I pulled up to the stucco gate that barred the deplorable masses from entering Arvida Parkway.

The gray-haired man with a crew cut inside the stucco gatehouse with the Spanish-tile roof wore a name tag that read Harold. He took one look at me and the pickup truck and his hand hovered near his gun. I'm used to it.

"Can I help you, sir?" he said.

"I'm here to see Pam Hayes," I said.

"What is your name, sir?"

I told him. He placed a pair of reading glasses on his nose and studied a clipboard. He took his time, allowing an uncomfortable silence to build, and then flipped some pages while frowning. I got the feeling he enjoys uncomfortable silences. My gut said retired cop.

"Do you have an appointment, sir?" he said.

"No," I said.

"Are you a registered visitor, sir?"

"No."

"I'm sorry, sir, but without an appointment, or being a registered visitor, or on my guest list here, I'll be unable to let you in."

"Look, Harold, I know you're just doing your job. Pam Hayes hired me to find her daughter Allie. You probably know Allie. You probably know she's missing. Well, I found her. I've been calling Mrs. Hayes all morning and getting no answer. This is good news for Mrs. Hayes. I've found her daughter alive and well and need to inform her because she's paid me a lot of money."

He looked at me for a long moment. Something in him decided I was telling the truth and he said, "Got an ID on you?"

I pulled out my Massachusetts Driver's License and handed it to him.

"One moment, please, sir," he said.

The window closed and he made a phone call. While he talked, I examined the five CD's in the space under the radio. I selected Gladys Knight and the Pips, put the CD in the player, and hummed along to "Midnight Train to Georgia."

The window opened.

"I'm sorry, sir," Harold said and handed me back my license, "but I can't find any authorization for your being here. I'm going to have to ask you to turn around and leave."

"You're kidding," I said.

"No, sir. I'm sorry, sir."

There was another long uncomfortable pause. I could ram the gate, but that would only bring the cops. Plus, I didn't know what other security awaits across the little bridge that leads down to the parkway where I knew the Hayes estate was.

"Can I leave a message for Mrs. Hayes?" I said.

"I cannot confirm nor deny that a Mrs. Hayes lives in

Gables Estates, sir."

I laughed. "Harold, you used to be a cop, right? You retired early and now you do this probably part-time, right?"

He smiled, but didn't say anything. I was right.

"Do you know Detective Sergeant Sofia DeJesus-Montero of the Miami Organized Crime Section?" I said.

"No, sir," he said.

"Do you know the Reverend Luther Williams of the Apostolic Rescue Mission Church of Miami Beach?"

"No, sir. Now, I'm going to have to ask you to—"

"Do you know Paulie DiNucci?"

His eyes lit up and he almost smiled. "You know Paulie?"

"I work for Paulie at Cap'n Jack's Seafood & Bar. At the bar. From one former cop to another, would you do me a favor and call Paulie and ask him if you can trust me?"

Harold stared at me some more, but didn't move to the phone. He leaned back and folded his arms.

"This missing girl," he said, "she talk back to you?"

I smiled. "Every other word was fuck," I said. "She told me in no uncertain terms what I could do with myself."

He chuckled. "She act like she's queen of the goddamned world and we're all tools to her?"

"Yeah."

"You think she's trouble?"

"Yeah."

He laughed. "Well, sir, like I said, I can't help you. I'll need to ask you to turn around and leave. But in the meantime, may I suggest a game of tennis? Do you play tennis, sir?"

"No."

"Well, that's a shame, because if I were to recommend a place to play tennis, it would be the Leucadendra Country Club. It's on Leucadendra Drive about a mile back. Oh, but you don't play tennis, so why am I telling you? Just being friendly and thought I'd make a recommendation. Now, you have a great day, sir."

I put the truck in gear and grinned at him. "Thank you, Harold."

"Say hello to Paulie from Harry Lyle."

"Will do."

I turned the truck around and pulled back out onto Old Cutler Road.

Paulie scores again.

22

I PULLED LUTHER'S truck into the Leucadendra Country Club. The large circular driveway was paved with Italian flagstone. There were several expensive cars, each with a driver waiting for various lords and ladies to finish an afternoon of the sport of kings. A couple of drivers stood and chatted while smoking. Others sat inside in the air conditioning, engines running.

A gray Mercedes was parked on the other side of the circle. I made a bet with myself that Chester would be behind the wheel in a gray suit and cap.

I pulled up alongside. Chester rolled down the window and sneered at me over gray lapels. I win.

"What are you doing here?" he said with just the right amount of indignant outrage.

"Looking for Mrs. Hayes," I said.

"I thought Mr. Hayes told you your assignment was complete."

"Wow, they keep you in the loop. Good for you, Chet. Thing is, Mr. Hayes didn't hire me. And I found Allie. Well, sort of. I know where she can be found at least one night of the week and I need to get this information to Mrs. Hayes."

"You can give it to me. I'll pass it along."

I laughed. "See, Chet, you're not Mrs. Hayes either, so that's not going to work. Why the sudden cold shoulder? Doesn't she want me to do the very thing she so gratuitously paid me to do? By the way, are you impressed? I bet you didn't think I could use the word gratuitously in a sentence, did you? It was a lot of money, Chet, a whole lot. You should know. You handed it to me. You must be bringing home the bacon yourself with a boss who can make it rain like that, huh? But seriously, how would you feel if you were just shut out for no reason? No explanation. Just like that, boom, done. I mean, picture it. Mrs. Hayes tells you to drive to—I don't know, Bal Harbour shopping mall—that's a place she might want to go, right? Halfway there, Mr. Hayes calls and says 'Chester, I want you to pull over, get out of the car, and walk away from it,' leaving Mrs. Hayes right in the middle of the highway. No explanation, no nothing. Just *hasta la vista*, Chester, don't call us, we'll call you. Wouldn't you be mad? I mean, just a little? Wouldn't you want to know why you were dumped mid-stream like that? Wouldn't you feel at least a tiny obligation to get Mrs. Hayes to the destination you were paid to take her to?"

"You are an annoying man," he said. "I'm calling the police." The window rolled up.

That did it. The crazy was on. I was getting really sick of these people.

I drove up two car lengths, pulled into an empty spot past a silver Audi A5, and got out. Sitting on a white Victorian wrought-iron bench in the shade of a white rose trellis was a short taut man with a scraggly tousle of salt-and-pepper hair over a wrinkly face. In fact, everything about him was wrinkly— a loose wrinkly white shirt, loose wrinkly tan pants that rode up his ankles, and white loafers with no socks. He smoked a cigarette motionlessly, watching me with a faint chiseled smile like a carved statue. I assumed he was one of the drivers, but whoever employs him needs to give him a raise so he can get his clothes pressed.

I walked past him and around the circle to the main entrance next to gold letters on expensive stone that read *Leucadendra Country Club*. The two blond security boys with stylish haircuts in blue polo shirts and white shorts looked like they weren't quite sure how to handle me as I stormed toward them. Understandable. Probably the toughest task they perform is to give rides home to members who've had too much to drink.

"Hey!" said one as I breezed past them. "You can't go in there!"

The other one followed me behind and to my right just as I saw Pam Hayes on an outside terrace, sitting at a patio table with several other posh middle-aged ladies. Lucky break. I wouldn't have to run around trying to find her. Tennis rackets lay propped by the chairs. The ladies sipped champagne from tall flutes.

The boy tried stepping in front of me. I'm big, but he was bigger, linebacker-size. He was also probably seventeen. I grabbed his left hand and twisted his little finger.

"Ow!" he said as I turned his arm away from the socket that holds it in place and held it like a briefcase as I walked him ahead of me onto the patio.

"Ow, you're hurting me!" he said.

"No I'm not," I said as we approached the table. "Trust me, if I was hurting you, you'd know."

"I'm calling the cops!" the other boy yelled from way behind us.

I never thought a mouth could open so wide as Pam Hayes' when she saw me.

"Mrs. Hayes," I said. "Sorry about the fuss, but I need to talk to you."

The other ladies were frozen with astonishment. Things like

this *just don't happen* at the Leucadendra Country Club. One of them didn't seem to mind, even forsaking her high position in life to smile at me.

I'll hand it to Pam Hayes. She composed herself quickly, stood up, and said, "I'll take care of this, girls. Titus and I are old friends. I'll be running along now."

Like it's a perfectly ordinary thing to do on a perfectly ordinary day. Longish-haired thugs with goatees are just another item on one's to-do list, ladies.

"Titus," she said with a warm smile, "let that boy go please."

I let him go. He said "Ow!" again.

"It's all right, Lucas," she said to him, patting him on the other arm. "Girls, really, everything is fine. This is a friend of mine. I'm going to leave for now. I'll see you next Thursday."

She took me by the arm like I was her date, her purse and tennis racket on her other arm.

The police had arrived. That was quick. They must have been fighting crime close by. They were talking with a tall white-haired man in a tuxedo who looked like the maître d'.

"Terrence," she said to him, "this is my friend Titus. Everything is fine. Just a misunderstanding." She turned to the two fresh-faced cops. "I'm sorry, officers. I've been neglecting my friend and he came to see me here. He gets a little agitated sometimes, but I assure you that everything is fine."

She and I walked arm-in-arm out to the car, her nose high in the clouds like the Queen of England with her Royal escort. Chester emerged from the Mercedes and stood, awaiting orders.

The man in the wrinkly clothes still occupied his place on the bench. He watched us without expression.

"Titus," she said in a cool voice, "I told you that everything is resolved and to stop looking for Allie. We found her and she's fine. All is well."

"No, Mrs. Hayes," I said, "you actually didn't tell me that everything is resolved and to stop looking for Allie. Your husband did, but he didn't hire me. You hired me, so I need to hear it from you."

"Well, now you're hearing it from me. Please, Titus, I wouldn't want to see you get hurt."

"That sounds like a threat."

She looked around, frustrated, pondering what to do next. She waved to Chester, who opened the rear door.

"Get in the car, Titus," she said. I stared at her. "Please." Big smiles, always gets her way. I got in the back with her. "Chester, give us a moment, please."

He nodded, turned, and shut the door.

"Titus," she said in a voice as icy as the car's air conditioning, "I will not have you rattling around frightening my friends and causing scenes that could ruin my husband's chances of being elected to the United States Senate."

"That's what this is all about, isn't it?" I said. "That's the most important thing to you really, isn't it? Keeping it all out of the papers. You really don't give a rat's ass about Allie or where she is. She's just a prop to you and your husband's quest for power. All that bullshit you dropped on me, it was all a sham. Rehearsed."

Her face swelled. I thought for a moment her head might explode, but she closed her eyes and brought it under control. When she spoke again, it was calm and warm with a gentle smile.

"Titus, now you know that's not true," she said. "I loved Allie. I wanted to help her. But there was nothing I could do. She was out of control."

"Loved? Past tense. You don't love Allie anymore?"

"Oh, of course I do. That didn't come out right. I still love her. I still think of her every day. It's just, I want this situation to right itself, and now I know where she is and everything can get better."

I decided to take a stab, rock the boat maybe.

"So you can get her to come home?" I said. "So she can be abused by her father again?"

"Is that what you think, Titus?" she said, the cool voice back.

"What should I think? Nineteen-year old girl ditches her rich life and education to be a dominatrix in a show where she whips and flogs people on stage."

"Titus, I won't hear any more of this!"

"Oh, you didn't know? I thought you knew what Allie has been up to."

"I know—what she likes. It's—disgusting. Revolting."

"Yes, but typically in my experience as a police officer, some people—maybe not all, but a good chunk—who fall into that lifestyle have been abused as children."

Her face lost all expression.

"Titus," she said, ice in her voice now, "get out of my car."

"I need to know, Pam," I said, "was Allie abused by her father?"

The words escaped her mouth like a lion storming out of a cage: "Not once! Not ever! Now get out of my car and leave us alone forever or I will—"

Her knuckles were white where she gripped the gray leather hand rest. She breathed heavily, near foaming.

"You will what?" I said.

"Just get out!" she said. "Get out!"

People just love telling me to get out of their cars, don't they? I raised my hands and got out.

Chester sneered at me as he shut the door.

"Chet," I said, "I've got to throw you a compliment. You are the best sneerer I've ever known. Did you go to sneering school? You could teach sneering. I'd sign up for a sneering lesson if you were the teacher."

He ignored me, got in the car, and they drove off.

I turned and looked at the two Coral Gables cops. They stood near the entrance and stared at me with folded arms.

"I'm going, I'm going," I said with my hands up as I got in Luther's truck.

I caught the eye of the wrinkly man with his scraggly tousle of salt-and-pepper hair. He hadn't moved. I wondered if he ever moved. Still the faint chiseled smile under cold gray eyes. I felt a twist in my stomach. The twist became a full-on tightening of my muscles all over.

As I pulled back out onto Old Cutler Road and turned right, I saw a black SUV parked near the corner with its engine running.

I got a sinking feeling.

You know what, though? Fuck it. I don't care anymore. I'm done. I'm out. This is too fucked up to continue. Done. Done done done. So fucking done with Pam Hayes, Rex, Allie, Jake Preston, Jason Stark, JoJo Burley, Eddie Corrado, and Morton Hinraker.

Fuck all of you.

Time to clear my head and shrug it all off. I threw in the next CD without looking at it. The Grass Roots' horn section kicked into "Midnight Confessions".

"Ha!" I said and hit the gas, breaking some local ordinances. I cranked the volume, shut the AC, and opened the windows. A hot breeze blew my hair all around as I belted out the lyrics, nobody listening but the old banyans and an occasional dog-walker as I sped past.

I'm free. Free and done. Time to focus on my unfinished task on West Lido Drive. Point, shoot, done. Bye bye Miami.

Just as I hit the soulless Dixie Highway again, the daily deluge crashed down. Headlights popped on everywhere as the world went dark. I rolled up the windows and pulled out into traffic, bolts of lightning shattering all around.

My phone rang. I looked at the name and smiled. Sofia.

Hot damn.

"I knew you'd give in sooner or later," I said.

There was a pause and she said, "Where are you?"

"On my way to your place with a bottle of wine."

"Seriously."

"Seriously? In a borrowed truck on Dixie Highway drowning in rain and traffic somewhere near Coconut Grove."

"You know where the Arthur Godfrey Bridge is? Where it crosses the Biscayne Waterway at 41st Street?"

"How could I forget?" I laughed. "That's where we first met when you pulled me over that night. I love it. Let's redo that night, just like in the movie *Groundhog Day*. You pull me over and arrest me, my punishment is you force me to take you to dinner. You name the place. I've got the cash."

"Titus," she said in a cutting business-like tone, "this is serious. Meet me there."

"Okay."

She hung up.

The sinking feeling returned.

23

I PARKED BEHIND a cruiser with its blues flashing and leaped out in the middle of the stopped cars on 41st Street. It had taken me a full forty-five minutes in the storm and traffic. The sun was back out, lighting an afternoon sea of commotion. A helicopter buzzed overhead. News vans were all over, reporters talking into cameras. A crowd lined the sidewalk on both sides—people watching, talking, and taking videos with their phones.

A line of yellow crime scene tape blocked off an area in a parking lot behind a bank that fronted the Biscayne Waterway, which ran under West 41st Street. A white tent had been set up on the grassy spot between the parking lot and the water. Uniformed officers surrounded the area while technicians in white baggy suits and booties walked around with various devices.

Across the waterway, painted on the side of an old building named the Roosevelt, was a graffiti art mural that read *Welcome to*

Miami Beach. Its cheery cartoon bird and smiling sun looked horribly out of place.

In the middle of the police activity, I recognized Sofia in her black pantsuit. She talked with several other plainclothes cops, their badges on belt hooks. I caught a glimpse of something on a long table in the tent.

My stomach sank

I walked up to the two uniforms nearest me, who were blocking people from the crime scene.

"You can't come through here, sir," one said. "You'll need to cross over to the other side."

"I was invited," I said. "Call her over there, in the black pantsuit."

"Who?"

"Detective Sergeant De Jesus-Montero," I said.

Sofia caught my eye and waved me over. I gestured toward the uniforms. She gave them a thumbs-up sign and waved me over again. They looked at each other and grunted. One gestured with his thumb backward for me to pass.

I walked around the metal railing down into the parking lot. Several bank employees had gathered by the door. One of them was crying. I went past the yellow pylons to the makeshift command center, my heart beating faster.

Sofia met me at the perimeter of the tape. She stood with a tall gray-haired man and a muscular black woman.

"Titus," she said, "this is Detective Belson from the Homicide Divison. He's in charge here."

I nodded, he nodded, both of us sizing each other up.

"This is Lieutenant Brown of OCS," Sofia said.

I nodded at the black woman, who shot eye-daggers at me.

"So you're the amateur investigator," said Lieutenant Brown. "I should arrest you right now."

I smiled. Her eyes bored into me. She stood like a prizefighter taunting an opponent. My instinct told me she'd be tough to take down.

"But I need you," she said, "to identify a body and then answer some questions. Follow me."

The four of us walked over to the tent, the rumble of helicopter rotors overhead. Halfway there, the Lieutenant turned and shouted at a uniformed sergeant while pointing up: "Davis, I told you to get that thing out of here!"

"Yes, lieutenant," Davis said, picked up a radio, and yelled into it.

I held my breath as we walked into the tent. The first thing I noticed were long male legs in dark jeans. I breathed a sigh of relief. Not that I wished harm on anyone, but if it was Allie I was afraid I'd drive back to Coral Gables and make an even bigger scene, one that would land me back in jail.

Lieutenant Brown uncovered his face, everyone staring at me as I looked down. His left eye—in fact, a huge chunk of the left side of his face—was missing. His other features were deformed from having been in the water, but I recognized him.

Testarossa is down.

"You know him?" said Lieutenant Brown.

"Jake Preston," I said.

She covered his face again and the four of us walked out of the tent to stand on the grassy spot near the riverbank. I felt naked as what seemed like half of Miami took videos of us.

"Sofia said you were looking for Jake Preston," said Lieutenant Brown.

"That is correct, Lieutenant," I said.

"Why were you looking for him?"

I gave her a brief overview of what I had been hired to do and what I had discovered, but left out the part about Allie at Hinraker's last night.

"Did you threaten Jake Preston?" said Lieutenant Brown.

"No," I said, "I only told him I'd find Allie."

"So you did confront him."

"Yeah, I talked with him at Sinz."

"Sins?"

"Sinz with a z. The club over on Ocean Drive."

One eyebrow went up. The lieutenant looked sharply at Sofia.

"Do you have any idea who might have shot Mr. Preston with a small-caliber handgun at close range?" said Lieutenant Brown.

"No," I said.

"You're a terrible liar, Titus. I will ask you once, and only once. Do you know where Allie Hayes is?"

"No."

She glared at me intensely.

"It's a good thing Sofia vouches for you," she said. "Because otherwise you'd be taken in for questioning right now. If Allie Hayes contacts you, you are hereby directed to inform the Miami-Dade Police Department immediately. Otherwise, you will stay away from this matter. If I even smell you anywhere near anything we are doing, you will spend a month living with some people who make alligators seem friendly."

"Oh, no worries there," I said. "I'm done with this whole thing, trust me."

"Are you giving me lip?"

"No, I'm serious. The Hayeses don't want me around anymore. They've been perfectly clear about that."

"Don't blame them. Just remember what I said."

She and Belson walked back to the tent. Sofia stayed with me, her arms folded.

"Why is OCS here?" I said. "Wouldn't homicide run this?"

"We were working on something involving Jake Preston," said Sofia. "Can't talk about it—even though now it's dead in the water. I can tell you that I don't think this has anything to do with that. This was an amateur job."

"When was the body discovered?"

"About three hours ago. Bank employee found him floating right there by the riverbank."

"I'm no forensics expert, but he looks like he hasn't been in the water long."

"So far, that's what the M.E. says but we can't be sure. We think he was dumped in the middle of the night. One thing's for sure. Whoever did the dumping had no clue how to get rid of a body so it isn't found."

"Yesterday was Tuesday, which was four days after I saw him at Sinz on Friday night. Today is Wednesday."

I stared across the waterway at a reporter making gestures toward the tent while talking into the camera. I shook my head and folded my arms.

"What are you thinking?" Sofia said.

"I'm not sure," I said. "Do you know an Eddie Corrado?"

"Yeah, lowlife thug. Works for Tommy Nero."

"I ran into him at Sinz, too. We didn't hit it off."

"You think he's involved with this?"

"He seems to want to scare me off. He's responsible for my new nose."

"I saw that. You okay?"

"Yes, and thanks for asking right away."

"Don't be a dick. What's with the Hayeses? Why do they suddenly want you to drop finding Allie?"

"Don't know," I said. "Tried to talk to Pam just an hour ago, but they suddenly hate me. Rex even tried to paid me a ridiculous amount of money to drop it, so I'm pretty much off the case."

Sofia bit her lip and looked down at the grass. I watched her bite her lip and look down at the grass.

"Do you think Allie killed Jake Preston?" she said.

"She'd be my number one suspect," I said, "but I'm not so sure. She and Jake have an odd relationship. I went into this with the idea that maybe Jake Preston manipulated Allie into all this shit, but now I wonder if it was the other way around. I'm thinking now that Jake was just a means to an end."

"Means to an end, how?"

"Allie has a fling with this Jake Preston boy who is a bad fit

178

for the parents. They hire a private investigator named Tom Langston, who finds her and brings her back. Everything returns to normal. Allie goes to college, dates a nice country club boy her mom finds for her, and becomes the family darling again. Then, something happens. I don't know what. Whatever it is causes Allie to flip, quit college, and run back to Jake. Maybe because she loves him. Or maybe she runs back to Jake because they're birds of a feather. Whatever it is, I think they work together to blackmail her father into paying for their love shack."

"Blackmail him with what?" Sofia said.

"Like I said, I'm only speculating here. I have no evidence, but my gut tells me that Rexford J. Hayes abused Allie and she has some sort of proof. That's why he pays their rent and writes checks like this."

I reached into my pocket, pulled out the big torn check from Foundation Investments LLC, and handed it to her.

"Holy shit," she said.

"I know," I said.

"You tore this?"

"I did."

Her eyes sparkled and she smiled.

"So what was with the mother hiring you?" she said.

"That's the part that doesn't fit," I said. "If Allie is living with Jake Preston in a house that's roundabout paid for by her own father just to shut the two kids up, then why keep it a secret from the mother?"

"Daddy-daughter secret?"

"Maybe. Pam Hayes reacted badly when I presented her with this notion. Maybe she doesn't know about the abuse. Maybe she wants to find Allie to confront her and find out if he really did it."

Sofia rolled her eyes. "God, this is why I don't want kids."

I looked up at the graffiti art, the cartoon bird still smiling at me and welcoming me to Miami Beach.

"Strange this happens here," I said, "the very spot where

you pulled me over that night."

Sofia glanced up at the mural. I felt an electrical charge hovering between us.

"Yeah," she said, "I noticed."

"Luther says there are no coincidences."

"What does that mean?"

"Not sure."

We looked into each others' eyes for a good long beat. The electrical charge grew. I'd better leave before I kiss her on live television.

"Okay," I said, turning to walk away, "I'm out of here."

"Can I keep this?" she said, holding up the torn check.

"Would you give it back if I said no?"

"No."

I smiled and headed across the parking lot toward the crowd.

"Hey," she said. I turned and looked back. "Keep me updated in case you hear anything."

"And risk the wrath of Bad Bad Lieutenant Brown? I thought both you and she wanted me to stay away."

"That's officially true. But keep me updated in case you hear anything," she repeated in a more demanding tone.

"Yes, officer," I said.

Was that a hint of a smile as she turned to walk away? Yes it was.

Hot damn.

24

I FILLED THE tank at the Chevron on Alton and dropped the truck back at the church. There was nobody there and the office was locked, so I hid the keys and texted the location to Luther.

Fighting the overwhelming urge for a cigarette, I walked up Washington Ave to the Art Deco Supermarket to buy dinner. At 5th Street, my phone vibrated with a text. I looked at it.

Shit. It was Bri:

> Hi madman. =)

I ignored it. At 7th Street, I got another one:

> Sash and I are at a
> private pool on a
> rcofdeck, 8th and

Ocean , come play

There were three emojis performing acts I didn't know emojis could perform. I texted back:

Thx busy

She sent another text: a winking emoji with a naked picture of herself. I didn't reply. I'm no prude, but sex is like scratching an itch to these kids. I did save the picture, though.

At 11th Street, my phone vibrated again. I was about to call Bri and tell her I can't do this "hookup" shit, but the new text was from an unknown number. It read:

> You are being
> followed by a pro
> cleaner who goes by
> the name of Z. Just
> the letter. Lean and
> short with gray hair.
> Age about 55. Drives
> a silver Audi A5.
> Watch your back.

My skin tightened all over. "Cleaner" is law enforcement slang for professional hired killer.

The world compressed inward on my location standing in front of the 11th Street Diner. I scanned all directions, senses heightened, hand near gun. No silver Audi A5 in sight.

Who would send a text to warn me? How would that

person know I'm being followed by a hitman? I got the feeling I
wasn't going to be able to let go of all this Allie Hayes bullshit
even if I wanted to.

I continued walking on high alert to the Art Deco
Supermarket, covertly scrutinizing my surroundings—every face,
every storefront, every car—hunting for signs of anything out of
the ordinary.

Once inside, I did a quick scan of the five other people
there. Nobody looked like a hitman. I took out my phone and
texted back to the unknown number:

Who are you?

The message instantly came back as undeliverable. Whoever
sent the warning is a pro, too.

I selected a meal of pork, rice, and zucchini with a lime
soda. I was at the cashier about to pay when a hand reached in
front of me from my left. I nearly grabbed my gun until I saw it
was a slender amber-skinned hand.

"I pay for him," said a soft female voice with a Latina
accent, handing the cashier a ten-dollar bill.

I turned and saw the sixteen-ish girl whose food I paid for a
few days ago. The world stopped on its axis.

It was Marisol.

She smiled, her lips thick around primordially white teeth.

Holy fuck. Marisol. No wonder she looked familiar in her
mother's pictures, but I also understand why she didn't click in
my brain. She was now older and more substantial. Not the girl
in pigtails anymore.

"I pay for him," said Marisol to the confused cashier, who
took her money. "I got into a little extra money this week."

She deliberately mocked the way I said it last time. I
couldn't help but laugh, admiring both her nobility and

183

intelligence. Her smile grew impossibly bigger and all my troubles momentarily vanished into a happy haze.

"Thank you," I said, grabbing the money from the cashier's hand and handing it back to Marisol. "But I can't let you do that."

I handed the cashier a twenty and she took it, shooting me a dirty look. Marisol reached over, grabbed the twenty, threw it down, and handed her the ten again. The cashier frowned and folded her arms.

"Yes you can," said Marisol. "I owe you from last week."

I decided to give her the satisfaction of paying me back.

"Thank you," I said.

The cashier gave her change and I took my bag to a spot by the front window near the door. I watched Marisol as she paid for her own food. She wore thick-framed dark glasses, loose jeans, a bright blue tank-top, and pink sandals. Her toenails were painted alternately pink and blue. Her body was oddly shaped with tiny shoulders and a skinny waist, but thick and big-boned from the hips down like her mother.

As she neared the door, she fumbled with her grocery bags. She hadn't noticed I was still there and looked up surprised.

"That was very nice of you," I said, "but you didn't have to do that."

"Yes, I did," she said with a smile that could melt a glacier. "My mother taught me to always, um, pay for myself. It's a Cuban thing. Never owe anybody anything."

I nodded. "Sounds like her. I offered her two hundred dollars just for food and she tried to turn me down. That's rare. Nobody does that."

Marisol's face expanded, eyes popping, mouth open.

"What did you say?" she said.

"Your mother," I said. "I've met her. She's looking for you. She stands on street-corners and at intersections holding up a sign that says 'Have you seen my daughter?' with a picture of a girl in pigtails. Your mother's name is Olivia Martinez-Valle.

Your name is Marisol. You're the girl in the picture."

Her eyes widened and she trembled all over. She ducked her head and bolted to the door.

Man, I sure know how to win them over, don't I?

"Marisol," I said as she went out the door and turned left, walking very fast.

I raced to catch up, moving alongside her in front of a shoe store.

"Marisol," I said. "Marisol, I told your mother I'd find you."

"Get away from me!" she said.

"Marisol, please stop and talk to me. My name is Titus. I've talked to your mother. She loves you. She's out here morning, noon, and night. She's going to die out here looking for you. Don't you care?"

She turned to face me. "It's none of your business! Get lost! Leave me alone or I'll scream."

"Marisol—"

She screamed. Several people turned to shoot me evil stares. I stopped and put my hands up, feeling like a dirty old man. She continued south down Washington Ave at a furious pace.

Shit.

I smiled and resumed walking, but super-slow. I took out my phone as if studying a text and kept my head down while keeping an eye on Marisol a block ahead.

I let her get even further ahead, continuing to follow from a distance. If I could figure out where she lived, then at least I'd have something to go on for her mother.

She turned right at 12th, which made it harder to follow her because there were less people in the residential area. I donned sunglasses and a camouflage head wrap and crossed to the opposite side of the street.

She turned left at the park onto Meridian, heading south. Oddly, the exact route I take home. Like she was going to my place. Who's following who here?

One thing was for certain—I was getting seriously fed up with these mother-daughter relationships. Why would a young beautiful girl like Marisol put her mother through so much torment?

At 10th, I sped up because I thought I might lose her. Then, she turned and stopped, glancing back. Her eyes fell across the street almost to my exact location. I side-stepped quickly to my right behind a banyan tree.

Little did Marisol know, but in that moment she saved my life. As I ducked behind the big tree, the unmistakable sound of a gunshot blasted through the air, blowing off a huge chunk of wood with a bone-jarring sound like an exploding bomb. I dove, grocery bag dropped, gun out, and crouched behind a parked car before I even thought about it.

Time slowed. Electrical impulses fired in my brain—seeing, recording, evaluating, strategizing. I was in a zone where a second became a minute, aware of every drop on every leaf, every crack in the pavement, every ridge of tree bark. I heard insects, the flutter of bird wings, and distant sounds of children at play, all in extreme slow-motion. On my haunches, I raised myself to peer through the windows of the parked car.

An old brown Buick was three-quarters past my location and accelerating. The front passenger window was rolled halfway down, a shotgun hanging out.

I raised myself to the roof of the parked car and fired three shots at the car. The back and rear right windows shattered. The Buick lurched to its left, side-swiping a red Volkswagen on the other side with a nasty crunch, but corrected and picked up speed, running the stop sign and barreling right at 9th. Two cars slammed on their brakes, nearly hitting each other. The alarm on the red Volkswagen screeched.

Windows opened. Eyes peered out. I could almost hear all the 9-1-1 calls being made.

I ran across the street, gun up, and looked for Marisol. No

sign of her. She must have either turned left at 9th or run further on down Meridian when she heard the loud gunshot. Either way, she was gone. She's likely safe. They were after me, not her.

I heard sirens coming from the west. I wasn't in any mood to deal with more police today, so I turned left at 9th, gun low and down. Once around the corner, I removed the head wrap and sunglasses, implementing a casual stride like a man out for a leisurely stroll. The sun vanished behind a wall of dark clouds and a hot breeze thick with the promise of rain caught the palm fronds and tossed them around.

At Washington Ave, I tucked my gun in its holster and crossed. I heard a cruiser with its sirens blaring and then saw it heading toward me from Collins Ave. I ducked into a clothing store on the corner and began to intensely browse. The cruiser flashed by in the window.

I grabbed a rainbow-colored shirt, a pink Panama hat with an enormous fluffy feather in the brim, and a pair of sunglasses with big square neon turquoise frames.

I paid the white-haired man behind the counter and stepped to the side of the cash register. Both he and a younger man stared at my muscles as I removed my black Henley t-shirt, plucked the garish shirt out of the bag, ripped the tags off, put it on with the Panama hat and the sunglasses, and walked out the door with a smile.

I felt like Elton John as I walked toward Collins, trying to gawk like a just-arrived tourist amazed to be in South Beach. Another cruiser blasted past. I turned right at Collins and south to 5th Street, where I turned right again. Light raindrops began to fall.

Shit, I forgot my grocery bag.

I left it there on the sidewalk at the foot of the big tree with the chunk blown out of it. They're going to find that and maybe question people at Art Deco Supermarket. Better not go back there for a while.

As I waited for a break in the traffic to cross 5th at

Meridian and down to my place, a car slowed to nearly pause in front of me.

It was a silver Audi A5.

My heart skipped a beat as my hand went to my gun. Cold gray eyes under a scraggly tousle of salt-and-pepper hair looked directly at me with a faint chiseled smile as the car slowly passed and then accelerated, heading east. It was the wrinkly man I had seen earlier at the Leucadendra Country Club.

The sinking feeling returned full force.

Gun out and close to my side, I continued on down Meridian to my building. Before going in, I circled the block to scan for anything out of place. The rain kicked in full.

Scraggly tousle of salt-and-pepper hair must be Z. Whoever tried offing me with a shotgun in that brown Buick was no pro. That was a local. A notch above Eddie Corrado maybe, but not on Z's level. I saw it behind the cold gray eyes as the silver Audi slowed—a cool calculated competence. The fact he even slowed and smiled at me was an irresistible taunt to display his high-level skills. His inflated ego wanted me to know he's top shelf—and that he's coming for me.

So who hired the locals in the brown Buick? Is it the same person who hired Z? Doubtful.

Great. Now I've got *two* enemies hiring thugs to kill me. One is Rexford J. Hayes, I'd bet the farm on it. But who's number two? Eddie Corrado? Maybe, but again doubtful. Eddie thinks he can do everything himself. Which makes me wonder: why hasn't Eddie returned for me? A guy like Eddie would take the beatdown I gave him as a personal insult to his identity as a lowlife thug and would need to finish the score.

What about Tommy Nero? Am I getting too close to something he doesn't want me to find?

Again, doubtful. Tommy's guys are on my level. They wouldn't use a shotgun. It would be quick and silent and nobody would find my body. Nope, not Tommy Nero.

Then who?

I had finished circling the block. Nothing. No silver Audi A5. No brown Buick.

At my building, I was about to step to my door when I noticed a light on inside my apartment through the open corner window built into the cracked green stucco. I stepped behind the sea grape tree in the courtyard, held my breath, and listened.

I heard something, a movement, from inside.

I crouched down and sneaked up to the door from the left. I put the key in one notch at a time, keeping my arm out of the doorframe. I took a deep breath, turned the knob, and kicked the door open, swinging my gun in front of me with both hands as I swiveled in.

I almost couldn't believe what I saw.

On her knees facing me from the other side of the room— pointing a small gun at me—was Allie Hayes.

25

"IS THAT YOU?" Allie said. "Titus?"

"Allie?" I said.

She giggled like a naughty schoolgirl, lowered the gun, and put it back in her purse. Then she giggled again.

"Nice outfit," she said. "I didn't know you were gay."

I holstered my gun, walked in, and closed the door behind me.

"What are you doing here, Allie?" I said.

She looked nothing like the girl in the space costume from last night, nor even the girl with the glowing eyes in the sprayed-on multicolored dresses from the pictures. She almost looked normal in a loose black dress made of light fabric, black-frame glasses, no makeup, blonde hair hanging down straight. A denim purse and an olive green duffle bag with red trim lay on the floor next to my airbed.

"I needed some help and I thought of you," she said.

"Last time I saw you," I said, "you didn't seem to want any

help, especially from me."

She looked down. "Yeah, I know. Sorry about that. I was high from the show last night—and some other stuff. I was really mean. You were just doing your job, and I'd like to make it up to you."

Alarm bells dinged in my head. "How did you even know where I live?"

"I asked your friend who was with you. He knows someone I know. I forget his name."

"Jason Stark."

"Yeah. God, he hates you."

"I'm good at making people hate me. It's a gift How'd you get in?"

She looked down and around. "I, uh, know how to get into places. Look, I know this is weird. I know I was really mean to you. And I know it's weird I'm in your place, but I really needed to see you because—this is going to sound strange—but you seem like a good guy and some of the stuff you said last night really made me think."

The lie detector in my ears rang off the scale. That's not the reason she was here. But whatever. She was here and I needed to deal with it. Better to use honey than vinegar. I locked the door and forced a smile on my face.

"Well," I said, "I'm not thrilled you pulled a B & E on me, but I am glad you're here, Allie. Time to get things finally straightened out."

"Yes," she said with an exaggerated smile.

"Where'd you get the gun?"

"Oh, that. A friend. I've had it for a while."

She bit her lower lip, chin down looking up at me with big eyes. She bent a knee and placed one bare foot on the wall. Christy Turlington.

"Can I see it?" I said.

"See what?" she said, the naughty schoolgirl voice back.

"Your gun."

"Oh. Why do you want to see that?"

"When people point guns at me in my own apartment, I get skittish."

"I only pointed it at the door because I didn't know who was coming through, silly."

She licked her lower lip and adjusted her pose, pushing her hips slightly off the wall. Cindy Crawford.

"Let me see the gun, Allie."

"Fine," she said with a sigh and rolled her eyes. She plucked the gun from her purse and handed it to me.

It was a Ruger .22 revolver, lighter than a grilled cheese sandwich, good for shooting butterflies. The serial number had been scrubbed. No visible residue, no brass filings. I sniffed. No gunpowder smell.

"This is a street gun," I said. "No serial number."

"Whatever," she said.

"I'm going to hold onto this for now, okay?"

Her foot went back up the wall, her knee protruding from under the dress again. She flicked her head to the side, causing a strand of blonde hair to fall across her face. She blew and it flipped up. Heidi Klum.

"You're lucky I don't call the police," I said.

"You don't really mean that," she said.

She shuffled around with a coy smile. Feet planted, hips out moving in small circles, hands behind back, head tilted. Gisele Bündchen.

I went over to the closet and opened it. I pressed on the spring hinge and the door to my stash spot fell open. I placed her gun on the shelf. She scooted up close to me on my left, peering over my shoulder.

"What's that?" she said.

Her hair flowed forward into my field of view, the scent of perfume invading my nostrils, her breath hot on my neck, her fingers grazing my back. A fire lit inside me, but quickly flamed out when I remembered the dominatrix with the Cage Girls and the slave boys.

"Nothing," I said.

"That's so neat," she said. "It looks like it isn't there but you've got a little shelf and everything. What's under the shelf?"

"Just space. I built the shelf so it'd be easier to reach things while standing up."

"What's in the envelope?"

I considered that for a moment and made a decision. I took out the manila envelope still full of Pam Hayes' money, removed five crisp one-hundred dollar bills, stuffed them in my front pocket, closed the envelope, and handed it to her.

"Yours," I said. "Minus five hundred for my recent expenses."

She opened it and looked.

"Oh my God," she said.

"It's what your mother paid me to find you. It's kind of a ridiculous amount. So there. I found you. My job is done. Your mother and father now want me to go away. They don't even want the money back. In fact, your father tried to pay me a whole lot more just to stop finding you but I wouldn't take it. So, this is yours."

"Thanks," she said. Her eyes went wide like she thought of something. She leaped forward and grabbed two fistfuls of my colorful shirt.

"Have you ever been to L.A.?" she said.

"No."

She pressed her body into me. "Oh, you should go. *We* should go. Right now. Let's just get on a plane."

"Allie—," I grabbed her wrists and pushed her away a foot. "Allie, what are you talking about?"

"Come on! It would be so much fun. You seem adventurous. Don't tell me you're one of those boring guys who stays home all the time. You would *love* L.A."

I gazed into her eyes, trying to figure out her game. Maybe I should just ask.

"What's your game, Allie?" I said.

She grunted. "God, I'm sick of Miami. I want to move to Hollywood."

"With a man you just met last night?"

She looked me up and down like she was considering buying me. "You seem like you'd come in handy."

"To protect you, right?"

She bit her lower lip and twirled on one foot with her hands twisted in front of her like a cheerleader flirting with the captain of the football team. "Sure, but not *just* to protect me."

I shook my head. "Subtle is not one of your skills, Allie. Why Hollywood?"

"A girl can make money out there."

"I heard that somewhere."

I closed up the stash space and grabbed a black Henley t-shirt from the small pile on the high shelf. I removed the rainbow shirt and tossed it in the trash with the Panama hat and garish sunglasses.

"Oh," she said, studying me shirtless, "you *definitely* need to come with me to L.A."

I put on the t-shirt and moved to the cabinet in the tiny kitchen where I took down the bottle of bourbon, which I hadn't touched since before Eddie Corrado's boot said hello to my nose. But there's nothing like the lip-loosening effects of alcohol to make words fall out of mouths—words that might help me. I poured some into two red plastic cups.

"Here's to me," I said, raising one. "I found you. Again."

She picked up the other one and sipped without a flinch.

"Uh-huh," she said, her voice sultry and low, and wriggled around the counter to me. "And it also looks like I—," her hand under the t-shirt drawing lines up my chest, "—found you."

Her eyes caught the flicker from the soft glow of the lone lamp on the table. The hard rain and silhouettes of palm fronds dancing in the windows only enhanced the effect. Lauren Bacall.

She was good, but her act was too calculated, too perfect. I was much too versed in the art of female hoodwinkery to fall for it.

"Sorry, Allie," I said, removing her hand from me. "Probably works on every guy who sees this show, but not me."

"So you *are* gay," she said.

"No. Allie, what's going on?"

She leaned in and hooked her right foot onto the back of my left calf. Same move that shoots fireworks in me when Jenny does it, but I got nothing.

"Allie," I said, "stop—just stop."

"I don't think you really want me to stop." Her voice was desperate now. She's not used to rejection.

I reached down and removed her leg while slightly backing away. "Yes, Allie. I want you to stop. You're going to stop right now."

We stared each other down. She glanced away, then tried the seductive look one more time, stupefied that it wasn't having its usual effect. I nodded no with a calmness that she recognized as genuine. She was good, this one. She sees shit others don't see and knows how to hit the hot spots that make men swoon and bow to her.

I'd bet tears next.

Sure enough, I watched the change as it happened. A faint tremble at first—not gushing, not overdone. Then, the crack grew wider and the first droplets scuttled down her cheeks right on cue. Claire Danes.

She spun away from me and sobbed uncontrollably, or so it would sound to most people. I let her run with it for a minute as I watched and listened. When she turned, her eyes were perfectly forlorn as they peeked at me for a reaction.

"Also not going to work," I said. "Not only can I tell the difference between real seduction and fake seduction, I can also tell the difference between real tears and fake tears."

The real Allie popped out with an angry blare.

"Asshole!" she shouted, her face red, her hands clenched

into fists.

"I'd bet threat of suicide next," I said. "Don't bother. I'll let you slash your wrists and watch, then call the ambulance. They'll call your mom and dad and then you're back at Gables Estates."

I wasn't serious about that, but I knew it would have the effect I wanted. She fumed, her big eyes nearly exploding out of her head with rage. Linda Blair.

"Okay, asshole," she said, "I need a place to stay for the night."

"Now that's the most truthful thing you've said to me yet," I said.

She made a sound like a cornered rat.

"I thought you were living with Jake Preston in a place paid for by your father," I said, not mentioning I've seen Jake in his current condition. "Why not go there?"

"Because Jake Fucking Preston is another fucking asshole. I fucking hate men."

Yep, the real Allie is in.

"Then why did you come here?" I said. "I'm a man."

She didn't answer, turned away from me, and bit her nail.

My phone vibrated with an incoming text. It was from JoJo Burley:

> I'm back in town. Call
> me. I have news.

I ignored it.

"Did Jake hurt you, Allie?" I said.

She shook her head.

"He bring in too many other girls for your taste?" I said.

"I could give a shit about that," she said, turning to face me. "I'm bi. I liked some of them, too. Jake is just like Rexford J. Fucking Hayes, and just like every other fucking man I've ever known. He wants me to fucking play along as he manipulates."

"Manipulates who?"

"Everyone. And the goddamned irony is that I fucking goddamned taught him how to do it. He was lame—useless without me. Before I came along, he was all cheesy pickup lines and hands in all the wrong places. I taught him how to go collect ten girls and bring them home to share."

"Nice to have a solid family life at home."

I sipped my bourbon. Ouch, it had been a while. What used to go down smooth nearly made me cough.

"Fuck you," she said. "You don't get it. You don't understand our lifestyle."

"You're right about that," I said, "nor do I want to. So if you haven't been with Jake, where have you been living lately?"

She stared at me and gritted her teeth. "I shouldn't have come here. You're all Mr. Questions. I'm leaving."

I had been trying to like her as she spoke—even just a little. It might be easier to like mosquitoes.

"Allie," I said, "it's okay. I'm on your side. I'm not going to call your parents, not that they would take my call anyway. Help me to figure some things out and I'll help you. How's that?"

She glared at me for another eternity, breaking the silence with:

"I want to hire you to protect me. I can pay you."

"With whose money?" I said.

She walked across the room and picked up the manila envelope.

"Let's start with this," she said and threw it at me. I leaned to my right and it crashed into the air conditioner behind me, landing on the linoleum. I just can't give this money away, can I?

"And besides that," she said, "I have my own money. More money than you know, asshole."

"Money from blackmailing your dad?"

Her eyes narrowed. She went to her purse and took out a pack of cigarettes. She lit one without asking if it bothered me.

"No," she said, "that was Jake. He was the one who got Big Daddy Rex to pay and he spent every last penny of it. It's all gone. Testarossa, my fucking ass."

"Oh," I said, "now I get it. Jake used you to blackmail your dad, spent all the money, and then tossed you aside."

She puffed out some smoke. It drifted toward me in long lovely wisps, triggering a craving I felt all the way down to my toenails. I gripped the countertop.

"But I did him one better," she said. "I figured out another way to get a ton of my own money. Fuck Jake Preston and his Testarossa. Thinks he's God."

"He does, doesn't he?" I said.

She laughed. "So you've met him, then?"

"Yeah, one night at Sinz."

"You—you were at Sinz?" She laughed hysterically.

"Yeah, I was looking for you. I met Jake and had a run-in with a guy named Eddie Corrado."

She froze, her face pale. She swallowed, stubbed out her cigarette, tossed it in the corner by the window, and resumed her previous pose.

"So you work for Pam Hayes," she said, "who's nuts, but you won't work for me?"

"Do you know Eddie Corrado?" I said.

She shrugged. "I think I've heard the name. Are you going to answer my question? Will you protect me if I hire you?"

"Protect you from who?"

"From Big Daddy Rex, from Pam Hayes, from the police."

"Why do you call your mother Pam Hayes?"

"Because—", she made a sound like a wounded wolf, "—Pam Hayes is a psychopath."

"Allie, I've met your mother. She doesn't strike me as the killer type."

"I told you. She tried to kill me. Her arms were around my throat. That's when I kicked her and got the fuck out of there."

"Why would your mother want to kill you?"

"Because I wouldn't marry this stupid rich kid she found for me. Joke's on her. He's really gay and just needs a 'beard' so his rich family doesn't find out. When her hands were around my throat, the gig was up."

"Gig?" I said. "What gig?"

"My gig as Allie Fucking Hayes," she said, "sweet blissful college girl who gets good grades and never does anything wrong so her daddy can be a big powerful pompous ass Senator."

"So after Pam Hayes tried to kill you, that's when you ran to Jake Preston, a guy you had dated before?"

She leaned on the counter and stared at the bourbon. She took a sip and looked down.

"Yes," she said. "I had nowhere else to go."

"And your father found you?" I said.

"Big Daddy Rex found me, begged me to come back, but no way. No fucking way. He insisted, but Jake came up with a plan—and surprise surprise—it was a good plan for once."

"The blackmail?"

"Yeah. He figured something out and used it against Big Daddy Rex, who paid. He paid big time."

She finished the bourbon and held it out to me like Zelda Fitzgerald to a busboy. I gritted my teeth, took it, poured another, and handed it back to her while trying my damndest to not throw it in her face.

"What did Jake have on your dad?" I said.

"None of your goddamned business," she said.

"Your father seems to like tossing money around. Why not just ask him for it instead of blackmailing him?"

"Because he wouldn't give it to me unless I moved back into that absurd mansion. I need to be fucking free. I need to be me, to do what I fucking want to do. To do my shows, to be with *my* people."

"So you go along with Jake in this blackmail scheme against your dad. Why?"

"Duh, asshole. For the money. Haven't you been fucking

listening?"

I felt the joy I would get from picking her up and throwing her into the street. I closed my eyes and took a deep breath.

"You know," I said, "calling me 'asshole' every two seconds and being condescending is not making me look forward to having you here all night."

She sipped and shrugged.

"Sorry," she said. "I've had a stressful day, okay?"

I sipped my bourbon and thought. "What I don't get, Allie, is why did your father keep your love nest with Jake Preston from your mother?"

"God, how dumb are you? Because she tried to kill me!"

"And Rex knows this?"

"You better believe he does. Look, can we get some food?"

"Sure." I thought about Z's chiseled smile out there somewhere in his silver Audi. "Do you mind delivery? It's a bad night out there with the rain."

"Don't you have anything here?"

"Stove and refrigerator don't work." I took out my phone and scanned for delivery.

"Why don't you get them fixed?"

"Because I'm not here long."

"You're weird."

I gripped the counter, squeezed hard, and forced a smile on my face.

"Pizza?" I said.

"Anything as long as we don't have to go out," she said.

"What do you want on yours?"

"Whatever, I don't care."

I dialed.

"Wait," she said. "No onions. No peppers. I hate peppers. No meat. Not too much sauce."

I called Primo Pizza and ordered a large cheese pizza for delivery.

Allie sat at the table and I joined her, bringing over the

bourbon. She still had some left in her glass. I finished mine and poured another, reminding myself to be careful.

"So you don't mind if I spend the night here?" she said.

"No," I lied. "As long as it's just tonight."

She looked directly at me and finished her drink. I refilled it. She kept on looking at me. I began to feel violated.

"You are different," she said. "I've never met a man like you."

"Different?" I said.

"Yeah, you're so—quiet. You don't talk much. Most guys babble on forever at me. You listen. Nobody ever listens to me."

I nodded.

"See?" she said. "You just nodded. Most guys would take that as a challenge and start trying to prove to me they're not quiet. You just nod."

I nodded. She laughed.

"You're funny," she said. "I think I might actually like you."

Time for a subject change.

"So you really hate Jake, huh?" I said.

"Oh God, more questions." She sipped. "Yes, he's a prick."

"How would you feel if he were, uh, no longer with us?"

Her eyes popped. She sat back in the chair. "You know, don't you? I didn't do it. I swear I didn't do it."

"Allie," I said, "I believe you. How did you know?"

"After Hinraker's last night, I went there—to his house—our house, what a joke—to get something. And somebody had shot him."

"You saw him dead?"

"Yes." She didn't seem bothered at all.

"What did you do?"

"What the fuck do you think I did? I got the fuck out of there, that's what I did. What would you do? They're going to try to pin it on me. They've been looking for me to ask me questions. I cancelled my shows and decided to go to L.A."

"You didn't dump the body in the canal?"

"Look at me. Do I look like I could dump a body in a canal?"

"Okay," I said, "you got me there. Have you been staying at Hinraker's?"

"No," she said. "I could anytime, but I've been staying with—"

"With who?"

"A friend." Her eyes narrowed and she lit another cigarette. "You wouldn't turn me in, would you?"

"Turn you in for what?" I said. "You say you didn't do anything. What would be the harm in talking to the police and telling them everything?"

"Oh, you're so goddamned naïve. None of that shit matters. The police work for Big Daddy Rex and every other goddamned rich asshole in Miami. They'll pin it on me and force me back there. Then, Pam Hayes *will* kill me."

"Allie, that's not true."

"Yes, it goddamned is."

There was a knock on the door. Gun out, I went to the window and peered out. It was a kid in a red polo shirt and delivery cap holding a pizza box.

I moved to the door, opened it, paid him, and took the pizza over to the table.

"I don't have any plates," I said.

"Of course not," she said. "That would be normal."

She grabbed a slice and chomped into it like a bear on a trash can. I inhaled, held it for a count of ten, and let it out. I sat down across from her, took a slice of pizza, and ate.

"What makes you think the police will do the bidding of your father?" I said.

"Because he owns them. They're in deep with him, all the local politicians—oh, and that fucking bitch in Washington D.C. who is the devil herself."

"Who?"

"Kelly Alves. She's a rich bitch who gets my dad out of

trouble. Looks like an icicle with a face. If she gets anywhere near me, I'll be sent to an asylum and they'll give me a lobotomy."

"Kelly Alves?" I said. "Never heard of her."

"She's a 'fixer.' An attorney in the pocket of everybody in Washington. Like Olivia Pope on that TV show *Scandal*. You know *Scandal*, right?"

"I don't watch TV." I took another bite.

"God, you're weirder than I thought."

We ate some pizza.

"So where are you from?" she said.

I froze, the question so oddly out of place.

"Did you just ask a question about me?" I said. "I'm shocked."

"Fuck you," she said. "But seriously, you're not from here, are you?"

"I was born in Georgia but I went to Boston when I was twelve, right after my mother died."

"Why did you go there?"

"To find my father."

I ate some pizza. She stopped mid-chew.

"Well—?" she said.

"Well what?" I said.

"Did you find him?"

"Yeah. He didn't want to have anything to do with me."

"What then?"

"Then, I was passed from foster home to foster home until finally my older brother took me in. He was at Harvard."

"What's his name?"

I took a deep breath, shocked that I'm actually talking about him without exploding into anger.

"Cassius," I said.

She laughed and almost choked on her slice of pizza.

"Cassius?" she said. "Seriously? Titus and Cassius?"

"Yeah," I said. "My dad had a—uh—weird sense of

humor."

"So did Cassius help you?"

"Yeah. He was like my mentor. Helped me to clean up my act."

"I had somebody like that."

"Who?"

Her face drifted away. I could tell she was visiting a memory, lost in time.

"Bumble," she said. "She was this—person—I knew—"

"Bumble? That's an odd name."

"That was my nickname for her. She called me her little Bug-boo. Her real name is Hayley. She's my big—uh—friend."

She smiled and looked at me. I started to almost like her. Didn't think it was possible, but I had managed to dig up a tiny fragment of human buried deep in there.

The pizza box was empty. I took it, got up, threw it in the trash, and sat back down. Allie was still a million miles away.

"So who was this Hayley?" I said.

I watched as the door slammed shut. She had begun to relax and open up, but I struck something that hit a nerve. She downed the rest of her drink.

"Fuck you," she said. Real tears began for a brief moment, but she squashed them and shut everything down.

She stood up, removed her dress like I wasn't even there, threw it over the back of the chair, and plopped onto my airbed in her bra and panties, curled up in a ball facing away from me.

Sweet dreams to you too, sweetheart.

I sipped my drink. I needed to learn to be more subtle. Although, I thought I was being subtle. Wasn't I subtle?

I flipped open my Chromebook and ran an online search for 'Kelly Alves.' High-profile Washington, D.C. attorney. Office on K Street. Kelly Alves & Associates. Advisor to three Presidents and a swamp of Senators and congressmen. Official title: crisis mitigation consultant.

Kelly Alves' face at her website looked like it was carved

from ice a thousand years ago. Cold eyes framed by rimless glasses, empty smile.

Does she fit in all this? Where? How?

I finished my drink, took off my jeans, turned out the light, and dropped to the right side of the airbed facing away from Allie.

I tried to make sense of all this for about an hour, and then drifted off to sleep.

Some time later—not sure when—I was awoken by a warm presence with its arms around me from behind.

Shit.

I was about to get up when I realized that the warm presence was crying. I flipped around.

"Allie," I said, "what's wrong?"

"I want to die," she said between sobs, real ones this time. "I just want to die."

I wiped a tear from her cheek. "Why, Allie?"

"I'm so tired. So so tired."

"Tired of what, Allie?"

"I'm tired of lying. I don't want to lie anymore."

"You don't need to lie anymore, Allie."

She pounded my shoulder with a fist.

"You don't understand," she said. "I do. I need to keep on lying. Lying forever."

She sobbed some more. I pulled her into me and held her tight. She squeezed me like a little kid hugging a parent.

We stayed like that for a long time. Eventually, she cried herself to sleep.

26

IN THE MORNING, I slunk out of bed and into the shower, making sure I took my Sig with me in case Z attacks—although I didn't think he would. He needed something first, but what?

I'm betting Allie. What else could it be? He's been tasked by somebody to bring her back and kill me in the process. Probably just like Tom Langston.

As I showered, I heard a thump against the wall. I shut the water and grabbed my gun from the toilet. I waited, but heard nothing more. Must be the wild boars upstairs.

I finished showering, threw on a pair of boxers, and walked out. Allie sat at the table, texting on her phone.

"Good morning," I said.

"Morning," she said in a monotone without looking up.

I threw on a pair of jeans and a black Henley T-shirt, then started the coffeemaker.

"You want to shower?" I said.

"Huh?" she said, texting furiously.

"Do you want to shower?"

"Oh. Yeah, sure. Just a sec." More monotone.

After a flurry of texting, she grabbed a pair of white shorts, a blue tank top, and pink panties that she must have laid out on the airbed while I was in the shower. Without a word, she went in the bathroom and closed the door.

Something was off. This was not the Allie who was here last night.

Once the water was running in the shower, I checked the stash spot. My Smith & Wesson and her Ruger were both still there, both loaded. I walked over to the corner of the kitchen, picked up the manila envelope, and opened it. Money still there too. Looked like all of it. Why was Allie so uninterested in this money?

I put the manila envelope back in the stash spot, closed it, and poured a coffee.

Allie came out, her blonde hair in wet tangles. She reached into her purse, took out a brush, and went back into the bathroom. Again without looking at me, like I'm furniture.

Once done brushing, she resumed her spot on the chair at the table and began a flurry of texting again.

"Coffee?" I said.

"Huh?" she said.

"Coffee?"

"Oh, yeah. Sure." More texting.

I poured a cup of coffee and placed it near her.

"I don't have any milk," I said. "Do you want sugar?"

"Huh?" she said.

"Allie! Look at me."

She looked up like she was seeing me for the first time.

"Just one sec," she said.

I again felt the urge to throw her in the street. For a brief moment last night, I actually liked her. Even started to care. Now, I had to force myself to push the idea of pouring hot coffee on her out of my head.

"Okay," she said and put her phone down. "What's up?"

"So," I said, "I have a friend on the Miami-Dade police force. She's a detective. She's not your typical cop. She's very nice. Let's go out, get some breakfast, and then I'll call her to meet with us."

"Okay."

Alarm bells again. Too easy.

"Okay?" I said.

"Sure," she said. "Where?"

"Ever been to Las Olas Café?"

"No."

"Everyone's been telling me to try their sweetbread, so let's go there."

"Okay. You want to go now or finish your coffee?"

Yep, something way off. Polite and agreeable are not Allie's trademarks.

"I'm going to finish my coffee," I said.

"Okay."

I sipped my coffee. She texted some more.

"How do you spell Las Olas?" she said.

"L-a-s-capital O-l-a-s," I said.

"What's that mean in Spanish?"

"Good question. My Spanish is terrible. Let's ask when we get there."

"Okay."

She twirled a stringy piece of hair and pondered that like it was one of the most interesting things she ever heard. Then, she resumed texting.

I got the feeling this was going to be another very long day.

I finished my coffee.

"Let's go," I said.

"Okay," she said and grabbed her purse, jumping out the door ahead of me while texting.

We walked in silence as I looked around for silver Audis, wrinkly clothes, and salt-and-pepper hair. Allie texted while we walked.

When we got to Las Olas Café, a couple was just finishing their breakfast at one of the outdoor tables facing Euclid Ave. They stood up to go.

"Let's sit outside," Allie said, plopping herself down at the table while texting.

"Okay," I said, looking over at the outdoor window and menu. "What do you want?"

"Huh? Oh, I don't care. Just coffee," she said.

I went over to the window and waited in line behind a young couple and a big man who looked like he could consume the entire establishment. I glanced over at Allie, who was still texting. I wondered if I should call Sofia now and have her show up here.

Yes, I decided—that's what I was going to do. I took out my phone.

Just as I was about to hit Send on Sofia's icon, a dark gray McLaren sports car screeched to a halt directly in front of the café. Its passenger side gull-wing door shot up.

Without a pause, Allie rose and dove into the car. The gull-wing door slammed down.

"Hey!" I shouted as I ran over, but too late.

"Bye, asshole." said Allie as both she and some kid I had never seen before shot me the finger. He revved the obscenely loud engine and hit the gas hard. The tires left streaks of hot rubber all the way around the corner onto 6th Street.

"Fuck!" I shouted loud enough for everyone in sight to turn and look at me.

27

TO CALM MYSELF down, I walked all the way to Dunkin' Donuts on Alton Road. Halfway there, I regained enough self-control to stop picturing my hands around Allie's neck. By the time I got there, I had a plan. I was also starved so I sat down and ate two butternut donuts. Then, I bought two iced coffees and a strawberry-banana smoothie and walked to the Apostolic Rescue Mission Church.

Luther and DaShawn had made progress on the right side wall. I noticed a new red-and-blue bike leaning up against the fence.

"Not bad," I said. "Not bad at all."

"And I tell you," Luther said, "you are Peter, and on this rock I will build my church, and the gates of hell shall not prevail against it. Matthew, chapter sixteen, verse eighteen."

"Actually, I'm Titus, not Peter. Different book. And you missed a spot. Up there, on the left."

DaShawn laughed. Luther shot me a dirty look.

"Speak with you a minute?" I said.

Luther made a show of putting down his can of paint and shaking off his brush with exaggerated annoyance.

"Hi, DaShawn," I said and handed him an iced coffee.

DaShawn said nothing and took the coffee without looking at me.

"Say thank you to brother Titus," said Luther.

"Thank you, brother Titus," said DaShawn.

"Nice bike," I said. "Is that new?"

I thought DaShawn might melt. He nodded, eyes down.

I shook my head and followed Luther inside to his office. I put the strawberry-banana smoothie on his desk.

"You bringing me a coffee?" Luther said. "You know how I feel about coffee."

"Does that look like coffee?" I said. "It's all pink and fruity with a little lowfat yogurt. It's kosher, or blessed, or whatever. You'll be fine."

"Sugar?"

"No—well, maybe—okay, yes—just drink it. Live a little."

He studied the drink carefully, reached into a drawer, removed two coasters, and placed one underneath each drink.

"Coasters?" I said. "Fancy."

"You know," said Luther as he sat behind his desk, "I do not wake up in the morning and say to myself, 'What can I do for Brother Titus today?'"

"You don't?" I said. "That's odd. Most people do."

"Are you here to discuss your decision to let go of your resentment and seek absolution from God?"

I sipped my iced coffee. "No. DaShawn steals bikes, you know."

His right eye glared at me harshly, and then wandered off.

"I know," he said. "Not all he steals. Boy is a mess. Wait. How do *you* know?"

"I, uh, liberated, a bike from him one night a while back," I said. "I wasn't going to say anything but I saw that new one out there. I promised him I'd smash his face in if he ever did it again but I don't want to do that on the Lord's property here. Just wanted you to know."

"Thank you, Brother Titus. It shall be resolved." Luther peeled the wrapping off his straw, stuck it in the top of the plastic cup, and sipped. "Not bad. Thank you for the refreshment. And you have my full blessing to smash DaShawn in the face if you ever catch him stealing again."

"I thought the Bible was against that sort of thing."

He sipped his smoothie. "Sometimes people who deserve to be smashed in the face need to be smashed in the face, only way they learn. Book of Luther, chapter one, verse one."

I laughed. "You kill me. Speaking of which, there's a pro cleaner following me around, name of Z. Ever heard of him?"

"No," he said. "You sure he's pro?"

"Definitely," I said. "Not like the two locals who fired a shotgun at me yesterday."

His eyebrows went up. "That was you?"

"Yeah."

"My my my, is there anyone who does not want you dead?"

"No. How'd you know about that?"

"It was on the Channel 7 news. Right after the body found in the waterway behind the bank parking lot. Which I believe be your boy Jake Preston."

"Uh-huh."

"So you were involved in the top two lead news stories yesterday. You going to be on the news today?"

"It's my daily goal," I said. "I've seen this Z. He's not itchy to off me, otherwise I wouldn't be sitting here. I'm not sure who he's working for. Whoever they are, I suspect, want to find Allie Hayes or determine what I know about Allie Hayes. Who, by the way, spent the night at my place last night."

Luther's bad eye turned in his head to look directly at me. I swear it has a will of its own.

"Tell me you did not commit a sin of the flesh again,

212

brother Titus," he said.

"Not if my life depended on it," I said. "Allie Hayes is my least favorite person on earth right now."

I told him about my afternoon after I borrowed his truck yesterday: Pam Hayes and Z at the Leucadendra Country Club, the mysterious black SUV I see everywhere, seeing Jake Preston's body, the text with the warning, getting shot at, seeing Z again, Allie showing up at my place, our conversation, and her running off this morning with some kid.

"Who this new kid?" Luther said.

"No clue," I said. "Probably another poor sucker she had her hooks into. She's good. She could get her hooks into most guys in Miami. I think she had her hooks into Eddie Corrado. Something in the way she reacted to his name tells me she knows him. Meantime, I want to talk to Tommy Nero. Ask him if he knows who might have hired the locals in the brown Buick. Know how to set up a meet with him, Mr. I-Know-Everybody-in-Miami?"

My phone vibrated. I looked. Call from JoJo Burley. I let it go to voicemail.

"You don't just call up Tommy Nero's secretary and make an appointment," Luther said.

"That's why I came to you, Brother."

"That's Reverend to you."

"Whatever."

"Let me make a call."

Luther took out a cell phone and called someone. I listened to JoJo Burley's voicemail while I waited. JoJo said he had something important to tell me so I walked out into the empty nave and called him back.

"Speak... speak!" said JoJo.

"That's how you answer your phone?" I said.

"Dude! I'm back in Miami."

"And awake. You do know it's morning, right?"

"I can't sleep, dude. Been awake for three days straight. I'm on a high of some kind."

"You? On a high? I don't believe it."

He giggled. "I know, huh?"

"By the way, I left your Sapphire Key with the concierge at your building."

"Got it, thanks. Dude, I got bad news."

"Yeah?"

"Vin Diesel is doing the *Miami Vice* reboot. And get this. It sounds just like ours."

"Dang," I said.

"Yeah," JoJo said, "it would have been sick. I still think my idea for *Miami Hotties* is going to fly. I talked to a couple of producers about it and they love it."

"Great. Listen, JoJo, I'd love to chat all day, but I've got to—"

"Dude!" JoJo said. "One more thing. I don't know if I should tell you, 'cause it's kind of freaky. It weirded me out, totally. You know that girl you were looking for?"

I inhaled sharply. "Yeah."

"Allie something, right?"

"Allie Hayes."

"I know where she is."

"You do?"

"Yeah, I couldn't believe it. Before I left for L.A., Eddie Corrado stopped by and she was with him."

"Are you sure?" I said.

"So sure, dude," he said. "And get this. She's the same girl in Hinraker's show. Mistress Tiffany."

"I know."

"You saw the show?"

"I saw it."

"Fucking amazing, huh?" he said with another giggle.

"Not the word I'd use," I said. "So you're sure she was with Eddie?"

"Positive, dude. My eyes like totally bugged out of my

freakin' head. Definitely her. The picture you showed me."

"So where is she?" I said.

"She lives with him. She's been living with him for a while."

"You got an address?"

"Yeah." He told me.

"Thanks, JoJo."

"Hey," he said, "I'm going to be at Sinz tonight. You should come by. I'll patch things up for you with Tony V."

"Thanks, JoJo," I said. "We'll see."

"Cool. It's the least I can do 'cause of the Vin Diesel thing."

"We'll survive. JoJo, get some sleep."

"Yeah, I probably should. Okay, later, dude."

I shook my head, hung up, and walked back to Luther's office.

"Tommy going to be at his restaurant at noon," Luther said. "He expecting us."

"Us?" I said.

Luther finished his smoothie and smiled. "Thought I might tag along."

"Thought you had painting to do and all."

"Haven't seen Tommy in a spell. Might be time to say hi-de-ho."

I glanced at my phone. 9:30 a.m.

"Want to visit Eddie Corrado first?" I said.

"Thought nobody could find Eddie Corrado," Luther said.

"A plump oval-shaped birdie with frizzy hair just told me where he lives."

Luther stretched his neck to either side, massaging it with his hands.

"You may need backup," he said. "Eddie Corrado nearly killed you once."

"Nearly killed me is a stretch," I said. "That was just a flesh wound."

"Your nose may disagree."

He sighed, folded his hands, looked at me squarely, and then got up. He motioned me down the short hall as he walked out.

I followed him to a door. He opened it with a key and we walked into a small room. There was a generator, a hedge trimmer, a large toolbox, an ancient rotary lawn mower, a table saw, and a smattering of supplies.

"Close the door behind you," Luther said. "Make sure it's locked."

I did.

He walked over to the wall on which a pegboard held various tools on hooks. He reached to the side of the pegboard and I heard a latch click. The entire pegboard swiveled outward on a hinge and there, behind thick wire-frame was a collection of guns hanging on hooks.

"You are so breaking the law," I said. "Not to mention a couple of commandments, Father."

"Reverend," he said. He grinned and unlocked the cage that held the guns. There were big guns, little guns, rifles, an AR-15, and an AK-47.

"Expecting an invasion from the Catholic Church?" I said.

"Be you prepared," he said, "and prepare for yourself, you, and all your company that are assembled to you, and be you a guard to them. Ezekiel, chapter thirty-eight, verse seven."

"You are the coolest preacher I've ever met."

"Truth."

He took down a pump-action Mossberg 500 and handed it to me. I opened the action lock and studied the craftsmanship.

"My all-time favorite," he said.

"Nice," I said and handed it back to him, "but I'm more partial to that Remington 870 there. Had one when I was a kid. Gift from my uncle."

"870 be classic," he said and handed me the shotgun. "But I like the tang safety on the Mossberg and the fact you don't have to wrap your hand up here to chamber that first shell."

"Yeah," I said, sighting a spot on the wall, "but this feels like home."

I handed it back to him. He took down a Springfield Armory M1911 EMP 4 and handed it to me along with a 9mm cartridge.

"Nice," I said, "but that's a Luger cartridge."

He grinned. "Would I steer you wrong, Brother?"

I put the Luger cartridge in the 1911 and it snapped right in with a solid click.

"Holy shit," I said.

"Uh-huh." He handed me a holster. "Hold onto it for backup."

"I won't argue with you," I said, tucked the gun into the holster, and clipped it to the other side of my gun belt opposite the Sig. I felt like Wyatt Earp.

He removed the Colt Python .357 Magnum with a 6-inch barrel from its perch, performed a press check, holstered it, and locked up the cage.

"Let's go see what Eddie Corrado be up to this fine morning," he said with a big smile.

28

THE ADDRESS JOJO Burley had given me was on SW 4th Street in Little Havana, an old four-story cement block building with a garish wraparound railing hugging the top three floors. The whole thing was painted yellow-brown, although something told me yellow-brown was not its original color.

Luther and I sat in his pickup truck across the street. We had been watching the building for fifteen minutes. Nobody had come in or gone out.

"Can't picture your little rich girl living here," said Luther.

"Allie is full of surprises," I said. "Ready? And don't give me a Bible quote about being ready."

He grinned and opened his door. I opened mine and we got out.

We walked across the street and onto a path lined with cracked yellow-brown pavers. We passed through a yellow-brown door into a tiny lobby with yellow-brown floor tiles that smelled like moldy excrement wrapped in seaweed and dropped into a steamer. The air conditioning was on life-support. A row of grimy mailboxes lined the left-hand wall ahead of an elevator and a stairwell. A hallway led straight through to a rear glass door with an outdoor pool area beyond it. A yellow-brown desk sat waiting for a front desk attendant. There may have been a front desk attendant the day Jimmy Carter was inaugurated. The most vibrant item in the lobby was a vending machine to the left of the desk, its hum loud in the small space. The cheerfully lit Cokes and Sprites seemed to beg to be rescued.

"I have a new appreciation for my place," I said.

"What number we looking for?" said Luther.

"Nine."

The entrances to the first floor apartments were dark brown doors stretched over a long yellow-brown corridor that cut across the hallway leading out back. One, two, and four were on the left. Three, five, and seven were on the right.

"No six," I said. "Strange."

"Nine must be on the second floor," said Luther. "If the numbering follows the same pattern, it's on the left in back. Only way up is in the center. Elevator or stairs?"

"Stairs. Elevator may not make it."

"Amen to that."

Halfway up the yellow-brown carpeted stairs my Sig was in my hand. I held it low to my side in case anyone was watching through peepholes, although it felt like we were the only people left after a nuclear reactor meltdown.

I turned left on the second floor, which had twice the yellow-brown charm of the first floor. The heat was thick and up here the steaming excrement odor was joined by a tinge of cooking spices.

Number nine was at the end. Luther and I moved down the hallway, the door on our right. It was perpendicular to a window with an iron grate over it. I crouched under the door's peephole and over to the other side by the window. I glanced outside, nothing visible but the balcony of the building next door.

Between the grate and the windowpane, a graveyard of dead insects floated like flak on puffy clouds of cobwebs over a sea of empty candy wrappers.

I nodded at Luther. His gun at his side, he placed his back against the far side of the hallway about six feet back.

I reached around, knocked on the door, and withdrew my hand fast.

Silence.

I knocked again, harder this time.

Again, nothing.

Luther glided with noiseless grace across the hallway to the other side of the door. He took a small case from his pocket and removed a bump key. He put it in the lock with the patience and skill of having done so many times before and the tumblers fell into place. Ten seconds, tops. Proficient. He turned the knob and the door opened. No chain.

Luther went prone against the wall again with his gun up. I tapped the door with the tip of my right foot and pointed my gun into the apartment with both hands as it swung open.

The smell that hit me in the face and churned my stomach told me what we would find. Still good to be cautious, though.

The air conditioning had been left on high by whoever was here last. The place was as cool as any room could probably be in Florida, but that didn't kill the stench of rotting flesh. A handful of big noisy flies swirled around us.

The living room directly ahead was clean and sparse—ancient couch, widescreen TV, round white coffee table, two lamps with square shades.

I moved forward and spun to my right toward a short hallway that led to what looked like a bedroom on the left and bathroom on the right. Luther came in behind me and turned immediately to his left, gun pointed toward the small empty kitchen.

We both froze, listening for any sound. Still nothing.

One forlorn orange tea kettle rested on the stove, but there was little else. Two large black trash bags leaned against the far wall. They were full of pizza boxes, Chinese take-out boxes, and assorted cans and bags. Whoever lived here had moved in recently and brought only the bare minimum. I got the sense they hadn't planned to stay long.

I moved down the hallway, glancing quickly into the bathroom. Empty.

I held my breath, the putrid odor permeating my sinuses as I neared the bedroom door. I gritted my teeth, preparing myself for the sight, and rounded the corner.

Eddie Corrado's lifeless right eye looked at me from where he sat on the double bed. His left eye was long gone, in its place a gaping hole that oozed something like petrified pink and gray bubbles. A gaggle of flies buzzed all over it, having a party.

Eddie sat up at an odd angle, like he had fallen to his side after being shot but his muscles locked up and stiffened him in place. Blood had trickled down to saturate his naked chest and blue plaid boxers. He wore no socks or shoes. His skin was blue-green.

There was some blood splatter on the bed, but not much. The small bullet from the small gun had gone right into his mushy brain and kicked around, probably still in there somewhere. There was a suitcase on the floor, half-packed. Several items of men's and women's clothing were strewn about. The closet was full of mostly women's clothes. I recognized a purple wig and a silver space costume.

"Allie was here," I said, pulling up my shirt to cover my nose and mouth from the stench.

"You think she did this?" Luther said, doing the same.

"Don't know. I'd guess small-caliber gun, fired at close range from someone Eddie knows. Allie had one, but it didn't appear to have been used lately—although she could have cleaned and re-loaded it."

"Or used another gun."

"Or that."

"Look like someone planning on going somewhere, but didn't finish packing."

"Yeah. Allie was fixated on escaping to L.A."

"So why didn't she just go?" Luther said. "Get on a bus or a plane? Why go to your place after shooting Eddie?"

"Maybe she was scared," I said. "Confused. Maybe she figured someone would call the cops after hearing the gunshot and be looking for her."

"People in this neighborhood don't call the cops."

"Fair point."

I walked to the back of the room. A large window looked out onto the wraparound balcony that stretched all the way around, the pool area below. It would be an easy drop for a lithe nineteen-year old girl with only a purse and a duffel bag.

Whoa, wait. What happened to the green duffel bag with red trim? Allie didn't have it with her this morning when she ran off with the kid in the McLaren. She must have left it at my place. I made a mental note to check that when I get back.

"Not much blood splatter," said Luther, "but she bound to have some on her if she shot him. Maybe that why she ran to your place—to shower."

"She could have showered here," I said. "No, I'm thinking she leaped out the window onto the wraparound balcony, jumped down, and ran across the back. She had to get out quick. The screen is torn. That's how the flies got in."

"That mean someone else was here doing the shooting."

"Exactly."

"So she ran out. How she get to your place?"

"Public transportation? No, too risky. She could have called an Uber or a taxi, also risky. Maybe Eddie had a car and she took it."

"And why run to your place? Still don't make no sense to run to your place."

I thought for a moment about that.

"Unless she wasn't lying to me," I said, "and my words

actually did have an impact on her the other night at Hinraker's. Maybe she did see me as a source of protection, seeing as this source was now defunct."

"My my my," Luther said, "somebody in this room think he 'The Girl Whisperer.'"

I walked around the room like I was on eggshells, careful not to touch nor disturb anything. I looked under the bed and found only dirt. I pulled out the drawers of a low chest to find nothing but a sparse collection of men's clothes. I recognized the shiny red shirt Eddie wore the night I met him at Sinz.

"Okay," I said, "I've seen enough."

"Good," said Luther. "Let's get out of here before we need to burn the clothes we wearing. You going to call five-oh? 'Cause if you do, I need to exit stage left."

"Yeah, but I'll do it anonymously. I'm not in the mood for an anal probe today, either."

Once back in the truck and on the road, I anonymously texted to Miami-Dade Crime Stoppers the location of a dead body.

"Think Tommy Nero know his boy be dead?" said Luther.

"Let's find out," I said.

29

IN TERMS OF atmosphere compared to where we had just been, The Saltwater Bay Crab Company may as well have been on Mars. Waiters in white shirts and bow ties whirled trays of seafood around white tablecloths, mahogany furniture, and glistening hardwood floors. Along the far wall was a spectacular view of the beach through a row of windows overlooking the boardwalk from three floors up inside the Jade Atlantic Hotel.

"Tommy Nero owns this restaurant?" I said.

"Uh-huh," said Luther, "but you won't find his name on no L-L-C papers."

"I'm sorry, sirs," said the young maître d' with acne in a tuxedo as he looked us up and down with a sad smirk. "Our lunch reservations are full."

"We have an appointment to see Tommy," said Luther.

"I'm sorry, sir. I don't know any—"

Phil, who will always be Thinning-Red-Hair to me, appeared behind the boy and placed his hand on his back.

"S'alrigh-," said Phil with some reluctance. The boy seemed to retreat inside a coccon of himself to the right of the podium.

Phil motoned us in. We followed. Today he was in a straw hat, dark red sunglasses with gold wire frames, a light green plaic sport coat over a brown shirt, tan pants, and brown shoes.

"Nice to see you, Phil," I said.

"Fuck you," he said.

"Such obscene language for such a fine establishment," said Luther.

"I know, huh?" I said. "You'd think two charming well-dressed gentlemen like us would be treated with at least a modicum of respect."

Armaud leaned against a wall. I smiled at him. He stared at me with no expression.

The crater-on-beach-ball silhouette at a window table was unmistakable against the brightness of the beach. Tommy Nero was cracking open the biggest pile of crabs I had ever seen, tossing the shells into a big glass bowl.

He looked up as we approached his table. A viscous white gob of crab had attached itself to a ridge on his puffy cheek.

"Luther," he said with a full mouth, "I'm surprised at you, hanging around with this lowlife. Thought you were a man of God."

"Tommy," said Luther, "man got something to say. Might do you good to listen."

Tommy chomped some more, wiped his face with a white linen napkin, and motioned us to sit in the two chairs opposite him. We did.

"You like my restaurant, Titus?" said Tommy.

"Figures you would own a place where lots of bones get cracked," I said.

"Funny. Joe's Stone Crab is closed in the summer, but *my* place is always open. I have Maryland blue crabs flown in. I like them better anyway."

"Eddie Corrado is dead," I said, trying not to stare at the

glob of crab still on Tommy's cheek.

"So?" said Tommy. "What's that to me?"

"Tommy," said Luther. "No need to play it hard. Titus be cool."

Tommy stared at both of us for a good long beat. We stared back. He picked up a crab leg and cracked it, slurped out some meat, and resumed chewing.

"Fine," Tommy said. "Eddie is dead. So what? I didn't do it."

"We know," I said. "It was an amateur."

"Who?"

"We don't know."

"So what does any of this have to do with me?"

"Last time we spoke," I said, "there was a hint that Eddie Corrado was skimming money off of you. You found out, but you let him continue. There are only two reasons you would do so, either A or B. A would be to find out if he was skimming for someone else. B would be to figure out where he hid the money so you could get it back. Which one was it?"

Tommy laughed.

"Let's just say," he said, "just for shits and giggles, that one of those is true. Why would I tell you?"

"Because maybe I can help you get your money back," I said.

He stopped chewing. His colorless eyes jiggled in his big head.

"I thought you found the idea of working for me distasteful," he said.

"It's B, isn't it?" I said with a smile. "Eddie Corrado stole a lot of money from you, beyond the basic skimming. That's the real reason you let him live. You needed to figure out where he hid it. If Eddie is dead, he can't tell you where it is, can he?"

Tommy wiped his face again and missed the glob of crab again. He leaned back in his chair with folded arms.

"You think you're so goddamned smart, don't you?" he

said.

"You said it yourself, Tommy," I said. "You love money. Everything you do is for money. The only reason you would let Eddie Corrado live one second longer than necessary would be for money."

Tommy leaned forward, glanced out at the ocean, and folded his hands.

"Okay," he said, "Eddie's been skimming off me for a while. I found out about two weeks ago and wanted to know if he was working for one of my, ah, competitors—so I let it slide for a few days. Big mistake. Eddie got his hands on a large amount and vanished."

"How much?" I said.

"Too much."

"If you tell me the amount, Tommy, I'll know what to look for. If I find it, I'll return it to you."

Tommy laughed. "You'll return it to me. Right. Mr. Bleeding-Heart who saves innocent girls is going to bring my money back. I'll believe that when I see it."

I leaned forward and rested my elbows on the table.

"If I find your money, Tommy," I said, "I'll bring it back to you. I don't respect you. I don't respect what you do. Phil is annoying, too. And you've got a glob of crab stuck on your cheek that's driving me insane. But I do respect my own word. If I say I'll bring your money back—if and only if I find it, that is—then you can bet you're going to get your money back."

Tommy wiped his cheek. The glob was finally gone.

"Fine," he said. "Two million. Now, what do you want from me?"

"I was ambushed the other day," I said. "Two guys in a brown Buick with a shotgun over on Meridian. Had to be local. They weren't very good."

"I saw that on the Channel 7 news. Looks like they missed. Shame."

"I'd love to know who hired them. Maybe you could ask

around, maybe find out."

"In exchange for my money returned?"

"I can't guarantee that, Tommy. Your money might already be in Belize for all I know. But whoever hired two guys in a brown Buick with a shotgun to ventilate me is somehow involved. Maybe that person has your money."

There was a long silence as we all stared at each other.

"I don't know," Tommy said, "'cause after that incident at my office last time, I was ready to ventilate you myself."

"Bad business decision," I said. "No money in it. There's money in this. Two million."

Tommy stared off at the ocean again and back.

"Fine," he said. "I'll ask around. But I need something from you. Call it a bonus."

"What's that?" I said.

"The name of the person who put Eddie Corrado up to it. 'Cause Eddie ain't smart enough to do it on his own."

I shook my head. "You'll settle for your money. Whoever got Eddie to do anything is irrelevant. Eddie's the one who did it. Maybe he was upset because the Fed raised interest rates."

Tommy smiled. "You just gave yourself away, Titus. You know who it is. It's the girl, isn't it? The one you've been looking for. Allie Hayes."

"Tommy," I said, "if anything happens to Allie Hayes, I will kill you. If it's the last thing I do."

"He's serious, Tommy," said Luther. "And if anything happens to Titus and I find out it's you, I cannot say what Biblical plague may befall you."

Maybe it was Luther's wonky eye, but I saw a glimmer of fear in Tommy Nero's face.

"Fine," Tommy said.

"Fine what?" I said. "I want to hear you say it."

He scrunched up a linen napkin and held it tight. "Nothing will happen to Allie Hayes by me. Just get me my money back. I'll have Phil call you when we find out about the locals."

I looked at Luther. He nodded. We stood.

"Tommy," said Luther.

"Luther," said Tommy. "I'd shake your hand, but I need some more wet wipes."

A waiter magically appeared with a basket of wet wipes.

"Have a nice day, Phil," I said as I passed him. "By the way, the 1970s called and they want their clothes back."

"Fuck you," said Phil.

"Phil's a real charmer," said Luther.

"Isn't he, though?" I said as we walked out.

30

LUTHER DROPPED ME off and went back to the church. I spent the rest of the afternoon walking around. I think better when I walk. I also think better when I drink, but I read somewhere that walking might be better for you. Maybe not when there's a hitman peeling around looking to ventilate you, but whatever. I took my chances and kept my eyes open.

As I walked, I pondered Jake Preston and Eddie Corrado. Both were shot by a non-pro—or by a pro who wants it to look non-pro—with a small-caliber gun. Both in the left eye.

Jake had been blackmailing Rexford J. Hayes with something. With what? I had previously suspected that he had proof that Rex molested Allie, but now I'm not so sure. Allie definitely has all the telltale signs of a girl who was brutalized by men from an early age. You get to know them as a cop. You can look at a girl and hear her voice and you just know. It's a pattern, a speaking rhythm, the way she darts her eyes. Just like how a pro can pick out the one hooker from a picture of eighty girls.

Allie tried to convince me it was Rex, but my gut told me she was covering up the real secret. Was it something to do with Pam?

Allie was street-smart. Too street-smart for a girl from Gables Estates. She spent some serious time doing some very bad things. She knew B & E. She knew how to hustle. She had an unregistered gun. Where would she have found the time to learn all this after class at Miss Favisham's Academy or wherever the hell little rich girls go to middle school?

Eddie stole from Tommy Nero. Where is the money? What's the connection between the fortune Jake pissed to the wind and Tommy's two million? Did Tommy kill Jake and make it look like an amateur?

No. Tommy Nero may be pond scum, but he's a businessman first and foremost. He wouldn't do anything that would compromise his reputation.

I felt a headache coming on. I went back to my place, flopped on the airbed, and stared at the ceiling as the afternoon storm kicked in. The couple upstairs must have been passed out from exhaustion because all I heard was the thunder and rain.

I did some deep-breathing, attempting to clear my mind to allow thoughts to come to me like all the meditation hucksters tell you to do. But instead, I fell asleep.

I awoke to sunshine and a knock at my door. I looked at the time. 6:01 p.m. Gun out, I sprang to the side of the door and listened, holding my breath. Another knock.

"Open up," said Sofia. "It's me."

I exhaled and opened the door. The sergeant appeared sweaty and tired. Her hair was a mess, face shiny, black pantsuit looking like it could use a tumble at the dry cleaner. She was thoroughly gorgeous.

"Well, hello stranger," I said. "It's about time."

"Can I come in?" she said.

"Do you have a warrant?"

"Shut up." She pushed past me and walked in. I closed the

door.

She looked around, her arms folded. It didn't take long to look around. There's not much to look around at.

"I usually don't answer the door myself," I said, "but my butler is off today. Cleaning staff too, so pardon the mess."

She turned and faced me. It felt good to have her in my private space. It felt very good.

"I saw another dead body this afternoon," she said.

I nodded and folded my arms. "Cops see a lot of those—or so I've heard."

"Shut up. It was Eddie Corrado. Someone texted it in anonymously. Any idea who that might be?"

I shrugged. "Sonny Crockett?"

"Shut up. Why didn't you call me?"

"I wasn't sure if Bad Bad Lieutenant Brown had your line tapped."

She thought about that and nodded.

"Belson got the case," she said. "I went and saw it. Whoever killed Jake Preston also killed Eddie Corrado."

"I know."

She folded her arms and turned to face the wall, tempting me to look at her butt. Which I did. Because how can you not? Wow. Then she took one step—which is all you can take in my place—and turned to face the corner window with the grime.

"Here's the thing," she said spitting the words through gritted teeth. "I put in an inquiry on Foundation Investments LLC."

"And?" I said.

"It was squashed. I've been told to focus on other things."

"Other things?"

"Yes, like rumors of an art theft ring ahead of Art Basel."

"Sounds dangerous."

"It isn't. I'm being sidelined. Again. We—Lieutenant Brown and the entire OCS department—have been directed to other matters by the higher-ups."

I nodded, again sensing the powerful magnetic field between us, as if either one of us stepped into it we'd snap together.

"Drink?" I said, clearing my throat again.

"No," she said.

"Sit."

I motioned to one of the plastic chairs. She hesitated but sat anyway. I sat across from her.

We stayed like that for a few thousand years. She gazed off into a distant world. I looked intermittently at the wall and then back at her amazing eyes. I chose her eyes and stuck with them. No contest.

"You know," she said in a voice like she was floating on a faraway ocean, "I used to be young and naïve."

"You?" I said. "Can't picture that. The naïve part, I mean."

"I used to think it was simple. Catch bad guys. Be a good cop. Do your job."

"Uh-huh."

"But how can you do your job when you're told not to do your job? How can you just look the other way? Why be a cop in the first place?"

"Perks, detail work, pension."

She sighed.

"That's exactly how so many of them think," she said. "They make checklists, get the bare minimum of clearances, kiss the lieutenant's ass, and go home counting the days until retirement, hoping maybe they'll fall down the stairs and bust a hip to get out early. But that's not why I became a cop."

"I know," I said.

"How do you know?"

"Because it's why I became a cop. I was solving puzzles and crimes in the fifth grade."

"Me too."

"But you're right. It's not why most cops become cops. You and I—they call us 'natural cops' and make fun of us."

She shook her head, like she needed to pull herself back to the present.

"There's just so much—corruption," she said. "Don't get me wrong. There's a lot of good people at all levels. But there's an equal number of assholes at all levels."

"Yeah," I said. "We know it going in, but we choose not to see it. Then, when we're sidelined for bullshit reasons, it hits us hard."

She looked at me like she was looking into my soul. "You couldn't take it. You quit."

"Yeah," I said. "I couldn't deal with it anymore. I kind of, uh—exploded—actually."

"I know. I read your file the night I pulled you over."

She smiled a smile that turned the brightness and contrast in the room up ten notches.

"I've got to know," she said. "How did it feel when you punched that FBI agent?"

I laughed. "Good. Real good. But on the flipside, not so good. Yes, he was being a prick. Yes, it was his job to be a prick and I knew it. But the sucky thing was we grew up together. We weren't best friends or anything, but I knew him from middle school up. I felt bad over that."

"What was his name again?" she said.

I glanced over at the window, my muscles tightening.

"Clark Erwin," I said.

"Right. Wow, that must have been something." She placed her hand on the table in an awkward resting position. "I think I know how you felt. Right now, I feel like I want to quit, to run, to get away. To fucking punch someone."

The way she said that sent a jolt through my jeans. I shifted in the plastic chair and cleared my throat again. Her face relaxed into a smile I hadn't seen yet—a soft and warm smile. A smile that could dissolve diamonds. All my problems instantly faded and I didn't care about anything anywhere else. I contemplated singing.

"That drink offer still good?" she said.

"Aren't you still on duty?" I said.

"I don't really know anymore."

I grinned, got up, took down the Rebel Yell and two red plastic cups, and brought them over to the table. I poured some in each, again noticing the amazing way her black pants bunch at the top of her thigh. I stifled a gulp.

"Nice glassware," she said.

"Thanks. I had these specially made to match the decor."

She laughed.

"You have a beautiful laugh," I said, unable to not say it. I raised my glass. "Cheers."

"Cheers," she said and sipped the bourbon.

She held my eyes for a good long heartbeat. I hoped it wouldn't end for a very long time.

Then, her hard face came back.

"But unlike you," she said, "I didn't punch anyone. I can't I need to keep going. I can't *not* be a cop. I can't lose this job. I need to be this. Just like my dad. He needed to. He still asks me about everything I'm working on every day when I come home."

"You live with your dad?" I said.

She nodded. "He was shot. Messed up his knee. Bad. Lots of surgeries. He'll never walk without a cane. He took disability but he didn't want to—there was no other choice. He hated it. All his friends patted him on the back, wishing they got shot in the knee. Meanwhile, he's this puzzle-solving beast without a home."

"Sounds like a great guy."

"He is."

"Where's your mom?"

"Gone."

"Sorry."

"My brother and I take care of my dad," she said. "You met my brother Jorge."

"I did," I said. "He's very—um—not your dad."

"Exactly. That's why I'm the one who gets to live with him."

"Now I know why you don't want me over."

She frowned. "It's not that I don't want you over. It's more complicated than that. The night I pulled you over, I was dealing with some shit. You were someone else too."

I sat up and took a deep breath. "Someone else?"

"Yeah," she said, "you were this fire-breathing dragon hell-bent on revenge. I could see it in your eyes. I know the look. Funny thing is, I felt kind of the same that night. I was in touch with it."

"That's why you followed me to West Lido Drive?"

"Yeah—I think—maybe. I don't know."

I liked that we were sharing. She usually keeps her walls up. She caught herself looking at me too long and moved her gaze past me as she sipped her drink.

"So why were you on uniform probation?" I said.

"I was getting too close to something," she said. "While I was pulling over drunks and suspicious guys in rental cars with broken taillights for a month, they swept it all under the table so when I got back everything sparkled again. No trace of it."

"Sucks."

"Yeah."

Our eyes met for another long heartbeat. She bit her lower lip. At that very moment, the couple upstairs commenced Act One.

"Right on cue," I said.

"What is that?" Sofia said.

"My neighbors upstairs have a theatrical sense of foreplay."

We both took deep breaths as the screaming escalated, our eyes locked on each other. A dollop of sweat broke out on her upper lip. She reached up with her tongue and licked it away. I finished my drink and poured another.

Sofia took a deep breath, shook her head, and sat up. Suddenly a cop again.

"So," she said, "it looks like Allie Hayes killed Jake Preston and Eddie Corrado."

I thought hard about my next words. I probably shouldn't. It would ruin the mood. In fact, I definitely shouldn't—but the cop inside me spoke first.

"Allie Hayes didn't kill Jake Preston and Eddie Corrado," I said.

Her hard stare returned. "You know this how?"

"Gut instinct," I said, kicking myself for opening this particular can of worms. "We talked about it, she and I. She—uh—spent the night here last night."

Sofia leaped to her feet. She glared down at the airbed with a combination of shock, surprise, and disgust. Then she turned back to me with a grimace I could feel in my spine.

"What did you say?" she hissed.

I felt myself blush. I didn't remember the last time I blushed.

"She just showed up," I said. "I was surprised, too. See, I had found her at Hinraker's the night before."

"What?" she said, her voice like metal sheathing being ripped off a roof. "You found her and you didn't tell me?"

I told her all about Hinraker's—the show, my confrontation with Allie, my suspicions. She folded her arms and shook her head.

"We've been trying to get to Morton Hinraker for suspected human trafficking for years," she said, "but no judge will ever authorize a warrant."

"Naturally," I said. "I'd bet a judge or three has a private room at Hinraker's."

"Still, you could have told me."

"I didn't tell you because I needed to get information from her and then convince her to go see you, which is a notch above just telling you. Allie and I were on our way to see you this morning."

"And?"

I leaned forward, my shoulders down, and stared at the corner.

"And—she, uh—outsmarted me," I said.

"Outsmarted you how?" she said.

"She ran off with some kid in a McLaren after trying to convince me to run off to L.A. with her and be her bodyguard. Yeah yeah yeah, on paper she looks good for Eddie Corrado. But I don't buy it. I know she didn't do it. She was there, but the window out back was open, back porch screen torn. The room was full of flies. I think she jumped out the back and escaped from whoever fired the gun that killed Eddie."

She sat down again. I could see her brain thinking. "You think it was Tommy Nero?"

"No," I said. "If Tommy Nero wanted to stage an amateur job, he could have, no doubt. But this was personal. I feel it. Whoever did it shot Eddie in the left eye up close, just like Jake Preston."

"So what do you think happened?"

"I don't know," I said. "Also, I can't be sure, but Allie's gun didn't appear to be fired. No smell, rounds chambered. In fact, I'm willing to bet on it."

I stood up, opened up the closet next to us, and pushed the spring lock that flipped open the stash space. I picked up Allie's .22 with two fingers and placed it on the table.

"Got a baggie on you?" I said. "I'm willing to bet this isn't the gun that killed Jake Preston nor Eddie Corrado."

"That's Allie's?" she said.

"Yep. She pointed it at me when I walked in."

Sofia stared at the gun, then at the floor, then back at the gun, then at me. She reached into her bag, removed a baggie, gently placed the gun in it, and stuffed it in her bag. I just knew she'd have a baggie. I bet there's a pack under her bed.

"Then you—convinced—her to talk to me?" she said, nearly spitting the words out.

"Yes," I said.

"How did you—convince—her?"

"I fucked her silly, of course."

"I knew it!"

Sofia stood up again and folded her arms, her face werewolf-like.

I laughed.

"Sofia," I said, "please. Come on, give me some credit. I'm joking. I couldn't get it up for Allie if I tried. She's used, abused, damaged—very damaged. Maybe beyond repair."

Sofia tapped her foot and stared at me like an interrogator to a terrorist with a car battery attached to his genitals. I held her eyes. They relaxed.

"I'm not sure if I believe you," she said, slowly sitting down again.

"You do," I said. "Here's another piece of the puzzle. Somebody's hired a pro cleaner named Z—just the letter—who has been keeping tabs on me."

"How do you know this?"

"Someone texted me to warn me. And I saw Z—twice. He's a cocky bastard, full of himself."

"You actually saw him?"

"Yeah. Once at the Leucadendra Country Club where Pam Hayes gave me marching orders, then later at 5th and Meridian when I was about to cross. He slowed just to stare me down and show me who's boss."

"Who warned you?"

"Don't know. Burner number."

We both stared and thought, rolling all this around. Her hand neared mine on the table again. The magnetic field was back. The couple upstairs were doing an enhanced version of the lead-up to Act Two. I took a chance and wrapped my hand around hers.

"I've got to go," Sofia said and stood up, almost knocking the chair over as she withdrew her hand. Her unfinished drink sat on the table. "I'll get this to the lab, not that anyone will test it for six months. They'll probably lose it, maybe even on purpose."

Before she got to the door, I stood up and blocked her way. I watched her nostrils flare as I took a deep breath and stepped directly into the magnetic field, my face an inch from hers. I smoothed a long stray hair behind her ear and followed the line with my fingers to the back of her neck.

She melted into my arms and I kissed her hard. Her body went slack under me, her hands running up my spine as she let go and pressed herself into me. I ran my hands down the back of her as I nibbled her face all the way up to her hair, where I took in a whiff of hot girl. Then, I bit her ear. She licked my neck and wrapped a leg around mine.

I was about to throw her down onto the airbed when something smashed and a girl screamed.

We both froze.

It was from upstairs. Then, a loud thump and a crash like broken glass. A male voice yelled. Another scream.

Shit.

31

GUN IN HAND, I was outside and up the steps in a heartbeat, Sofia behind me with her Glock 17.

Another scream. I turned the knob, but the door was locked. I rammed my right shoulder into it, which only hurt my shoulder. And again. Sofia gave me a "1-2-3-go" signal and we both threw our weight into it. The old jamb cracked and the door swung open.

We splayed into the room. A Latina girl with dark hair was on the floor holding a big ceramic mug she had been about to throw at the same Latino kid with the gang tattoos that I had stared down before. Blood ran down her face. Smashed glass was everywhere. The kid held a broken beer bottle in his right hand. He lunged toward me.

I stepped slightly to my left to allow his right arm to sail past me. I spun right, grabbed his wrist with my left hand, and kneed him in the groin. He made a sound like "Unk!" as he went down. I placed my left boot onto the right side of his face, holding him in place on the floor.

"Got a zip-tie?" I said to Sofia. She nodded and holstered her sidearm. I just knew she'd have a zip-tie.

I looked over at the bleeding girl, who was crying and screaming at me.

Holy fuck.

She was right above me the whole time.

"Marisol," I said.

"Take your foot off him!" Marisol said as she smashed the ceramic mug on the side of my head. I saw a burst of stars and went down backward.

The kid used the opportunity to lunge at Sofia, who slipped right and hit his face with a one-two left-jab, right-hook combination. He met the carpet again, very quiet this time.

Marisol screamed at Sofia in Spanish and looked around for something to throw at her. Sofia stepped into her space and slapped her. Then Marisol slapped Sofia back. Sofia grabbed Marisol's wrist and twisted it. Marisol fell to her knees and Sofia pulled out a zip-tie, bound her wrists behind her back, and threw her down on the couch like a used pillow. During all this, they continued to scream at each other in fast vile Spanish.

"You okay?" Sofia finally said to me.

"Yeah," I said, stars still there but clearing. I put my hand to my throbbing temple. No blood. Just a swelling bump.

I sat up. Sofia zip-tied the boy's arms behind his back and threw him onto a chair opposite the couch. He was conscious, but just barely.

More yelling in Spanish erupted between Marisol and Sofia. There were references to me, I could tell, but without subtitles I was lost. I did pick out parts of the Miranda warning.

"Sofia," I said, "wait. Don't take her in yet."

"Oh, they're *both* going in!" said Sofia.

"Wait. Just wait."

I took out my phone and called Marisol's mother. She picked up on the third ring. I tried to ask her where she was but the language barrier got in the way. I handed the phone to Sofia.

"This is Marisol's mother," I said. "Please tell her where we are."

Sofia took the phone and had an epic conversation with her. Marisol breathed heavily, near hyperventilation, and beamed me a feral hate stare through gritted teeth. Wisps of foam bubbled at the corners of her mouth.

Sofia handed me back the phone and I put it away.

"You are a real piece of work," she said.

"She told you?" I said.

"It wasn't enough to find one missing girl. You had to be out there looking for another. Why didn't you tell me? I could have helped, especially with the Spanish."

"You seemed busy."

She smiled a beautiful smile and our magnetic field found its way to this sad bloody scene. I felt even closer to her than when we had kissed downstairs.

"How far away is the mother?" I said.

"Close," said Sofia. "She'll be here soon."

Marisol launched another angry tirade at Sofia, who shot back an equal one that ended with Marisol staring at the floor.

I sat there on the floor and stared at the bleeding girl throwing eye-grenades at me. What happened to the pretty face in pigtails I first saw in the middle school picture at the intersection that night?

"Why is she like this?" I said.

"Because she loves this dirtbag," said Sofia, rolling her eyes. "See those neck tattoos and the one on the chest? MS-13."

"I don't get it. Why do beautiful young sweet girls want murderous scumbags? He cut her. He was maybe even going to kill her. It makes no sense."

Sofia shrugged. "I don't get it, either. Some girls get off on this bullshit. They're fucked in the head. They equate being a criminal with masculinity. Oh, get this—Marisol here just told me she's pregnant with this asshole's child."

"Oh, no fucking way."

"Yep."

"I hate you!" screamed Marisol at me.

Sofia railed at her in Spanish again. The kid remained half-conscious, staring at nothing.

Marisol's mother arrived. More Spanish. More yelling. Sofia and I stepped outside onto the second floor landing, leaned on the rail, and gazed down into my dirty little courtyard, daylight giving way to the Meridian Ave streetlamps. We stayed like that for a long time, standing with our shoulders almost touching, while the three people behind us hammered it out. In all the chaos, life felt good there with her.

Finally, Marisol's mom came out to us. She thanked me profusely and asked if Marisol could come home with her.

Sofia didn't want to, but relented after a stare-off with me, in which I employed my seldom-used puppy-dog look. She rolled her eyes, nodded, and snipped the zip-ties off Marisol, who had become docile. Marisol's mother thanked and hugged me with a hundred or so *Dios te bendigas*. I offered to pay for a cab and there was more thanking and blessing as I called. It took less than five minutes and they were gone.

"Did you tell her to go to the hospital to get that stitched up?" I said to Sofia.

"I did," she said, "but they won't."

"She's going to have a scar."

Sofia shrugged and walked back into the apartment, where she said something in Spanish to the gangbanger, and then got him up off the couch and down the steps to her unmarked SUV.

I walked with her. A light rain began to fall. She shoved him in the back and closed the door, then turned to face me.

"This was great," I said. "I had a really good time. What do you want to do for our second date? Maybe a shootout with a drug kingpin down at the docks?"

She folded her arms, looked down, and stepped back from me a little. Uh-oh.

"Yeah, about that," she said.

"Don't say anything," I said, and played with the same wayward strand of her hair as before. She reached up and took it away from me, tamping it down.

Ouch.

"Titus, I can't," she said.

I nodded, not sure what I was nodding to.

"I'll run the weapon and let you know what they find, if they even try," she said as thunder clapped and the raindrops became steady.

"Sure," I said and leaned in to kiss her, even if on the forehead, but she pushed me back.

Double ouch.

She got in the SUV and rolled down the window.

"I'll—uh—see you," she said.

"Sure," I said and watched her as she drove away.

Triple ouch.

32

I WALKED BACK inside my apartment and turned on the little lamp on the table. Sofia had barely touched her drink. I scoffed it down in one gulp. Then, I drank my unfinished one and poured another. I could almost hear Luther's disapproval, but fuck it.

I noticed I had left the stash spot open.

There was a clap of thunder and a flash of lightning. Full of unresolved sexual tension, I growled like an animal and bashed the spring door hard. The hinge broke and the whole thing fell off, slipping down into the tiny space underneath the shelf.

Fuck. Why did I do that?

I ran my fingers through my hair and took a deep breath. I bent down and reached in to pick up the door, which rested on something. I pulled it out and peered in, squinting. In the tiny space underneath the shelf, barely visible in the dim light, was a nebulous mass.

I reached down and felt something soft and plastic with

straps. I got hold of it and yanked it up through the narrow opening.

It was Allie's green duffel bag, the one with the red trim. The one she had with her last night. I brought it up, placed it on the table, and carefully zipped it open.

Holy fuck.

Heart pounding, I zipped it shut and carried it over behind the curve of the kitchen counter onto the floor in front of the stove, away from the window where nobody could see in from outside. I dropped to my knees and opened the bag again.

Holy fuck. Still there.

Cash. A lot of cash. Too much cash. Cash that shouldn't be in one place all together like that—ever. The kind of cash that most people never see in a lifetime.

I listened to the raindrops as the money and I sat there on the floor. A profusion of Ben Franklins smirked up at me from the tops of stacks of other Ben Franklins banded tightly under them, all sitting on a pile of more stacks of Ben Franklins. All those smirks and not one of them said anything.

In addition to the cash, there was a plastic bag with some papers in it. I removed it from the duffel, placed it to the side, and decided to count the money. Gingerly, I laid out stacks of bills, nothing but hundreds. Two million one hundred seventy-five thousand dollars. I counted again, just to be sure. Two million one hundred seventy-five thousand dollars. One more time. Two million one hundred seventy-five thousand dollars.

A thunderhead crashed and made me jump, gun out. I peered over the top of the counter toward the window. Nothing.

I re-stuffed the duffel bag. Once all the stacks were back in, I zipped it up and shoved it into the inert oven for now. I didn't like having that much money in my possession. I felt like everybody in Miami could see me and the money, as if a giant spotlight was on me—even though the only real light came from the tiny table lamp and the fluorescent streetlights behind the dancing silhouettes of palm fronds tossing about in the hot wet wind.

I turned my attention to the thin plastic bag. Inside were some photographs and papers. I got up, walked over to the table, opened the bag, and removed the papers.

The first document was a birth certificate in the name of Tiffany Connors. Born July 19, 1998 in Newark, New Jersey.

There were a handful of pictures of Allie as a child. The first was a baby in a blue bonnet with eyes like Allie's.

She was maybe five in another, wearing a winter coat. In another, she was closer to seven standing under a banner with several other kids. The banner read "HAPPY BIRTHDAY, TIFFANY!" Several more pictures spanned her childhood from probably age eight all the way up to about thirteen. Then, they stopped.

The thunder clapped. The rain fell. The palm fronds danced. The wind whistled.

I counted the pictures. Eleven all together. I flipped through them again.

Allie looked about twelve in the most recent one. She stood with a forty-ish blonde woman and a man with dark movie-star looks in front of a sign surrounded by palm trees that read *Welcome to Lakewood Ranch*. The blonde woman had the same distinctive big eyes as Allie. Allie was nineteen now, so that must have been seven years ago.

There was a plump girl in several pictures. From the age progression, I surmised she was about five years older than Allie. She got plumper as the years went by. She had dark red hair and freckles, but the same big eyes.

I finished my drink and poured another.

I booted up my Chromebook and ran an online search for Tiffany Connors from Newark, New Jersey. Nothing.

I modified the search to Tiffany Connors from Lakewood Ranch, Florida. I found a death notice from 2011. Tiffany Connors died when she was thirteen years old, six years ago. Killed by a drunk driver. Horrible accident. At the Legacy site, two relatives were named: her mother Jean Connors and her sister Hayley Thurlow. I copied the names into a text document. I finished my drink, poured another, and studied the palm frond silhouettes some more.

If Tiffany Connors died when she was thirteen years old, six years ago, then she'd be nineteen today if she had lived. Same age as Allie Hayes.

Six years ago. Six years ago. Something about the phrase replayed in my mind. Where have I heard that phrase recently?

No distractions like six years ago.

I leaped to my feet. Pam Hayes at the outdoor table. Six years ago, Rexford J. Hayes was running for the Senate. He lost. Now, he's running again. *No distractions like six years ago,* she had said to me.

An idea hit me. I'm not sure where it came from, but it landed on me and I felt compelled to follow it. I sat down and looked up Pam Hayes on two of the big people-lookup sites.

Pam Hayes had two sisters, both still in Connecticut—Monroe and Greenwich. A brother in Newport, who owns an art gallery. Father died ten years ago. Mother still alive. Eighty-one years old. Lives in Stonington, Connecticut.

I looked up her number and dialed, the buzz of the bourbon hitting me full force. As the phone rang, I wondered what I was doing. I seemed to be making this up as I went along. I didn't even know what I was going to say. Pam Hayes' mother picked up on the eighth ring.

"Hello, Mrs. Elliott," I said, falling into the voice of a man I knew well who speaks in a thick Boston accent. "This is Agent Clark Erwin from the FBI."

"Oh God," she said. "What now?"

"What do you mean by that, Mrs. Elliott?"

"I mean I thought I'd never hear from you again, Agent Erwin."

Shit, Pam Hayes' mother knows Clark Erwin. Hadn't expected that. Bad call to impersonate Clark Erwin. Very bad call. This was going to be tricky. But I needed to run with it as far as I could get.

"Well, Mrs. Elliott," I said, "I was just cleaning up some records here. We're moving offices and some of these cases are near expiring. I just came across yours and I wanted to follow up before we destroyed it."

"We finished this matter a long time ago," said Mrs. Elliott. "Alison came home to Pamela and Rexford and that was that. My daughter Pamela isn't as evil as you suspected her to be. This is an odd call in the evening. What are you fishing for, Agent Erwin?"

Sharp old lady.

"Right," I said, trying to channel what Clark Erwin would say. "Okay. Well, as long as you say everything is fine, then everything must be fine. How's Allie been?"

"Alison has been wonderful. She's in college now. She regrets running off with that group of hooligans. Two months she was gone, but she returned home almost reborn. Alison is now a fine, healthy, well-balanced young woman."

Mrs. Elliott obviously hasn't spent much time with Allie.

"Oh," I said, "so you see her a lot?"

There was a long silence.

"Nobody visits an eighty-one year old woman anymore," said Mrs. Elliott. "They're all too busy staring at the screens of their ridiculous little devices. So busy. So so busy. Busy busy busy. Truth be told, Agent Erwin—and I don't know why I'm telling *you* this, of all people—I haven't even seen my own granddaughter in five years."

"Five years?" I said.

"Yes, Pamela and Rexford never come up here anymore and I refuse to travel south of Manhattan."

"But as far as you know everything is fine with Allie and Pam and Rex?"

There was another silence on the other end of the line—a longer and stranger one. Then, Mrs. Elliott said, "You're good,

Agent Erwin. You bring the soap, and then you bring the steel wool. Fine, I'll tell you. I'll tell you because I'm a lonely old woman and I have nobody else to tell. Nobody ever listens to me anyway."

"That's frustrating, I'm sure."

There was a long pause. I thought I had lost her, but then she said, "It was just so strange at the time."

"Strange at the time?" I said.

"Pamela and Rexford were here for a wedding with Alison. It was, oh, what was it? Five years ago. The last time I saw Alison. Alison looked—different. Like she had had a facelift or something. I know children these days have plastic surgery, but it was ridiculous for fourteen-year old Alison. I started talking to her and she acted odd, like she didn't know me. I could swear it wasn't even her, almost a girl who looked like her who was playing her part. She had big eyes. Alison doesn't have eyes that big. Then, Rexford and Pamela came by and whisked her away from me. I thought that was strange."

"When did you see Allie again?"

"I told you. I haven't."

"Oh. Okay. Well, I guess we'll purge this file now. Mrs. Elliott, if you wouldn't mind, could you forget I called? We're not supposed to make calls like this."

"Of course, Agent Erwin. Thank you so much, and I'm sorry for being snippy with you. I know you were only doing your job, suspecting my daughter of things that shall go unmentioned. Thank you so much again for your help—and your discretion."

"You bet, Mrs. Elliott. Thank you very much. I wish you the best."

"Goodbye."

Whew, that was close. Not to mention weird.

The picture was getting clear. But I needed one more piece of the puzzle.

I went back online and again looked at the list of bereaved

relatives of the late Tiffany Connors, who had been buried at the Eternal Pine Cemetery in Lakewood Ranch. I again visited the people-lookup sites, both confirming that Tiffany's mother Jean Kirkwood—formerly Jean Connors—formerly Jean Thurlow—formerly of Newark, New Jersey—currently lives at 48101 Cherry Farm Road in Lakewood Ranch, which is just north of Sarasota.

According to her Facebook page and various links, "Jeannie" Kirkwood is a real estate agent. With her big smile and piled-high blonde hair in a red blazer, she posed in front of a beige stucco house with a Spanish-tile roof, her right hand extended in a *voila!* gesture. Jeannie Kirkwood will find the right home for you in beautiful Lakewood Ranch, guaranteed.

She was the same woman in the picture with thirteen-year old Allie. I right-clicked and saved the picture, and then zoomed in on her eyes. They were big and nearly glowed behind a weathered face with lots of cover-up and maybe some airbrushing.

I called Luther and asked for a favor—two favors, actually. He agreed, but only if I promised to attend service on Sunday. I reluctantly said yes.

I called Bruno and asked him if he wanted my shifts at Cap'n Jack's for the next few days. He gladly accepted. Nobody seems to be throwing manila envelopes full of money at his head nor hiding duffel bags full of millions in his closet.

I went online and reserved a rental car for the morning. Then, I walked over to T.J. Maxx at Fifth and Alton and bought a sport coat to take the edge off my appearance.

One missing daughter found. One to go.

33

IN THE MORNING, I picked up a black Toyota Corolla rental from the Avis on Collins at 23rd. Then, I followed Google Maps' directions through Little Haiti and Miami Shores to I-95 North and over to I-595 in Davie, which became I-75 all the way across the state of Florida. Three-and-a-half hours later, I was in Lakewood Ranch.

I got off at the Fruitville Road exit and followed the Google voice as it directed me to the Eternal Pine Cemetery. I pulled in to an empty parking lot in front of a tiny but elegant gate. There were a lot of pine trees. I wondered which one was the eternal one. Nobody was in sight anywhere.

I got out and walked through the gate, my footsteps oddly loud on the soft grass in the hot morning sun, joined intermittently by the croak of a tree frog. The headstones were the flat uniform kind, rows of identical gray marble. Three had flowers recently placed on top of them.

It took a while, but I located the right one:

TIFFANY JANE CONNORS

JULY 19, 1998 – AUGUST 27, 2011

I bowed my head, hands clasped in front. I thought maybe I should say a prayer, but I wasn't sure I remembered how. So I stayed silent and listened to the tree frog.

After a minute, I sat on my haunches and touched the smooth headstone. It was cool, even in the direct Florida sunshine.

"Found you," I said and patted it. "For real this time."

34

I GOT BACK ON I-75 and drove up one more exit to University Parkway, which I followed to Lakewood Ranch Boulevard, turned left, left again onto Ranch Club Boulevard, and right onto Cherry Farm Road. The sky was that bright Florida summer gray with a hot wind kicking around but no rain.

It was a suburban development, somewhat recent, a living tribute to beige stucco. Endless rows of McMansions with red Spanish tile roofs fronted perfectly mowed lawns behind wide sidewalks and islands, an identical pool under an identical cage-like structure in every back yard. Not shabby by any means, but the houses looked like they had been manufactured on an assembly line and clicked into place like giant Lego pieces. I wondered if anyone ever walked into anyone else's house by accident.

48101 Cherry Farm Road had lawn sprinklers on high in a wide arc, feeding perfectly uniform blades of grass in front of two flower beds, each with the obligatory palm tree. I parked on the street, walked up the long driveway and along the path to the coral front door, which was framed by two large white pillars. I rang the doorbell.

No answer.

I rang it again. Nothing. I looked at my phone. 12:45.

I drove to a nearby shopping plaza built to look like an old Main Street in a real town somewhere else. I parked and walked around a fake city hall in front of a fake monument surrounded by park benches on which nobody sat.

Between a pizza shop and a hair salon was the real estate office where Jeannie Kirkwood was listed as an agent. The girl behind the desk was about twenty-two with brown hair and freckles. She wore a red blazer and a name tag that read Becky.

"Good morning," she said with a perky smile and a happy lilt in her voice.

"Good morning," I said. "Is Jeannie Kirkwood in?"

"No, I'm sorry." She seemed genuinely sorry. "But can I help you with anything?"

"Well, I was talking to Jeannie about a property over on Ranch Club Boulevard. Can you tell me when she'll be in?"

"Um," Becky said, twirling her hair, "let me check."

She got up and disappeared around the corner. I looked around. There was only one other agent at her desk, a sixty-ish woman with short hair and bifocals in a red blazer three sizes too big for her. She tapped at a computer with two fingers and ignored me completely.

Becky returned with a plump woman in her fifties with big brown hair, bright red lipstick, and a tired face. She carried glasses in her right hand and a ream of papers in her left. She wore a red blazer over a white blouse with black pants. Her name tag read Helen Whitney – C.R.E, C.I.P.S., S.R.E.S.

"Jeannie isn't here," said Helen Whitney – C.R.E, C.I.P.S., S.R.E.S.

"Oh," I said. "It's just that I had spoken to her about a property over on—"

"Look, I don't know what you're selling." Her voice was sharper than a chef's knife. "Jeannie Kirkwood hasn't listed a property with us in years. Whatever you're peddling, we don't need it. Now, if you're really interested in property—and I doubt you are if you're looking for Jeannie—then Becky here is our newest broker and will be happy to help you."

Becky smiled perkily. I smiled back.

"I'm sure Becky is fantastic," I said, "but Jeannie is listed on your website and—"

"Do you know how many agents work out of this office?" said Helen. "Thirty-five. Do you know how many actually sell houses? Four. I'd love to kick the deadbeats off the site, but the corporate office has its rules. Now, what property can Becky help you with today?"

Becky smiled again. She looked as comfortable as a rabbit in a coyote den.

"I'm sorry," I said. "The truth is, this is a, uh, personal matter."

Helen Whitney – C.R.E, C.I.P.S., S.R.E.S. slapped the ream of papers against her substantial hip, causing Becky to jump.

"My God," she said, "what magic does that woman have? I've been married twice to two scum-of-the-earth losers but Jeannie has men like you walking in here at least once a month looking for her. I just don't get it."

"Excuse me," said Becky as she slunk away and disappeared.

"It's not that at all," I said. "I just need to serve some papers to Mrs. Kirkwood."

"Oh, a process server?" said Helen. "That's a new one. Look, maybe you're telling the truth. Maybe you're not. Either way, I don't have time. Jeannie Kirkwood is usually at Linksters Tap Room this time of day, but you'd better hurry"–she looked at her watch—"she's probably already got her teeth into somebody by now and is headed to his place. Try again tomorrow, but get there before noon."

Helen Whitney – C.R.E, C.I.P.S., S.R.E.S. turned and disappeared around a corner.

"Thank you," I said to nobody.

The older woman with the short hair and bifocals kept tapping with two fingers. I wondered how many letters she had next to her name, turned, and walked out.

35

LINKSTERS TAP ROOM was in one corner of a large square strip mall with no pretensions of being a fake Main Street, but felt fake anyway. The bar was half-outside half-inside. I walked in and looked around, but didn't see Jeannie Connors.

I thought about asking, but the smell from the grill reminded me I hadn't eaten since Miami. I sat at one of the outdoor tables and drank two tall Sierra Nevada IPAs with a medium-well burger and fries, served with a bright smile from a sweet girl named Vanessa.

I asked her if she knew Jeannie Connors. She did. I had just missed her, but Vanessa said she'd likely be back tomorrow. I drank another beer and left a big tip.

Walking back to the car, I caught a fleeting glimpse of a silver Audi A5 out of the corner of my eye as it scooted out of the parking lot. My hand involuntarily tapped the gun on my hip.

I got in the Toyota and looked at the clock. 2:45 p.m. I drove back to Jeannie Kirkwood's house on Cherry Farm Road.

I rang the bell again while looking around. Nobody answered. Nobody peered out of their windows at me. Nobody even tried to shoot me.

I got back in the car and wondered how long it would take for Jeannie to do what I surmise she's doing, if Helen Whitney – C.R.E, C.I.P.S., S.R.E.S. is correct about her proclivities.

I drove around some more. I followed University Parkway to its end, turned south on Highway 41, and looped around out Fruitville Road and back up I-75, eye out for a silver Audi A5. I didn't see it, but I had the unmistakable sixth sense it was nearby.

An hour later, I was back in front of Jeannie Kirkwood's house a third time. Nothing had changed. I waited some more.

An hour later, I looked at my phone. 4:45 p.m. The neighborhood sprang to life somewhat. A man walking his poodle with a bag of dog poop in his hand looked at me with squinted eyes. A mother with three kids arrived home next door. She carried a baby out from a white SUV while a boy about four blew bubbles and a girl about three screamed her head off.

At 5:57 p.m., a gray SUV pulled into Jeannie Kirkwood's driveway. It parked and the lift-back went up to reveal a grocery bag. I got out of the rental car.

A blonde woman about forty-five got out of the SUV and walked toward me walking toward her, pointing at me with a big smile. She wore lots of makeup over a face that up close had more wear than noticeable from the online pictures. Her substantial hair was piled messily on top her head. She wore a loose white off-the-shoulder dress with a faint flower print. Her tanned legs glistened. They were nice legs.

"Hello, Mrs. Connors," I said.

She looked me up and down, the smile growing wider, drawing circles with her finger. Definitely Allie's eyes.

"Kirkwood," she said. "I remarried and re-divorced. Long story, hun. And call me Jeannie, for God's sake."

"My name is Titus," I said.

"Oh, of course," she said. "I remember you, hun. You're that feller from Atlanta, right? You fly planes."

"No. I'm from Miami. I'm a, uh, private detective."

"Oh, right," she said with a big laugh as she took the grocery bag out of the back of the SUV and closed it. It contained three bottles of wine and nothing else. "I'm sorry hun. I have a bad memory. I meet so many people being a real estate agent and all. Oh, I remember you. It's so good to see you." She moved right up to me and planted a kiss on my face while squeezing her body into mine and running her hand up my back. I whiffed an odd mix of alcohol, perfume, and sweat. "So glad you stopped by."

Then, she turned and swung her substantial hips to the front door and unlocked it. I remained still. She opened the door and turned back to me.

"Well, don't just stand there, stranger," she said. "Come on in and we'll catch up."

Feeling like I had wandered into a scene from the movie *Memento*, I followed her inside. It was a tastefully decorated home with all the basics where they should be, a perfectly matched suburban mix of modern and classic decor. Simple, unadorned, ready for anyone to move in, more like a show home than a place where people actually live.

"Last time you were here, hun," she said as she placed the bag on a large counter that separated the kitchen from the living room, "I probably called myself Mrs. Connors because I was mad at my ex-husband. But don't you worry. There ain't no Mr. Kirkwood. He ran off with the daughter of the bitch across the street. I took care of her, let me tell you. Sorry, hun. I babble sometimes. You must remember that about me."

"Of course," I said.

She unscrewed the cap from a wine bottle and got out two glasses.

"Pinot Gri okay?" she said. "I'm out of the hard stuff."

"That's fine," I said.

She poured the wine and handed me a glass.

"Cheers," she said and raised her glass.

"Bottoms up," I said, raising mine. We clinked.

"Ooh," she said with a wink, "you *do* remember me." She downed half her glass in one gulp. I took barely a sip.

She held her glass between her sizable breasts, looked up at me, and squinted.

"Your name's not Titus," she said.

"It isn't?" I said.

"No, it's Branson. Or Brandon. Or Brad. I'm right, right? God, I could swear you fly planes. I remember your uniform with the stripes on the shoulders. But you say you're from Miami and you're a police officer."

"Private investigator—of sorts."

"Hm," she said and finished her drink. She poured another. "So, I thought about changing my name back to my maiden name Thurlow, but Thurlow is so stuffy. Jeannie Thurlow. I always hated that. My third grade teacher always said 'Miss Thurlow' in this big ol' nasty voice." She laughed again and ran her hand up my chest like we were old lovers. "Nope, just don't work for me, hun."

Her words slurred. She squeezed my shoulder muscles.

"My, but you fill out that sport coat in a thuggish sort of way," she said. Her hand moved to my neck and fingered my longish hair at the nape.

"Have you heard from your daughter?" I said.

She froze for a moment. Then, she laughed again.

"Hayley?" she said. "Was she here when you were here last? She was with that tattooed bearded swamp rat she calls a man, right? I'm sorry about that. No, I haven't heard from Hayley. She's up there in Lake Heron in the boonies."

"Oh, yeah," I said, playing along. "What was his name again?"

"Vernon." She finished another half-glass and threw her head back laughing. "White trash name. Hick boy who shoots possums and eats squirrels. God, and that beard. I never got the whole big long beard thing." She poured another glass of wine. "You ain't drinkin' fast enough, hun. Come on, catch up with me."

"What was Vernon's last name again?"

"Shores," she said with a laugh. "Vernon Shores. If Hayley marries him, which I'm sure she's done by now, she'll be Hayley Shores. Sounds like a condo on the beach. Sign up now for your own timeshare at Hayley Shores." She laughed herself silly again and slapped my knee, squeezing my thigh.

"How about your other daughter?" I said. "Heard from her?"

Her face dropped. Her hand left my thigh. She backed up an inch.

"Ginny?" she said.

"Yeah," I said. "How's Ginny?"

The air had changed. Jeannie Kirkwood shook her head and put her glass down. She took a deep breath and looked around the house as if she was seeing it for the first time. She placed both hands on her thighs.

"Ginny's fine," she said in a serious tone. "I haven't heard from her in ten years since she married that rich man and moved up north. Did I ever mention Ginny to you? I never talk about Ginny."

Nice family.

"Wait," I said, pretending to remember, wondering how far I could push this. "No, it wasn't Ginny. You have a third daughter. The youngest one. Tiffany, right?"

She took another deep breath, stood up unsteadily, and walked past me around to the other side of the counter. The room suddenly felt like it was filling with concrete. I pushed things too far again, didn't I? I've got to learn to be more subtle.

"Tiffany is dead," she said in a voice as cold as a bag of ice. "Wait, wait, wait. Who did you say you are again?"

Uh-oh. Definitely pushed it too far. I stood up. She moved

to her right and reached down into a cabinet. I glanced at the door and backed up a little.

"My name is Titus," I said. "I'm a private investigator."

"Uh-huh," she said with a tone of finality like she made a decision. She shook her head again as if to clear away the alcohol. "What are you looking for?"

"Not what. Who. I was hired to find a girl named Allie Hayes, and I'm pretty certain I know where she is."

At the name, I thought both of Jeannie Kirkwood's eyes would explode out of her head. She reached down and lifted a double-barreled shotgun, pointing it directly at me.

She was quick. I had steeled myself to dive to the door, thinking I had time considering her state of inebriation but I didn't expect her swift action, much less a shotgun. The two big barrels stared at me with cold malice.

"You get out of here right now!" Jeannie Kirkwood said. "I got nothing for you. I don't know no Allie Fucking Hayes. My daughter Tiffany is dead. Dead. You go back to whoever sent you and you tell them my daughter is dead. She's dead. She was killed by a drunk driver. A drunk driver hit her and she was killed. And that's it. That's how it is. That's how it will always be. You tell them that. Now get out."

"Jeannie," I said, "there's no need for this. We're on the same side. I'm doing this for Allie. And for Tiffany. Don't you want to see your daughter again?"

"I told you. My daughter is fucking dead. Now get the fuck out!"

I put my hands up and backed toward the door, pulse pounding. I opened it, stepped outside, closed it, walked swiftly to my rental car, started the engine, and got the hell out of Lakewood Ranch. I breathed again only when I was back on I-75, heading north.

Well, that went well, didn't it?

36

THE HOUSE WAS in Lake Heron, which wasn't much of a town. More like a big patch of woods with one paved road cutting through it, just north of Starke.

It wasn't much of a house, either. More like a series of ragged square stones piled on top of each other by a sleepwalker with bad vision. The roof was corrugated aluminum and looked like a hearty sneeze might blow it off. An inside light glowed through a window in the dusk.

According to the online database, the deed was in the name of Vernon Shores. A lean man about twenty-five was working on an old orange-red Ford Bronco in the front yard—if you could call it a yard. Slough or dirt-pit might be more accurate. The young man was shirtless in faded jeans and brown boots. Sleeve tattoos graced both arms and some sort of metal band had been riveted up his nose like a horseshoe, two prongs hanging down like shiny silver snot. He had a long beard and wore a tattered black baseball cap.

He glanced up when I pulled the rental car off the side of the road. I put on my warm trustworthy face as I got out of the car and walked toward him.

"Hi," I said, "I'm looking for Hayley."

"The fuck you want with Hayley?" he said, moving away from the Bronco with a large wrench in his hand.

Man, can I ever win them over.

"I'm from a law firm in Miami," I said. "Hayley may be the beneficiary of a large sum of money, but we're not sure."

Vernon Shores held the wrench like he was considering using it and took two steps toward me, chewing something.

"What the fuck are you talking about?" he said mid-chew.

"Money. There may be some money for her in a fund. There are three Hayley Thurlows in Florida and we need to determine if she's the correct one so she can claim it."

He chewed some more and looked at me, thinking that over. Thinking was always going to be a bother for him.

"How much money?" he said as he turned and spit.

"I'm only allowed to speak to Hayley Thurlow about the matter," I said, "and only after determining she's the correct Hayley Thurlow. She may not be."

He thought some more. The sun went down a little. Crickets chirped.

"You aren't the guy fucking her, are you?" he said.

I stifled a sudden urge to laugh hysterically. Not sure why. It's just been that kind of a day.

"No," I said with as straight a face as I could muster.

He chewed and thought some more, the gears churning very slowly.

"Fine," he said, turning back to the Bronco. "She's at the Horseshoe, working her shift at the bar. Go ahead, I don't care. Fuck her. I just don't care anymore. She's all yours, bud."

I didn't know what to say to that so I turned, got in the car, and drove away.

37

THE HORSESHOE LOOKED exactly how a bar named The Horseshoe should look. It was a low brown brick building in an unpaved clearing surrounded by tall pines. One door, no windows. I felt somewhat inadequate as I parked my Toyota rental, dwarfed by massive pickup trucks all around.

Just as I expected, on the inside were pool tables surrounded by good-ol'-boys in cowboy hats swilling longnecks and making sure I knew from their stares that they didn't like my haircut. The bar was long and strangely shaped, running all along the back and then jutting out in the middle before ending near the far left corner. The place was busy.

There were three bartenders on duty, all female. I picked the one who most closely resembled the plump girl in the pictures and took a stool near her, over to the right near the pool tables. If it was Hayley, she's gotten a whole lot plumper. Not obese yet, but on the fast-track. I'd guess her age at about twenty-five.

A napkin landed in front of me.

"What can I get you, hun?" she said with big eyes that seemed to glow, even though her face was different from Allie and Jeannie. Freckles and long red hair, but definitely the plump girl in the pictures. Her pretty smile radiated warmth and kindness.

"PBL draft," I said.

"Tall?"

"There should only be tall."

"Sure thing, hun," she said with a sweet laugh. I liked her. I watched her as she filled the glass from the Pabst Blue Ribbon tap and placed it in front of me. "Want to run a tab?"

"Sure."

"Want to see a menu?"

"No, thanks."

I sipped my beer and watched her work, pondering the best approach. My batting average wasn't high today, so I gave it some thought. I finished my beer.

"Another one?" she said as she came over to me.

"Sure," I said. "I'm Titus, by the way."

She finished pouring and paused, something out of the ordinary string-of-life bullshit being said.

"I'm Hayley," she said, placing the glass down with another big smile.

"Nice to meet you, Hayley."

"Same here."

"You know, you look like an intuitive person. I bet everybody comes to you for advice, don't they?"

"Oh my God," she said, rolling her eyes. "You have no idea. I am *everybody's* problem-solver. Sometimes I think I should be a psychiatrist. I'd probably make a ton more money."

"Probably. Well, I've got a problem and I could use some help. I know I don't know you, but sometimes it's good to talk to a stranger."

She pointed at me with one hand, the other on her hip.

"You're right. Give me a minute, hun. Let me take care of these boys and I'll be right back."

A crew of guys with the aroma of having put in a twelve-hour shift outdoors somewhere had lined up to my right. I predicted they would become loud and boisterous sooner rather than later.

I looked around for who could take care of them. I spotted him right away. He sat in the right hand corner in a black hat, black shirt, jeans with a big buckle in the front, and cowboy boots. Fifty-ish, but extremely fit with a trimmed neat white beard. He didn't seem to be drinking or doing anything at all besides looking around. The way he sat, completely at ease but with a certain readiness, told me he would be a formidable opponent. I know a pro when I see one.

Hayley finished setting up the new crowd and came back to me.

"So, Titus," she said, "the doctor is in."

"I'm trying to help somebody," I said. "Somebody who's involved in something way beyond her control."

"Story of my life, hun. Go on."

"See, there's this girl I know who is in trouble. I want to get her out of it because I'm afraid of what could happen to her. She's surrounded by some very bad people."

Hayley squinted. "She's your girlfriend, right?"

"No."

"Wife?"

"No," I said. "It's a long story. I know her through a friend of a friend. The thing is, she told me about her—mentor—someone she loves deeply who she hasn't seen in a long time. I'm thinking if I can get in touch with that mentor and somehow get them together I can help her."

She rolled her eyes and smiled, leaning down on the bar. The way she genuinely listened to me and dove into my problem made me like her a whole lot more.

"Honey," she said, "first of all, you can't help anyone if

they ain't willing to help themselves. Everyone digs their own graves and they jump right on in. I say move on."

"Yes," I said, "I've considered moving on. But let's just say for a moment that you, Hayley, are the mentor and you don't know how much trouble your former student is in. Wouldn't you want to know so you could help?"

She thought about that. "Yeah, I guess I would, but coming from a stranger it would be weird."

"Exactly. I can't just jump into the mentor's life and say 'Do you remember So-and-So? She's in trouble.' That would be weird."

"Definitely weird."

"So how would you go about doing that?"

She frowned, thinking. "Hm, I don't know. Let me work on that." She went off and served some more customers.

The boys next to me began to get louder. Two of them shot dirty glances my way. Nobody else in the bar wore longish hair nor a sport coat. I looked at the guy over in the corner. He was keeping an eye on the loud boys, but he had become fixated on me. He stared at me like a statue with no expression.

I finished my beer. A few minutes later, Hayley returned and poured another one without asking.

"Hun," she said, "I thought it over. You need to forget this girl. It's going to be super-weird for you to get involved."

"Okay," I said, "but I have a picture of her with her mentor. They were kids. Her mentor is actually her older sister. Mind if I show you?"

"Sure," she said with a twitch in her eye.

I dropped the 'HAPPY BIRTHDAY, TIFFANY!' picture on the bar. Hayley picked it up and looked at it.

Her face dropped. She shuddered.

"I'm trying to help Tiffany," I said. "She loves her older sister and she's in trouble."

Hayley folded her arms and backed up a little. I could feel her withdrawing into herself.

"Are you a cop?" she said.

"No," I said. "I'm a friend of Tiffany's. She's in trouble. She needs your help."

Hayley folded her arms and shook her head. I watched the raw fear as it enveloped her. The walls slammed down.

"I can't help you," she said, trembling. "Look, I got to get back to work."

I sat some more and sipped my beer, watching her from the corner of my eye. She threw quick glances over at me. She was frightened. I didn't mean to come across as frightening. My instinct told me that it wasn't me she was frightened of.

Whatever the hold is on this family, it's strong. I heard someone yell at her for bringing the wrong order. Then she disappeared into the kitchen and was gone for a while.

I glanced over at the corner. The guy in the black cowboy hat with the white beard was gone.

Hayley didn't return. Another girl took over her end of the bar. Nobody offered to refill my drink. It's just not my day, is it?

I took out a pen and wrote my phone number on the back of the picture along with a note:

Bug-boo needs her Bumble. Please help.

I folded two twenty-dollar bills under it, reached over and left it on the underbar station next to the taps facing up.

The guy in the black cowboy hat with the white beard reappeared, walking straight through the group of loud boys like they weren't even there. He stopped directly to my right. The position of his hands and the way he stood with his weight centered and his shoulders loose only confirmed my suspicion that he was a pro. I could also tell he knew I was a pro.

"I'm sorry, sir," he said. "I've had a request for you to leave the premises."

I get that a lot, don't I?

"No problem," I said, hands up. "I was just leaving anyway."

We walked to the door together. He pushed it open.

"Have a nice night," he said.

I nodded and walked to my car. When I backed out of the space, I noticed the man was still standing out front with his arms folded, watching me. I felt his eyes on me all the way out of Lake Heron and south to Starke, where I rented a room for the night.

38

THE SUN STREAMED in through the window of my room at the Best Western in Starke, where I sat on the bed waiting. 10:55 a.m. No call from Hayley.

The night before—while eating a ridiculously good steak sandwich from an old-school place next door called Powell's Dairy Freeze—I had bet myself Hayley would call by my 11:00 a.m. check-out time.

Looks like I'm losing the bet.

I sat and stared at Powell's and at the cars going by on Florida Highway 301. A silver Audi A5 drifted by. In the moment I saw it, I made a decision.

I got out my phone and ran an online search for 'sporting goods.' I quickly found what I was looking for.

I picked up my duffel and left a ten on the bed for the housekeeper, walked to the front desk, dropped off my key, and headed out to the rental car.

At 10:59 a.m., my phone rang. Unknown number.

"Hello, this is Titus," I said.

"Hi," said a female voice. "It's, um, Hayley from last night. From the Horseshoe."

"Hi, Hayley."

There was a long pause.

"Is Tiffany okay?" she said in a voice that had been crying.

"I don't know," I said. "That's why I came here. I need your help. I can't help her without you."

"Why? How? What's going on?"

"Where can we meet? I'll tell you all about it. Pick a place you feel safe. Anywhere you want. Bring anyone you trust."

There was a long silence. I waited, my stomach churning as I watched a man in a Guns 'n Roses T-shirt eating a sandwich at an outdoor picnic table next door.

"Meet me at Hendree's in Starke," she said. "But I won't be able to get there until after three. I'm working the morning shift at the dollar store across the street. I won't have long because I'm at the Horseshoe again tonight."

"Two jobs back-to-back," I said. "You must be tired."

"I have no choice. I have a baby and my husband—well—I have no choice."

"Okay. What time?"

"Three-fifteen?"

"I'll be there."

I thought about leaving, but the guy in the Guns 'n Roses T-shirt changed my mind. I walked next door to Powell's Dairy Freeze for another steak sandwich. Because it's too delicious for words.

Then, I spent the afternoon driving around Starke, familiarizing myself with the general layout—especially the area around Hendree's and the surrounding streets. Behind Hendree's was a stretch of woods that went back to a side-street with small cinderblock houses. My plan took shape.

Next, I drove to the Walmart Supercenter, made some purchases, and donned what I bought in a stall in the men's room.

At 2:00 p.m., I pulled into Hendree's and drove around the building, scanning for security cameras. I saw only one. There was nobody at the Drive-Thru. Wearing dark sunglasses and a camouflage head wrap, I stopped the car, dove out, and smashed the security camera with the same crowbar that almost crushed my skull a few nights ago. Then, I got back in the car, pulled up to the dumpster out back, and tossed my duffel bag in. Then, I left and drove around Starke for another hour.

At 3:00 p.m., I pulled into Hendree's again and parked on the side. I removed the camouflage head wrap and sunglasses and walked inside. I ordered a coffee from a tall pretty black girl and sat in the front window.

Hendree's was your typical fast-food chain with a location in almost every town from Florida to Texas. Big windows looked out on Florida Highway 301. I remembered how excited I used to be as a kid in Georgia when my mom took us to Hendree's for a burger and a shake. I wasn't excited today.

At 3:11 p.m., a silver Audi A5 glided past.

At 3:15 p.m., a Starke police cruiser pulled into the lot. A young pudgy blond cop in dark sunglasses got out. The tall pretty black girl went outside and talked to him, pointing at the area of the smashed security camera. They drifted out of sight.

I sipped some coffee.

At 3:19 p.m., a battered red Honda Civic pulled in and parked next to my Toyota. Hayley climbed out and walked inside.

She sat down in front of me with eyes swollen from crying.

39

"SO YOU'RE A private eye," Hayley said. "Like on those old TV shows."

"Sort of," I said. "Well, no—not officially. And nothing like the old TV shows. I'm a cop—well, I used to be. Detective, that is. I was hired by a rich lady to find her daughter Allie Hayes. I found Allie Hayes—or who I thought was Allie Hayes, anyway. The pictures seem to indicate she may be your sister Tiffany. She is running from the rich lady. She says the rich lady tried to kill her. She's gone from boyfriend to boyfriend and even tried to get me to move to L.A. with her."

"Sounds like Tiff." Hayley chewed her nail and looked out the window. "Do you believe her?"

"Strangely, I do. Everyone in Miami seems to be looking for Allie—I mean, Tiffany—and they're all lying to me. If Tiffany is in danger, I'd like to get her out of danger." I took out the birth certificate. "Tiffany left this with me. It was in the safe of a dead kid named Jake Preston who was using it to blackmail

Rexford J. Hayes, the guy running for Senate."

I placed it on the table, along with the other pictures. When Hayley unfolded it and read it, she burst into tears.

Hendree's wasn't busy, but the handful of people there glanced over at us. I got up and took some napkins from the dispenser. I walked back, sat next to Hayley, handed them to her, and placed my arm around her. She leaned into my shoulder sobbing as she looked at the pictures.

We sat there in the window for several minutes. I watched steady streams of tourists headed south to paradise. The pudgy young cop left and the tall pretty black girl resumed her duties behind the counter. The silver Audi drifted past again. Nine-minute intervals.

"I can't take it anymore," Hayley said. "No more of this."

"No more of what?" I said.

"The lies. I miss my sister. She was all I had, and they took her away from me. I loved her. It's all my mother's fault."

"Jeannie Kirkwood?"

"Jeannie Thurlow, Jeannie Connors, Jeannie Kirkwood—whatever the fuck her name is now. She's an evil bitch whore." She stroked the picture, her finger lingering on her little sister.

"That bad, huh?"

She nodded.

"You're from New Jersey, right?" I said. "Newark."

"Not just Newark," she said. "We moved like ten times when I was a kid. Sometimes Philly. Sometimes New York. My mom went from man to man to man. Several of them were—really bad men."

Her eyes filled up again.

"Then," she said, "along came Tiffany. The sweetest baby. I thought mom would change. She married Hank Connors, the man who was supposedly Tiff's father but I don't think so. Hell, I'm not sure who *my* father was."

She sobbed some more, stroking the picture of Tiffany as a baby. I waited and hugged.

"Tiff was my world," she said. "My little Bug-boo."

"She looked up to you a lot," I said.

"I tried. But Tiff had one thing going for her that I didn't. She was smart. I mean, not just ordinary smart, but people-smart. She figured out how to manipulate early on, just like mom. Tiff got total strangers to pay for movies for us at the mall when she was eight. She'd go on the subway and pretend she was homeless and beg for money with this long sob story about mom dying of cancer. She'd come home with two hundred dollars sometimes. Nine years old. Two hundred dollars, like it was nothing. She could do accents, sound like she's from Texas or England if she wanted. She made stories up on the fly that were so good sometimes even I believed them."

I took the picture of Tiffany when she was twelve, standing with Jeannie and the man with movie-star looks in front of the Lakewood Ranch sign.

"Who's this?" I said.

"Bobby Kirkwood," she said. "My mom's third husband. I hated him. He moved us down here to Florida. He had hands that went—everywhere. He was why I ran away with Vernon."

"What happened to Tiffany?"

"One day, she just up and ran away. She was obsessed with the idea of South Beach. I was worried, but not worried. I knew Tiff could take care of herself, and she was better off away from mom and that Bobby bastard. Sure enough, three weeks later, Tiff calls me from Miami. Says she found a job that pays a lot of money."

"Then what?"

"Then things went quiet for a while, a long while. Life went on. Then, one day my mom shows up at Vernon's house and tells me Tiff died in a car crash."

"In Miami?" I said.

"No," she said, "home in Lakewood Ranch. Which is really weird, because it was never in the papers. Nobody heard of it. We had a funeral and buried her. And that was that. I was devastated. I cried for months. Then—one day, out of the blue—Tiff calls me."

"That must have been a shock."

She sobbed again for a while. I held her.

"I nearly had a heart attack," Hayley said. "Tiff says she's on someone else's phone and can't talk. She says she's alive and made a mistake, that she's getting paid a lot of money to pretend she's someone else and she thinks the woman killed her daughter, the girl she's being paid to impersonate. She said the husband is a pervert, too. Something about sex parties."

"Then what?" I said.

"Then I had a visit." She looked around, the fear enveloping her again. "Three big men in suits. A tall older woman with this awful short white hair told me that I needed to keep my mouth shut or—"

"Or what?"

"Or they'll kill me. I believed them."

"A tall woman with short white hair?"

"Yes."

I took out my phone and looked up Kelly Alves online.

"Is that her?" I said, turning the screen toward her.

Hayley looked like she saw a ghost and nodded.

"Yes," she said, "that's her."

Hayley jerked and sat up. She looked at her watch. She wiped her eyes and moved to leave.

"I have to go," she said, "I have to get to my shift at the Horseshoe I'm on till two. I don't even know why I told you all this. That woman and those men will probably show up again and kill me."

"Hayley," I said, "I have a plan—a way to free you and your sister from all this. But I need your help."

"A plan? What kind of a plan?"

"A good one. Will you help me?"

She fought back more tears, nodded, and squeezed my hand.

40

I WATCHED HAYLEY get into her car and drive away from Hendree's. I sipped my coffee and waited.

At 4:13 p.m., the silver Audi drove by again. I sat and waited and sipped some more. At 4:22 p.m., it passed again. Z was as precise as a Swiss-engineered timepiece. I was counting on it. As soon as he passed, I finished my coffee and went to the men's room.

There, I removed my shirt and pants to reveal the camouflage clothes I had bought at Walmart. I put on the head wrap and dark sunglasses again. I removed the gun belt from my jeans and secured it over the pants, which were as light as underwear. I checked my guns and ammo, holstered them, and tied my clothes into a tight ball.

Nobody in Starke seemed to notice the Army Ranger-type who walked casually out of a Hendree's in the middle of the day. I think I pulled it off. I went out the side door, past the smashed security camera and Drive-Thru toward the dumpster. There, I retrieved the duffel bag I had dropped earlier and continued on into the woods about a hundred yards.

I stuffed my clothes in the duffel and removed a tactical bag, which I attached to my belt. I got out the Remington 870 I had borrowed from Luther and loaded it with 00 shells. Next, I threw together a makeshift brush fort with dead tree branches, removed a pair of binoculars from the duffel, zipped it shut, and hid it under a pile of leaves. I looked at my phone. 4:30 p.m. I went to my chosen hiding place and focused the binoculars on the road in front of Hendree's.

At 4:31 p.m., the silver Audi drove by.

Then again at 4:40 p.m. Then every nine minutes until 5:34 p.m.

The woods were quiet. They were oddly similar to woods back home up north. Lots of oak leaves, pine needles, and underbrush. The only major difference down here was the squirrels. They're red and fearlessly approach you. Back home, they're gray and run from you.

At 5:43 p.m., the silver Audi A5 pulled into the parking lot and parked next to my rental car. I couldn't see his face through the tinted windows. He just sat there.

I was hoping he was shitting his pants about now, thinking he lost me. If he was the egotist I believed him to be, he would need to figure out what I did and how I did it.

That wouldn't be the sensible thing to do. Sensible would be to wait until Hayley walks out of The Horseshoe at two a.m., shoot her from a distance, drive back to Miami, and relocate me there.

But Z was not sensible. He was cocky. The fact he had sat out in the open at the Leucadendra Country Club watching me with a smile, as well as the slowdown on 5th Street, told me all I needed to know about him. He thought he was unbeatable. I was counting on his overinflated ego to obsess over how I got away. If I was wrong, then I'd have to get over to The Horseshoe before two a.m and somehow get Hayley out of there.

I was betting that wouldn't be necessary.

At 6:03 p.m., Z got out of his car. Unmistakably him, scraggly tousle and all. Clothes still wrinkly. He looked around and walked into Hendree's.

If I were a sniper, I could have taken him right there. I'm good, but I'm no sniper.

I pictured him inside, likely sitting in the same window seat where Hayley and I had sat, probably facing the same direction, trying to think like me. The thought of him sitting there baffled made me smile.

At 6:23 p.m., he walked out and got back in his car.

A squirrel crawled down a tree and perched on my head. His little paws dug through the head wrap like tiny needles. I jumped and jerked the shotgun. The squirrel scuttled off.

Shit.

If the barrel of the gun caught the sunlight, it may have glinted in his direction and alerted him to my hiding spot. My breathing got heavy and fast. I did my best to slow it down.

At 6:43 p.m., Z backed out of the parking spot, drove around Hendree's slowly, merged into traffic on Highway 301, and was gone.

My pulse quickened, sweat glands kicking into high gear. I took a sip of water from the bottle in my tactical bag, attempting to prevent dehydration.

At 6:52 p.m., he didn't drive by. Nor at 7:01 p.m. No more nine-minute intervals.

Where is he?

My breathing became unsteady and lightheadedness washed over me. My muscles had been locked in the same position for so long that they were beginning to twitch. I forced ten deep breaths, focusing on relaxing my body.

I tried to think like Z. He probably went back to the Best Western and looked for signs of me there. I'd bet he went to the Horseshoe to see if Hayley made it there. He'd confirm that and find a space to hide so he could shoot her when she leaves.

I should go, maybe get over there. That's what I should do, right? He's over there, right? Should I go?

Nope, I'm sticking with the plan. He's not over there, no way. He's got it out for me, and he's going nuts right now wondering where I am.

At 7:15, the daylight began its long slide. It was still an hour or so before sunset, but the shadows were longer. I watched and waited as the world slowly turned red, then purple, then blue-gray.

At 8:11 p.m., I heard something. In the past three-and-a-half hours, I had become one with the unique sounds of this little patch of woods. I knew the squirrels by their footsteps and the birds by their tweets. I had even named them. But this was a new sound.

My mouth was drier than the Sahara, but I couldn't take a sip of water now. I needed all my energy for pure focus.

I listened and waited. Listened and waited.

I heard the sound again. Over near the dumpster, I think. I trained my sights over toward its bulky mass. Something moved. Sweat poured from my fingertips around the trigger of the shotgun. I could hear my heart beating in my ears.

Then I saw a silhouette moving into view. It's him. He stepped out from the side of the dumpster.

I knew it. I knew he'd come back. He couldn't let it go, just like I thought. I know you, you bastard.

He had been looking inside the dumpster, maybe thinking I was hiding there. I had thought about it, but I liked where I was better.

He took his time, slowly pacing the parking lot. His gun was out, low and to his side, a long silver handgun. A Luger, I'd bet. He finished inspecting the parking lot and then glanced over toward my location in the woods.

My heart skipped several beats.

Steady, Titus, steady. Wait.

I could almost hear his thoughts. He's flabbergasted that I

eluded him. He's wondering if I walked through the woods and out onto the next street, which was about three hundred yards behind me. It must be tearing him up that my rental car is just sitting there.

He walked to the edge of the woods, only about fifty feet from the brush fort now. I sensed his muscles as they tensed. It was all I could do to prevent myself from shaking.

He moved in graceful slow-motion, soaking in every sound. He wasted no energy, allowing his instinct to guide him as he slithered from tree to tree in a zig-zag pattern. Something inside him knows I'm here. He's good. He knows how to move around the trees and shadows so that he's never a clear target. That's why I still need him to get closer. I had sweat completely through the camouflage clothes now, my pulse pounding in my ears. I tried to swallow, but there was nothing there.

I heard his sharp inhale as he saw the brush fort. Then, I saw the glint in his eye as he emerged from behind a tree, turned a little to his right, and fired two shots into the pile of branches and leaves.

"Wrong," I said as I stepped out from behind a different tree.

He was quick, turning his gun toward me from where I stood facing his left side ten feet away.

But he wasn't quick enough.

I fired the shotgun. His silver gun swirled into the air as his entire middle, wrinkly shirt and all, exploded in a mass of red. The shocked expression on his face said it all. He died in sheer disbelief that I had outwitted him.

His body, nearly cut in half from the brutal force of the shotgun shell at so close a range, plopped down almost silently onto the leaves. Then, everything got very quiet.

I had a sudden urge to vomit, but I swallowed it down and waited. I had no idea if anyone heard the shots. They were surely loud, but the Hendree's was as quiet as the woods.

I listened some more. Nothing changed.

Then, my knees wobbled and I fell. I couldn't hold it back this time, the bile crashing up through my throat and out onto the ground.

I began to shiver in full-body spasms. I was suddenly very cold, even though it was still a blisteringly hot summer evening in central Florida. The clothes I had been wearing were soaked through. I was breathing, but I felt like I was underwater, or like a bag was over my head even though I was out in the air.

Everything took about ten fast spins around. I felt lightheaded and recognized the sickly sensation of unconsciousness coming on. I gripped the tree hard, pressing my hand into it, concentrating on the sensation of the spindly bark digging into my skin to keep myself from passing out.

Two minutes later, my head and body were just lucid enough for me to collect my belongings and walk to my rental car. I got in and closed the door. Sitting behind the wheel of the tiny car felt like a luxurious suite, all anyone would ever need.

I was lucky. I wasn't sure if the sound of gunshots in the woods are common in Starke, but nobody seemed to have heard them. Even so, I'd better get out of here before that pudgy cop returns.

It took another five minutes for my hands to stop shaking enough to turn the key and start the engine.

41

RIGHT AFTER THE Port St. Lucie exit on the turnpike heading back to Miami, my phone rang.

I looked at it. Unknown number.

"Hello," I said, "this is Titus."

"Where the fuck is it?" said a female voice I recognized.

"Hi, Tiffany."

"What did you do with my fucking duffel bag, asshole?"

"I have it. It's safe, no worries."

"I bet it's fucking safe, dickhead. Where the fuck is it? I need it—now!"

I laughed.

"So," I said, "let me get this straight. You hide two million one hundred seventy-five thousand dollars in my apartment—yes, I counted it—and *you* are mad at *me* because I found it? Is that what I'm hearing, Tiffany?"

"You weren't supposed to fucking find it!" she said. "You said you never look down there."

"I don't. But I did."

"You're such a fucking asshole! That's my fucking money. Hey wait. Whoa. Fucking whoa. Why did you call me Tiffany?"

"That's your name, isn't it?"

There was a long pause.

"That's my show name," she said. "Mistress Tiffany. Why are you calling me by my show name?"

"Because it's your real name," I said. "Tiffany Connors from Newark, New Jersey, daughter of Jeannie Connors, sister of Hayley Shores."

The amber highway lights flickered by for a good long time. The baby woke and began to cry.

"Fuck you!" said the girl I knew as Allie Hayes, but I heard tears behind it. I pictured her with some confused lackey kid she had bamboozled into taking her to L.A., both of them standing right now in my dinky little apartment.

"Tiffany," I said, "please—please let me help you The only way I can help you is if you let me. We need to develop some trust. I took this case to find you. I found you. I found the real you. I also found the real Allie, but I was six years too late to save her. It's time for all of us—including me—to become real and fix things. It can all be fixed. We can make this right for all of us."

"Fuck you!" she said again. But she didn't hang up.

"Tiffany," I said, "there's someone here who wants to say hello."

I handed the phone to Hayley, who was leaning between the front and back seats to feed the baby in the car seat. With a mother's skill, she took the phone with one hand while keeping the bottle in the baby's mouth with the other.

She glanced at me for a brief moment with eyes full of tears.

"Tiff?" she said. "It's Hayley. Yeah, it's really me. Yeah, I'm with Titus. Sorry, I'm feeding the baby. Yeah, I had a baby girl. You have a niece, Tiff. You need to see her. Her name is Tiffany just like yours, and she's beautiful." Her voice cracked. "Tiff, it's okay. Titus is helping us. He's a good man. You need to listen to him. He has a plan. A good plan."

I smiled over at Hayley, tears in my own eyes as the faint glow of Miami grew brighter on the horizon.

42

REXFORD J. HAYES' office on the 29th floor of an obscene glass skyscraper in downtown Miami wasn't quite as spacious as the deck of an aircraft carrier. Floor-to-ceiling windows presented a spectacular view of Brickell Key, the port, South Beach, and the Atlantic. Opposite the windows, a wood-paneled wall was covered with pictures of Rex cutting ribbons in front of construction projects, Rex shaking hands with former Presidents, and Rex smiling broadly on the covers of business magazines. Romanesque furniture sat on a round stately blue-and-gold rug with a spread-winged bald eagle carrying an American flag that matched a bronze sculpture of the same on the wall behind the desk.

The desk was the size of Delaware. Each leg wore the head of a dour-looking carved lion. There were three leather-clad Dante chairs on either side. Rex's was a high-backed leather CEO special, pushed over to accommodate the two ladies who sat on his left.

Pam Hayes wore a peach pantsuit, Rex a blue blazer with gold cufflinks and a Delta Kappa Epsilon crest over a white shirt and spotted red ascot. All he needed was a white captain's hat and pipe to be on the cover of *GQ*, circa 1957. A tall thin woman sat between Rex and Pam. Short white hair, purple suit, no jewelry. She was sixty or so with a long rectangular face under rimless square glasses. Her jaw looked like it had been added to her face with sutures and wires as an afterthought. A leather-bound journal lay open in front of her on the desk. Next to it were several official-looking documents and a voice recorder with a steady orange light. She smiled coldly, her eyes like ice cubes.

Pam Hayes' eyes flared at the sight of Tiffany and Hayley as they walked in with their arms around each other.

"Titus, this is Kelly Alves," said Rex. The tall thin woman didn't stand up nor offer her hand.

I nodded. She nodded.

"Sit, please," said Rex.

The three of us sat across from the three of them.

"So you're the unlicensed amateur detective and disgraced former police officer who spent ten months at a maximum security correctional facility," said Kelly Alves.

"Medium security," I said. "Not that it was pleasant. Oh, and nice to meet you, too."

"Titus," said Rex Hayes with the Southern good-ol'-boy charm turned up to high, "I hope you don't mind but Kelly here is going to represent the Hayes family today."

"Smart," I said, giving him a thumbs-up.

"Titus," said Kelly Alves with a cold competence, "I represent Mr. and Mrs. Hayes on behalf of my firm Kelly Alves & Associates. We are a crisis mitigation firm located in Washington, D.C. We are here today to discuss the ramifications of, as well as the immediate termination of your continued and troubling intrusion into the lives of Mr. and Mrs. Hayes, which has occasioned a considerable traumatizing effect on their personal well-being."

Kelly Alves had the air of a prosecutor in a large courtroom requiring a heady amount of voice projection. Her voice sounded like two strips of sandpaper rubbing together, her words meticulous and succinct with long pauses and full glottal stops at the end of every sentence. I bet she sees periods and commas in her head as she speaks.

"Um," I said, scratching my head, "I thought *I* was the one who requested this meeting."

"As required by the law of the State of Florida," she continued, ignoring me, "I am officially informing you that this meeting is being recorded."

"Digital or analog?" I said.

"Excuse me?" she said.

"Is the recording digital or analog? I prefer analog myself. It's got that warm inviting sound, like when the record player needle makes that beautiful crackling noise right before the soft soulful piano kicks in and Sam Cooke sings 'Bring It On Home to Me.'"

Kelly Alves removed her glasses in slow-motion, a move calculated to make lesser foes quake with fear. Her facial expression remained unchanged. She made a nodding jerk-like movement and said:

"I've been warned that you think you're funny, Titus, but you won't be laughing soon."

"Ms. Alves," I said, "I represent Tiffany Connors and Hayley Shores, who sit here with me."

Ignoring me, she flipped one of the papers over across the desk to face me. I didn't look at it, keeping my gaze locked on the ice cubes.

"This," she said, "is a court order for you to discontinue your offensive and brazen intrusion into the business and personal matters of Mr. and Mrs. Hayes. You are hereby and forthwith ordered to cease and desist." She flipped over another paper. "This is a Federal restraining order requiring you to maintain a distance of at least one mile from Mr. and Mrs. Hayes pursuant to this meeting."

"She's a pistol," I said to Rex with a wink.

He remained perfectly still.

"This document," she said a decibel louder as she flipped it over, "is an instigation of inquiry and warrant for your arrest for interfering with a Federal investigation, harassment of a United States candidate for office, and trespassing on private property. There are agents on the premises who will be taking you into custody pending further inspection and inquiry."

"Do you see periods in your head when you speak?" I said. "Your glottal stops are amazing. Shakespearean, even. You'd make a great Lady Macbeth."

She smiled, unfazed. Two men in dark suits, FBI badges clipped to their lapels, appeared on either side of me. I smiled at them. Neither smiled back.

"Okay," I said and sat up straight, "enough of this gay banter. Hayley Shores, is that the woman who threatened you?"

"Uh-huh," said Hayley, her stare fixated on Kelly Alves.

"Hayley, please say yes or no for the lovely lady's recording device."

"Yes, that's her. That's the bitch who ruined our lives."

Kelly Alves turned her attention to Hayley as if she had just beamed down from outer space.

"I'm sorry, have we met?" said Kelly Alves.

"That's her," said Hayley. "Are you all listening? She came to my home and said I'd be killed unless I kept my mouth shut."

Kelly Alves shut the recorder off and closed the book in front of her.

"I believe we are done here," she said.

"Oh, Kelly-Kelly-Kelly," I said. "I think not. In fact, we've only just begun."

"You're not hosting this meeting, Titus. *I* am, and I declare it over."

"This meeting isn't over until the murderer of Allie Hayes is arrested."

"Now you're being ridiculous, Titus. Allie Hayes is sitting right next to you."

"Oh, Kelly-Kelly-Kelly, you know better than that. Allie Hayes was killed by her mother six years ago. She had suffered sexual abuse at the hands of her father for years and threatened to tell."

"Titus!" said Pam Hayes, leaping to her feet, her limbs shaking.

"It's true, Pam," I said, counting on this trigger-reaction. "Rex sexually abused Allie and you killed her so it wouldn't get out. Y'all are so goddamned rich that you got Kelly Alves here to cover everything up neatly for you. Kelly Alves specializes in fixing things for her political clients."

"That is not true, Titus. Not true at all!"

"Pam," said Kelly Alves, tugging on Pam's sleeve. "Sit, please. He has nothing."

Pam sat, near-foaming as she launched eye-daggers at me.

"Six years ago," I said, "right after the murder of Allie Hayes by her mother, and while Rex was in the middle of a nasty campaign for the Senate, Kelly Alves found an almost exact lookalike to replace the dead girl. Tiffany Connors, then thirteen-years old, had run away from her home in Lakewood Ranch and was at a SoBe nightclub trying to look twenty-one and pulling it off easily. Tiffany Connors learned early on she had to provide for herself, so she's always been very clever. She had looked for ways to make a living and lucked into a lucrative one when approached to replace the murdered daughter of an up-and-coming Senator."

"I'm leaving," said Kelly Alves, standing up and gathering her papers and binder into a leather briefcase. "Agents, arrest him and remove his two cohorts from the premises."

The FBI men didn't move.

"Now!" she said, slamming the briefcase shut. But nobody moved.

"Kelly-Kelly-Kelly," I said, slower this time, shaking my head.

She picked up the briefcase and walked around Pam toward the exit, but the two FBI agents stepped in front of her.

"What is this?" she said. Her face looked like it was about to crack. "Arrest him!"

"Not yet," said Clark Erwin as he stepped into the room. He stood to my right directly in front of Kelly Alves and nodded at me. I nodded back. "I'd like to hear what Titus has to say."

43

"WHO THE HELL are you?" said Kelly Alves.

Clark Erwin was my age. We went to Somerville High School together in ninth and tenth grades before I moved to Cambridge. I once bullied a peanut butter and jelly sandwich from him in the school cafeteria, but we became friends anyway. I hadn't seen him since the day I punched him in the face two years ago, but he looked good. Nice FBI suit, black hair in a crew cut with only a few flecks of gray, square Irish face that always needed a shave, broad shoulders, maybe ten pounds heavier than before.

"Clark Erwin," he said holding up his FBI badge. "Senior Special Agent, Criminal Investigative Division. Sit down please, Miss Alves."

"I will not," Kelly Alves said. "I'm leaving. This is ridiculous."

One agent placed an arm up. She slapped it but he didn't flinch.

"Sit down please, Miss Alves," said Clark Erwin.

Pam Hayes burst into tears as Kelly Alves resumed her seat at the desk. Rex remained motionless, as if he had been whittled from stone centuries before.

"Please do continue, Titus," said Clark Erwin. "Oh, and by the way, Miss Alves, this meeting is still being recorded—just for the record."

"I didn't authorize another recording device," she said. "It's against the law."

"Actually, by agreeing to be recorded on your device you gave your consent to be recorded by another. Not that any of that matters. We are the FBI, you know. We invented recording. Go on, Titus."

"You did well, Kelly," I said. "Amazingly well. It was ballsy. You cleaned everything up, found a girl who looked exactly like Allie Hayes, or close anyway—enough so the press wouldn't ask questions. Allie Hayes was buried as Tiffany Connors in a quiet little grave in Lakewood Ranch. Tiffany was said to have died in a car crash. Rex and Pam moved the new Allie to a different school surrounded by different friends. The new Allie, who I will refer to from this point forward as Tiffany Connors, didn't get quite the honor roll grades that the original one did and ended up in public high school, which worked because nobody there had ever seen her before. One thing they had going for the scam was that Tiffany Connors was smart. Not book-smart, but street-smart. The book-smart part can always be faked by tutors and professional test-takers and research paper writers. Just ask the Kennedys. But Tiffany knew how to con, how to play a part, and how to sucker a mark from growing up on the streets of Newark, Philadelphia, and New York City. One person wasn't fooled, though. Allie's grandmother Constance Elliott, Pam's mother, knew Allie had changed somehow—she wasn't quite herself—which is why Rex and Pam stopped visiting the elderly lady in Connecticut. Meanwhile, Tiffany's unstable mother Jeannie Connors received a steady stream of payments to keep her daughter's identity secret. Hayley Shores, Tiffany's older half-sister, was threatened in person by Kelly Alves and promised a painful death if she ever breathed a word. Hayley, not quite as street-smart as her younger sister—," I leaned over and patted Hayley's hand, "—and that's a good thing—clammed up and led her life. Enter Tom Langston, private investigator. He had been hired four years ago by Pam Hayes to find Tiffany the first time she ran out. Tiffany couldn't keep up the façade of cocktail parties, tennis, golf, and general marble-mouthery. By this time, Tiffany was fifteen and met a boy named Jake Preston. They had similar backgrounds coming from crazy rich parents and they hit it off. They did drugs, went clubbing in South Beach, and fell in love—sort of. With the help of Tom Langston, Rex and Pam were able to locate Tiffany and convince her to return home. Everything seemed to resume its proper course to Hunky-Dory Land, disaster averted. Although not for poor Tom Langston, who two years later put the pieces together brilliantly. He almost made it. It was a piece of the puzzle that kept him awake nights. 'Why,' he said into his voice recorder in the form of a journal, 'why were there large payments from a company named Foundation Investments LLC to Jeannie Connors in Lakewood Ranch?' Tom Langston had a natural curiosity, the kind of curiosity that gets people killed. Someday, the same curiosity is going to catch up with me, but not today. Tom Langston found the answer. Foundation Investments LLC is a shell company. You can't find the owner no matter how hard you try, but Rexford J. Hayes had written a check to Tom Langston from Foundation Investments LLC. Tom being Tom, he looked it up. Nobody knows exactly how he pieced it together nor how he showed his hand, but Kelly Alves decided he needed to be killed—likely by a professional killer who goes by the name of Z, who does occasional work for Miss Alves. Or used to, anyway."

Kelly Alves laughed. "This is ridiculous," she said. "Me? Hire a professional killer?"

"Oh, yes indeed," I said. "You, Ms. Alves, had Tom Langston killed, probably after a panicked phone call from Rex. Phone records indicate a call from Gables Estates to you three days before Tom Langston's body was found."

"What? That's ridiculous. How do you know this?"

Sofia walked in and placed a document on the desk in front of all of us. I felt a happy jolt to the room's cold air like the entire brightness control of the world was just turned up a few notches.

"Miss Alves," I said, "I'd like to introduce Detective-Sergeant Sofia DeJesus-Montero of the Miami-Dade Organized Crime Section. Detective-Sergeant DeJesus-Montero had been recently piecing the murders of Jake Preston and Eddie Corrado together. Based on a check written to me by Rex to bribe me to stay silent, Detective-Sergeant DeJesus-Montero reopened the investigation into Tom Langston's death in coordination with the Coral Gables Police Department. There, buried beneath a pile of papers in an evidence box was Tom's voice recorder, not unlike yours with its little orange light. On it were his detailed thoughts about the fate of Allie Hayes."

Pam Hayes fell into another fit of tears, burying her face in her hands.

"This is bullshit, Titus," said Rex.

"How can *you* say that?" said Tiffany to Rex. "*You*, of all people, you sick fuck! How can you fucking say that?"

"Allie," said Rex.

"Don't call me that! I'm Tiffany. I'm not playing your stupid fucking game anymore."

"Then Tiffany," I said, "ran off again just recently. She and Jake had developed a scheme to free her permanently so she could partake in, uh—activities—that she enjoys. Tiffany and Jake somehow got their hands on Tiffany's birth certificate and some photos of her growing up, photos that included her half-sister Hayley. Tiffany and Jake used these to blackmail Rex to pay for a house where they lived together. Rex kept this a secret from his wife Pam, postponing the explanation until he figured something out. Rex is not the best communicator when it comes to anything besides writing big checks from shell companies. When Pam got wind of Rex's deception, she hired me to find out where Tiffany and Jake Preston were living."

"Titus," said Pam Hayes, "I have no idea what you are talking about. I only hired you to find out that my daughter was safe."

"Actually no, Pam, that's not why you hired me. You wanted me to find Tiffany's location so you could go kill her. And Jake Preston."

"That's a lie!" said Rex. "I won't have you slandering my wife like that, Titus."

"See," I said, "Tiffany and Jake Preston weren't lovers in the traditional sense this time around, more like business partners. Tiffany provided Jake with the ammo to blackmail her father into paying for their house, where they lived together but each pretty much went their own separate ways. Tiffany did her, uh—performance art—while Jake spent his time penetrating every willing female orifice in South Beach. Everybody was happy, but Pam was bearing down on Tiffany—hiring thugs like me to find her so Pam could kill her. Rex got wind that Pam had hired me. He got nervous and called Kelly Alves who sent Z, the aforementioned professional killer. Meanwhile, Tiffany had her claws into Eddie Corrado, a young man who she met through Jake Preston. Eddie had, uh—saved up—some money. Tiffany saw this as her 'Escape to L.A.' fund. Somehow, Pam finds where they were living, goes there, and kills Jake. Bang. One .22 round to the left eye. Tiffany comes by, finds Jake dead, gets her birth certificate and photographs out of his safe, stuffs them in a green duffel bag with red trim, and calls Eddie Corrado. Eddie arranges a cleanup of sorts, but not a very good one. Jake Preston's body was found rather quickly by the Miami-Dade police department underneath the 41st Street Bridge. Tiffany goes to Eddie's apartment, where she has been living. She convinces Eddie now is the time to run with her, get out of Miami, head to L.A. and start a new life. She was manipulating Eddie because he was supposedly a street thug and could protect her, although Eddie turned out to be not a very good protector. Someone had located Eddie Corrado's address for Pam Hayes. Tiffany and Eddie were packing to run, but were interrupted by Pam's little gun. Bang. Another .22 round into another left eye, Eddie's this time."

"Titus," said Rex. "Let me get this clear. You are accusing my wife of killing not just one—but *two* people?"

"Yes. Jake Preston and Eddie Corrado were both shot up close with a .22-caliber handgun. Pam Hayes knew Tiffany had a .22. That's why she used one to kill Jake Preston to make it look like Tiffany killed both Jake and Eddie. To make this work, though, she was going to need to replace Tiffany's gun with the one she had used. She shows up at Eddie's, but Tiffany hides. Pam Hayes shoots Eddie, who in his final moments, gives his life for the girl he loves. Pam Hayes can now frame Tiffany for the murders of both Jake and Eddie, but she really wants it to be a posthumous frame. She wants to kill Tiffany herself, knowing she can work out with Kelly Alves how to spin and sell it so that the grieving parents who 'lost their daughter to the drug trade fueled by the opioid crisis'—or some-such media bullshit—boosts Rex Hayes' chances at the polls. But Tiffany escapes and runs to me. She spends the night and secretly hides her birth certificate and pictures in my apartment where I have a very secure hiding space. At the time, I still didn't know about her true identity. She needed a new bodyguard, so she tried to convince me to move to L.A. with her, but I said no, let's talk to the police. She gets pissed, realizing she can't con me so she calls Steve, another boy from her manipulation roster—one of many—and hides out at his place, fully intending to return to my apartment to retrieve her items. She didn't count on my finding them, though. Or maybe deep down she wanted me to find them. Maybe that's why she left them with me. Maybe it was a cry for help. Either way, the photos and birth certificate led me to Tiffany's real mother Jeannie Connors, her real sister Hayley, and her real identity."

Kelly Ayes looked like she had swallowed a chipmunk. Then, she slowly recovered and sat up with folded hands.

"Very well done," she said. "Brilliant story. You should write fiction, Titus. But you can't prove any of it."

"Oh, Kelly-Kelly-Kelly," I said. "That's how you're going to play this? Seriously? Because all we need is the gun. Clark Erwin here has already uncovered the paper trail of money from Foundation Investments LLC to Jeannie Connors. We could even go further. We could exhume Allie Hayes' body."

I looked at Rex and saw something I didn't expect. He was crying. Tears streamed down his face.

"I loved Allie," he said. "I didn't abuse her. I didn't kill her. I loved my little girl so much."

"Is that right, Pam?" I said.

Pam Hayes shook like she was possessed by a demon. Then, she regained control and her eyes filled with tears. She opened her purse, and removed a tissue.

"Yes," Pam Hayes said, "It's true. Rex didn't abuse Allie. He abused *this* trollop here, that's for sure. Although the slut started it. But Rex didn't kill Allie. I did. She would not obey me. She would not attend fundraising events. She was"—Pam made a noise like a dying animal—"pregnant with the child of some strange boy with long hair. I couldn't help it. I hit her. She fell and struck her head. And she was dead. I didn't mean to kill her, I swear. I'm sorry, Rex. I ruined everything for you. But you couldn't keep your hands off *this* tramp, could you? You and your sex parties with those girls at that awful man's house. You ruined it *this* time, not me."

I nodded at Sofia. Clark threw me a faint smile.

Pam Hayes wiped her eyes again, tucked the tissue in her purse, and removed a small revolver. She pointed it at Rex's left eye and shot. A gush of blood poured out from his face and he slumped over, his head smacking the big table with a sickening thud.

Next, she turned the gun toward Tiffany and shouted, "You little whore!"

Which were the last words Pam Hayes ever spoke. The two FBI agents both shot Pam Hayes simultaneously. Her suit exploded in red, splattering blood all over the desk and all over us. Hayley and Tiffany screamed and held each other with their heads down.

Sofia and I looked at each other.

"Shit," we both said at the same time.

44

CLARK ERWIN AND I sat facing each other at a bland desk in a bland office inside FBI Headquarters in Miramar, a ridiculous complex of glass buildings shoved together at odd angles It looked like it belonged on the planet Krypton. I had just finished a nauseating four hours with three separate agents who were as thrilled to interrogate me as I was to be interrogated. I told them all I knew, minus the bit about Tommy Nero's money. I felt like a wet rag wrung dry.

"Are you okay?" Clark Erwin said.

"Yeah," I said, glancing down at the blood stains on my shirt and pants. "You just never get used to it."

"No, you don't. So did you know it was Pam and not Rex?" said Clark.

"Rex was always good for it," I said. "I smelled sleaze from him from the start. But my gut told me Pam did Jake and Eddie. The only way to find out was to do what I did and level the abuse accusation at Rex. She freaked when I accused him of it before."

"It worked."

"Yeah, but who benefits? Tiffany and Hayley are scarred for life now. They shouldn't have been there, shouldn't have seen that. Nobody should see that."

"Christ, Titus. Nobody should ever see bad shit, but bad shit happens every day all over this world. None of us thought Pam Hayes was going to pull a gun."

"We can tell ourselves that all day long, but Tiffany and Hayley are going to be paying the price for years."

"They were going to be paying the price anyway," Clark said. "They drew a shitty straw being born to Jeannie Connors. If you want to put the blame on someone, put the blame on her."

"I guess," I said and sighed.

"Your gut was spot on about Rex Hayes. Foundation Investments LLC shows up in some skanky paperwork."

"Where's Kelly Alves?"

Clark laughed. "Fun gal, ain't she? She's in the hold. We've got enough to send her away for life, but she'll likely call in some favors, do two years at a country club prison, and get disbarred. I'm betting she'll be back in D.C. in four years at a lobbying firm with an advisory title."

I looked out the window at the vast parking lot full of black SUVs.

"New topic," I said. "How did you know I was in Miami?"

Clark laughed again, a tad too merrily.

"I, uh, had a tracer on you," he said. "When your ID was pulled up by a Miami-Dade patrol officer who pulled you over for a broken taillight, the system flagged me."

I smiled. "That was Sofia."

"No way. The same chick who was with us in there?"

"Yeah."

"What was she doing on uniform patrol?"

"Doing too good of a job."

Clark tilted his head and squinted. Then, he grinned. "You got something going on with her, don't you?"

"Naw," I said.

"Yes you do. You can't fool me. Good. I'm glad. It's been long enough. I know how much you loved Ariel, but it's time."

For a moment, I was back in the cold mountains, Ariel's red hair across my face. I swear I could smell her in this nondescript dull room years and miles away.

I shook my head to snap myself out of it.

"So," I said, "you've had one of your guys following me around in a black SUV, huh?"

"Yeah right," Clark said, "like the FBI can afford to follow you around." He paused and his face dropped. "Oh, you're serious. What black SUV?"

"Cut the shit, Clarkie."

"No shit, Titus. I'm serious. We haven't been tailing you. Why would we?"

My heart skipped a beat.

"The text warning me about Z?" I said. "That was you, right?"

Clark leaned forward.

"No," he said, "that wasn't me, either. I saw that in the transcript from your interview with Donegan. That's weird, huh?"

"Don't fuck with me, Clarkie."

"Hey, ease up. I'm not fucking with you. Nobody from the Bureau texted you, God's honest truth."

I stared out the window again, a sick feeling starting up in my stomach. The world realigned as the answer came to me. I broke out into a sweat.

"You sure you're all right?" Clark said.

"Yeah," I said, not believing myself. "Come to think of it, how did I get involved in all this? Why did you tell Pam Hayes who I was, where I worked, and certain bullshit characteristics about me?"

Clark Erwin blushed. "Look, Titus, I, uh, know you had some problems transitioning back out and I just thought I might want to, uh, I don't know—help. She called me up and asked me to run a trace on Allie's credit cards. I didn't want anything to do with it. I don't like Pam Hayes. Never did. So I sent her to you."

"To give me something to do?"

"There was that, you could say. But I knew Pam was a rotten egg. I knew it the first time around when I worked Allie Hayes' first disappearance six years ago. The real one. The story they shot me about her running off with some hooligans was bogus. Suddenly everything was ship-shape and they didn't need me anymore. Allie was magically home—replaced by Tiffany—and I was assigned a different case. I knew it was bullshit somehow, but I couldn't prove it and I had everybody working against me here. I also knew that if anyone could find anything and not let go of it like a pit bull, it was you. Hey, I got a question. How did you get Old Lady Elliott to talk to you?"

"Pam's mother?" I chuckled, brushed my face with my hand, and glanced down at the gray wall-to-wall carpet. "I, uh, pretended I was someone else."

Clark Erwin sat up, his face deadly serious. "Don't say another word. There are some things I should not know."

We laughed again.

"Speaking of things I shouldn't know," he said, opening a folder from a stack to his right to read from it, "the body of a fifty-two year old man from Belarus identified as Zinoviy Belenko was found in Starke in the woods behind a Hendree's—or what was left of it, anyway. Cut in half by a shotgun."

"Never heard of him," I said with a shrug.

"Well, that's that then."

"If you say so."

He smiled, closed the folder, and returned it to the stack.

"You know," he said with a fond stare, "all these years and you haven't changed."

"Neither have you."

There was a long pause, the memories flashing before us as two old friends gazed at each other.

"Have you seen him?" Clark Erwin said.

"Who?" I said.

"You know who."

The sudden craving for a cigarette hit me hard.

"No," I said. "I was on my way, but got sidetracked."

"You should talk to him," he said. "You both live in the same town now."

"Not for long."

"What's that mean?"

"I'm leaving."

"Going back home?"

"No," I said as I stood up. "Someplace else. Not sure where. When I get there, I'll be sure to get pulled over right away so your computer dings."

We shook hands. I opened the door, but turned back.

"Clarkie," I said.

"Yeah?" he said.

"What brought you over to the good side?"

"I don't know, Titus. All I know is the day you punched me in the face, you impressed the hell out of me. I didn't realize it right away. It took some time, but the fact you were willing to stand up for what was right while I went along with everything. It made me realize you were really one of the good ones. And I was—uh—sick of not being one of the good ones."

"Bullshit. You were always the goody-two-shoes. I was always the troublemaker."

"Yeah, but in the end, who went to jail for all the right reasons?"

"True," I said. "but who helped get me out behind-the-scenes for all the right reasons?"

"True," he said.

We looked at each other for a long beat, the years too much to take now.

"My jaw still hurts, you know," he said.

"Aspirin," I said.

"And I still haven't forgotten about the peanut butter and jelly sandwich."

"I'll see if I can find it in my stuff and get it back to you."

We both laughed.

"Take care, Titus," he said.

"You too," I said. "Say hi to Theresa for me. And to your two kids I haven't met yet."

"You bet. Say hello to You-Know-Who for me when you see him."

"Sure."

I walked out.

45

AT GROUND LEVEL, the sea of black SUVs made the FBI parking lot resemble a Chevrolet dealership.

As I walked out, trying my damndest to push away the thought of sweet smoke pummeling its death particles into my lungs, one of the SUVs pulled in front and stopped in front of me. The window rolled down to reveal one of my favorite sights.

"Hey," said Sofia. "Come here often?"

"Hey," I said. "So you do have a sense of humor after all. I just lost a bet with myself."

She smiled, almost even laughed. "Need a lift?"

"Only to the middle of the highway. I can walk the rest of the way." I leaned on the open window with my elbows. "But this time, can you do me a favor and let me out in the fast lane? It'd be more of a challenge."

"Yeah. Sorry about that. I was having a bad day."

"Oh, *now* you're sorry. Now that I've delivered you a case on a silver platter that's going to get you a promotion to lieutenant."

"Not likely." There was a pause as we stared at each other. "Get the fuck in."

"I've been waiting for you to say that."

"Shut up."

We drove slowly to the highway—a feat of which I didn't think Sofia was capable, based on our last ride. We didn't speak again until we were on the turnpike heading south. I liked being quiet with Sofia. It felt natural, like we had grown comfortable enough with each other to enjoy silence together.

"You know," she said as we passed Hard Rock Stadium, "besides the blood and guts and all, what you did today was pretty cool."

"Oh my God, did you just compliment me? Who are you and what have you done with Sofia?"

"Shut up. I'm serious. You owned that square-faced old cunt."

"Whoa, hey. You're not supposed to say that word. Nobody is ever supposed to say that word."

"I'll arrest myself later," she said. "I just want you to know that the way everything went down was perfect."

"No," I said, "it was far from perfect."

"There was no way you could know Rex's old lady was going to do what she did."

I scratched the back of my neck. "I wish I could agree."

"Let it go."

I turned and smiled at her.

"Look at you," I said, "comforting *me*. You were about to shoot her yourself."

"Yeah, I didn't have a chance. Those Fed boys are fast."

"No shit, huh? You were pretty fucking awesome yourself, Detective Sergeant. Your timing couldn't have been more perfect. The way you strutted into that room and slammed the evidence down. Pow!"

"Why, thank you. Oh, and by the way, your two brown

Buick guys were found in an empty lot in Miami Gardens. They had been shot with a Luger. Still sitting in the Buick with the shotgun."

"Shocking. So much crime these days."

"We figure Pam hired them. They probably guarded her when she went to Eddie's. Then, Z stepped in and cleaned them. Speaking of Z, the FBI was strangely silent about what happened to him. They wouldn't tell me, but acted like they knew."

I shrugged. "Must still be out there somewhere, shooting people. Pop-pop-pop."

She glanced at me with a squint and a smile. Nobody does the squint and smile better. I smiled back with another shrug.

"Fine," she said, "don't tell me."

We passed the I-195 interchange. Our time together was diminishing. I hate when our time together diminishes.

"You are seriously something else," she said. "First, you rip up Rex's check. That was hot. Then, you promise a poor woman you'll get her daughter back and you do. Even hotter. Then, you solve this big case that got a bunch of people killed before you came along. Super-freaking-hot. Got to say, I'm impressed."

"So this is probably a good time to ask," I said with an overeager smile, "will you go to the Prom with me?"

She burst into laughter, slapped the steering wheel with her right hand, and then my thigh. My thigh twitched with joy. I turned and looked at her for a good long minute. Her smile was gleeful. Her face should have a gleeful smile on it all the time.

We were on the MacArthur passing the Museum of Science.

"So," she said with a furrowed brow, "I hear you gave your notice at Cap'n Jack's."

"Where'd you hear that?" I said.

"I have my sources."

"Who?"

She shook her head.

"Yeah," I said.

We didn't say anything else until we were in front of my building. She put the SUV in park.

"Want to come in for some cheap bourbon in a red plastic cup?" I said.

"I can't," she said, biting her lip. "I've got to finish my report. The FBI got their fill, but the Lieutenant won't be satisfied until I've crossed all the i's and dotted all the t's. Not to mention made the appointment for the obligatory shrink visit."

"Oh," I said, my hand on the door handle. "Well, thanks for the ride."

"Wait," she said. "Don't get out yet. I need to ask you something."

She took a deep breath and sat facing me, her hands clasped tight between her thighs. My heart nearly stopped.

"Yes?" I said.

"Where are you going?" she said.

"Going?"

"You're going. I can tell."

I brushed my chin with my hand and looked out the window at the sea grape tree. Just above it, the door to the second floor apartment had been boarded up.

"It's just time," I said. "I can't do Hamlet here for much longer. Somebody may think I'm a professional actor. Couldn't have that."

She nodded. "I've got something to say."

"Okay."

Another long pause. She scowled, staring directly ahead, as she struggled to say whatever it was she was trying to say. Another near heart-stoppage enveloped me.

"Are you going to say it," I said, "or are we going to grow old here?"

"I have issues," she blurted out. "I lost someone. Someone very close to me."

"Me too."

"I'm not over it. But, that doesn't mean that I don't know

I'm still alive and need to go on."

"What was his name?"

She inhaled deeply and sighed. "Rick."

"What happened?"

"I don't want to talk about it."

I nodded.

"But," she said, "I—uh, well—I appreciate your being there that night. You stopped me from doing something stupid."

"Whoa," I said. "Wait. I thought you stopped me from doing something stupid."

"I did," she said. "But so did you. You just didn't know it until right now. That man at the Betsy Hotel that I had you help me identify—I was going to give him some information that would have made him do something very bad, not to mention very illegal. But I didn't. Because of you."

"We saved each other."

"Maybe. I also wanted to say that if you wanted to stay in Miami—that wouldn't be so bad. Maybe set yourself up as something."

"Like what?" I said. "Professional face-buster?" The hint of a smile appeared at the corner of her mouth. "Or maybe something more elegant like Thuggery, Inc.?"

She laughed. "Seriously, I could help you get licensed as a private investigator."

I chuckled and rolled my eyes.

"I'm serious!" she said and slapped my thigh again. "You could solve crimes on the side."

"Your crimes? So you can gain accolades in Doral while I do all your dirty work?"

She hit me in the shoulder. She can hit me in the shoulder anytime.

"Shut up," she said with a giggle.

"You'd like that, wouldn't you?" I said. "Me all stamped, approved, all that B.S. When are you going to figure out I'm not a stamped nor approved guy? I don't work well with authority."

"But seriously—"

She touched my hand. We both felt it. That same magnetic field again. Our eyes met and we stayed like that for a few heartbeats.

"It wouldn't work," I said, pulling back my hand. "Like you said, you have issues, I have issues."

She sat up, shoulders squared, face deadly serious.

"You're not going back up there to West Lido Drive, are you?" she said.

I twitched.

"I—uh—" I said.

"Get out," she said, sudden venom in her voice.

"Hey!" I said as she leaned across me and threw the door open, pushing me out.

"Get out! Just get out! Get out of fucking Miami! Get out! Go! I thought you had changed. I was wrong. You're still the moron I pulled over that night. Go!"

I grabbed her hand. She kicked my shin and heaved me out the door. I nearly fell on the sidewalk. She reached over and yanked the door shut.

I got up and was about to lean in the window to say something, but she hit the gas and screeched off.

I paused for a moment in the dirty little courtyard before going in. The black SUV was parked across the street by the corner, engine running.

Sorry to disappoint you, Sofia. I've got one more task to perform in Miami.

Only one.

46

"OKAY," I SAID as I picked up several dirty glasses and placed them into the bus tray, "I give up. What's wrong?"

"Nothing," said Jenny as she added her receipts, standing in that 'Can't-you-see-I'm mad?' stance with her weight on one hip.

"Did you break up with Matt again?"

"No. We're back together. We're happy. I love him."

"That's good. So what is it?"

"Just shut up, okay? Just shut up and leave me alone."

She grabbed her receipts and cash and stormed out back, blonde ponytail in a flip-floppy huff.

I had hoped it wouldn't end this way, but what can I do? I already said goodbye to Paulie and Trina last night. This was my last shift at Cap'n Jack's Seafood and Bar.

A cheer erupted from the afternoon beer guzzlers as the Marlins scored.

"Did you see that play?" said Marty from Jersey.

"Yeah," I lied.

"Fucking amazing," he said with a nod to set him up again. I poured a Bud Light draft and placed it on a napkin in front of him.

I looked around for Jenny and wondered if she left out back without saying goodbye. Whatever.

I tied up the trash bag and walked out into the afternoon steam bath.

I opened the gate and got that old familiar longing for a cigarette. I inhaled a deep breath of viscous Miami air and breathed it out on a ten count. Somewhat better, but I needed to find some real air soon.

I tossed the trash in the bin, remembering both Pam Hayes standing on the step and Eddie Corrado making my nose a landing strip right on this spot. Was that only last week? Feels like ten years ago.

I turned and nearly bumped into Jenny, who stood facing me.

"I'm leaving," she said in a sharp voice with a frown.

"Okay," I said. "Bye."

"Bye."

"See you."

"Yeah, see you."

She stormed off, her bubbly butt bouncing in those tight jean cutoffs. Doesn't hurt to look.

I locked the gate and turned and she was back, maybe an inch from me. She grabbed me by the shirt and pulled me down to her mouth, kissing me as fully as a person can be kissed. I think I felt her tongue in the back of my brain.

Then, she pushed me away.

"You suck!" she said. "You're going away. Not fair."

"Jenny," I said, "it's 2017. We can text, SnapFace, InstaTwit, or whatever you kids do these days."

"It's not the same!"

"I know. You'll get over it. Besides, you have Matt."

"Matt sucks."

"You just said you love him and you're happy."

She moved forward and threw her arms around me, a nice warm hug. I hugged her back.

"Take care of yourself," she said.

"You too," I said. "Don't ever change."

She smiled "Come back and visit, okay?"

I nodded, although I knew I'd probably never see her again. She turned and walked away. I went back inside.

My final shift was the usual deep-fried beer-pouring adventure. I had to break up one fight and toss out two guys who argued over the size of their outboard engines.

At last call, Marty from Jersey turned half-away from the big-screen TV and said, "So you're leaving, huh?"

"Yeah," I said.

"That guy Bruno—I don't know. Not the same. I may move up to The Abbey full-time. Well, anyhoo, best of luck, yeah?"

He reached out his hand. I shook it.

"Yeah," I said. "Thanks, Marty."

He turned his attention back to the TV for his final beer. That was the deepest conversation I ever had with Marty from Jersey.

He and the others left and I shut the TV off. Pablo had already gone home without saying goodbye. I was about to lock the door when Bri and Sash walked in.

They were both in skin-tight sequin dresses, Bri glittering in orange and Sash dazzling in purple.

"Hi, madman," said Bri.

"I'm closing the bar," I said. "It's nice to see you two and all, but I've got to lock up."

"Haven't you ever wanted to fuck two horny girls on barstools?"

Sash locked the door. Both of their dresses fell to the floor. They wore nothing underneath.

"Hey!" I said. "Put those back on."

"You don't really want us to put anything back on," Bri said as they both gravitated to me and dropped to their knees.

The adolescent in me got all excited, but I told him to grow up.

"Put your clothes on," I said, firm this time.

They both threw me sad-little-girl pouts.

"Look," I said, "I need to apologize. I took advantage of both of you and I feel really shitty about it. You should both be with boys your own age. What happened never should have happened. I'm better than that."

"You're apologizing for fucking us?" Bri said. "Seriously?"

"Yes. Well—no. I mean—you're taking it the wrong way. You're both amazing. It's just—I can't do the hookup thing. Your generation treats sex like eating candy. It should be more than that. Look at yourselves in the mirror sometime. It's going to get old and empty fast. People are going to use you and someday you're not going to be able to do the things you do now and it's going to suck. You're going to walk down the street and not every guy is going to fall all over you. There's more to life than this. Not to mention accidental pregnancy and STDs."

Bri put her hand up as if to shut me up.

"I've heard enough," she said, standing up, clearly angry. "Come on, Sash, let's go."

They put their dresses back on. Bri seethed. Sash stared at the floor.

Bri led Sash to the door. Sash sheepishly glanced back at me. Oddly, even though I thought I was trying to impart wisdom, I felt like the worst human being alive.

Then, Bri turned back and stomped right up to me.

"You have no right to lecture me or Sash!" she said with her finger in my face. "Who do you think you are, my father? You're *so* not fun. You have no right to tell me or Sash what to do or how to think. Life is short, old man. My mom paints pictures of ducks while drinking wine because nobody wants to fuck her anymore. Well, guess what? That's going to be me someday, wishing I could go back and look like this for just *one* night. I—unlike you—am taking every opportunity to enjoy life. I'm going to get as much as I can while I look like *this*—and you, buddy, just lost out. Come on, Sash."

I started to speak but she interrupted me and said, "Don't even—"

Bri stormed out the door. Sash followed, paused, turned back, and silently mouthed *call me* with a phone gesture and a wave.

"Sash!" called Bri from outside. Sash went out and closed the door.

Well, I sure told them, didn't I?

I locked up one last time, feeling like a very old man indeed, but oddly okay about it.

I took the long way home, trying to forget that entire conversation by absorbing all the sights, sounds, and smells of my final late-night stroll through the heart of South Beach's tropical hedonism.

As I turned up Jefferson, I heard a clanging sound from behind a tree.

No, it couldn't be.

I ran across the street toward it. This time, DaShawn was faster than me and pedaled into the middle of the street before I could get to him. He said nothing as he raced off on somebody's bike.

I shook my head, getting a strange feeling that I'm not used to. Like my work here isn't done. Like maybe I should stick around.

I shrugged it off and continued to my apartment. Once inside, I undressed, lay on the airbed, and looked around for my little lizard buddy. I hadn't seen him in a while. He must have moved out.

Don't blame him.

47

I TRIMMED MY hair. Not much, just a neatening, still not short like it used to be. I showered and shaved, including the goatee, and got dressed. I slicked my hair back and looked in the bathroom mirror. I hardly recognized myself in the new white linen suit I had bought yesterday from *Da-veed*, who was thrilled to see me again. I could see why. I looked damned good. Don Johnson, kiss my ass.

I packed my duffel bag and left the apartment keys on the countertop for the landlord with a thank you note.

I walked to the Apostolic Rescue Mission Church under bright sunshine and a clear blue sky. I didn't feel the heat today. Maybe I was getting used to it. I hoped I wasn't getting used to it.

Today the sign read:

AIN'T NOBODY LOVE YOU BETTER THAN THE LORD

ALL WELCOME SUN 10:00 AM

THE REV LUTHER WIL I AMS

I stood behind an oak tree across the street and watched Luther as he greeted the parishioners. I really didn't want to do this, especially considering where I was headed afterward.

But a promise is a promise.

I waited until the church door closed and the first hymn began. I recognized it from my childhood in a different tiny white church on a hill in a tiny Georgia town, holding my mom's hand as we sang "Just a Closer Walk With Thee."

I took a deep breath, picked up my duffel, walked across the street and up the steps, and tiptoed inside.

Candace led the tiny choir, who were still off-key—although the piano sounded better. DaShawn wasn't there. I took a seat in the back. If Luther noticed I was here, he gave no indication.

Once the hymn ended, Luther took the podium and asked everyone to rise in prayer. He was splendid, also in a white suit with a blue shirt and white tie.

As everyone bowed their heads, I looked around. There were about fifty people. The jaw of an old man in a Stetson trembled as he leaned on his cane. Only parts of his face were shaven. A large black woman in a lavender flower-print dress with a big white hat reminded me of a woman I used to know as a kid. A little girl in pigtails smiled at me. I waved and smiled back.

"Amen," said everyone in unison and sat.

"Good morning," said Luther. "Today's subject is retribution."

Oh, here we go. Really? Do I have to stay and sit through this?

As if it heard my thoughts, Luther's wonky eye found me and sliced me open with a deadly stare.

"Let us turn to the words of the Apostle Paul," Luther said, "in his Epistle to the Romans, chapter twelve, verse nineteen."

A rustling sound filled the rafters as everyone got out their Bibles and flipped pages. A boy to my right noticed that I didn't have one and offered to share. I shook my head with a smile.

"Beloved," Luther continued, "never avenge yourselves, but leave it to the wrath of God. For it is written, 'Vengeance is mine. *I* will pay them back', says the Lord."

And so it went for an hour. Luther was good, I'll admit. Nobody here would suspect that in ten seconds, he could pick the lock of an apartment door. His passion shone through. He believed every word and it showed.

He knew his Bible, too. He had uncovered every verse on vengeance, resentment, bitterness, retribution—you name it. And he lobbed them all in my direction like grenades of salvation. Knowing me, you'd think I would have been uncomfortable, right? But instead, a calmness washed over me. I just sat and listened, drinking it all in.

After a final prayer, Candace stepped back to the piano and banged the keys into a rousing rendition of "Oh Happy Day." The congregation erupted and got funky. I couldn't help but smile when the large black woman in the flowered dress let it out. She tipped the scales and may have saved a few souls herself with her amazing voice, shaking her big booty under the dress with a blessed flair.

"Let the Lord walk with you every day," said Luther as he dismissed the crowd.

I slinked out the door and hustled across the street back to my spot behind the oak tree. It was a full twenty minutes before Luther finished shaking hands with everyone, including several long intense conversations in the tiny little grassy spot with a variety of people of all genders, shapes, and colors. He picked up crying kids and bobbed them up and down until they giggled. He dropped to a knee to talk to an old woman in a wheelchair, cradling her withered hands in his own. He posed for a picture with a young widow who held a portrait of a soldier over the heads of two kids.

Once everyone was gone, he turned toward my hiding spot. I walked out and crossed the street.

"You clean up good," he said. "Barely recognized you, brother Titus. Almost respectable."

"You and I should pose for *Esquire*," I said.

"Be a run on white suits. Stores sell out quick."

I nodded and laughed. I was having difficulty looking at him for some reason. I focused my attention on an egret feeding on the grass. Then, I summoned the courage and looked into both his eyes. They both looked back at me evenly.

"You leaving," he said.

"That obvious?" I said. "I need to work on my poker face, apparently."

"That and the duffel bag. Besides, I know when the Devil been around. You talking to him again."

"Nope. Used to talk to him all the time. We had some pretty deep conversations. But he hasn't been around lately. Not sure where he went."

"You did that. He spoke to you and in your own way you said 'Get thee behind me, Satan', as did Our Lord and Savior Jesus Christ. Now, put away your need for vengeance and let God save you."

"I'm tough to save."

"God saves all."

"Hope so. Nice service, by the way."

"Nobody is without sin. Nobody is without redemption. If I can help but even one of God's children, then I've served His purpose for me here on Earth."

The egret got bored with the grass and took off.

"Where's DaShawn?" I said.

Luther bit his lip and looked away.

"Don't know," he said. "Up and gone."

"Stole a bike again last night," I said. "Quicker this time. Couldn't stop him."

Luther gritted his teeth and shook his head. "Harder to save some people than others."

"Yeah."

"Heard Tommy pleased to get his money back."

"How did you hear that?"

Luther grinned.

"I know everything happens in Miami, remember?" he said. "What did you do with the extra one hundred seventy-five thousand that you forgot to mention to Tommy?"

"His fault," I said. "He said two million. He should have been more specific. I took out a handful to buy this suit and gave the rest to Tiffany."

"She going to be okay?"

"I don't think she'll ever be okay. She's one very messed-up girl. But she has Hayley and she can be herself again. They're going to live together for a while. Maybe they'll sort things out."

I looked across the street at a young couple pushing a baby carriage. The girl licked an ice cream cone.

"Black SUV still with you," said Luther. "Block up, four spaces in on the left, engine running."

"I know," I said.

"Need help?"

"No, I got this one. I know who it is. But hey—" I stuck out my hand "—thanks."

"For what?" he said, taking my hand in both of his giant ones.

"You helped me more than you'll ever know."

"You helped yourself, brother. I just a humble messenger in service to the Lord."

We unclasped hands and I began to walk away, facing

north. I passed the sign, turned back, and gestured to it.

"God a big Rufus and Chaka Khan fan too, huh?" I said.

Luther grinned.

I took one more step before he called out to me in his big deep voice.

"Brother Titus," he said.

I turned back. "Yeah?"

"Don't do it. It won't solve any problems. It won't bring her back. You'll only lose your soul."

I nodded and continued walking.

"God bless you, brother Titus," he said.

"You too, Reverend," I said and headed toward West Lido Drive.

The black SUV pulled out from its space and followed me at a distance.

48

THE DOOR BUILT into the coral-colored fence between cobblestone pillars beckoned me again. There was a black wrought-iron gate on a coded security system across the wide stone driveway, but the door in the fence to the left of it interested me more. It would be easier.

The night was remarkably similar to my first night in Miami several weeks ago when I stood on this very spot across the street from this very house here on West Lido Drive—burning with a desire to kill. The insects were loud, the smells fragrant, the breeze hot, and distant flashes of silent heat lightning lit high cloudscapes at rough three-second intervals.

But there was one thing missing.

I looked around for Sofia, but she was nowhere in sight. Nobody was going to save me from my fate tonight.

The house was lit with an effervescent glow from a variety of spotlights that had likely been designed by a lighting consultant who charges more than I've ever made in a year. Palm trees gleamed in spaced rows behind crisp squares of glass and concrete. It wasn't a Hinraker mega-mansion nor a Gables Estates small nation. This neighborhood was nothing but average Miami bayfront mansions for average Miami multi-millionaires.

Unlike last time, I didn't smoke. Oddly, I had no cravings. First time since I quit.

I turned to my left and smiled at the black SUV parked three houses up. I waved.

Then, I took a deep breath and removed my Sig from its holster. Time to get this over with, once and for all.

I walked across the street prepared for a challenge—any kind of a challenge—but I didn't have to jimmy the fence door nor even pick a lock. At my touch, it gently swung open. No alarms.

I stepped into a Japanese garden with a pathway running alongside the house. The lighting designer earned his keep for sure, a multitude of colors projected at artful angles around a koi pond surrounded by blue gemstones that reflected the light like a sea of candies.

An enormous Easter Island-like carved face stood at the head of the pond. Its expression was grim, as if saying "Such a pity."

I nodded in agreement.

A stone lantern sat at the head of the garden in front of a large carved water basin. In the pond, the koi swam back and forth, rippling the water ever so softly. They didn't seem concerned about me.

I continued through a small thicket of big leaves that rustled louder than I would have preferred. Not that he didn't know I was here. He was making this very easy for me.

I rounded the corner and saw him. He sat in a lounge chair facing away from me, an iPad in his lap. He scrolled absently while sipping from a large martini glass. His coiffed blond hair shimmered in the warm glow from the floor-to-ceiling windows behind him. I bet he has it foiled and trimmed once a week at the cost of a few hundred dollars.

Strangely, this is just how I pictured the whole scene would look when I got here—him, the lounge chair next to the aquamarine pool lit by underwater lights, the yacht moored just over to the right so as not to spoil the view of distant downtown skyscrapers in brilliant splendor across the bay, the gentle lapping of the waves against the dock pilings, the occasional flash of red taillights on cars crossing the Venetian.

Something else was missing, though, come to think of it. The voice that had prompted me on before was now silent. Was Luther right? Had I truly got the devil behind me?

I stepped out from the shrubbery and raised the gun. I wasn't afraid. My breathing was easy, heart rate low.

I took two steps forward to his left, almost into his field of vision, and studied his face.

Hard to believe I was so close to this face—a face I had obsessed about in prison, a face that once meant so much to me, and yet the same face I dreamed about smashing into pieces every time I pictured Ariel's lifeless body on that damned medical examiner's table.

I took another step forward, the gun pointed at his head.

"What are you waiting for, Titus?" he said in an even tone without looking up from the iPad. "Pull the trigger."

"Hello, Cassius," I said.

My brother looked up at me for the first time. He hadn't changed. His blue eyes shone brightly in the lights of the patio. Ripples from the pool lights danced across his face. He wore a plain white shirt and tan slacks. He was barefoot.

We looked at each other, a lifetime passing between us. He was as calm as I was. As if we were both relieved to be getting this over with.

"Well," Cassius said, "go ahead, Titus. It's what you came here for. I've made it easy for you. I disarmed the security system and I have no weapon. Kill me."

I laughed, not sure why. It all seemed so silly now. It had been so dramatic in my head every time I rehearsed it, but right now it struck me as comical.

"I had it all planned," I said. "I sat there in my cell rehearsing this moment. I knew exactly what I was going to say. I knew exactly how you would react. I went over it a thousand times, at least. Then another thousand times in cheap motel rooms, on buses, and in rental cars from the sidewalk along Route 2 in Concord all the way here to Miami. You would say this, I would say that. You would use your Harvard Law School skills on me. You would get me to agree to X, I would twist out from under your legal trap and say Y. And then I'd shoot you. Bang. Point, shoot, done."

"Then what?" he said, sipping casually, like people walk onto his patio pointing guns at him all the time.

"Then," I said as a brief flash of heat lightning lit the sky on fire, "then I—don't know. I had never moved past the part where I shoot you. I couldn't see it. Would I turn the gun on myself? Would I even bother trying to get away? I just don't know, Cassius."

"Why are you telling me this, Titus? Why don't you just shoot me?"

I sighed, lowered the gun, and holstered it. I clasped my hands in front of me and kept on looking at him.

He placed the iPad and the martini glass on the table next to him and stood up. He was still an inch taller than me at six-two. His eyes met mine head on.

"I rehearsed this moment, too," he said. "I knew you'd come to kill me. I pictured me, right here, waiting. I had some good lines in mind, some from movies like 'Go ahead, Titus. Kill me. You'd be doing me a favor.' I even worked on my Humphrey Bogart inflection. Thought you'd appreciate that."

He looked down and away, a pained expression on his face.

"Funny thing is," he continued, "I meant it. If this was right, you'd kill me. It was my fate. I refused to allow myself to prevent you. I couldn't *not* let you. I had to give you every chance."

"Why?" I said.

"Because I had faith in you, Titus. You're not a cold-blooded killer. I couldn't deny you the opportunity to prove to yourself that killing me isn't going to bring Ariel back. I knew you'd snap out of it. I knew you'd return to the land of the living. The only way to get you back was to put my life on the line. And if you pulled the trigger, then you pulled the trigger. I wouldn't want to live in a world where my own brother could kill me like that."

I glanced over at the Venetian. A cop had just pulled someone over. I wondered if it was a busted taillight.

"So here we are," I said.

"So here we are," he said.

Bugs chirped. Frogs croaked. Water lapped.

"So," he said, "what changed, Titus?"

"I don't know," I said. "I heard voices. Voices telling me what to do. Ever since Ariel died. Dark voices. I lost it. I lost everything. Including my mind, for a while. Then I came here and—I don't know—lately I've become someone else. I became a part of something that has nothing to do with you and me and Ariel and I, uh—felt—something."

"Felt what?"

"Something I haven't felt in a long time. A kind of—I don't know—belonging. Everything is turned on its head."

Cassius folded his arms, glanced down at the expensive stone walkway surrounding the pool, and then looked me in the eyes again.

"So," he said, "where do we go from here, Titus?"

"What happened to Ariel?" I said.

"I told you, Titus. I don't know. I swear to you on the grave of our mother. I—don't—know. I didn't kill Ariel and I don't know who did. I blame myself as much as you do for getting her involved. I never thought she was in danger."

"I may not shoot you, but I can't forgive you."

"I don't blame you. I acted badly. I crossed the line. But, I loved her, too."

"Don't go there."

Cassius put his hands up, folded his arms, and stared at me. He reached into his pocket and took out something small and rectangular.

"This is for you," he said and tossed it to me.

"What's this?" I said as I caught it. It was a thumb drive.

"Everything Ariel was working on—files, records, notes, recordings. Stuff the police and the FBI don't even know about."

My heart skipped a beat.

"Why did you keep this from them?" I said.

"You know why, Titus," he said. "I'm not exactly Mister Clean. There's stuff in there that could put me away."

"Why are you giving this to me?"

"Because I trust you. I know that sounds ridiculous after all we've been through, but I really have nobody else. Stay here. I've got a room for you in the house. Work with me and let's solve this. Let's find out what really happened to Ariel. Let's find out who killed her. Together. My legal skills plus your street skills. We can do it. What say?"

I spun the thumb drive in my hand.

"I wouldn't live in this gaudy monstrosity if it were the last place on earth," I said.

"Suit yourself," Cassius said. "But let me help out."

"No. Your money is dirty. I wouldn't take a dime of it. But maybe I'll—uh—look into this. Thanks."

I pocketed the thumb drive and turned to walk away.

"Where are you headed?" he said.

"Don't know," I said. "Away from this place."

"Aw, come on, Titus. Stay. Seriously. Don't do it for me. Do it for her."

I turned back at the hedge. "You've been following me."

He scratched his neck. "Not me, personally. But if I'm going to be killed, I like a little advance warning. Who do you think sent you the text about Z?"

My head spun. I took a step toward him.

"You?" I said. "That was you?"

"Yes, me," he said. "My guy tailing you spotted him and identified him. So I had him text you from an anonymous number."

"You were looking out for me?"

"Been looking out for you since you were fifteen and showed up at my door beaten to a bloody pulp. Besides, I didn't want you to miss out on completing your task here."

I watched as the police cruiser on the Venetian drove away in a flurry of flashing blues. The ticketed violator sheepishly pulled back out into the road.

"Thanks," I said. "But I don't need you to look out for me anymore. I'm leaving."

Cassius raised his hands in an 'I-give-up' gesture.

"Fine," he said. "I can't make you stay."

"No," I said. "You can't."

I turned and walked back through the hedge, past the koi pond, and across the street. I picked up my duffel from behind the bush where I had left it and walked up the street. The black SUV was gone.

I walked onto the Venetian Causeway and to the bus stop. From here, I'd take the bus to the terminal and from there to a different city—any different city. The Intracoastal glistened between the tall buildings on my left and the low sparkling water of the canals that ran between the houses of the Sunset Islands to my right.

At the bus stop, a heavy-set short woman and a tall younger woman sat on the bench talking in Spanish. They went silent when I stood near them.

I removed the thumb drive from my pocket and twirled it around again.

What's on this?

My curiosity fired up, even though I had promised myself I was leaving Miami tonight.

What good would it do? *Vengeance is mine, says the Lord.* That's what Luther would say. I should just get on this bus, go to the bus terminal, and get out of town.

As if to answer my question, the bus arrived. The two women got on. I paid the driver and sat down. There were only five other people. I sat in an aisle seat.

The doors closed and the driver put the bus in gear. We passed West Lido Drive and were almost to San Marino Island when I stood up.

"Stop!" I said as I approached the driver.

"No stop here," said the driver. "Only at bus stops."

I opened my suit coat to show him my gun in its holster, being careful so that the other passengers couldn't see.

The driver slammed on the brakes.

"Son of bitch," he said.

He opened the door, shaking his head. I got out and the bus continued on. As I passed, I glanced over at the deck on which I had recently stood. Cassius had gone inside. The pool and patio lights were off.

I walked past Rivo Alto Island and Belle Isle Park, and over to 17th Street. I turned right at Meridian and back down all the way to my apartment, hoping my Chromebook was still sitting on the table where I left it.

Once there, I noticed a light in the window. I hid behind the sea grape tree and sneaked across the courtyard to the corner, where I peered in. A heavy-set shirtless man with a bad comb-over was in his plaid boxers walking around and eating from a McDonald's bag.

Damn. Landlord didn't waste any time. Didn't even clean or paint. Makes sense when you think about it, though. It's not that kind of building. Not those kinds of tenants.

There was no sign of my Chromebook. Bet he sold it.

I continued on, back to the little park at the corner of Washington Ave and 2nd Street. I found the bench on which I had spent my first night in Miami and sat down.

I got out the thumb drive and looked at it again.

I'm going to have to stay here and finish this, right?

Which meant I was right back where I started. Same park bench. Same cash problem. No job. No place to live. Here we go again.

Maybe Paulie and Trina will stroll by and get mugged again so I can save them again and Paulie can offer me a job again.

No, it was going to have to be different this time.

I put my duffel bag on the bench and fell to my side, using it as a pillow. I closed my eyes and allowed the hot breeze to lull and relax me.

Somewhere between reality and sleep, I heard Ariel's voice.

"I told you," she said.

I opened my eyes.

"You were right," I said.

I closed my eyes and went to sleep.

ABOUT THE AUTHOR

JOHN D. PATTEN occasionally skipped class because he was glued to a Spenser mystery by Robert B. Parker. He was late for work because he got caught up in a Travis McGee adventure by John D. MacDonald. He memorized Philip Marlowe lines from hard-boiled detective stories by Raymond Chandler. Now, after all these years, he's finally figured out what he should really be doing. He's currently working on the next Titus thriller. Say hello at:

https://johndpatten.com

. . . where you can sign up for the Meridian Breeze Lounge, the official "Titus Fans Only" Newsletter.

Made in the USA
Monee, IL
13 December 2022

21586372R00204